A FIGHTING CHANCE

WILLIAM C. DIETZ

ACE BOOKS, NEW YORK

THE BERKLEY PUBLISHING GROUP
Published by the Penguin Group
Penguin Group (USA) Inc.
375 Hudson Street, New York, New York 10014, USA
Penguin Group (Canada), 90 Eglinton Avenue East, Suite 700, Toronto, Ontario M4P 2Y3, Canada (a division of Pearson Penguin Canada Inc.) • Penguin Books Ltd., 80 Strand, London WC2R 0RL, England • Penguin Ireland, 25 St. Stephen's Green, Dublin 2, Ireland (a division of Penguin Books Ltd.) • Penguin Group (Australia), 707 Collins Street, Melbourne, Victoria 3008, Australia (a division of Pearson Australia Group Pty. Ltd.) • Penguin Books India Pvt. Ltd., 11 Community Centre, Panchsheel Park, New Delhi—110 017, India • Penguin Group (NZ), 67 Apollo Drive, Rosedale, Auckland 0632, New Zealand (a division of Pearson New Zealand Ltd.) • Penguin Books, Rosebank Office Park, 181 Jan Smuts Avenue, Parktown North 2193, South Africa • Penguin China, B7 Jaiming Center, 27 East Third Ring Road North, Chaoyang District, Beijing 100020, China

Penguin Books Ltd., Registered Offices: 80 Strand, London WC2R 0RL, England

A FIGHTING CHANCE

An Ace Book / published by arrangement with the author

PUBLISHING HISTORY
Ace hardcover edition / November 2011
Ace mass-market edition / December 2012

Cover art by Bruce Jensen.
Cover design by Judith Lagerman.

ISBN: 978-0-425-25612-1

ACE
Ace Books are published by The Berkley Publishing Group,
a division of Penguin Group (USA) Inc.,
375 Hudson Street, New York, New York 10014.
ACE and the "A" design are trademarks of Penguin Group (USA) Inc.

PRINTED IN THE UNITED STATES OF AMERICA

10 9 8 7 6 5 4 3 2 1

Praise for William C. Dietz and the Legion of the Damned novels

A FIGHTING CHANCE

"Superb . . . An exciting, action-packed tale . . . Fast-paced."
—*Midwest Book Review*

WHEN DUTY CALLS

"The action is as brisk as ever in a Legion yarn. Standard-issue military SF doesn't get much better than this." —*Booklist*

"Fans of military science fiction on other worlds will thoroughly enjoy *When Duty Calls*, the latest Legion of the Damned space-opera thriller . . . William C. Dietz keeps his long-running saga fresh to the delight of military science fiction fans."
—*Midwest Book Review*

WHEN ALL SEEMS LOST

"A fast-paced, deep-space military tale with enough sci-fi details to fire the imagination." —*The Kansas City Star*

"A pedal-to-the-metal plot jam-packed with intrigue, deep-space adventure, and futuristic combat." —*Publishers Weekly*

"[*When All Seems Lost*] starts at hyperspeed and accelerates from there into a fabulous, graphic military science fiction opus in which readers will need seat belts." —*SFRevu*

"Pleasant, straightforward adventure in space with military undertones. Dietz's characters are better drawn than in most similar books." —Don D'Ammassa, *Critical Mass*

continued . . .

"This is classic Dietz, which means classic military SF for all fans of the brand." —*Booklist*

"Military sci-fi at its best . . . The horrors of war are described convincingly. A brilliantly plotted story and escalating suspense provide a highly satisfying story." —*RT Book Reviews*

FOR THOSE WHO FELL

"Careful plotting and realistically messy detail . . . Dietz expertly jumps from one theater of combat to another, one side to another, to show the opponents planning but then improvising as plans go awry." —*Publishers Weekly*

"The usual fast-paced adventure we have come to expect in the series and from Dietz." —*Booklist*

"An excellent story, well written and rich in detail that sets the scene both militarily and against the background of a galaxy-wide war . . . It is a great tribute to William Dietz's skill that he is able to make [the story] seem possible and believable." —SF Crowsnest.com

"William C. Dietz raises the bar of excellence for military science fiction with every book he writes . . . A superb, action-packed thriller." —*Midwest Book Review*

"If you . . . take comfort in reading about mayhem on an interstellar scale, then this is probably a good bet for hours of slack-jawed, drooling entertainment." —*The Agony Column*

FOR MORE THAN GLORY

"Plenty of conflict and mayhem . . . Rewarding." —*SF Site*

"Thoughtful . . . Plot conscious." —*Chronicle*

"Dietz has created an intricate tapestry of local and star-faring culture with top-notch action sequences." —*Publishers Weekly*

"Exciting military SF fare. Series readers and *Starship Troopers* fans will want this." —*Booklist*

Praise for

BONES OF EMPIRE

"For those who enjoy science fiction that deals with lots of character-driven stories, political intrigue, and military action, I would highly recommend *Bones of Empire* and give it a five-star rating—keeper status!" —*Night Owl Reviews*

"Fast-paced space opera. Action, adventure, alien politics, and a bit of romance move the plot forward. Violent, blood-spattered scenes lead to the satisfying conclusion." —*RT Book Reviews*

"An action-packed, faster-than-the-speed-of-light . . . space thriller." —*Midwest Book Review*

AT EMPIRE'S EDGE

"A testosterone-soaked tale of violent retribution." —*Publishers Weekly*

"Entertaining police-procedural space opera . . . Fans who enjoy a blood-spattered science fiction thriller will want to read the first of a two-part saga as William C. Dietz provides an exciting but out-of-control opening act." —*Midwest Book Review*

"An excellent novel for first-time readers of Mr. Dietz . . . The story moves at a nice clip and contains plenty of future tech and strange creatures. This novel should satisfy a wide range of readers." —*CA Reviews*

Ace Books by William C. Dietz

GALACTIC BOUNTY
FREEHOLD
PRISON PLANET
IMPERIAL BOUNTY
ALIEN BOUNTY
McCADE'S BOUNTY
DRIFTER
DRIFTER'S RUN
DRIFTER'S WAR
LEGION OF THE DAMNED
BODYGUARD
THE FINAL BATTLE
WHERE THE SHIPS DIE
STEELHEART
BY BLOOD ALONE
BY FORCE OF ARMS
DEATHDAY
EARTHRISE
FOR MORE THAN GLORY
FOR THOSE WHO FELL
RUNNER
LOGOS RUN
WHEN ALL SEEMS LOST
WHEN DUTY CALLS
AT EMPIRE'S EDGE
BONES OF EMPIRE
A FIGHTING CHANCE
ANDROMEDA'S FALL

Dearest Marjorie . . .
Thank you for the journey,
the things we experienced along the way,
and the voyage ahead.

1

Some of the most important battles are the most obscure.

—Hoda Ibin Ragnatha
Turr truth sayer
Standard year 2206

PLANET O-CHI 4, THE CONFEDERACY OF SENTIENT BEINGS

A pair of destroyer escorts popped out of hyperspace off O-Chi 4 where they were joined moments later by the combat supply ship *Lictor.* The vessel was nearly two miles long and carried a crew of more than a thousand. When fully loaded, the vessel could transport up to three million tons of cargo, including as many as eight disk-shaped TACBASEs. One such fortress was filled to capacity with the men, women, and cyborgs of Alpha Company, 2nd Battalion, 1st REC. It was about to drop into O-Chi 4's atmosphere, and all of them were strapped in.

Major Antonio Santana was seated in the op center on the top deck of TACBASE-011767, where he could see the video that was being fed to them from the *Lictor*'s bridge. He could see a large part of O-Chi 4, and the general impression was of a heavily forested planet, much of which was shrouded by clouds. Santana's orders were to land, join forces with the local militia, and destroy a Ramanthian installation. That was how it was supposed to work. But such operations rarely went according to plan.

Santana's thoughts were interrupted as the image of O-Chi 4 was replaced with a head shot of the *Lictor*'s commanding officer. She had short gray hair, steely blue eyes, and high cheekbones. A retread most likely. One of thousands who had been brought out of retirement to battle the Ramanthians. She looked tired. "It's been nice having you and your troops aboard, Major. I have no idea what you hope to accomplish down there but good luck. As you know, the bugs control about sixty percent of the surface and have for the last six months or so. A flight of CF-184 Daggers will keep the enemy fighters off your back. But once you drop through thirty thousand feet, they'll break off and return to the ship. You'll be on your own after that. Any questions?"

"No, ma'am," Santana answered stoically. "Thanks for the lift."

The navy officer smiled. "Anytime. Make sure your people are strapped in. It'll be a rough ride." And with that, the video monitors snapped to black, leaving the tech data to scroll.

Santana turned to his Executive Officer. Captain Eor Rona-Sa was a 250-pound Hudathan who had been allowed to join the Legion despite the fact that his race had attempted to annihilate the Confederacy in the past. But the Hudathans had been defeated. And having failed to take what they needed, the big aliens were forced to join the same alliance they had previously sought to destroy.

The decision to accept Hudathans into the Confederacy's armed forces had been partly political but was a practical matter as well. The war with the Ramanthians wasn't going well, and the Confederacy was in desperate need of soldiers. Especially good ones.

Rona-Sa had a large head, a wide froglike mouth, and the

vestige of a dorsal fin that ran front to back along the top of his skull. And when Santana looked into Rona-Sa's eyes, he could tell that his XO was way ahead of him. "Are the troops strapped in?"

"Yes, sir," Rona-Sa rumbled. "I checked them personally."

"And the cyborgs?"

"Secured, sir."

"Good. Thank you. Now all we need is a nap."

Sergeant Major Dice Dietrich was seated to Santana's left. The comment might have been sufficient to elicit a chuckle from the hollow-cheeked noncom except that he was already asleep and snoring gently. An apparent lapse that would have earned him a tongue-lashing from another commanding officer. But Dietrich had served under Santana for many years and had certain privileges.

Behind them, and strapped to D-rings set into the deck, was a recon ball. Her name was Lieutenant Sally Ponco. Thanks to her special abilities, the cyborg could tap into the TACBASE's circuitry and the *Lictor*'s so long as the vessels were connected. "The bugs are coming up to play," she said laconically. "And the Dags are engaging them. Hang on . . . We are twenty from launch and counting."

The onboard computer began a countdown that could be heard in every compartment. And for reasons known only to the combat habitat's manufacturer, the machine had a female voice. "Attention all personnel. TACBASE-11767 will launch in ten, nine, eight, seven, six, five, four, three, two . . ."

The last was followed by a violent jerk as the self-contained fortress fell free of the *Lictor* and the influence of the supply ship's argrav generators. Santana felt his stomach flip-flop as the artificial gravity disappeared and his body rose. The six-point harness held him in place.

Then came a sudden jolt as the computer fired a combination

of steering jets, and video blossomed on the monitors. The planet framed in the center monitor began to swell as the flying fortress entered the exosphere. After ten minutes of acceleration, the disembodied voice flooded the PA system again. "TACBASE-011767 is about to enter a planetary atmosphere. All personnel will remain in their seats with harnesses fastened until further notice."

"Here it comes," Ponco predicted. And she was correct. Shortly thereafter, the hull began to vibrate, then rattle. Finally, it shook like a thing possessed as the flying fortress slip-slid down through heavy cloud cover. The battering continued for what seemed like an eternity but was actually less than half an hour.

As Santana began to wonder if the trip would ever end, the disk-shaped hull steadied. Wisps of cloud blew away, and hundreds of square miles of verdant forest appeared on the monitors. The land was divided into asymmetric shapes by ribbons of blue that connected lakes with the sea. He could see that much. But the TACBASE was traveling too fast for him to discern very many details.

Santana gripped the armrests of his chair more tightly as a saw-toothed mountain range appeared in the distance, and the TACBASE flew straight toward it. The so-called drop box was equipped with steering jets and repellers. But it didn't have engines—and it couldn't climb. So, as the mountains rushed at them, Santana wondered if they were about to die before the mission really began. He could see gaps between the jagged peaks, but none was wide enough to accommodate the flying fortress. It was a struggle to maintain his outward composure as the final seconds of his life ticked by. He thought about Christine Vanderveen, wondered where she was, and how the news would affect her.

Then, without warning, the flying disk flipped over onto its side, slipped between two neighboring pinnacles of rock, and righted itself again. "Holy shit," Dietrich said. "I hope this thing lands soon. I need some fresh underwear."

"I think you're going to get your wish," Ponco observed, as foothills gave way to thick forest and the TACBASE continued to lose altitude. "But Baynor's Bay wasn't much before the war, and I doubt things have improved much."

The flying fortress was only three hundred feet off the ground by then. Santana saw what might have been a plantation, a stretch of dirt road, and a distant hill. Within a matter of seconds, the disk passed to one side of the elevation and flew over a sprawl of one-, two-, and three-story buildings. Then the drop box flashed out over Baynor's Bay before circling back for a landing. "TACBASE-011767 is taking fire," the computer said emotionlessly, as the hull shuddered.

"Contact the Baynor's Bay port authority," Santana ordered. "Give them the recognition code and order them to cease fire. All personnel will prepare for a crash landing followed by surface combat."

"That message was sent," the computer responded, "and a confirmation was received. But TACBASE-011767 continues to take fire."

The flying fortress shook violently as a barrage of cannon shells and missiles slammed into it. But the durasteel hull was built to take a lot of punishment and did. "I'm trying to contact the locals as well," Ponco put in. "But no luck so far."

"TACBASE-011767 is running low on fuel and will have to put down within three minutes and seventeen seconds," the computer announced. "Please designate a landing zone."

Santana swore and made use of the small joystick on his armrest to scan Baynor's Bay. Then, based on what he could see, he chose what millions of military leaders had chosen before him. And that was the high ground. "Put us down on top of that hill."

"I have a contact," Ponco announced, as the fortress passed over the town and neared the hill. "Or contacts. It seems there are *two* militia groups on the ground. One is ordering the other to stop firing."

A couple of homes could be seen on top of the hill, along with a small water tank and the remains of a com mast. All of the structures disappeared as the computer triggered a dozen drop tubes—and an equal number of specially designed "weed cutters" laid waste to the hilltop. "That ought to get their attention," Dietrich said darkly.

Suddenly, the main monitor went to black as the TACBASE was consumed by a rising cloud of smoke. There was a *thud* as the fortress landed. The deck tilted to one side but came level again as hydraulically controlled supports probed the ground, found solid footing, and made the necessary adjustments. Moments later, the computer began to drone its way through a status report. "Sensors, on. Ground defense system, on. Com system, on . . ."

But Santana wasn't listening. He hit the release on his harness and was up on his feet by the time Ponco spoke. "I have a link with a Colonel Antov, sir. He says he's sorry about the mix-up, but says everything is under control now. You are to report to him by 1600 hours local. He will provide transportation."

Santana made a face. "Tell him I'll be there." There were a lot of things about the mission to O-Chi 4 that he didn't like. And reporting to a militia colonel was at the top of the list. He had even gone so far as to appeal that part of the assignment to General Mortimer Kobbi on Adobe, where the company had been assembled. The older officer had been sympathetic but firm. "I hear you. But we don't have a battalion of regular troops to drop onto O-Chi 4. So you're going to need the locals to get the job done. And don't forget . . . They know the place a lot better than you ever will.

"Plus," Kobbi continued, "judging from his record, Colonel Antov was a reasonably competent officer before he left the marines to take over the family plantation. So it isn't as if you'll be reporting to the local pub owner or something. Have another drink. It'll make you feel better."

But Santana *didn't* feel better as he and his staff left the command deck and made their way down a flight of metal stairs to the lower level where the Trooper IIs and bio bods were assembled. The four quads were too large to fit inside the TACBASE and were slotted into recesses in the hull. There was some comfort in knowing that their weapons, plus those controlled by the drop box's computer, would be more than sufficient to repel most ground attacks.

Two corridors divided the main deck into four sections. They ran quad to quad across the hull. That meant the bio bods and T-2s could access the huge cyborgs in a matter of seconds.

Alpha Company was led by Captain Jo Zarrella, a combat veteran whom Santana had been lucky to get. The unit consisted of two platoons, each led by a lieutenant and a staff sergeant. A typical platoon included eight bio bods, eight T-2s, and a quad. But such numbers were deceptive because the total firepower possessed by a single platoon of highly mobile legionnaires was equal to an entire company of 175 foot soldiers.

A noncom yelled, "Atten-hut!" as Santana appeared, and all of the bio bods and T-2s crashed to attention. Some were veterans, but all too many of the legionnaires were barely out of advanced infantry training and green as grass. That included some of the seven-and-a-half-foot-tall Trooper IIs. They had a vaguely humanoid appearance, but form follows function, and there was no mistaking their arm-mounted machine guns and laser cannons for anything other than what they were.

Some of the T-2s were criminals who had chosen life in a brain box over death. Others were the victims of accidents or, having been "killed" in action, had seized the opportunity to live on as cyborgs. Santana took the opportunity to say a few words. "At ease. Welcome to O-Chi 4. How do you like it so far?"

That produced some grins and a guffaw or two. Santana nodded. "The good news is that we were able to put down safely. The bad news is that even our friends are shooting at us. Fortunately, the friendly-fire problem has been resolved. But the bugs are only 150 miles away. So stay sharp.

"As you know, we were sent here to take part in a joint operation with a local outfit called the O-Chi Rifles. I will learn more about them when I report to Colonel Antov at 1600 hours. During my absence, Captain Rona-Sa will be in command—and it's my guess he'll find ways to keep you occupied."

Everyone knew Rona-Sa was a stickler for maintenance, so the last comment elicited outright laughter from everyone except the officer in question. He lacked both the inclination and the capacity to smile. Dietrich had served under Santana for a long time and knew the pep talk was over. "Ten-hut!"

The troops came to attention. "Dismissed."

"Sir?" As the troops began to disperse, Santana turned to find that his clerk, an earnest youth named Corporal Colby, was waiting to speak with him.

"Yes?"

"There is a vehicle and three militiamen waiting outside, sir. They're from Colonel Antov."

"Or so they claim," Ponco put in as she drifted to a halt. Her sphere-shaped war form was covered with a mottled forest green paint job and equipped with two skeletal tool arms plus a variety of weaponry. "For all we know, they're part of the group that was shooting at us. I think you should ride in a quad, sir."

"I hear you," Santana acknowledged. "But how would that look? We wouldn't want the locals to think we're scared. I'll ride Sergeant Joshi. That should strike the right balance.

"Corporal Colby, if you would be so kind as to fetch my body armor and weapons, I'd be grateful."

Colby took off at a trot, and Santana turned to Rona-Sa. "You know what we came here to accomplish, Captain. If I fail to return, carry on. Is that clear?"

It was the type of order that any officer should understand, but because Rona-Sa was a Hudathan, Santana knew the command would be followed regardless of cost. Even if it meant every man, woman, and cyborg in the unit had to die. The XO nodded. "Yes, sir."

Fifteen minutes later, Santana was high on Joshi's back with his harness fastened. A hatch whirred open, a ramp slid down to meet the rubble below, and the Trooper II followed it down to the smoking ground below.

From his position above and behind Joshi's head, Santana could see the sturdy-looking ground vehicle that had been sent to pick him up. It was a boxy affair that consisted of an enclosed engine, a passenger compartment protected by a roll cage, and huge tires, which kept the car high off the ground. All three occupants were male, armed, and dressed in standard-issue camos. And, as Joshi carried Santana over to the all-terrain vehicle (ATV), the locals looked wary. Chances were that they had seen pictures of T-2s but never been exposed to the real thing. And Joshi *was* intimidating. "Good afternoon," Santana said politely. "I'm Major Santana."

The man in the front passenger seat was wearing a civilian bush hat. He stood, and thanks to the jungle buggy's ground clearance, rose to the same level as Santana. The militiaman had a blocky build, black hair, and brown skin. His manner was friendly but guarded. "It's a pleasure to meet you, sir. I'm

Captain Motu Kimbo. The colonel sent me to collect you. I was going to offer you a ride—but it looks like you brought your own transportation."

"You lead, and we'll follow," Santana replied. "Let's meet on channel two."

After a quick radio check, Kimbo's driver started his engine, put the ATV in gear, and executed a tight turn. Joshi could run up to fifty miles per hour without difficulty, but as Santana eyed the slope ahead, it didn't seem likely that the cyborg would need to go even half that fast. A two-lane heat-fused road switchbacked down toward a jumble of pastel-colored buildings below. Some of the structures were intact, but many showed signs of blast damage or sat next to rubble-strewn craters. It didn't require a military genius to figure out that the bugs had been by more than once.

With nothing to do other than compensate for the back-and-forth motion of the ride, Santana took the opportunity to scan his surroundings. One of the first things he noticed was a twenty-foot-high fence that followed the curve of the bay and was made out of metal beams. They had been welded together into self-supporting X-shapes that were dug into the ground. The obstacles stood shoulder to shoulder as if to protect local residents from something big. Ramanthian tanks? Or native life-forms? Having read up on O-Chi 4, Santana knew that some of the local triturators stood around fifteen feet tall, weighed up to eight tons, and had nasty tempers. So they wouldn't be welcome in town. Or anywhere else for that matter.

Another thing stood out as Joshi and Santana followed the ATV through town. That was the way Baynor's Bay's townspeople came out to greet them. And no wonder since most had been witness to the TACBASE's rather noisy arrival, not to mention the landing on the hill.

But as the road curved and followed the beach toward the

southwest, most of the gawkers waved cheerfully, and a few were armed with Confederate flags. So if these people were friendly—who had attempted to bring the TACBASE down? It was an interesting question but one that would have to wait.

The ATV slowed, passed between a couple of stone pillars, and entered a curved drive. It led to a sprawling one-story house. The home was not only larger than most of the places Santana had seen but was perched on the edge of the bay, with a glorious view of the water. As both vehicles came to a halt under a portico, two native O-Chies hurried out to meet them.

The locals were about five feet tall and looked like animated skeletons. Large light-gathering eyes were located on both sides of their oval heads. That meant they could look in two directions at once. A rather useful adaptation for sentients who had reason to fear large carnivores. And as Santana freed himself from the harness, he saw that the indigs had three chevron-shaped nostrils centered in the middle of their faces. Their slitlike mouths were very wide, and if they had teeth, there was no sign of them as the nearest O-Chi spoke. The native's voice had a soft, raspy sound. "Welcome to Bay House. The colonel is waiting."

Santana got the impression that Antov didn't like to wait for things; he ordered Joshi to stand by and held up a pocket com for the T-2 to see. The cyborg's armor was painted forest green dappled with random ribbons of yellow. Like most vets, rows of bug skulls had been stenciled onto his slablike chest. One for each confirmed kill.

The noncom nodded a huge head. His computer-generated voice sounded like a rock crusher in low gear. "Just say the word, sir, and I'll join the party."

Santana grinned at the thought. "Thank you, Sergeant. That's very comforting."

As Santana turned toward the front door and made his way

toward Kimbo, he could see the militia officer's frown. "You look troubled, Captain . . . Is something wrong?"

"No, sir . . . But I'm afraid I'll have to ask that you leave your weapons here. They will be kept under lock and key. The armor is up to you."

Santana wasn't pleased, but he understood. Trust had to be earned. So he slid the carbine off his shoulder and gave both it and his pistol to Kimbo, who placed them in a cabinet. The clamshell-style armor made a *thump* as it hit the floor. His helmet went on top. "Okay, Captain . . . At least I got to keep my pants. Please lead the way."

The house had white walls, gleaming hardwood floors, and was furnished with beautiful O-Chi-made rattan furniture. But what immediately drew Santana's eyes were the hundreds of animal trophies, both large and small, that glared down at him from every angle. Some had fur, and others were covered with scales. And because none of the creatures were familiar to him, Santana assumed all of them were native to O-Chi 4.

But, as Santana discovered when he was shown into a cavernous living area, the heads in the hallway were nothing compared to the beast that eyed him from the far end of the room. The reptile was about eight feet tall and equipped with four muscular legs. Yellow eyes were set into a bony head. And there were lots of sharp-looking teeth inside a yawning mouth. A meat eater for sure.

"It's a velocipod," a male voice said. "I took it down with a .50-caliber Hawking. Anything smaller just pisses them off. The range was about a hundred feet. Closer than I would like—but that's how it is with velocipods. They're damned fast, so you only have seconds in which to fire."

When Santana turned in the direction of the voice, he saw that a pair of easy chairs was positioned in front of a large window looking out onto the bay. One of them was occupied by a middle-aged man dressed in civilian khakis. He had a receding hairline with a prow-shaped nose and appeared to be in good shape except for the leg propped up in front of him. It was encased in a cast that produced a thumping sound when struck with a swagger stick. "I was gored," the man explained. "A stupid mistake. But when another member of my party missed his shot—I went into a thicket of brush to finish the tusker off. It damned near went the other way!"

The last was said with a smile and obvious amusement. "Please have a seat. I'm Colonel Antov. And I assume that you are Major Santana."

Santana confirmed that he was and took the chair next to Antov's. They were separated by a side table that held a lamp, the swagger stick, and a pair of binoculars. "Can I interest you in a cup of O-Chi caf?" Antov inquired. "We produce the best beans in the Confederacy. Or did back before the bugs landed."

"I would love a cup of O-Chi caf," Santana replied. "It's difficult to get a decent cup of coffee anymore."

"Heedu!" Antov said loudly. "Fetch the major a cup of caf."

The servant had been so quiet, and his slightly shimmery skin had blended so well with the wood paneling, that Santana didn't know the O-Chi was present until he spoke. "Yes, Colonel. Right away, sir." Then he was gone.

"So," Antov said. "We gave you something of a warm welcome didn't we? I was sitting right here when your TACBASE passed over the bay. It was quite a sight. My people knew the score. But it appears that Major Temo forgot to tell her troops about your arrival, so they mistook the TACBASE for a Ramanthian ship and opened fire. It was a regrettable mistake but an understandable one. Air superiority shifts back and forth all the time. And when the bugs are on top, they love to shoot the place up."

Santana's eyebrows rose as Heedu returned with a tray. "Major Temo?"

"Major Temo was my XO," Antov explained. "Back before Governor Hardy was killed. Then, based on a very fanciful interpretation of the law, she named herself to replace him. Here, take a look through these . . . You can see the Temo family's pharmaceutical plant on the north side of the bay. They make a number of drugs based on extracts from O-Chi plants. That's how they make their money. Lots of it."

Santana brought the military-style device up to his eyes as Heedu placed a steaming cup of caf on the table next to him. When he pressed the zoom button, the other side of the bay seemed to leap forward. He saw a businesslike dock, a jumble of low-lying buildings, and some higher ground beyond. "That's where all of the AA fire was coming from," Antov commented. "Back before she tried to supplant the planetary government, Temo was in command of the O-Chi Scouts. They're good people and excellent soldiers.

"But most of the scouts are employed by Temo Pharmaceuticals. And the family continues to pay them even though they can't ship any pharmaceuticals off-planet at the moment. That buys a lot of loyalty."

"Maybe I should talk to her," Santana said, as he put the glasses down.

"You're welcome to try," Antov replied, wryly. "But I don't think you'll get very far."

"No? Why not?"

"You may have noticed that there was a group of houses on top of Signal Hill before you cleared it," Antov replied. "The largest belonged to the Temo family."

"Shit."

"Exactly. But it gets worse. Major Temo's grandmother was living there."

Santana winced. "I'm sorry to hear that."

"You had no way to know," Antov said philosophically. "And you were under fire. Plus, that drop box must have been running low on fuel. How much burn time did you have left?"

"A little over two minutes."

"There you have it," Antov put in. "The Temos will file a formal complaint once they get the opportunity. But I will submit an after-action report to General Kobbi indicating why it was necessary to land on the hill. That should prevent any fallout."

"Thank you, sir."

"You're welcome. But you won't thank me for what I'm going to say next. Unfortunately, given my leg, I won't be able to accompany you. And, before you depart, it will be necessary to do something about Temo. My Rifles keep the O-Chi Scouts out of Baynor's Bay. But if they were to depart, Temo would take over the south-bay area in a matter of hours. Then, having named herself governor, she would use the Scouts to take over what remains of our planetary government."

Santana felt a rising sense of anger. The need to deal with what amounted to a civil war before tackling the real mission was frustrating to say the least. But it wouldn't do any good to say that, and he didn't. "Yes, sir. Assuming we are able to resolve the Temo problem—what can you tell me about the mission itself?"

Antov grinned approvingly. "Spoken like the fire-eating officer that Kobbi says you are. Let's adjourn to my study. There's something I want to show you. Heedu! Bring my crutches."

Between the slight, thin-limbed O-Chi and the more muscular Santana, they were able to hoist Antov up onto his good leg. Then, with the aid of sturdy crutches, the militia officer thumped his way into a well-furnished study. The walls were hung with trophies, animal skins covered most of the floor, and a huge gun cabinet stood in a corner. There was a desk as well. But it had been pushed back out of the way to make room for the table at the center of the room and the meticulously crafted object that sat on top of it.

Rather than a holo projection of the sort the Legion's Intel people would put together, it was a handcrafted model reminiscent of those that military leaders had employed thousands of years before. What looked like a small mountain had been painstakingly texturized to make it look real. Miniature fortifications could be seen, and a very convincing paint job had been applied to all of the component parts, including hundreds of miniature trees.

As Santana circled the table, Antov offered a running narration. "The mountain didn't have a name until the bugs landed six months ago. Now we call it Headstone, because that's where more than a thousand of our citizens are buried," Antov said grimly. "That may not sound like a lot to you. Not given the millions who have been killed during the war. But it's a large number for us. The planet had a population of about sixty thousand people before the war began."

Santana looked up. "Was that the *total* population? Or the human population?"

"I don't know," Antov admitted. "It's hard to say how many sticks live out in the bush."

"Sticks?"

"We call them 'sticks' because they look like sticks," Antov said irritably. "What difference does it make?"

Santana looked over to where Heedu was standing with his back to the wall. He was more visible now that the officer knew what to look for. The O-Chi was wearing a brown fez, matching vest, and a breechcloth. Heedu didn't have a facial expression as far as Santana could tell. Although he had spent enough time with nonhumans to know that such perceptions were almost always wrong. Most species employed some sort of nonverbal communications. "The number of O-Chies could be important," Santana said mildly. "It is their planet after all."

Antov produced a snort of derision. "Please, Major . . . Spare me the social nonsense. This is war. We don't have the time or resources to count indigs, initiate assimilation projects, or conduct anthropological studies. I suggest that you focus your attention on the task at hand."

The tone was harsh, and Santana could tell that Antov was angry. "Yes, sir."

"There are two ways to attack Headstone," Antov said, as he picked up the narration. "By air, which is how the first assault went in, or on the ground. Unfortunately, an airborne attack is out of the question at the moment. Simply put, we lack the aircraft required to carry one out. Not to mention the fact that the bugs have had plenty of time in which to install antiaircraft batteries. Our scouts have gotten fairly close and report that the STS installation is surrounded by them."

Santana knew that "STS" stood for surface-to-space, as in surface-to-space cannons. They were weapons so powerful they could reach into the void and destroy ships thousands of miles out. And according to the briefing he had received before leaving Adobe, if a cannon was constructed on top of Headstone, it would be able to fire on the neighboring O-Chi jump point.

That was important because even though ships could enter hyperspace just about anywhere, jump points were like shortcuts, which could save both time and fuel. So capturing and controlling such sites was important to both sides. "Okay," Santana replied. "An air assault is out. But what about air cover? Will there be any?"

"We have five CF-150 Daggers and an in-atmosphere transport generally referred to as *The Hangar Queen*. That's it,"

Antov replied. "The good news is that the *Lictor* dropped some much-needed parts and ammo into the atmosphere—and we were able to retrieve all but one of the containers. So the 150s will remain operational for a bit longer, and we have enough ordinance for the mission and plenty of field rations."

Santana nodded. "I'm glad to hear it. We brought supplies of our own—but not enough to equip your forces as well. So tell me about the ground attack. What's the best way in?"

Antov's crutches made a thumping sound as he moved in closer. "I've spent a lot of time thinking about it," he said. "Unfortunately, I don't see any alternative to a direct assault up the west side of the ridge. The first half mile won't be too bad. But then you'll come to a very steep section *here*. The bugs know that's the most likely route, of course, so they'll be firing down on you from prepared positions."

Santana eyed the nearly vertical slope, knew the quads wouldn't be able to negotiate it, and felt a growing emptiness in the pit of his stomach. "And then?"

"Then you'll be on this flat area," Antov said, pointing a blunt finger. "As you can see from the model, that's where the Ramanthians placed their support structure. Two-thirds of it is located underground. So you'll have to force your way in and clear it. Then you'll be able to access the lowest level and a corridor that leads to an elevator. That will take you up into the STS battery itself.

"Meanwhile," Antov continued, "I suggest you send part of your force up along the ridge to create a diversion and pull most of the defenders in that direction. That should do the trick."

The last was said so casually that Antov could have been describing a walk in a park rather than a hellish assault that was certain to claim hundreds of lives even if successful. For one brief moment, Santana wondered if Antov's wound was real.

But Kobbi swore by the man, and there was no denying his record in the Marine Corps.

No, the injury was real. And consistent with the man's personality. Just as he had been willing to enter a thicket of brush looking for a wounded tusker—Antov would think nothing of attacking Headstone with little more than a swagger stick.

Santana was about to ask a follow-up question when Captain Kimbo charged into the room. "Sir! A Ramanthian submarine surfaced in the middle of the bay. It's firing on the TACBASE."

Then, as if to emphasize the seriousness of the situation, a siren began to wail. Baynor's Bay was under attack.

2

A monarch should be ever intent on conquest; otherwise, his neighbors will rise in arms against him.

—Akbar
Mughal Indian emperor
Standard year circa 1572

PLANET HIVE, THE RAMANTHIAN EMPIRE

As the destroyer *Star Taker* dropped into orbit, the War Ubatha looked up through a viewport to the planet floating over his head. The mission to Bounty had been a waste of time and energy. But there was no way to have known that in advance.

Security around Hive had always been tight, but in the wake of the surprise attack that the Confederacy had launched eight standard months before, even more ships had been assigned to protect it. A show of force was necessary, of course, but the War Ubatha thought that another attack was unlikely, especially since the humans and their despicable allies were losing the war.

A patrol vessel issued a challenge to the destroyer. Codes were exchanged, checked, and double-checked. Then, and only then, was the *Star Taker* allowed to proceed to one of twenty-four heavily armed space stations that orbited Hive. It took the better part of an hour to dock and match locks. Finally, the War Ubatha was allowed to disembark. He, like all other incoming personnel, regardless of rank, had to pass through a Detox Center, where highly sophisticated sensors were used to detect off-world pathogens, cyborgs, and cleverly designed intelligence-gathering nanos. Some of which were only microns across.

Once cleared, the officer was released into the station proper. Rather than being forced to wait for a regular shuttle, the War Ubatha was escorted onto a military transport that departed moments later. The ship bumped its way down through the atmosphere and entered a high-priority flight path.

The War Ubatha never tired of looking at his home planet and peered through a viewport. In marked contrast to the ugly cities that covered Earth, it was the very picture of perfection. Rivers went where they should go, fruit trees marched in orderly rows across low-lying hills, and crops grew within irrigated circles.

All of which was made possible by the fact that Ramanthians preferred to live underground. A basic instinct that maximized the use of arable land and made their industrial base more difficult to attack. Not impossible, as had been proven months earlier, but more difficult.

Despite the race's carefully managed infrastructure, however, there was one variable they couldn't control. And that was the Ramanthian reproductive cycle. Because in addition to the three eggs produced by each tripartite family unit, the race had a secondary means of procreation as well. Every three hundred years or so, the Queen would produce *billions* of eggs. The result was a population explosion so massive that previous hatchings had triggered social change. Some birthings had positive effects. Like the one that led to interstellar travel. And some had led to famine and civil war.

Now, having been gifted with an estimated five billion new

souls by the great mother, the empire needed planets for them to live on. The race knew from bitter experience that Hive couldn't accommodate such a large number of additional citizens without negative consequences. Especially given the antisocial tendencies the newly hatched nymphs were known for.

The War Ubatha watched as the transport sped east, lights appeared below, and darkness cloaked the land. It wasn't long before the aircraft slowed and began a gradual descent. Eventually, the shuttle flared in for a vertical landing on a landing pad defined by a circle of amber lights. Once the skids made contact, a platform lowered the vessel into the ground.

Minutes later, the War Ubatha left the terminal, entered a government vehicle, and was whisked away. The funeral was scheduled for the next morning. That left just enough time to get some sleep and, if the gods were willing, a few hours of peace. Because even if the animals were millions of light-years away, he still fought them in his dreams.

THE PLAIN OF PAIN

The sky was clear, the sun was beating down, and the deep *boom, boom, boom* of the heart drums could be heard. The War Ubatha and the Egg Ubatha were seated toward the front of the seats reserved for members of the royal family, senior government officials, and members of the priesthood. Airborne cameras hovered here and there, beaming video to the citizens of Hive and the rest of the empire as well. It was a sad day. Having buried the great mother within the past year, the Ramanthian people were now forced to confront the death of her successor, the so-called Warrior Queen. She'd been a young, and some said reckless, royal who had been wounded on Earth and brought back to Hive. Unfortunately, the empire's finest doctors hadn't been able to save her. Or so the government claimed.

As her funeral cortege made its way up out of the Royal Reliquary, where the embossed casket had been on display for the requisite three days, a deafening clatter was heard as five hundred thousand citizens began to click their pincers. They were seated in a bowl-shaped amphitheater at the center of the Plain of Pain, where the pretenders had been slaughtered almost a thousand years earlier and all of the nest clans had been brought together under a single queen. Ancient weapons and chunks of fossilized chitin were still being found as scouring winds removed layers of sand and soil.

It was a moving sight as members of the funeral procession, all clad in imperial livery, shuffled up out of the underground complex and made their way toward the conical hill at the center of the dry lake bed. From there it was necessary to follow a spiral pathway to the top, where the Queen's remains would be cremated. The clatter had faded by then, but the mournful sound of the kleege pipes could still be heard, along with the occasional snap of a pennant as a persistent breeze blew from the east.

All of which was very touching except for one thing: The Queen was still very much alive. Or so the War Ubatha assumed. Although there was the possibility that the royal's paralysis had worsened and she had died. But there was no way to be sure. And that made her a threat. Because, were the royal to surface after the state funeral and the coronation of her carefully selected successor, both he and his allies would be tried and executed for treason. Thereby ensuring that the monarch's incompetent rule would continue, the empire would fall to the animals, and the thousand years of darkness that Nira the truth-bringer had warned of would begin.

The very thought of it made the War Ubatha feel cold even though he was seated in direct sunlight. The processional had arrived at the top of the hill by that time. The priests formed a circle and began the prayer for the dead as the richly decorated coffin was placed on a metal grating. The body inside was that of a female Skrum, or untouchable, who had been abducted and killed so that the casket would weigh the right amount. Plus, there were the remains to consider. Though spectacular, open-air cremations were notoriously inefficient. There were often beaks, bits of chitin, and toe claws left over. *Details are important,* the War Ubatha reminded himself. *Perfection can be achieved.*

Like all Ramanthians, the War Ubatha had excellent peripheral vision. That meant he could see the Egg Ubatha and her posture. As with all Ramanthians, her body language was quite eloquent if one knew what to look for. Even the slightest tilt of the head had meaning. But as one would expect of an upper-class female, the Egg Ubatha's body was expressionless. *What is she thinking?* he wondered. *About the funeral? About him? Or about their mate, Chancellor Itnor Ubatha?* The high-ranking government official had been listed as dead for weeks—even if no body had been recovered from the wreckage of his air car. Which raised an interesting question. If one of her mates was dead, why hadn't the Egg Ubatha spent more than the minimum required time in mourning?

The War Ubatha's thoughts were interrupted as a priest held the ceremonial spear of truth aloft, a tongue of fire shot up from deep inside the hill, and the casket was consumed in a ball of fire. Flames crackled, and gray smoke poured up into the sky, where, much to the satisfaction of the mourners, it was blown to the west. Thereby ensuring the Queen's speedy passage into the afterlife. *Or the Skrum's afterlife,* the War Ubatha thought to himself, as the Ramanthian people waited for the ceremony to end. The War Ubatha had killed her himself to make sure the job was carried out properly. Not a pleasant chore but a necessary one. Such was the life of a warrior.

THE PLACE WHERE THE QUEEN DWELLS

The royal eggery was empty and had been for many months, ever since the great mother's inevitable death and the Warrior Queen's ascension to the throne. But as the War Ubatha entered the royal residence and submitted himself to a biometric scan, he could smell the lingering egg odor. It was a reminder of the fact that billions of recently hatched Ramanthians were depending on him to do the right thing for them and the rest of the empire. No matter how difficult that might be.

The thought served to reinforce his sense of resolve as he shuffled up a series of ramps to the ornate platform where the grotesquely swollen great mother had been confined during the last months of her life. It was empty, and would remain so until another three hundred years had passed and another Queen was required to make the ultimate sacrifice.

A liveried functionary was waiting for him there and led the officer through an arched entryway into the private chambers beyond. It was there, within the royal reception hall, that the council of advisors was waiting for him. They were more than that, of course; because for all practical purposes, they were in control of the government. Not publicly. That would have to wait until their Queen officially named them to the posts they had chosen for themselves.

But thanks to the positions they had held during the great mother's reign, and the networks of cronies created then, the advisors were very much in control. It was a good thing, too. Because, unbeknownst to the average citizen, the empire was in grave danger, and urgent action was required to save it.

As the War Ubatha entered the reception hall, he saw that a curtained enclosure had been put in place on the raised platform normally occupied by the Queen's throne. That meant the Queen was seated within and would be able to hear the ensuing discussion. Not for the purpose of ruling, which the council would do on her behalf, but in order to play the part of figurehead with skill and grace. The draped cloister was a pretence, a way to have the royal-in-waiting present without having to defer to her.

Most of the council members were already present. That included Su Ixba, the onetime head of the Department of Criminal Prosecution. He was already hard at work vetting candidates for hundreds of important positions and identifying potential loyalists, who would soon find themselves living on remote nursery planets.

Ixba was seated next to Cam Taas, who had been in charge of the Department of Transportation until the Warrior Queen let him go. Though hidebound and averse to anything new, he was very dependable. And given the challenges before them, that was a valuable quality.

Also present were Admirals Tu Stik and Zo Nelo plus General Ma Amm. All were students of the third-century mystic warrior Haru Nira. There were greetings and formal bows all around. Then, as if determined to make an entrance, ex-Governor Oma Parth shuffled into the room. Though old enough to have age spots on his chitin, his movements were precise, and he exuded energy. Space black eyes darted from person to person. "You're all here . . . Excellent. We'll hear from Commander Ubatha first. His report will be followed by a strategic review. It's important to make sure all of us understand the current situation." Ubatha suspected the last was a reference to the queen-in-waiting.

"Please," Parth continued. "Take your seats. Commander Ubatha?"

Ubatha chose to remain standing as the others sat on matching saddle chairs. There was a skylight overhead, and sunshine pooled on flagstones worn smooth by thousands of shuffling feet. In keeping with his reputation for unflinching directness, the War Ubatha made no attempt to soften his report. "I am sorry to report that my mission to the hive world Bounty was a failure. As you know, the Warrior Queen was, or is, extremely popular there. So there was a distinct possibility that, having learned of our plan, Chancellor Ubatha might have taken the Queen to the planet. But such is not the case. Thanks to Su Ixba's intervention, members of the local police were *very* cooperative—and made use of their resources to scour the entire planet. A large cell of denialists was identified and dismantled. But there was no sign that they were hiding anyone."

All of the council members were aware that there were thousands, perhaps *hundreds* of thousands, of citizens so devoted to the Warrior Queen that they refused to believe that she was dead. Such individuals were generally referred to as denialists. Ixba clacked a pincer approvingly. "Well done."

"Thank you," Parth said, as he came to his feet. "I know I speak for the entire council when I say that Commander Ubatha's mission shouldn't be considered a complete failure. At least we know of one place where the Warrior Queen *isn't* hiding. We will return to that very important subject later on. In the meantime, let's review the strategic situation, which, in spite of numerous military victories, can only be described as poor.

"I suggest that we begin with a discussion of planet Earth. Truth be told, there were some things the Warrior Queen did right. One of them was to invade Earth's solar system, destroy the fleet positioned to protect it, and attack the planet itself. But then, rather than glass the pus ball, she made the decision to occupy it. That was worse than wrong—it was stupid. And I can prove it."

Those were strong words to direct against a monarch, even a failed one, and the War Ubatha wondered what the queen-to-be was thinking. But there was no way to know as Stik, Nello, and Amm all clacked their pincers in agreement.

"First," Parth continued, "by occupying Earth, we are tying up twenty divisions desperately needed elsewhere. Because, while our troops chase resistance fighters around the surface of the planet, there's evidence that the Confederacy is starting to target our nursery planets. Some of which are quite vulnerable. And that isn't all. In addition to the soldiers killed in action on Earth, we're losing personnel to some sort of disease. General Amm . . . What can you tell us about that?"

Insofar as Ubatha knew, Amm had never fired a shot in anger but had risen through the officer ranks by virtue of his administrative abilities and cold-blooded willingness to do whatever was necessary. A philosophy that was apparent in the way he answered the question. "We are investigating the nature of the problem, sir," Amm replied. "In the meantime, rather than run the risk of infecting additional personnel, or allowing the pathogen to reach other Ramanthian planets, a quarantine is in place. No additional troops will be sent to Earth—and no troops will be allowed to depart until this matter has been resolved."

"That's unfortunate," Parth said, "but it can't be avoided. Please let me know the moment more information becomes available."

Parth's eyes swept the small audience. "I'm sorry to say the challenges we face don't end there. All of you know that the Hudathans have surrendered their independence to the Confederacy in return for help in dealing with their increasingly uninhabitable home world. Meanwhile, thousands of so-called volunteers have been allowed to join the Legion. And they are very formidable warriors. So that has to be counted as a win for the Confederacy."

Was the new Queen taking all of it in? The War Ubatha hoped so as Parth tackled the next subject. "But, fortunately for us, the Hudathans are relatively few in number. That isn't true where the Clone Hegemony is concerned, however. Which is one of the reasons why the Warrior Queen chose to attack Gamma-014, where General Akoto's forces were victorious.

"But while that campaign was taking place, the Clone Hegemony's heretofore insular government was overthrown, and the rebels elected to join the Confederacy. That means we will be facing a unified command. One that is likely to make effective use of the clone military caste. So, as you can see, we face some formidable challenges. Did I leave anything out?"

"I think the Thrakies are worth a mention," Ixba said. "There's considerable evidence to suggest that they played a role in spiriting the Warrior Queen away. The question is whether the individuals who did so were acting on their own or with the knowledge and consent of their government. That would be very worrisome indeed. Because if they *know* the Warrior Queen is alive and where she is, the Thrakies could reveal that information and attempt to return her to the throne."

Parth clacked his agreement. "I think it's safe to assume that our furry friends are waiting to see what will happen, with plans to benefit either way." He turned toward Ubatha. "We can't allow the Thrakies to have that kind of power over us. Or to run the risk that the denialists will learn that the Queen is alive and coalesce around her. So, much as it pains me to do so, I'm afraid I must ask you to have a conversation with the Egg Ubatha. Believe me, I understand how painful such a situation is, but having failed to find the Warrior Queen any other way, we are left with no choice. If anyone knows where Chancellor Ubatha is, she does. And once you find your mate, the Queen will be nearby."

The War Ubatha had seen it coming but felt a heavy weight settle into the pit of his stomach nevertheless. Because despite everything Nira had written regarding the need for complete detachment, he was still in love with the Egg Ubatha. It was a weakness. He knew that. And one he would have to confront in order to pursue the Hath or "true path," a discipline so strict that devotees were expected to sever all ties with their mates. That had been relatively easy to do where Chancellor Ubatha was concerned, but this was different. He forced himself to reply. "I will speak with her."

"When?"

For one brief moment, the War Ubatha hated Parth and all the rest of them. "Soon," he clicked. "When the time is right."

Parth looked as if he wanted to challenge the reply but apparently thought better of it and chose to let the matter drop. "Good. Let's discuss the coronation."

THE PLACE WHERE THE QUEEN DWELLS

During the three days since the Warrior Queen's funeral, thousands of functionaries had worked day and night to prepare the underground city for the new Queen's coronation. And now their efforts were about to pay off. Tradition called for the processional to start at the small cavern that was one of the earliest known nests on Hive and a potent symbol of the long climb up to an interstellar civilization. From the cave, the royal was required to demonstrate her humility by shuffling through more than three miles of twisting, turning streets while the commoners looked on. During the journey, which was said to represent the challenges that a ruler must face, she would be required to climb a steep ramp, navigate her way around a mythical monster, and pass through a narrow corridor lined with mirrors. All the while wearing royal regalia that weighed thirty pounds and being tracked by airborne cameras. Along the way, a cheering populace would pelt her with sath seeds in hopes of bringing about an era of prosperity.

Meanwhile, streaming along behind her were hundreds of senior government, military, and religious figures, who by their presence signified their support for the new monarch. Parth, Ixba, Taas, Stik, Nelo, Amm, and Ubatha were at the very front of the column, all wearing formal robes or uniforms. Ubatha's consisted of a red pillbox hat, gold epaulettes, his medals, a pleated kilt, and a chromed pistol. His sword hung crosswise across his back.

To be there, to be on the receiving end no matter how indirectly of such enthusiastic applause, was heady stuff. And the War Ubatha felt a profound sense of pride as the Queen neared a contingent of soldiers from the *Death Hammer* Regiment, and they crashed to attention. Yet even as he took it all in, Nira's teachings haunted him. Because, according to the mystic, the warrior's true enemies were ego, possessions, and relationships. Such thoughts were sobering, and he gave thanks for them as a group of rarely seen Skrum prostrated themselves on the pavement.

Having successfully shuffled up the steep ramp that was symbolic of all the resistance the new Queen would have to overcome, it was time for her to confront the mythical monster. According to legend, the Kathong was the only thing that could destroy the royal house. The richly imagined statue was located in the middle of a traffic circle, where it was usually little more than a well-executed curiosity. But thanks to hundreds of years of tradition, the Kathong took on additional significance whenever a coronation was under way.

In some respects the beast looked a great deal like any Ramanthian, except that it had four tool arms rather than two, and a tail that was brandishing a trident. In keeping with tradition, the Queen stopped in front of the huge statue as if daring the Kathong to bar her way. The idea was that, if the beast disapproved of the Queen, it would suddenly come to life and devour her. It hadn't happened, of course, and never would, but Ubatha knew that news commentators would be talking about it nevertheless.

Having confronted the Kathong without being eaten, the royal continued on her way as thousands clacked their pincers—and she led the processional into the hall of images. The double rows of full-length mirrors were cautionary in nature, symbolizing all of the different ways in which truth could be expressed and the danger of falling victim to the sort of royal narcissism that some of her predecessors had been subject to.

From there it was a short distance to the royal dwelling, where the final ceremony would take place and the young female would become Queen. The only problem was that she wouldn't be the *real* Queen until such time as Ubatha could find the missing royal and kill her.

A full day had passed since the coronation. As the ground car stopped in front of the upscale dwelling, the War Ubatha steeled himself against what was to come. Two members of the military police were riding on a platform to the rear. He waited for one of them to step down and open his door. Slowly, and with a feeling of reluctance, he got out of the vehicle. It was a test of sorts. He forced himself to look at the familiar facade and monitor his emotions as he did so. Was he happy?

Or sad? No. Home was no longer a physical place but something he carried inside him. "Sir?" the noncom named Nenk inquired. "Should we accompany you?"

"Yes," Ubatha answered evenly. "And bring the satchel. We might need it."

Ubatha followed a short but scrupulously clean path to the front door. A single pair of sandals had been laid out in front of it. *His.* Because Chancellor Ubatha was dead. Or supposed to be. The War Ubatha entered a number into the key pad and waited for the door to move aside. Then, with two soldiers at his back, he entered what had once been his home.

He could smell the incense in the air, the faint odor of newly baked wafers, and what? A whiff of the Egg Orno's perfume? Ubatha felt a pang of regret, hurried to repress it, and made his way forward. First came the carefully arranged rock garden, followed by a hallway with heirloom prints on both walls and a formal reception room. The Egg Ubatha bowed as he arrived. Her click speech was both precise and elegant. "I'm sorry . . . I had no idea you were coming. I would have met you at the door."

"The fault was mine for not letting you know," the War Ubatha replied. "I suggest that we retire to the sitting area."

The Egg Ubatha made no move to obey. It was both literally and figuratively *her* house. "And your soldiers?"

"They are with me."

Bringing soldiers, especially enlisted soldiers, into the most intimate recesses of the house was unprecedented, and subtle changes in the Egg Ubatha's posture signaled her disapproval. "And your weapons?"

"They are part of me," the War Ubatha replied. He normally left his sidearm and sword on an antique rack designed for that purpose.

There was a good ten seconds of silence as she studied him. Then, having reached some internal decision, she turned and shuffled away. That was intentionally rude. But anger, like love, was something that Ubatha had forsworn. He followed.

The chamber beyond was large enough to seat twenty. Something the space had often been called upon to do back during the days when the Chancellor had been in residence. Saddle seats surrounded a tiled area that was empty at the moment but could be configured in a number of different ways. The Egg Ubatha stopped in the middle of it and turned. She was beautiful, or had been back when the soldier had been captive to such things. "Now what?" she said defiantly.

"Now you will tell me the truth," the War Ubatha replied coldly. "The Chancellor is still alive. Where is he?"

"How strange," she replied. "The government notified me of his death. Yet you believe he's alive. *Why?*"

The War Ubatha took three steps forward, brought his right pincer back over his left shoulder, and struck the side of her head. The Egg Ubatha fell and slid across the tiles. "Pick her up," the warrior ordered. "And hold her."

The troopers hurried to obey. The War Ubatha saw that the blow had pulped his mate's right eye. That hadn't been his intention. But what was, was. Perhaps it was for the best. She would take his questions seriously now. Blobs of viscous goo dripped down onto her otherwise-pristine gown. "I'm going to ask the question again," Ubatha said harshly, as his mate sobbed. "Where is the Chancellor? He would never leave Hive without telling you where he's going. Speak or suffer some more."

The Egg Ubatha was half-blind. But somehow, in spite of the intense pain, she managed to raise her head. "So this is what you have come to . . . I am to be dishonored by common filth."

"No," the War Ubatha replied. "You are to answer my questions. Turn her around."

The troopers, who were none too pleased by the way they had been described, wrestled her into position. The War Ubatha ripped the gown away. That exposed the Egg Ubatha's wings and the shiny chitin of her back. With that accomplished, he shuffled over to the satchel, rummaged around inside, and removed a pair of clippers.

Then it was back to where his mate was being held. The War Ubatha raised the tool so she could see it with her remaining eye. "Unless you answer my questions I am going to remove your right wing. Where is the Chancellor?"

She continued to sob but made no answer. The Egg Ubatha was defying him. And the War Ubatha couldn't help but admire her. Because deep down he knew that what she was doing for the Chancellor she would do for *him.* And her strength, as well as moral clarity, was worthy of a warrior. But to show pity was to violate the way. The War Ubatha took hold of a wing, cut it off, and felt a pang of regret when he heard her high-pitched scream. "Look," he said, as he held the appendage up for her to see. "Where is the Chancellor?"

The Egg Ubatha sobbed and said something unintelligible.

The warrior came closer. "Say it again."

She did.

"That's where he is?"

She answered in the affirmative.

The War Ubatha drew his sword. The weapon made a whispering sound as it left its sheath. "Release her."

The soldiers did so. The blade rose. Light glinted off the slightly curved blade as it came around. There was a loud *thunk* as it struck, and the Egg Ubatha's head fell free. Her body barely made a sound as it hit the floor. The War Ubatha bent to wipe his blade on her gown. Then, having returned the weapon to its sheath, he shuffled away. The Egg Ubatha's head lay on its side. A glassy eye watched him go.

3

War without allies is bad enough—with allies it is hell!

—*Sir John Slessor*
Strategy for the West
Standard year 1954

PLANET O-CHI 4, THE CONFEDERACY OF SENTIENT BEINGS

Having clumped into the living room of his waterfront home, Colonel Antov snatched the binos off the side table and brought them up to his eyes. A Ramanthian submarine! In the middle of Baynor's Bay. It didn't seem possible. Yet there the humpbacked apparition was, sitting on the surface and shelling his town.

Santana didn't have glasses. But the submarine was large enough that he didn't need them. The warship was about 150 feet long and mounted two auto cannons. One forward and one aft. They were firing three-round bursts at targets Santana couldn't see from his position. "Is this sort of thing common?" Santana inquired, as the com set in his pocket started to vibrate.

"No, sir," Captain Kimbo replied. "Air attacks, yes. But this is the first time the bugs have sent a submarine. We didn't know they had one. I wonder where it came from?"

"Odds are that the Ramanthians assembled it here," Antov said grimly as he lowered the binos. "They see the TACBASE as a harbinger of things to come and want to destroy it right away. Get on the horn, Captain. Order our people to open fire. Maybe we'll get lucky."

Santana removed the com set from his pocket but didn't open it. He knew Rona-Sa was on the other end and wanted to open fire. And judging from the water spouts that had appeared around the submarine, the people in the north-bay area already had. "Could I make a suggestion, sir? Before you open fire?"

Antov frowned. "Yes? What is it?"

"I suggest that we keep our troops on standby for a minute or two. Let's see what happens."

"You surprise me," Antov replied. "Why the hell would I . . ." Then a look of comprehension appeared on his face. "Why you tricky bastard! If we let them battle the sub by themselves, the bugs will concentrate their fire on the north side of the bay. And that will soften up Temo's followers for us."

"Exactly," Santana replied. "Meanwhile, with your permission, I'll send the Ramanthians a very nasty surprise."

The submarine's black hull was still wet and glistened in the sunlight as its auto cannons roared, explosions flashed across the surface of the TACBASE, and columns of dirt shot skyward all around it. Then the TACBASE disappeared inside a cloud of blue smoke as a dozen smoke grenades went off.

That wasn't going to stop the Ramanthian bombardment, of course, since the bugs had a clear infrared image to fire at, but it did give one of the Legion's quads an opportunity to disengage from the hull and head downslope without drawing as much fire attention as it would otherwise. The four-legged cyborg was twenty-five feet tall and weighed fifty tons. It was armed with self-loading missile launchers, a minigun that could be raised well above the massive hull, and a variety of antipersonnel weapons.

The cyborg's cargo compartment was large enough to accommodate tons of supplies, a mobile surgical suite, or a fully armed squad of bio bods and T-2s. But what made the quad a *truly* fearsome weapon was the fact that it was controlled by a biological rather than an electronic brain. Because human brains can improvise, break rules when necessary, and imagine things that machines can't. Even if Private Edwin Durkee was a convicted murderer.

That was what Earth's criminal justice system had said. And it was true. Eighteen standard months earlier, Durkee had been lying in wait when his stepfather entered the little frame house located just outside of Chico and shouted his wife's name. Or *his* version of her name, which was "bitch." As in, "Hey, bitch, where's my fucking dinner?"

It was a significant phrase because it inevitably signaled the beginning of a nightmarish evening. First came dinner, followed by half a bottle of vodka, and beatings for both his wife and her teenage son.

But not *that* night. Because Durkee was waiting. And one second after his stepfather said the word "dinner," a three-foot-long section of rusty pipe slammed into the older man's yellowed teeth and broke his jaw. Then, fueled by months of pent-up frustration and rage, Durkee beat his stepfather to death. Once the killing was over, Durkee made himself a peanut butter and jam sandwich and called the police. He was still in the process of eating it when they arrived. And that was how he earned the prison nickname "PJ."

The trial lasted four minutes and thirteen seconds. It was carried out by an artificial intelligence known as JMS 50.3, which received the facts gathered by the police and agreed to by Durkee in a carefully monitored confession, and came to the conclusion that the accused was guilty of premeditated murder. "Yes," JMS 50.3 agreed in response to a request for leniency from Durkee's court-appointed attorney. "There were extenuating circumstances. But since neither the accused nor his mother was under attack at the time of the killing, there is no way that citizen Durkee can claim self-defense."

So Durkee was sentenced to death. And in keeping with the letter of the law, the execution consisted of a carefully staged reenactment of the murder. Only with Durkee playing the role of victim this time. It was televised live for the purpose of preventing homicides. Except everyone knew that most of the people who watched the judicial channel did so because they enjoyed watching executions.

Durkee was strapped to a special X-shaped stand and his head was clamped in place as the piece of pipe smashed through his teeth. That was when he screamed, or tried to, but a second blow put an end to that. Moments later, Durkee was dead. Well, mostly dead. Because Durkee had been offered a reprieve of sorts. The agreement was simple. He couldn't have his biological body back. That wouldn't be fair to his victim. But he could enlist in the Legion, become a cyborg, and continue to exist. So his brain had been salvaged, installed in a high-tech life-support box, and trained to "wear" a quad.

As Durkee guided his huge body down a boat ramp and into the water, his onboard computer opened a series of valves that allowed water to rush into the saddle tanks located on both sides of his hull. That was sufficient to compensate for the air trapped in the tightly sealed cargo compartment so that the cyborg could walk on the seabed.

As Durkee prepared to enter combat for the first time, he was conscious of all sorts of things, including the data that scrolled down one side of his electronic "vision," the way the six-inch-deep muck pulled at his foot pods, and the fear in his nonexistent belly. Here he was, a kid from the projects, about to tackle an enemy submarine all by himself.

The mission was simple, or that was what Captain Rona-Sa had said. "All you have to do is stroll out there, put a missile in that thing, and walk back. They'll never know what hit them."

The plan sounded good. Real good. And it seemed to be working as Durkee's lights crept across the bottom, and a fish with an enormous jaw burst up out of the mud, gave a powerful flick of its eel-like tail, and disappeared into the surrounding gloom. What looked like a dimly lit wall appeared up ahead. Except it wasn't a wall. The barge, which was covered with a thick layer of marine growth, had clearly been there for a long time and was stretched lengthwise across Durkee's path.

That forced the cyborg to turn right to bypass the obstruction, a detour that would consume valuable time. Meanwhile, Durkee's sensors were feeding him information on the water temperature, a current that was running left to right, and the target's position relative to his. All he had to do was think about the targeting grid in order to summon it up. The submarine was a sausage-shaped blob of orange light located at the center of the crisscrossing amber lines. A tone sounded as Durkee rounded the north end of the barge and came into range.

The multipurpose missiles loaded onto Durkee's racks could be used in a wide variety of environments, including the one he was in. But the cyborg knew that the surrounding liquid would slow the missiles down. And once the bugs became aware of the attack, they would use the lengthy "flight" time to employ countermeasures. So Durkee wanted to close the distance between himself and the sub. It was something Rona-Sa had been emphatic about. "You will have the advantage of surprise the first time you fire. But not the second."

Of course, if Durkee waited *too* long and the sub got under way, the opportunity to destroy it would disappear. So a compromise was in order. And, because the target was currently broadside to him, Durkee decided to go for it.

He paused, brought his missile launchers online, and "felt" them deploy from recesses located along the top surface of his hull. Then, as the ready lights appeared, he fired. There was an explosion of bubbles as the missiles sped away. Durkee "heard" a tone and felt a momentary sense of jubilation as the weapons locked onto their target. But that emotion was snatched away as the sub began to turn toward him. The chits knew! They had been a little slow on the uptake, just as Rona-Sa predicted they would be, but they were reacting now.

The cyborg swore as the sub fired a salvo of minitorps from side-mounted tubes. The underwater flares exploded, forcing the guidance systems in Durkee's missiles to choose between the original heat source and new ones. One of his weapons fell for the ruse and veered away. The other hit the sub and exploded. But it was still in the process of turning. So even though some damage had been done, the Ramanthian ship remained operational.

That was too bad. So was the fact that the sub was equipped with torpedo tubes in addition to deck guns. Durkee's onboard computer had a tendency to belabor the obvious. "Two enemy torpedoes have been fired and are running. Estimated time to impact is thirty-two seconds. Thirty-one . . . Thirty . . . Twenty-nine . . ."

Despite the fact that Durkee's war form could operate underwater, it hadn't been designed to battle submarines and had no defense against incoming torpedoes other than the thickness of its hull. So all Durkee could do was fire another salvo of missiles in hopes of scoring a lucky hit. Meanwhile, he was backing around the sunken barge in an attempt to take shelter behind it. The strategy worked to some extent as one of the Ramanthian torpedoes hit the wreck and exploded.

Durkee's brain registered the momentary flash of light and "felt" the resulting concussion. But his senses were immediately overwhelmed by a searing pain as the second torpedo struck his right foreleg and blew it off.

Durkee knew that when his war form took a hit, the onboard computer was programmed to provide him with negative feedback by stimulating his thalmus and somatosensory cortex. The idea was to force cyborgs to protect their extremely expensive bodies. The fact that it was artificial didn't make the pain any less excruciating, however.

What happened next was more a matter of instinct than logic. Even though Durkee had lost a leg, he could still move, albeit not very gracefully. Alarms battled for his attention, and the stump flailed wildly as Durkee ordered his body forward. One of the follow-up missiles had scored a hit. And there was a momentary lag as the Ramanthians reacted to the blow. Precious seconds during which Durkee was determined to close with the sub and get directly beneath it. Because once in place, it would be impossible for the bugs to fire on him without endangering themselves as well.

Mud dislodged by Durkee's foot pods rose to cloud the water, a dark ribbon of bloodlike hydraulic fluid trailed away from his stump, and there was a terrifying *thud* as a Ramanthian torpedo hit the quad. But, rather than going off, the weapon simply fell away. That raised the possibility that Durkee had entered the zone where an explosion would threaten the sub, a theory reinforced by the fact that the cyborg was "looking" up at the enemy vessel by that time.

The realization that he was safe, for the moment at least, was followed by an overriding question: How could he destroy the sub? At close range, his missiles were just as impotent as the Ramanthian torpedoes were. Then, like a bolt out of the blue, the answer came to him. Durkee blew his tanks. And as a large quantity of water was forced out of the war form's hull, it shot upwards. Durkee shut his eyes, or tried to, and waited to die.

Santana was worried. And for good reason. He was standing on the seawall out in front of Colonel Antov's home. The Ramanthian submarine shuddered, as if it had been hit from below, but continued to shell the north side of the bay. Nearly fifteen minutes had elapsed since Private Durkee had entered the water. And rather than the quick kill that he had envisioned, a protracted battle was under way. Now, with the benefit of twenty-twenty hindsight, Santana knew it had been foolish to pit an inexperienced legionnaire against a Ramanthian submarine.

One aspect of the plan had gone well, however. True to his prediction, the sub's commander had turned both of his guns on the north side of the bay in an attempt to suppress the fire coming from that direction. But he couldn't let that continue for much longer. Not if there was to be any hope of bringing Temo's O-Chi Scouts back into the Confederate fold. Plus, there was the matter of civilian casualties to consider. So he was about to recommend that *all* of Antov's forces including the TACBASE open fire when something unexpected occurred.

As Santana and hundreds of others looked on, something struck the Ramanthian ship from below and lifted it out of the water. The submarine seemed to hang there for a moment, as if suspended in time, before breaking open and spilling some of its contents into the swirling sea. A terrible groan was heard as the metal hull was torn apart, and both halves of the submersible took a final dive. Onlookers caught a brief glimpse of a boxy hull before it, too, slid beneath the waves.

"Damn," Antov said from a couple of feet away. "What was that?"

"*That* was a quad," Santana replied as he lowered a pair of binos.

"Really? How many did you send?"

"One."

Antov looked incredulous. "Only one?"

"There was one submarine."

Antov laughed. "What now?"

"We'll regroup," Santana replied. "And get some rest. Then, first thing in the morning, I'll pay Major Temo a visit."

The night passed without incident. Santana's alarm went off at 0400. After a shave, a shower, and some of the O-Chi caf that Antov had provided, Santana was ready to face another day. Captain Zarrella was already in the process of inspecting the first platoon as he made his way across the base to visit Durkee.

Having returned home under his own power, the quad had been able to back into his parking bay and successfully reintegrate himself with the fortress on top of Signal Hill. A damage assessment had been carried out, and the results weren't good. There was no way to recover, much less repair, the missing leg—and the TACBASE was too small to carry a full array of spares. A significant amount of damage had been sustained when the cyborg surfaced under the submarine as well. So rather than hand the job off to Zarrella, Santana had assigned himself the task of delivering the news.

Durkee's cargo bay was open. Santana entered, went over to the fold-down seat intended for use by the quad's platoon leader, and sat down. After pulling a headset on, he spoke. "Private Durkee? This is Major Santana . . . Do you read me?"

There was a slight hesitation, as if Durkee had been caught

unawares or was worried about getting in trouble. "Sir? Yes, sir."

"Good. I'll get right to the point. First, you did a damned good job yesterday, and I was very impressed. So was Captain Rona-Sa. And he doesn't impress easily."

Durkee sounded relieved. "Thank you, sir."

"Second, I'm promoting you to corporal effective today, and I'm putting you in for a DSM. Of course, the approval process takes time—so you may be forty by the time you actually get it. That's the good news.

"The bad news is that we can't repair your leg. So, rather than accompany us on the mission, I'll have to leave you here. But I understand the bugs come by to shoot the place up every now and then, so stay sharp. I'm counting on you to protect the TACBASE and the local civilians."

Durkee was both surprised and pleased that Santana would come to visit him. *And* put him in for a medal. His mother would be proud.

As for the leg, and limited duty, well that was something of a mixed bag. Durkee didn't know them very well as yet, but he still felt a sense of kinship with the other legionnaires and wanted to accompany them. Still, he had a bad feeling regarding the mission and knew he'd be safer in Baynor's Bay. "Yes, sir. Thank you, sir. I'll do my best."

The sky was gray, a steady rain was falling, and visibility was limited to a half mile as Captain Jo Zarrella and Lieutenant Bo Betz led the first platoon down the hill and north through the part of Baynor's Bay that Santana hadn't seen the day before. The force consisted of eighteen bio bods and an equal number of T-2s. All of the quads had been left at the TACBASE because Santana wanted to emphasize mobility over brute force.

After years as a company commander and a platoon leader before that, it felt strange to ride in the four slot. And to know that if the column came under fire, it would behoove him to keep his mouth shut unless asked for advice. Otherwise, Santana would run the risk of undermining Zarrella's credibility.

Having been sent along in the role of advisor, Captain Kimbo and his T-2 were to Santana's right. Kimbo's visor was up, and he looked a bit green around the edges, leading Santana to suspect that he was seasick. It was a common occurrence for anyone not accustomed to riding a T-2. But practice makes perfect, and Santana felt sure that the last thing the militia officer would want was sympathy.

Santana allowed his weight to rest against the harness as Joshi carried him past the homes that lined the beach, occasional businesses, and piles of rubble. Computer-controlled antiaircraft weapons were located at half-mile intervals. They swiveled left or right as large seabirds triggered their sensors.

After a fifteen-minute jog, the patrol arrived at a barricade that consisted of an old fishing boat, two wrecked vehicles, and at least a ton of assorted junk. Kimbo appeared to be feeling a bit better—and pitched his voice so Santana could hear it. "This marks the border between the area controlled by Colonel Antov's Rifles and Major Temo's Scouts. It's more symbolic than anything else. There hasn't been any combat. Not yet anyway."

"We'll try to keep it that way," Santana replied, as the column of T-2s snaked its way around the barricade and returned to the highway. The legionnaires were wearing long slickers over their body armor, but cold rainwater still found its way past Santana's collar and began to trickle down his back.

This time there were no clusters of welcoming citizens. The locals were present, though. They peeked from windows or stopped what they were doing to watch the off-world troops splash past. None of them smiled or waved. Santana understood. The locals had every reason to support Temo given how important her family's pharmaceutical plant was to the local economy. But, after months of being attacked by the Ramanthians, they had to feel a little better now that some Confed troops were on the ground. Maybe that would help to bring them around. Santana's thoughts were interrupted by a burst of static and the sound of Ponco's voice. "Zulu Seven to Zulu Nine. Over."

Ponco was scouting ahead. And when Santana brought his HUD (heads-up display) up, he could see a delta marked A-2 superimposed over a map of north bay. It was about half a mile ahead. "This is Nine. Go. Over."

"A platoon of O-Chi Scouts is blocking the road. Their PL, a lieutenant named Milly Yorty, wants to speak with you. Over."

"She's a good officer," Kimbo put in from his position to Santana's right. "But not one of Temo's favorites. Which is a good thing in my opinion."

Santana opened his mike. "Tell Lieutenant Yorty that I'd be happy to speak with her. We'll be there shortly. Over."

As the distance between the houses began to close, Santana saw gaps where dwellings had been destroyed. One of them was at least three homes wide. What had been a fortified gun battery was positioned at the center of the still-steaming rubble. It appeared to have taken a direct hit, and the crew was almost certainly dead. Probably as a result of the manner in which Santana had manipulated the situation.

He felt a sudden surge of guilt, wondered if he'd been wrong to engineer the bombardment of north bay, and what Christine would think of the strategy. She was a diplomat, but a tough one, so it was impossible to know.

Then the column began to slow and came to a complete halt as Captain Zarrella's voice came over the platoon push. "Alpha Six to Alpha One-Six. We're going to pause here. Have the first squad take up defensive positions. Over."

Zarrella clearly had a good grasp of the situation, and Santana felt pleased, as Lieutenant Betz acknowledged the order. Then, as Joshi came to a stop, Kimbo's T-2 sidled up next to him. "Would you like me to go forward, sir?" Kimbo inquired.

"Thanks, but no thanks," Santana responded. "If you were to serve as a go-between, the Scouts might conclude that the Legion is taking sides. I'd like to avoid that if possible."

Kimbo nodded. If he felt disappointed, there was no sign of it on his face as Ponco arrived. Her rain-streaked body coasted to a stop a few feet away. "The lieutenant is waiting, sir."

"Okay," Santana said as he hit the harness release. "I'll go forward on foot. Sergeant Joshi can be somewhat intimidating."

"Who, *me*?" the T-2 growled innocently.

Santana grinned, jumped to the ground, and made his way past Zarrella and her T-2 to the point where a couple of olive drab ATVs blocked the road. The heavily armed vehicles *looked* imposing. But any one of the T-2s could have cleared them away in seconds. The lieutenant was a small rain-soaked figure who came forward to meet him as her troops looked on. She was wearing a black beret with a crossed-machete insignia on it, a glistening poncho, and jungle boots. Water splashed away from them as she stomped both feet and came to attention. The salute was crisp and perfectly executed. "Lieutenant Milly Yorty, *sir*!"

Santana returned the salute. "At ease, Lieutenant. I'm Major Santana. Thanks for coming out to meet us. Especially in this downpour."

Yorty had brown hair, a round face, and wide-set eyes. Santana thought he saw relief in them. Maybe she had been expecting a fire-breathing fanatic or something. Yorty nodded hesitantly. "You're welcome, sir. Normally, Major Temo would be here. Or Captain Omo. But they aren't available right now."

Santana could tell there was more. And Yorty wanted to tell him. All he had to do was ask. "I see. If you don't mind my asking, where are your senior officers?"

Yorty's eyes flicked away and came back again. "There was a disagreement, sir. When it became clear that the Legion had landed, some of us felt that we should report to you for orders. Others, the major included, believe the Scouts should operate independently until certain matters have been resolved."

"Meaning Major Temo's claim on the governorship?"

Yorty nodded. "Yes, sir."

"I see. Well, Lieutenant, here's the situation as I see it. Governors are named by the president of the Confederacy—and must be confirmed by the Senate. That means the lieutenant governor is in charge of civilian affairs for the moment. And it's my understanding that she resides in the city of Tal, about a thousand miles west of here. True?"

"Yes, sir."

"Good. That's settled then. As for the Scouts, this is a time of war, which means they fall under the senior officer on O-Chi 4. And, like it or not, that's Colonel Antov. But, as his executive officer, I can assure you that you and your troops will be treated fairly."

"Sir, yes sir. And the others? Those who followed the major into the bush?"

"I want them to return to duty," Santana answered. "We

were sent here to tackle an important mission, and we're going to need all the support we can get. But if Major Temo's troops fail to report within two local rotations I will list them as deserters. And, if they attack anyone other than the Ramanthians, I'll charge them with treason. So you might want to pass the word."

Yorty swallowed. "Yes, sir. And Major Temo?"

"The same applies to Major Temo. Although she's likely to face charges no matter what happens. But that won't be up to me. Where is she anyway?"

Yorty looked at her boots and back up again. She was clearly conflicted. "May I ask what will happen if I tell you?"

"No," Santana replied levelly. "You can't. Please answer the question."

There was a long moment of silence as Yorty studied her boots again. Finally, her eyes came up to meet Santana's, and she began to talk.

It was nighttime. But, thanks to the three moons that were slowly arcing across the sky, a silvery glow pervaded the upper reaches of the forest. However, lower down, within the inky blackness that lay between the trees, nocturnal animals were locked in life-and-death battles as Ponco hovered some fifty feet above. The surface of O-Chi 4 was a dangerous place regardless, but the darkness made the cacophony of screeches, howls, and gibbering noises even more unnerving.

More than two days had passed since the landing. Roughly half of the O-Chi Scouts had reported for duty, choosing Colonel Antov and the Confederacy over the rebellious Major Temo. That was progress of a sort. But, with a group of well-armed renegades out in the bush ready to attack Baynor's Bay at the first opportunity, Santana couldn't go after the Ramanthians.

So with time ticking away, the decision was made to track Temo down and capture or kill her. However, first they had to close with her. And the Temo clan's hunting lodge was up ahead. But before charging into the area with guns blazing, Ponco took a moment to look around. She had been killed twice before and had no desire to go through the process again.

Her first death had taken place when the assault boat that she and her platoon were riding in was shot down during the attempt to retake Savas Prime. Fortunately for her and a couple of other legionnaires, the navy pilot had been able to crash-land within a quarter mile of a Confed field hospital. That was when Ponco's brain had been surgically removed from her shattered body and shipped to Adobe, along with more than twenty others.

A few days later, Ponco woke up to discover that most of her body had been left back on Savas Prime, and she was wired to a life-support system. It was a terrible shock. She wanted to cry, to sob herself to sleep, but lacked the means. A computer took note of her brain waves, administered a sedative, and put her under.

Three days later, a cheerful noncom stopped by. He offered her a job as a T-2. The other choices were to buy a civilian-style body she couldn't afford or remain bodiless and wait. Maybe, if she and others like her were lucky, the government would grant them utilitarian spider forms as part of the much-debated veterans bill presently stalled in the Senate. Or maybe she would eventually die of old age. The choice was no choice at all.

Then, seven standard months later, Ponco had been killed all over again when a shoulder-launched missile hit the middle of her chest and exploded. Fortunately, a bio bod had had the presence of mind to find her severed head, pull her protective brain box, and hand it over to a medic. It was during the subsequent recovery process that Ponco had been invited to join military intelligence. And now, after months of additional training, she was risking her life again. *How many lives do I have left?* she wondered. There was no way to know. But she liked Santana. And was happy to serve under him.

Having checked the area, Ponco ghosted forward. Her sensors were on high gain and sensitive to even the slightest bit of heat, movement, or electronic activity. The problem was that, because they were set on max, her detection systems were producing a great deal of clutter. And all of it had to be evaluated. Most of the heat signatures belonged to local life-forms and could be ignored.

But when Ponco saw what looked like a string of lights hanging between two giant trees, she knew she was looking at a chain of proximity detectors that could pick up on the metal in her body, thereby distinguishing her from the local wildlife. That brought her to a full stop. Her voice was internalized and made no sound whatsoever. "Zulu Seven to Zulu Nine. I can't advance without triggering a chain of proximity detectors. Over."

There was a momentary pause followed by the sound of Santana's voice. "This is Nine . . . Roger that. We're almost in position. Give us three minutes and go in hard. Take out any bio bods you see. Especially those on the elevated weapons platforms that Lieutenant Yorty warned us about. Over."

As part of Santana's effort to make peace between the two factions, members of both the O-Chi Rifles and Scouts had been intentionally barred from participating in the mission. And that was fine except for the fact that it left the Legion to carry the load and absorb all of the casualties. "Roger," Ponco replied. "Three and counting. Over."

Time seemed to slow as the recon ball allowed herself to drift in among some branches. Ponco knew that the ground-assault team had to slip past the huge X-shaped animal barriers that ringed the lodge before it could proceed. Then, as the final seconds ticked away, Ponco went on the attack.

Consistent with her orders, the Intel officer sped past the chain of proximity detectors, followed a leafy passageway into the clearing beyond, and "saw" a huge blob of heat. The elaborate tree house was located about fifty feet off the forest floor, where it was safe from even the largest predators and well positioned to repel a human ground attack. No wonder Temo had taken refuge there.

But lofty though the lodge might be, it was still vulnerable from the air. And, as a Klaxon began to bleat, Temo's soldiers were already dying. Wooden platforms had been established high in the branches of the surrounding trees. Each supported an automatic weapon and a two-person crew. All of whom were positioned to fire on the assault team below.

Ponco's initial shots were fired from long range as she swept into the clearing that fronted the lodge. A gunner was snatched off his platform and thrown into the darkness, quickly followed by his loader, who crashed through a succession of branches before thumping into the ground.

Then the attack became increasingly personal as Ponco passed within feet of a second crew-served weapon. The gunner shouted something incoherent as Ponco dropped a grenade at his feet and accelerated away. There was a flash of light as the resulting explosion lit up the forest, and the assault team entered the clearing. The chatter of machine guns blended with the staccato bark of assault rifles to create a hellish symphony.

Ponco couldn't deal with all of the aerial gun platforms, however. Not and take care of her primary mission, which was to prevent Temo from escaping in the family's private air car. The orange-red blob was sitting on a circular landing pad, adjacent to the lodge, ready for takeoff.

The defenders had Ponco in their sights by then, and two streams of tracers rose to greet the recon ball as she prepared to release a thermite bomb from her small drop bay. She only had one of the weapons, so accuracy was important. A bullet slammed into Ponco's casing, glanced off, and whined away. But the impact was sufficient to knock the recon ball off course and send her spinning.

The tracers sought to follow her as Ponco fired her steering jets. Then, once the cyborg had regained control, she went in for the kill. The bomb fell, landed right in the middle of the open air car, and detonated. The result was a column of fire that shot straight upwards as a mixture of powdered red iron and aluminum was ignited. The air car was destroyed in a matter of seconds as Ponco entered a spiraling climb, paused a hundred feet off the ground, and looked back. "Zulu Seven to Zulu Nine. Objective destroyed. Over."

Santana experienced a momentary sense of satisfaction as Ponco's report came in. But the emotion was short-lived as someone fired from above. Geysers of loam shot up all around Santana, Dietrich, and their T-2s. Thanks to his onboard computer, Joshi could pinpoint the exact spot the fire was coming from. His arm-mounted energy cannon came up and sent blips of coherent energy into the treetops. Dietrich's T-2 joined the effort, and Santana watched as the blue blobs converged on each other.

He heard a scream, followed by a sequence of crashing noises as a severed branch fell. The limb was at least twenty-five feet long and two feet thick at the butt end. That made it large enough to crush Private Morton *and* his T-2. Both of whom vanished from the Integrated Tactical Command (ITC) system on Santana's HUD.

That was bad, but things were about to become worse, as

the surviving cyborgs charged across the clearing and grenades fell around them. Though random, the bombardment was effective. A headless bio bod continued to ride the T-2 off to Santana's left as an explosion blew a cyborg's foot off. He fell, taking his rider down with him, while geysers of dirt rose all around.

Then, as Joshi began to close with the enormous tree trunk, the number of explosions started to dwindle. Santana thought he knew why. Ponco was still at work high above, as were his Naa snipers, both of whom had orders to stay back and fire on targets of opportunity.

The tree trunk that supported the lodge was at least fifty feet in diameter, and the lowest branches were twenty feet overhead. "Okay," Santana said, as Joshi came to a halt. "This is where I get off. Watch your six."

"Roger that," Joshi replied. "Give me a holler when you're ready to leave."

Dietrich was next to him as Santana followed the trunk around to the right with his CA-10 carbine at the ready. There were two ways to reach the lodge according to Yorty. An elevator, which was sure to be off-line, and a spiral staircase that circled the tree. It would have been nice to send a T-2 up to clear the way. But the cyborgs were too big and heavy.

A few moments later, Santana and Dietrich arrived at the foot of the stairs, where a squad of bio bods was gathered. "What's this?" Dietrich demanded harshly. "A circle jerk? The enemy is up there—not down here. Follow me and keep your heads on a swivel."

Dietrich was carrying a drum-fed shotgun, which was ideal for close-in work. So Santana took the two slot and chinned the mike switch as they began to climb. "Zulu Nine to Zulu Seven. We're on the stairs. Clear the way if you can. Over."

There was no response as a grenade fell from above, hit a

railing, and bounced into the gloom. That was followed by a flash of light, a loud explosion, and a series of woody thuds as pieces of shrapnel struck the tree trunk. Then came the rattle of an automatic weapon, which Dietrich answered with three blasts from his shotgun.

The firing stopped, and two bodies were sprawled on the blood-slicked platform when Santana arrived. He followed Dietrich as the noncom led him upwards. It was a steep climb, and the officer was struggling to catch his breath when Ponco's voice sounded in his helmet. "Zulu Seven to Zulu Nine. I think I have the target located. Mark my position. Over."

Santana took a moment to scan the ITC. The recon ball was about fifteen feet above and south of the main trunk. "Roger that . . . We're on the way. Over."

Dietrich heard, continued to lead the way upwards, and arrived on a generously proportioned observation deck moments later. A tribarreled minigun had been set up there. But, judging from the dead bodies scattered about, either Ponco or one of the snipers had been able to silence the weapon.

The darkened lodge was on their left as they followed the deck to a suspended walkway. The bridge was supported by cables fastened to the branches above and started to sway as the legionnaires crossed it. Santana was forced to let his weapon dangle from its sling so that he could get a firm grip on the side ropes. The ITC system was still displayed on his HUD, and he could see Ponco's Z-7 marker pulsing on and off about fifty feet in front of him. Major Temo was within his grasp. Or so it seemed until Ponco shouted a warning, a powerful light flooded the area, and a windstorm descended on them.

"It's a transport!" Dietrich shouted. "They're coming for Temo." And as Santana looked up into the dazzling spotlight, he realized that the noncom was correct. A ship was about to rescue Temo. But how could that be? The local militia had one cargo vessel, and it was called *The Hangar Queen* for a reason. But what if . . .

"Watch out . . . I think the ship is Ramanthian," Ponco said over the radio. Suddenly, fire lashed down from above, the rope bridge parted, and Santana began to fall.

4

No good deed goes unpunished.

—Human folk saying
Standard year circa 1800

ABOARD THE CONFEDERACY TRANSPORT *GALAXSIS* IN HYPERSPACE

The *Galaxsis* was more than three miles long and had once been a very posh passenger liner. But with the coming of the war, she'd been taken over by the navy for use as a transport. That meant most of the fancy cutlery, dishes, art, furniture, and expensive carpets had been replaced with less expensive equivalents. But even without all of the finery, there was no doubt as to the ship's pedigree. The *Galaxsis* was all about class, which was apparent in her glossy wood trim, solid brass fittings, and marble decks.

The ship's official capacity was fifty-four hundred passengers. But by assigning three people to cabins intended for two, and converting the space formerly occupied by an onboard shopping arcade into stacked berths, the navy had been able to cram another five hundred passengers aboard. And Foreign Service Officer-2 (FSO-2) Christine Vanderveen was among them.

But thanks to her status as a high-ranking civil servant,

plus some good luck, she had been slotted into a cabin with only one other occupant. Captain Marcie Jones was a doctor and a member of the Legion's 2nd REI (2nd Foreign Infantry Regiment) currently conducting training exercises on Algeron. The planet that had long served as the Legion's home—and was the current seat of the Confederacy's government.

Both women were getting ready for their final dinner aboard the *Galaxsis*. No one expected the sort of lavish meal that had been typical before the war. But the food promised to be a welcome change from the monotonous cafeteria-style meals of the last week. And, as Jones had put it moments earlier, the dinner was likely to be ". . . a very good hunting ground." By which she meant an opportunity to meet men.

But as Vanderveen put on her red lipstick, she was only interested in *one* man. And he wasn't on the ship. The woman who looked back at her from the mirror had shoulder-length blond hair and blue eyes. They were bracketed by the beginnings of tiny wrinkles. It was the price paid for her service on planets like LaNor and Jericho, not to mention the shortage of good skin creams. She sighed. "So what are you after? A colonel perhaps?"

"Don't be silly," Marcie replied from inside their tiny bathroom. "Colonels are too old! A major perhaps . . . Or a handsome lieutenant."

"But you're a captain," Vanderveen objected. "Captains can't date lieutenants."

"For the moment," Jones agreed as she stepped into the stateroom. "But not forever. Once the war is over, most of us will go back to whatever we were doing before it started. And some lieutenants were doing very well indeed! How do I look?"

Jones was petite, with military-short brown hair and a pretty face. Her uniform looked as if it had been sprayed on. "You're the hottest captain in the Legion," Vanderveen replied. "Bring your sidearm. You'll need it."

Jones laughed. "Look who's talking! That's a very nice black dress . . . And those diamond earrings. Someone likes you."

"Yes, he does," Vanderveen replied. "And I call him 'Daddy.' Are you ready? Let's go."

A side corridor led the women out onto what was still called the Galactic Promenade. Even if the majority of the beings strolling along it were wearing uniforms rather than fancy evening dress. Vanderveen wasn't the only civilian, however. Far from it. The crowd included business types, a delegation of nearly identical clones, a group of Thrakies, and a pair of brightly plumed Prithian merchants.

Foot traffic slowed as those assigned to the second sitting jammed the approaches to the dining room. But not for long, as identical androids scanned ID bracelets and led the passengers to their tables. The dining room occupied a duraplast blister on the ship's skin. While in orbit around a planet, passengers could look out upon the world below. And when in hyperspace, as they were at the moment, a sensaround was projected onto the curving viewport to give the impression of a starscape. That was why the spectacular Horsehead Nebula appeared to be all around them.

As Vanderveen followed the formally attired robot down one of the spokelike corridors toward the center of the wheel-shaped room, she saw that the ship's social director was still doing her job. Those tables located on the outer rings were traditionally occupied by relatively-lower-status beings. In this case, enlisted personnel from all the various branches. Junior and midlevel officers came next. That included Jones, who waved gaily as a waiter led her over to a table occupied entirely by men.

Vanderveen envied the doctor in a way since military officers were a known quantity, and one could tell who outranked whom by looking at their uniforms. Her world was a good deal more complicated. Was the ambassador the one to court? Or was the title more honorary than real? Perhaps the less flashy Adjunct for Interspecies Communications had the *real* clout. One rarely knew when meeting foreign dignitaries for the first time.

So as Vanderveen was led to a six-person table only three rings from the center of the room, she felt a mild sense of apprehension. Though not on duty, she was never truly off duty either. And that made it difficult to relax. At her approach, three of those seated at the table rose to greet her. The nearest and therefore the first to introduce himself was a Legion general named George Tuchida. Judging from the chromed plate set into the right side of his skull, and the whirring noises that accompanied his movements, Tuchida was a "partial." Meaning a cyborg who was still using significant parts of his original body. He turned to announce her name and title to the rest of those seated at the table.

And even though she hadn't seen him in many years—it turned out that Vanderveen already knew the second man who came forward to greet her. His name was Rex Soro, the eventual heir to the Soro computer fortune and a classmate from her college days. He looked a bit older, but still handsome, and was impeccably dressed. She caught a whiff of expensive cologne as he leaned in to hug her. "Vanders! What a wonderful surprise. You look gorgeous. And no ring. Let's mate."

"I never mate prior to dinner," Vanderveen said primly, "but thank you for the invitation. I see you haven't changed." Soros laughed.

"My name is Hambu Tras Gormo," the frail-looking Dweller said. His sticklike body was supported by the high-tech exoskeleton that made it possible for him to leave his low-gravity home world and travel to other planets. The device emitted a soft whining sound as the Dweller offered a formal bow.

Vanderveen recognized the name. "*Senator* Tras Gormo? It's an honor to meet you."

Tras Gormo bowed again.

"And this," Soro said, as he gestured to the only other female present, "is the famous Misty Melody."

"It's a pleasure to meet you," Vanderveen said, as the woman in question looked up from a gold compact. She had shoulder-length silver hair and had been poured into a matching dress. Her breasts were not only unnaturally large but almost entirely exposed. "I have all of your albums," Vanderveen said truthfully. "You have a beautiful voice."

Melody's smile was unexpectedly genuine. "Why, thank you . . . It's the only part of me that's real."

The comment was so unexpectedly honest that Vanderveen had to laugh. "Miss Melody is going to perform for the troops on Algeron," Tuchida put in. "And we're very grateful."

"We'll see if the general feels the same way once the screeching is over," Melody said with a grin.

"And last, but not least, we have Trade Representative Imbia," Soro intoned.

The plainly dressed Thraki was sitting on a booster seat and apparently enthralled by the antics of his robotic "form." It was doing cartwheels across the table in front of him. Vanderveen knew the six-inch-high machine was a technical work of art that had probably been assembled by its owner. Such toys were something of a passion where the Thrakies were concerned. The Thraks claimed to be neutral but had been caught providing support to the Ramanthians and clearly expected them to win the war.

But because President Nankool and his advisors had no

desire to push the Thrakies into open conflict, especially given the strength of their navy, they were allowed to travel freely inside the Confederacy. It was a constant source of concern for Madame X—Nankool's chief of intelligence.

The Thraki looked up to acknowledge the introduction with a curt nod. So Vanderveen allowed Tuchida to seat her and let the social process carry her along. There was a menu to choose from, the usual small talk about the war, the hand that Soro placed on her left knee. Vanderveen removed it and turned to Tuchida. It didn't take long to discover that they had numerous acquaintances in common, something Vanderveen was quick to capitalize on. "So," she said, as the first course arrived, "do you know Captain Antonio Santana by any chance?"

Tuchida was no fool and sensed that the question was something more than a casual inquiry. He had black eyebrows, and they rose slightly. "I know a *Major* Santana. Not well, mind you—but both of us were on Gamma-014. He was one of the last people to make it out. Aboard a ship owned by Chien-Chu Enterprises if I'm not mistaken. General Kobbi thinks highly of him."

"Yes," Vanderveen agreed. "If anyone deserves a promotion, he does. I wonder where he is now?"

Tuchida smiled gently. "If I knew, I couldn't tell you. I'm sorry."

Vanderveen felt herself color slightly and was grateful when an android requested permission to pour some wine. The next hour passed comfortably enough and was capped off by a variety of desserts and a performance by Misty Melody. There was thunderous applause as she left the table and made her way up onto the platform at the center of the room. The lights dimmed, the stage began to rotate, and a huge holo of the planet Earth appeared. It was transparent and seemed to encapsulate the performer. Then, as Melody began to sing "My Home," Earth morphed into Gamma-014, which dissolved to another planet and so on until *all* of the worlds ravaged by the Ramanthians had come and gone.

There was a standing ovation as Melody hit the final plaintive note, and Imbia's miniature robot somersaulted across the table. Senator Tras Gormo caught the form, closed a power-assisted fist round it, and crushed the toy. Electricity crackled around his hand, which didn't bother him in the least. When the applause was over, the Dweller dropped the mangled object onto the table. It landed with a *thump*.

Imbia stood on his chair and was clearly going to object, when General Tuchida leaned in to speak with him. It was impossible to hear the exchange. But once it was over, the Thraki jumped to the floor and stalked away. Vanderveen turned to Tuchida. "What did you say to him?"

Tuchida grinned. "I told the little bastard that if he said a single word, I would shove what's left of that form up his ass. Was that a breach of diplomatic protocol? If so, I apologize."

Vanderveen laughed. "No apologies required insofar as I'm concerned. Well done."

People were streaming out of the dining room by then. And as both of them stood, Tuchida took a look around as if to make sure that no one could hear him. Then his eyes swung back to Vanderveen. "O-Chi 4. The major is on O-Chi 4." And with that he was gone.

PLANET ALGERON, THE CONFEDERACY OF SENTIENT BEINGS

The *Galaxsis* was far too large to pass through a planetary atmosphere and take off again. So, having dropped out of hyperspace and into orbit, it was necessary to shuttle passengers down to the planet's surface. Though classified as "earthlike,"

Algeron was a very different planet, primarily because it completed a full rotation every two hours and forty-two minutes. The rotation was so fast that centrifugal force had created a mountain range around the equator. The indigenous Naa called them "the Towers of Algeron," some of which were higher than Everest on Terra or Olympic Mons on Mars.

The once-obscure Fort Camerone was located in the northern hemisphere. It had been destroyed many years before, and a larger structure was built to replace it. Even so, the complex had been too small to accommodate the Legion *and* the sudden influx of civilians that took place after the ship housing the Confederacy's space-going capital was destroyed. There were other planets, of course. *Hundreds* of them. But none wanted to be elevated to the status of target number one.

So Naa Town had been leveled to make room for the addition commonly referred to as "the new fort." A full-scale spaceport was under construction west of the old fort, and a huge training complex was taking shape twenty miles to the north. All of which could be seen as Vanderveen's shuttle circled the area before coming in for a landing.

Vanderveen had been there before, of course. But everything looked strange as she entered baggage claim. That was where she spotted her father, who forced his way through the crowd to greet her. Charles was tall, slim, and had a long, narrow face framed by a full head of silvery hair. Vanderveen hadn't seen him for a year or so. But it looked as though he had aged five in that period of time, and she knew why. Because as the war continued to drag on, there was a never-ending temptation for the more vulnerable races to declare neutrality or align themselves with the Ramanthian Empire. That meant diplomats like her father were locked in a continuous struggle to strengthen alliances, pave over differences, and hold the network of existing relationships together.

There was a happy collision as father and daughter came together. Vanderveen took comfort from the familiar smell of him, the strength of his arms, and the sound of his voice. "Welcome to Algeron, sweetie . . . It's been too long."

Vanderveen pulled back in order to take a second look at him. "You need a haircut. How's Mom?"

Charles smiled. "I haven't actually spoken with her. Hypercom time is way too scarce for that. But, based on what Sergi Chien-Chu tells me, she's working with the resistance. I asked how, but he wouldn't say."

Vanderveen felt a stab of concern. Even though her mother might *look* like a helpless socialite, she was an active horsewoman and possessed an inner toughness. But working with the resistance? Shooting Ramanthians? That was hard to imagine.

"I hope you're hungry," Charles said as he took control of her rolling suitcase. "Because I made dinner. It may be humble, but my cooking beats the Foreign Service mess. You're staying with me by the way. I scored a one-bedroom apartment back when such a thing was still possible. And the couch is yours."

"Sounds good," Vanderveen said as she took his arm. "We have a lot of catching up to do."

The apartment was located in the so-called old fort. It was small but included a kitchenette, bathroom, bedroom, and a sitting area. A far cry from the one-room "boxes" that were presently being constructed. And while the decor would never have passed muster with her mother, Vanderveen thought the comfortable mix of Naa artifacts, outdoorsy paraphernalia, and leather-covered furniture was just right for a bachelor dad.

The main course had been simmering for hours. It consisted of a hearty dooth stew, chunks of fresh bread purchased in New Town, and a bottle of Napa Valley red that had been given to Charles as a gift six months earlier. The whole thing was delicious and took nearly two hours to consume as they told stories and caught up.

Eventually, it was one such story that led Vanderveen to mention the issue foremost on her mind. "So you're plugged in. What have you heard? Where am I headed?"

Charles looked uncomfortable. "I don't know, hon. For some reason, people don't talk about you when I'm around."

Vanderveen could see the concern in his eyes and felt a sudden sense of apprehension. "Come on, Dad . . . Level with me. You know something."

Charles shrugged. "No, I don't. Not really. But I can make an educated guess. Odds are that Nankool and senior members of his team are rather conflicted where you're concerned. And that's understandable," he said clinically. "The way I hear it, you formed a relationship with members of the Clone underground on Alpha-001 during a state visit. And after meeting with them, you came to the conclusion that their efforts to overthrow the government might be successful.

"So you shared that opinion with your superiors and recommended that they agree to some sort of a deal. They said 'no.' So you went AWOL. Ultimately, your judgment was proven to be correct. And thanks to your relationship with the rebels, the new government became part of the Confederacy. But, had the revolt failed, your actions could have done considerable damage to our relationship with the Alpha Clones. Is that a fair summation?"

Vanderveen could see the disapproval in her father's eyes, and it hurt, largely because she knew he was correct. Her actions had been very dangerous indeed. And she had come to regret her relationship with the rebel leader, Alan Freeman. An affair that might have influenced her judgment—and violated the implicit agreement that she had with Santana. It was difficult to meet her father's eyes. "Yes, that's a fair summation."

Charles leaned back in his chair. "Okay, then. So you can see the president's dilemma. Should he punish you for disobeying a directive? Or reward you for bringing a powerful ally over to our side?"

"Which means?"

"Which means that your fate is probably up in the air. But that's just a guess."

There was a long moment of silence as Vanderveen looked away. Finally, when her eyes came back, his were waiting. "So I screwed up?"

Charles nodded. "I would break you down to file clerk 1."

Vanderveen forced a smile. "Mom wouldn't let you."

Charles laughed. "No, she probably wouldn't."

"I'll check in first thing tomorrow. Or four days from now, as the case may be."

Charles laughed and raised his glass. "Confusion to the enemy."

Vanderveen wondered which enemy he was referring to. The Ramanthians? The Foreign Service? Or something inside of *her*? She took a sip of wine. It was anything but sweet.

Her father's couch wasn't all that comfortable. And she had a lot to think about. So about three hours passed before Vanderveen was able to fall asleep. And when she awoke, it was to find that her father had already eaten breakfast and left for work. That made her feel guilty. Because she was used to working and working *hard*.

So she showered, put on a conservative suit, and made herself a light breakfast. Then, with a mostly empty briefcase in hand, Vanderveen locked the door behind her and went looking for the so-called government block, where Secretary of State Mary Yatsu's office was located. Not that she would get to meet with the secretary. Because while Vanderveen was fairly senior, especially for a person her age, she wasn't *that* senior. No, chances were that she would be handed off to an assistant secretary of state. And that was fine so long as it wasn't Richard Holson, who had been in charge of negotiations on Alpha-001 and been very upset with what he referred to as her "antics" there.

The corridors were eternally crowded, and even though Vanderveen thought of it as morning, it was dark outside. Just one of the things Vanderveen would have to adjust to as she made a series of wrong turns and was forced to ask for directions. Ten minutes later, she arrived at the suite of offices assigned to the Foreign Service.

Blastproof duraplast doors sensed her presence and slid out of the way. The lobby was equipped to meet the needs of a wide variety of races and was already full of sentients who wanted someone to grant them a favor, explain an obscure law, or stroke their egos.

Vanderveen navigated her way around a table and the vase of flowery branches that sat on top of it, made her way over to the reception desk, and waited for the gray android to look up from the screen in front of him. The name CHET was stenciled across the center of his chest. "Yes? How can I help you?"

"I'm FSO-2 Vanderveen," the diplomat replied. "I was ordered to report to Algeron from Alpha-001."

"Welcome to Algeron," Chet said tonelessly. "One moment please."

A few seconds passed as the robot consulted his screen. "Ah, yes, here we are. You have an appointment to see Secretary Yatsu at 1500 hours local, five standard days from now."

Vanderveen was surprised to hear that the appointment

was with someone so senior and disappointed regarding the date. "*Five* days? You don't have anything earlier than that?"

"No," the machine said unapologetically. "Will there be anything else?"

Vanderveen considered pitching a fit but knew it would be pointless. So all she could do was to say, "Okay, thank you," and leave the office.

Disappointed, but determined to accomplish something, Vanderveen took the opportunity to visit the Foreign Service's research library, where employees could access data on every known planet and culture. It was a long, rectangular room with partially screened workstations to either side, about half of which were occupied.

Having been told that Santana was on O-Chi 4, she sat down at a terminal. Once Vanderveen verified her identity, she was free to read about the planet, the products it was known for, and a rather superficial analysis of O-Chi civilization. There was a military summary as well, but it had been written in the immediate aftermath of a disastrous attack on a Ramanthian base and was badly outdated. Further efforts to find out what was taking place on O-Chi 4 were met with a polite, "The information you requested is not currently available," which was govspeak for "mind your own business."

All of which led Vanderveen to believe that Santana was on a special-operations mission of some sort. To attack the Ramanthian fortress mentioned earlier? The diplomat feared that was the case. She wanted to cry and bit her lower lip to prevent herself from doing so.

The walk to her father's apartment was long and depressing. And when Vanderveen entered, it was to discover that an envelope with her name on it had been slipped under the door. She tore it open. The note was written in what looked like a feminine hand.

Dear Christine,

My uncle Sergi has known your parents for a long time and my husband has mentioned your service to the Confederacy more than once. I know from personal experience that Algeron can take some getting used to. I have some errands to run at 1300 hours. Perhaps you would like to join me? I could show you around.

Sincerely,
Maylo Chien-Chu

Vanderveen had agreed to meet Maylo Chien-Chu in the old fort at the entrance to the Hall of Honor. It was a corridor really, both sides of which were lined with photos of the Legion's heroes, along with descriptions of what they had done. Having arrived a few minutes early, Vanderveen followed the hall all the way to the end, where two legionnaires stood guard over a wooden display case. Their backs were ramrod straight and their eyes were fixed on the other end of the corridor as Vanderveen paused to look down through clear duraplast.

The wooden hand had once been worn by Captain Jean Danjou. Arguably the Legion's most important hero. A man who, like most of those in the Hall of Honor, had been killed in action. "It's strange, isn't it?" a female voice inquired. "I've been married to a legionnaire for years, and I still don't understand."

Vanderveen hadn't heard any footsteps. But when she turned, Maylo Chien-Chu was there. She was one of the most photographed people in the Confederacy. So there was no mistaking the glossy black hair, the high cheekbones, or the full lips. But she was thinner. Some observers said gaunt. And Vanderveen thought she saw something like sadness in Maylo's eyes. Because she was married to General Bill Booly? And, therefore, to the Legion? Probably. "Yes," Vanderveen replied. "It's both wonderful and horrible at the same time."

"Ah," Maylo said understandingly, "so you have one, too."

Vanderveen was astonished by the speed with which Maylo had uncovered her relationship with Antonio Santana. "Yes," she said. "If he's still alive."

Maylo winced and nodded. "These are very difficult times. I'm Maylo Chien-Chu."

"And I'm Christine Vanderveen. It's a pleasure to meet you."

"Come," Maylo said as she took the younger woman's arm. "You've been to Algeron before?"

"Yes, but it has been a while."

"Well, I'm sure you remember Naa Town."

Naa Town had originally been little more than a collection of Naa dwellings that had grown up next to the old fort. A place where legionnaires could have a meal, get drunk, and blow off some steam. There were dangers, too, because the relationship between the Naa and the Legion had traditionally been a tumultuous one although things were better now that the locals had a measure of independence. "I remember it well," Vanderveen said. "It was easy to get lost down there."

"Yes, it was," Maylo agreed, as they left the hall. "I think you'll find that New Town is far easier to navigate now. My job, *our* job, is to wander about and see how things are going. You're a diplomat, so you understand the importance of staying in touch with the local population. Especially those who live and work near an installation like this one."

Everyone knew that Maylo was an ex-officio member of the administration, a philanthropist, and a patriot. The kind who would actually pitch in and do something rather than simply stand around and talk about it. So Vanderveen wasn't surprised to learn that Maylo was an unofficial ambassador to the local business community. "That makes sense," Vanderveen agreed.

The women continued to chat as they took an elevator down to a brightly lit subsurface walkway. A moving sidewalk carried them a quarter of a mile north, to the point where they could board an escalator. That conveyed them and a scattering of other people up to a heated lobby. It had transparent walls that let in the dim sunlight.

"We could have built everything underground," Maylo said, as they stepped out into the frosty air. "But that would make New Town like thousands of other malls. The goal was to reimagine a Naa village in a way that would look and feel genuine while introducing some modern elements."

The next hour was spent walking through well-marked streets, window-shopping, and pausing to speak with small-business owners. And, judging from the way many of the Naa came rushing out of their stores to greet her, Maylo was a very popular figure.

The final stop was a restaurant called the Gor's Head. Stairs led down into a generously sized room. A large Naa-style fireplace dominated the center of the room, where all of the guests could see it and feel at least some of the surrounding warmth. Light fixtures fashioned from gor antlers hung over each table, and the air was heavy with the odors of good food. "This is Bill's favorite restaurant," Maylo explained. "My husband is something of a carnivore—so we come here when we can."

Was there a wistful quality to Maylo's voice? As if such occasions were all too rare? Vanderveen thought so, as the restaurant's proprietor came bustling out of the kitchen to greet them. She was middle-aged, somewhat plump, and her brown fur was shot through with streaks of black. There was a smile on her vaguely catlike face. "Madam Chien-Chu! This is an honor."

"I brought you a new customer," Maylo said, as they

embraced. "This is Christine Vanderveen. Christine, this is Bakewell Goodeat. She owns the restaurant."

Having collected a hug of her own, Vanderveen followed Maylo and a solemn-looking waiter, who led them to a table next to the fire. What followed was an excellent meal. There was a salad made from assorted marsh greens, a meat pie with a wonderfully flaky crust, and a generous slice of cake. Vanderveen was still in the process of finishing her dessert when a female Naa arrived at the table.

A good deal older than Goodeat, she was slightly stooped over, and her eyes were somewhat rheumy. Her fur had once been jet-black but was now shot with gray. It was clear that Maylo knew her. "Christine . . . This is Dreamsee Futurewalk. She can throw the Wula Sticks. And, more importantly, read them. Let's move our plates. She'll need some room."

Vanderveen didn't believe in fortune-tellers, but it appeared that Maylo did. Or was this a simple act of charity? A way to help an aging female make some money? It was impossible to tell as Futurewalk placed a one-legged stool next to the table and rested her weight on it. She upended a tube and black Wula Sticks came pouring out. They were about twelve inches long and wound up in an untidy pile.

Then Futurewalk began to remove sticks in what looked like random order, sliding each one back into the brightly decorated tube as she did so. Two or three minutes passed before she began to speak. Her voice was surprisingly youthful and melodious. "Your fates are bound together," she announced. "But not here. The moment of truth will occur in a distant place, where fire rules the sky, and death dances the land. One of you will gain everything, and the other will lose everything, as billions of lives hang in the balance."

The words, and the way they were said, sent a chill down Vanderveen's spine. And as Maylo's eyes came up off the tangle of sticks, Vanderveen saw fear in them. And that was even more troubling. Because if Maylo Chien-Chu had reason to be afraid, what about *her*?

"Well," Maylo said with a grim smile, "to hell with the calories. We might as well finish our desserts."

With nothing productive to do, and her fate hanging in the balance, Vanderveen had been forced to wait for what seemed like an eternity. But finally, for better or for worse, the day of reckoning had arrived. So Vanderveen was dressed in a conservative suit, and ready for just about anything, as she entered the reception area and made herself known to the android named Chet. "FSO-2 Vanderveen. I'm scheduled to meet with Secretary Yatsu."

A suspenseful moment followed as Chet consulted the screen in front of him. What if Yatsu was ill? Or had been called away? Or any of a dozen other possibilities?

Vanderveen felt a rising sense of apprehension as the seconds ticked by, and she confronted the possibility that it might be necessary to wait for another week. Then came a feeling of relief as Chet spoke. "Here we are . . . The secretary is running about ten minutes late. Please take a seat. I'll call your name as soon as she becomes available."

Ten minutes passed. Then twenty. Eventually, after more than half an hour of watching people come and go, Vanderveen heard her name. She stood and made her way up to the desk where a flesh-and-blood person waited to meet her. The woman had carefully coiffed hair, dark eyes, and coffee-colored skin. "It's a pleasure to meet you," she said. "I'm Nanci. Secretary Yatsu's assistant. Please accept our apologies. The meeting with the Prithian delegation ran over. I'm sure you understand."

Being an FSO-2, Vanderveen *did* understand. Even if the

wait had been painful. She forced a smile. "Of course. Thank you for squeezing me in."

"Please follow me," Nanci said, and Vanderveen did so. Their heels made clicking sounds as they made their way down a corridor and past more than a dozen offices. Eventually, they entered an open area, rounded a desk that had Nanci's name on it, and passed between a pair of large double doors. It was a nice office by local standards. There was a circular conference table, which was made out of local wood and was intended to put everyone on an equal footing. A massive desk could be seen beyond that, backed by a large Confederacy seal and flanked by appropriate flags. Just the thing for official photos.

"Please have a seat," Nanci intoned. "The secretary will be back shortly—and Assistant Secretary Holson will be joining you as well. Can I get you anything? Some caf perhaps?"

Vanderveen had been feeling slightly positive about the meeting up until that point. Because even though Yatsu was tough, she was also known to be fair. But Holson had been *very* angry about her activities on Alpha-001. Partly because of her refusal to follow orders, which was perfectly understandable, but also because of the way that he had been left standing on the sidelines when the rebels took over. It was a grudge he would have an opportunity to settle. So as Vanderveen sat down, she could feel the world closing in around her. If her own father would reduce her to file clerk—what would Assistant Secretary Holson do? "No, thank you. I'm fine." Nanci nodded pleasantly and left the office.

Vanderveen was still mulling her fate when Yatsu and Holson entered the room two minutes later. Yatsu was a tiny birdlike thing, with a mop of black hair and bright, inquisitive eyes. Her teeth were very white and flashed when she smiled. But there was strength lurking behind the girlish charm, which was why Yatsu was referred to as the "Iron Maiden" behind her back.

Holson had brown hair, some of which flopped down over a high forehead. His wide-set eyes were slightly hooded, as if to conceal what he was thinking, and a carefully trimmed mustache served to emphasize a slashlike mouth.

Vanderveen stood and found herself on the receiving end of a warm handshake from Yatsu and a cold stare from Holson, who had chosen to sit across from her. "There will be one more participant," Yatsu said, "and here he is now."

Vanderveen turned toward the door and was astonished to see President Marcott Nankool enter the office. He'd shed thirty pounds on Jericho and a few more as Earth fell to the Ramanthians, but it appeared as though his weight had stabilized. His face still had a gaunt appearance, however, and the smile was in marked contrast to the sadness in his eyes. It was no secret that the never-ending stream of bad news was taking a toll on him. "Christine!" he said warmly. "I heard about this meeting and asked Secretary Yatsu if I could sit in. I hope you don't mind."

Vanderveen *didn't* mind. Nankool was upset with her. She knew that. But the fact that they had survived the horrors of Jericho together meant there was a bond between them. One that Holson was clearly aware of judging from the way he frowned when Nankool gave her a hug.

But Vanderveen wasn't out of the woods. She knew that. In spite of the relationship that existed between them, Nankool couldn't allow his diplomats to do whatever they pleased. So as they took their seats, her future was still in doubt.

All eyes went to Yatsu. She consulted a hand comp before looking up again. Her expression was serious. "I must say that in all my years of Foreign Service experience I haven't run into anyone quite like you. On the plus side, you more than distinguished yourself while serving on LaNor during the Claw uprising. Then there was the partnership with His Excellency Triad Hiween Doma-Sa, which resulted in an important intelligence coup. That was followed by your imprisonment on Jericho, where the president described your actions as 'heroic.' All capped off by the recent one-diplomat effort that culminated in a historic agreement with Clone Hegemony. It's a very impressive record, and that's why you're the youngest FSO-2 in the Foreign Service."

Yatsu paused at that point, formed a steeple with her fingers, and frowned. "That's the good news. The *bad* news is that while you were stationed on Alpha-001, you disobeyed a directive, which, had things gone the other way, could have been disastrous."

Holson smiled thinly. And there was no mistaking the hostility in his half-shuttered eyes.

"Nor was that the first time," Yatsu added sternly. "For example, your work with Triad Doma-Sa was unauthorized, and your superior put a letter to that effect in your P-1 file."

"Assistant Undersecretary for Foreign Affairs Wilmot was later convicted of treason, Madam Secretary," Vanderveen put in.

"She has you there," Nankool said, as he spoke for the first time.

"With all due respect, Wilmot's conviction came well after the time the letter was written," Holson commented darkly.

Yatsu nodded. "The point is that discipline is important to an organization such as ours. Just imagine if all our FSO-3's and 2's were running about cutting deals on their own! Say what you will about our bureaucracy—but it exists for a reason."

Vanderveen felt there had been extenuating circumstances associated with all of the situations that Yatsu had mentioned, but knew the secretary was correct where the need for a disciplined approach was concerned. She nodded contritely. "I know. I'm sorry."

"Good," Yatsu replied. "So with all of that in mind, we are faced with a very difficult decision. And, given what we do for a living, you won't be surprised to learn that we settled on a compromise." It was a joke, and Vanderveen managed to produce a weak smile.

"The president wants to reward you for bringing the Hegemony into the Confederacy," Yatsu added. "So, effective today, I'm promoting you to FS-1. But Richard feels that it would be inappropriate to reward your behavior by posting you to one of the core worlds. And I agree."

"As do I," Nankool added sternly.

"So we're sending you to Trevia," Yatsu announced. "It's a rim world, which is located outside the boundaries of the bug empire but has a significant population of Ramanthian expatriates. Eccentrics mostly, plus a scattering of political exiles and members of other races."

Vanderveen felt a crushing sense of disappointment. They were sending her to prison. A place far from civilization, where she could be left to rot for who knew how long.

Nankool saw the look in her eyes. "It's more than a holding cell," he assured her. "We need eyes and ears out there. So make a lot of contacts. And who knows? Once the war begins to go our way, one or more of your new friends might prove to be useful where negotiations are concerned."

"Or, depending on how things go, you may find yourself living *inside* the Ramanthian Empire," Holson said unsympathetically. "But I'm sure you'll manage given your well-known capacity to take care of yourself."

That earned Holson a dirty look from Nankool. But if the diplomat regretted his comment, there was no sign of it on his face.

"I guess that handles it," Yatsu said blithely. "Congratulations on your promotion—and have a nice trip."

5

The measure of an officer is not in victory but in defeat.

—Grand Marshal Nimu Wurla-Ka (ret.)
Instructor, Hudathan War College
Standard year 1958

PLANET O-CHI 4, THE CONFEDERACY OF SENTIENT BEINGS

There was a violent jerk as his half of the rope bridge struck something solid. Santana lost his grip, fell backwards, and crashed through multiple layers of branches. When he hit the ground, the impact drove all of the air out of his lungs. But thanks to his helmet and the foliage that slowed his fall, he was uninjured.

As the Ramanthian transport rose, Santana could see the platform where Temo had been standing. She had somehow been able to establish contact with the bugs and cut a deal. The bitch. The lights were extinguished, and Santana knew the renegade had escaped.

A spectral form appeared above him. "No offense, sir," Dietrich said. "But you're lying down on the job. An officer should set a good example for the troops."

Santana accepted the proffered hand, allowed himself to be pulled up onto his feet, and was pleased to discover that he could stand unassisted. No broken bones, then. That was good. "Thank you, Sergeant Major. I'm glad to see that you survived the fall—and are keeping a sharp eye out for slackers. Have you seen my weapon by any chance? I lost it."

"It was barrel down in the ground," Dietrich replied as he gave the carbine over. "So don't try to fire it. Orders, sir?"

"Pass the word . . . There's no point in blundering around in the darkness. Tell our people to count heads, collect the wounded, and muster below the lodge. We'll search it and the clearing at first light. Then we'll have some field rats and get the hell out of here."

"Yes, sir."

"And one more thing."

"Sir?"

"That's the last time I follow you out onto a rope bridge."

More than a day had passed since the failed attempt to capture or kill Major Temo, and the battalion was back in Baynor's Bay. One thing had been accomplished, however. With the exception of a small number of O-Chi Scouts who had escaped with their leader—the rest of Temo's loyalists had been captured or killed. And that meant Santana was free to go after the STS cannon. Assuming he could integrate the O-Chi Rifles, O-Chi Scouts, and legionnaires into a single fighting force. And do so quickly.

The sun was still rising in the east and a gauzy mist was floating just off the ground as the troops made their way out onto the athletic field adjacent to the Baynor's Bay trischool. They hadn't been ordered to form up. But as Santana climbed onto the top of a quad named Sy Coto and looked out over their heads, he wasn't surprised to see Scouts with Scouts, Rifles with Rifles, and legionnaires with legionnaires. Once Santana was in position, Dietrich bellowed, "Ten-hut!" The legionnaires looked pretty good as they came to attention, but many of the militia men and women were somewhat sloppy.

Santana was wearing a lip mike. And when he spoke, his voice could be heard over Coto's PA system. "At ease. You'll notice that you weren't required to muster as part of a unit. That's because, as of this morning, you are members of a battalion-strength expeditionary force called the O-Chi Raiders. It will consist of three companies, each having three platoons, with three squads to a platoon."

Based on facial expressions and body language, Santana could tell that none of the soldiers liked that. Especially *his* troops, who saw themselves as part of an elite unit and were proud of the Legion's long history. He smiled grimly. "And that isn't all. Not only will you become part of a single organization, you will serve in a company, platoon, and squad with people from the other units. A table of organization (TO) will be distributed at the conclusion of this briefing. At that time, you will report to your platoon leaders, who will go over their expectations with you.

"Then, after a word from your company commander, you'll be heading into the bush on a three-day training exercise. Each company will have a flag, and the objective will be to capture as many flags as you can and deliver them to me. During this evolution, you will be unarmed. Should you run into serious trouble with the local wildlife, a quick reaction force comprised of T-2s will be available to respond. The rules governing this field exercise will be delivered to squad leaders and above along with the TO charts. Lieutenant Ponco will serve as referee, and, should there be some sort of dispute, her decisions will be final.

"Finally," Santana added, "remember this . . . About five days from now, we will depart on a very important mission. This is your chance to prepare for it. That will be all."

RAMANTHIAN BASE 46791, AKA "HEADSTONE," THE PLANET O-CHI 4, THE CONFEDERACY OF SENTIENT BEINGS

The pit was utterly dark except for the beams of light that slanted down through the metal grating to make a pattern on Major Temo's face. Ever since the last-minute rescue from the clearing, she'd been waiting to learn her fate. The cell was about four feet wide, six feet long, and eight feet high. There was no furniture and no conveniences other than the floor drain located in one corner.

So as Temo crouched on the floor and listened to the shuffle of Ramanthian feet and occasional bursts of click speech, she had no way to know what would happen next. The fact that she was still alive could be credited to the family's business manager. A shrewd Thraki named Eban Rhaki. As a member of a race that was officially neutral, he had been able to forge a friendly relationship with the bugs on O-Chi 4 months earlier. But whether that would be enough to save her life remained to be seen.

Shadows rippled across her face as the grating was removed, and a Ramanthian noncom peered down at her. Like all of his kind, the soldier had compound eyes, a parrot-shaped beak, and two short olfactory antennae that projected from his forehead. "You stink," the Ramanthian said contemptuously. His standard was wooden but serviceable. "Take your clothes off."

Temo was about to refuse when a blast of cold water hit her from above. Suddenly, there was reason to hope. After all, why bother to hose her down if the bugs were about to put a bullet in her head?

So she stripped off her filthy clothing, shivered as the water blasted her body, and forced herself to perform a slow 360. Then, as suddenly as the shower had begun, it was over. The noncom said, "Catch," and a bundle of clean clothes fell into her arms.

Temo discovered that it was civilian clothing, which, though slightly too large for her, was a lot better than the filthy uniform that lay on the wet concrete. She had finished tucking the shirt in and was fastening the trousers when her combat boots thumped onto the floor. There weren't any socks to go with them, but Temo wasn't about to complain as she tied her laces.

Once she was dressed, a ladder slid down into the pit and came to rest about a foot away. "Commander Dammo will see you now," the noncom announced. "Climb the ladder."

The Ramanthian-style ladder consisted of a long pole to which crosspieces had been fastened. V-shaped supports provided stability at both ends. Temo climbed up, stepped out onto a concrete floor, and saw that two escorts were waiting for her. They stood on their hind legs and clutched Negar III assault rifles with their pincers. Their uniforms consisted of armor plates held together by sections of metal mesh and harness-style ammo bibs. "Go with them," the noncom ordered. "And do as you are told."

Having been born into a wealthy family and educated on Earth, Temo wasn't used to being addressed in that fashion. So she felt a flash of anger but managed to conceal it as the troopers took charge. One led the way, which meant Temo could see the long, seldom-used wings that were folded along his back and smell the wax that had been applied to them.

Temo had participated in the disastrous attack on Headstone during which more than a thousand of her fellow citizens were killed. But she had never been inside the complex. So it was natural to pay close attention to everything around her, and she was impressed. The corridor was clean. Racks of weapons were located at regular intervals. First-aid stations stood ready in alcoves. Side passageways led to what might have been gun emplacements and missile launchers. And the troops who passed her in the hall appeared to be well fed. All of which was consistent with what Rhaki had been telling her for months: The Ramanthians were going to win the war. And that, according to Rhaki, was why companies like Temo Pharmaceuticals should establish meaningful relationships with the Ramanthians while such a thing was still possible.

Those were Temo's thoughts as she followed the first soldier into a side corridor. A ramp led up to a door, where two sentries stood at the Ramanthian equivalent of port arms. They remained motionless as Temo passed between them and entered a spacious office. The walls were hewn from solid rock and had been left rough, a look that Temo knew to be consistent with the underground dwellings the bugs preferred.

Two beings were waiting to receive Temo, one of whom was Rhaki. He was seated on a Ramanthian-style saddle chair and stood as she entered. The Thraki's brown fur was shot with gray. He had pointy ears, a short muzzle, and was dressed in a white business suit. A jacket with a high collar hung down over a pair of neatly bloused pants. The pull-on boots he wore were well polished and way too nice for the bush. "Donna!" he said warmly. "Commander Dammo and I were just talking about you."

Having known the Thraki for years and having learned to read his nonverbal expressions, Temo recognized what she thought of as his sales mode. Without being told, she knew it was her job to play along. Not ideal, perhaps, since it put her under Rhaki's control, but what choice did she have? Temo forced a smile but knew it wouldn't mean anything to the other person in the room, a stern-looking Ramanthian with a bulging prosthesis in place of his right eye. "I don't know what you were saying—but I hope it was nice."

"Of course it was," Rhaki said jovially. "Commander Dammo, please allow me to introduce Major Donna Temo."

Temo looked at the Ramanthian. Here was the officer responsible for taking part of what she considered to be *her* planet—and killing more than a thousand of its citizens. She should tell him to screw himself. But not if she wanted to survive and see Temo Pharmaceuticals prosper. "It's an honor to meet you, sir."

Dammo was silent for a moment. He was seated on a saddle chair. The officer's scarlet uniform fit just so, his leather cross belts were polished, and everything about him conveyed a sense of controlled power. And when he spoke, his standard was so good that Temo suspected that he had spent time on one of the Confederacy's planets prior to the war. A military attaché perhaps—or something similar. "I suspect those words cost you dearly," he said. "But you were able to utter them nevertheless. Many of my peers would judge you harshly for that. Especially those who are members of the *Nira* cult.

"But I have no time for such nonsense. I, like citizen Rhaki here, am a pragmatist—a person more interested in results than process. And based on what I've heard about you, as well as what I've seen so far, it appears that you and I may be similar in that regard."

Temo was impressed with what the Ramanthian had to say and the way in which it was said. "Yes, sir."

Dammo nodded. A nonverbal gesture that the two races had in common. "Good. You humans have a saying. One I learned while stationed on Earth. 'Talk is cheap.' So I'm going to give you an opportunity to prove yourself."

Temo looked at Rhaki and saw the concern in his eyes. The Thraki was worried. Everything was on the line. Her eyes swung back. "Thank you, sir. What do you have in mind?"

Dammo's artificial eye whirred softly. "We're going to attack the town you call Baynor's Bay. And *you* will lead the way."

**THE TOWN OF BAYNOR'S BAY, PLANET O-CHI 4,
THE CONFEDERACY OF SENTIENT BEINGS**

It was a beautiful day, which made it perfect for flying. But as the transport skimmed the leafy treetops and the noise of its engines sent flocks of blue flits into the air, Temo barely noticed them. Her thoughts were elsewhere as she stood in the open hatch and allowed the slipstream to tear at her clothes. If she was willing to sacrifice herself, she could turn and open fire on the Ramanthian soldiers seated in the cargo bay. Then it would be a simple matter to go forward and shoot the pilots.

But it wouldn't make any difference. Not according to Rhaki. Because the chits would still win the war. *So focus,* she told herself. *Make the best of a bad situation. Members of the Temo family have been killed,* she reminded herself. *And now it's payback time.*

That thought generated a fierce sense of anticipation as the transports flashed past Signal Hill, flew out over the bay, and circled back. The TACBASE that sat atop the ruins of her grandmother's house had opened fire by then. But it, along with all of the legionnaires within, were about to die.

Corporal Durkee was off duty, watching one of the vids stored in his onboard computer, when the shit hit the fan. Because most of the battalion was in the jungle, playing war games, only six people had been left behind to defend the TACBASE. That number was deceptive, however. Especially since the computer-controlled fortress could fend off minor attacks on its own. But it couldn't cope with three loads of Ramanthian troops plus two Ramanthian aerospace fighters without support.

Still, the TACBASE had already begun to fire surface-to-air missiles (SAMs) at the enemy ships by the time Staff Sergeant Nello's voice came over the intercom. "Look alive, people—the bugs want to play. Let's blow their pointy asses out of the sky."

Durkee could fire while parked in the bay—but only at a limited array of targets. Ideally, had the other quads been present, all four quadrants would have been covered. But his peers were out in the jungle somewhere, which left Durkee to do the job alone. He opened a com link. "Roger that, Sarge . . . How 'bout I go out and teach 'em a lesson?"

"I dunno," Nello replied doubtfully, as a missile hit the TACBASE and exploded. "We call you 'gimpy' for a reason."

"All I have to do is get clear of the base, divide their fire, and let 'em have it," Durkee countered. "Besides, I promised the major I would take care of things."

The TACBASE shuddered as more missiles hit, 25 percent of the computer-controlled AA batteries went off-line, and Nello's voice grew tighter. "Okay, Corporal . . . Feed the bastards a SAM for me."

Having ordered his onboard computer to disengage from the TACBASE, Durkee crab-walked out into the roiling smoke. The enemy transports were busy landing troops, but the top of Signal Hill was taking a pounding from the Ramanthian fighters.

Durkee put an electronic tag on one of them, sent two fire-and-forget SAMs after it. He was about to fire on the second aircraft when a remotely piloted bunker-buster missile arrived from a base located more than three hundred miles away and scored a direct hit. The TACBASE and everyone inside of it ceased to exist. The resulting shock wave picked Durkee up and threw him off the hill. His fifty-ton body cartwheeled down the slope, skidded to a stop, and blew up.

But even as the legionnaire was dying, his missiles hit a Ramanthian fighter and exploded. The fighter vanished in a flash and puff of smoke. Had he known, the ex-murderer, legionnaire, and cyborg would have been pleased.

After landing, the Ramanthian soldiers split into smaller teams and shuffled their way through the streets, intent on razing the community of south bay so that the humans couldn't use it as a staging area. And, based on the deal struck with Commander Dammo, Temo was in charge of a squad-sized group of them.

Temo heard the boom, felt the ground shake, and smiled approvingly as she turned to watch a column of black smoke rise from the top of Signal Hill. Her grandmother's death had been avenged. Now with a half file of troopers to do her bidding, she was about to settle another score. Resistance had been lighter than expected. That meant the legionnaires and Antov's Rifles were elsewhere. Out on a training exercise? Or marching toward Headstone? One of the two. It didn't matter. Antov wasn't in the field. Not with his leg. That was all she cared about. Weapons rattled, people screamed, and the slaughter began.

Behind Antov's waterfront home, and on the other side of Bay Road, a steep trail switchbacked up a slope to the spot where he and his wife had enjoyed occasional picnics. He hadn't gone up there in years. Not since her death.

But the hill would give him the advantage of height and a place from which he could harvest as many Ramanthian lives as possible. Maybe he would stuff one of the bastards and put him next to the fireplace!

First, however, he had to drag his ass up the hill, which was hard to do on crutches, and get into position. Santana would return, of course. And bring the newly formed battalion back with him. But it would be too late by then. The TACBASE was gone, along with all of the supplies stored inside. The three-legged quad had given a good account of himself, though—before being blown off the hilltop. All of which had been reported to CENTCOM using one of only four hypercom sets on O-Chi 4.

Antov looked back over his shoulder as the remaining aerospace fighter circled above. Heedu was about fifty feet to the rear, carrying two heavy rifles plus a backpack filled with ammo and other supplies. "Pick up the pace," Antov ordered. "I'm on crutches, for God's sake. You should have passed me by now."

Heedu made no reply as Antov turned back and redoubled his efforts. He arrived at the picnic spot three minutes later. Someone else might have been tempted to pause and look out over the destruction, but Antov wanted to kill some bugs. Sightseeing could wait.

So he chose his spot, flopped onto his belly, and called for the Hawking. Having just arrived, Heedu knelt, gave the long-barreled rifle over, and began to load the second weapon.

Antov felt a grim sense of satisfaction as he put his cheek to the rifle and looked through the telescopic sight. Houses were on fire, and smoke was drifting across the scene below, but at least half a dozen targets were shuffling south.

Rather than alert the entire file by shooting their leader, Antov guided the crosshairs onto the spot where the last bug was about to be and squeezed the trigger. The stock slammed into his shoulder, and the Ramanthian went down as if poleaxed. Antov smiled as he worked a second cartridge into the chamber. The report had been loud, but thanks to the incessant chatter of Negar assault rifles all around, it had gone unnoticed.

So Antov killed the next trooper, and the *next*, until a trail of five bodies lay in the road. All head shots. Then, with a single bullet remaining, Antov prepared to take the leader down. But, as he made the necessary adjustment and the final target filled his vision, Antov saw something entirely unexpected: Major Temo's face! The rotten bitch had not only gone over to the enemy—but was taking part in an attack on her own people.

Well, not for long, Antov told himself, and pulled the trigger. But that was the moment when Temo turned to look back over her shoulder. The bullet missed by less than inch, she saw the bodies, and broke right. Antov swore, put the Hawking aside, and said, "Give me the Walby. Quickly now." Nothing happened.

Antov swore again, rolled over onto his side, and was about to rip into Heedu when he found himself staring into the Walby's barrel. The weapon was steady, and, judging from Heedu's stance, he'd been practicing with it. "What the hell?" Antov inquired. "Have you lost your frigging mind? Give me that weapon. We'll discuss this later."

"There will be no later," Heedu replied woodenly. "Not for you." And with that, he pulled the trigger.

Temo was scared. And for good reason. Every single one of her Ramanthian troopers had been killed by a sniper located on the rise behind Antov's house. Could it be Antov himself? Quite possibly. He was arguably the best shot on O-Chi 4. So if she were stupid enough to raise her head above the concrete retaining wall at the side of the road, he would blow it off. Fortunately, there was a simple solution to her problem.

Temo removed the Ramanthian radio from an ammo pouch

on the front of her chest protector, fumbled with the squeeze-style mike control, and identified herself. Then, speaking distinctly so as to avoid any possibility of a misunderstanding, she gave the necessary order.

Moments later, the fighter made a lazy swing to the south, came north again, and began to lose altitude. The dart-shaped aircraft was no more than a hundred feet off the ground when its pilot released the fuel bomb. There was a flash of light as the top of the rise was consumed by a rising ball of fire. Rivers of red flowed downhill, set the brush ablaze, and stopped just short of the road.

Confident that the sniper was dead, Temo stood and continued up the road. The plan had been to find Antov and kill him. But when she arrived at the house, she found that the front door was open, the servants had fled, and its owner was nowhere to be found. That made her feel even more confident that Antov had been killed.

Temo left through the front door and walked away. It wasn't until three minutes later, when she was halfway to the Ramanthian extraction point, that she gave the final order. The fighter swooped in, a bomb fell, and the Antov house ceased to exist. The mission was complete.

From Santana's perspective, the first two days of the field exercise had gone fairly well. By giving Alpha Company to Captain Jo Zarrella, Bravo Company to Rifles Captain Motu Kimbo, and Charlie Company to Scouts Captain Corin Ryley, he had been able to spread the leadership responsibilities around. And by assigning each company commander a quad, six T-2s, and eight legionnaires, Santana had been able to ensure rough parity among the three units. It was a strategy intended to build morale and ensure operational flexibility. Because it would be a mistake to rely too heavily on any one company.

In an effort to make the exercise easier to control, the war game had been held on the Antov family's coffee plantation. The trees were laid out in orderly rows, and there wasn't any underbrush to contend with, which made it easy to move around. Weapons, food, and other gear were stored in a half-empty warehouse, where they were kept under guard.

The rules of engagement were not only simple but very similar to a game called capture the flag that Santana had played as a boy. The main difference was that the battalion was divided into *three* teams rather than two.

The first thing each team had to do was take control of the territory assigned to it and hide its flag in keeping with Lieutenant Ponco's rules. Each company commander could divide the force into groups of attackers and defenders, using whatever criteria and percentages they considered to be appropriate.

With that accomplished, it was time to hide the unit's flag, position defenders around it, and send people out to capture enemy flags. Individuals who were caught and tagged were placed in prisons where they were held, traded for other POWs, and sometimes freed by opposing special-ops teams.

The rules were intentionally simple so that the company commanders could demonstrate initiative and creativity, which they immediately did by forming alliances, employing spies, and launching sneak attacks. There were verbal conflicts and some fistfights, but Ponco was able to keep things under control, which left Santana free to observe.

Zarrella's Alpha Company emerged as the overall winner, having captured both enemy flags. And, given all of her experience, Santana would have been surprised by any other outcome. But both Kimbo and Ryley showed considerable promise, with Kimbo being the stronger of the two. Of equal importance was what the three company commanders learned about the men, women, and cyborgs in their respective units. Strengths and weaknesses that would help them place the right people in the right positions.

It had been Santana's intention to use the last day as an opportunity to review what had been learned and brief the troops regarding the upcoming mission, but that plan was put aside when Sergeant Nello's report came in. The TACBASE was under attack, Durkee was going out to fight, and three enemy transports were inbound.

Santana had questions but never got to ask them as Nello was cut off in midsentence. So Santana put in a call for air support, dispatched Ponco to Baynor's Bay to investigate, and ordered the battalion to rearm itself. Then, having summoned Joshi, he led the quick-reaction force west. The rest of the troops were to follow as quickly as possible. But all of his efforts were for naught. Because by the time the elderly CF-150 Daggers arrived overhead and Ponco entered the town, the bugs were gone.

Santana winced as the damage reports came in but had no way to appreciate how bad things really were until he saw the black smoke pouring up into the sky and Joshi topped the final rise. Then, as the force of bio bods and T-2s flowed downslope, the full extent of the devastation became apparent.

The top of Signal Hill, which was off to his left, looked like a blackened stump. Now, in contrast to the spotty damage suffered earlier, the entire waterfront had been reduced to a swath of smoking rubble. Bodies lay in the road. Many had been executed, judging from the way they were clustered together, and in one case Santana saw a child crouched by her mother, sobbing hopelessly. All because of his decision to leave the town with only a minimal defense.

The knowledge was like a black hand that took hold of his spirit and crushed it. Here, lying in the streets, was the evidence of something he had feared but never confronted. Just because he'd been able to lead a platoon, then a company, didn't mean he could handle a battalion. Somebody else, Kobbi perhaps, or Antov, would have done things differently. And most of the people who lay scattered about would still be alive.

The certainty of that rode the pit of his stomach as he ordered Rona-Sa to send all of the battalion's medics forward on T-2s in order to get them on-site more quickly. Then he dispatched Ponco to north bay along with a request for assistance and allowed the Daggers to leave.

Finally, once everything Santana could do had been accomplished, he took a radio and set off for the crescent-shaped beach that lay half a mile beyond what had been Antov's home. There was quite a bit of driftwood, thanks to all the dead trees, branches, and other detritus that was carried down rivers and into the sea during the rainy season. So Santana sat on a log and stared at the slowly sinking sun. It was bloodred. And, as the stars began to appear, he could feel the darkness closing in around him.

The crunch of footsteps came, followed by a noticeable tilt of the log as a heavy weight was added. "Permission to join you, sir?"

Santana looked to the right and saw Rona-Sa. He didn't want any company but couldn't say "no" to his Executive Officer. "Permission granted."

The Hudathan nodded. "Permission to speak freely, sir?"

Santana scowled. "How many more permissions are you going to request, Captain? Okay, go ahead and get whatever it is off your chest."

If Rona-Sa was offended, there was no sign of it on his craggy face. "We have a problem, sir," Rona-Sa said bluntly. "And the problem is *you*."

Santana started to object but stopped as Rona-Sa raised a huge paw. "I have permission to speak freely. Remember? And

I intend to do so. What took place here was terrible. And I understand why you feel bad about it. But it couldn't be helped. You were sent here to carry out an important mission and to do so using troops from what my people would consider to be three different clans. There was no way to protect Baynor's Bay *and* take the battalion into the field. And there was no reason to expect a major attack. Which, based on eyewitness accounts, was led by Major Temo. An act of treason no one could anticipate.

"But, even if you had known in advance what the bugs were going to do, it would have been your duty to prepare the battalion for the upcoming mission rather than protect the town. Because the deaths suffered there today are nothing compared to the importance of the O-Chi jump point. So I respectfully suggest that you suck it up and do what battalion commanders are supposed to do, which is lead. Sir."

It was the longest statement Santana had ever heard Rona-Sa make. And the fact that the Hudathan felt strongly enough to try to intervene meant a lot. But Santana was unconvinced. "Thank you, Eor. I appreciate what you're trying to do. But the truth is that I may lack some of the qualities required for the job at hand. You might be a better choice."

"I would be an excellent choice," Rona-Sa rumbled, "*if* Headstone were a mile away and all we had to do was storm it. But the job is a good deal more complicated than that. You have already made considerable progress at bringing three disparate units together, and that would be difficult for me. But ultimately, it comes down to this. Look around, think about the individuals who are available, and ask yourself the following question: 'If not me, then *who*?'"

Santana thought about it. There was a certain logic to what Rona-Sa had to say. He wasn't perfect. Far from it. But there weren't any other choices. Not really. He forced a smile. "You know something, Eor?"

"Sir?"

"You have a tendency to run your mouth. Especially for a Hudathan. But thank you. I will do my best to heed your advice."

Both officers were silent as the sun dipped below the horizon, waves lapped against the beach, and a thousand stars dusted the sky.

6

He who fights and runs away will live to fight another day.

—Demosthenes
Standard year 338 B.C.

PLANET EARTH, THE RAMANTHIAN EMPIRE
THE SAN PEDRO CHANNEL, OFF THE COAST OF CALIFORNIA

Except for the stars and the blinking red lights mounted on top of the sensor towers the Ramanthians had put up, that section of the California coastline was entirely dark. It hadn't been that way just a few months earlier. Back then, before the Ramanthians landed, anyone looking east from a boat would have seen the sparkling lights of Long Beach stretched out in front of them.

But the city was mostly rubble now. Just part of an urban wasteland that stretched all the way down into what had once been Mexico. *But not forever,* Commander Leo Foley thought to himself, as an ocean swell lifted the seventy-five-foot hydrofoil up out of a trough. *Not forever.*

Foley's thoughts were interrupted as a barely seen figure materialized out of the gloom. The man was an employee of Chien-Chu Enterprises, which was owned by the legendary Sergi Chien-Chu and run by his niece, Maylo. "The drone entered the atmosphere," the crewman said. "We should have splashdown in roughly five minutes."

"Good," Foley replied. "Your crew is ready?"

"Yes, sir."

Foley wasn't surprised. Chien-Chu's people had proven themselves to be very adept at programming drones to enter hyperspace thousands of light-years away, exit inside the moon's orbit, and splash down before the Ramanthians could intercept them. Nearly 100 percent of the unmanned spaceships made it through at first. But as the bugs became aware of the strategy and sharpened their defenses, the success rate had been reduced to about 60 percent. That was still pretty good, however, and likely to remain constant because two-thirds of Earth's surface was covered with water. And that made the incoming drones very hard to find. Not to mention the fact that the objects blew themselves up when the Ramanthians tried to recover them. A nasty surprise indeed.

So thanks to the hypercom technology used to coordinate the drops, the program had been very successful. Pickups were normally handled by Foley's subordinates. But this load was different. Because if it came down safely and the crew managed to retrieve it, a whole lot of bugs were going to die. And Foley wanted to make sure of it. As the seconds ticked away, the crewman reappeared. "Sorry, sir, but we have a problem. Two high-speed surface targets are closing from the north."

"Bugs? Or pirates?"

"It's impossible to be absolutely sure," the man responded, "but I'd put my money on pirates. The Ramanthians don't use boats very often."

Foley knew that to be true. The chits had a need for drinking water but didn't like to travel on it. Perhaps that was because they weren't very good swimmers. And ever since the government-backed Earth Liberation Brigade had begun to receive supplies from off-planet, it had become a target for various militias, gangs, and competing resistance groups, most of whom were more interested in acquiring power and making a profit than in defeating the bugs. So identifying and eliminating spies had become a full-time job for members of Foley's staff. And it appeared that, despite their efforts, there was a leak somewhere, a leak he would plug with a bullet once the traitor was identified.

In the meantime, there were a couple of choices: They could fight or instruct the drone to submerge and resurface later, a perfectly acceptable plan under normal circumstances. But not at the moment because the incoming cargo was critical to Operation Cockroach. A plan that might be compromised if Foley failed to trigger it soon. All of that flashed through his mind in an instant. "Let's turn and fight. We'll pick up the drone once the battle is over." *Assuming we're still alive,* Foley thought to himself.

If the crewman was concerned, he gave no sign of it. "Yes, sir. You might want to join the skipper on the bridge. It's going to get rough out here."

Foley didn't know if the man was referring to the ride or the impending battle—not that it made any difference. The crew wanted him out of the way. "Roger that. I'll join the captain."

The boat was already up on its winglike hydrofoils and entering a sweeping turn as Foley passed a gun tub on the port side. A short ladder led up to the blacked-out superstructure and bridge. As he slid a door out of the way and stepped inside, Foley felt the boat's speed increase. He knew that the twin engines could send the foil skimming over the surface at a speed of fifty knots. The *Interceptor* had been a yacht until Chien-Chu's people "borrowed" the boat from a shot-up marina and turned her into the equivalent of a small warship by adding a missile launcher in the bow, half a dozen guns, and a second launcher in the stern. Some extra armor had been welded to the front and sides of the bridge. But that was the limit of what they could do without compromising performance. Because when all was said and done, the *Interceptor*'s main virtue was speed.

The captain was a woman named Kate Prosser. She'd been a tour-boat operator before the war, taking tourists out to the Channel Islands, Catalina, and as far south as San Diego. Prosser gave Foley a sideways glance as he entered. Her face was bottom lit by the screens arrayed in front of her. That gave her normally pleasant features a ghoulish appearance. "I suggest that you sit down and strap in," she said. "Evasive maneuvers will begin shortly."

Then Prosser was all business as she turned back toward the screens and gave the orders necessary to fire a salvo of missiles. Flames appeared and winked out as the weapons raced away. "Tracking," the crew member said. "Uh-oh, the bastards fired flares."

What looked like balls of fire could be seen up ahead and lit the wave tops with red light. Foley knew the purpose of the flares was to distract the heat-seeking missiles by providing them with false targets. And the strategy was successful. "There goes one and two," the crewman intoned disapprovingly, as a pair of explosions strobed the night. "No hits."

"Okay," Prosser said matter-of-factly, as she opened the intercom. "This is the captain . . . The missiles missed. We're going right up the middle. Prepare to engage both targets."

Foley knew that luck would play an important role in what was about to take place. Because with all the boats rushing toward each other at combined speeds of seventy-five to one hundred knots, it would be very difficult for the gunners to aim. The best they could do was fire a lot of shells and hope that the enemy collided with some of them.

Then the time for thinking was over as the blips on the nav screen came together and the guns began to fire. The incoming tracers were red. And because the guns that fired them were in motion, they curved into the darkness like beads on a string. Except that *these* beads were lethal. Shells hammered the starboard side of the boat's superstructure. Some of them hit the gun tub located there, blew a window out, and sent splinters flying. A piece of trim speared the helmsman. He stumbled away, hands to his throat, as Prosser stepped in to replace him.

Then the moment of violence was over as the *Interceptor* passed between her adversaries and began a wide turn. Foley felt the deck tilt as he freed himself from his harness and went to help the wounded helmsman. But it was too late. The crew member had bled out by then, and there was nothing Foley could do but struggle to remain upright on the blood-slicked deck as the *Interceptor* completed the turn and began to accelerate. The engine noise increased, and Prosser had to shout in order to be heard. "They're after the drone! Should we sink it?"

"I need it," Foley replied tightly. "I need it tonight."

"Roger that," Prosser replied. "Check the starboard fifty . . . We're going to need it."

Foley grabbed a handrail, followed it over to the starboard door, and pushed it out of the way. The wind tore at his clothes, and safety glass crunched under his feet as he removed a small flashlight from a vest pocket and directed the beam into the tub. The gunner was slumped to one side, and the fifty was pointed at the sky.

A headset and mike clattered to the deck as Foley climbed into the tub and pulled the body free. Once the corpse was clear, he pulled the earphones on and spoke into the mike. "This is Foley. The gunner was killed. I took her place."

"Roger that," came the reply. "I don't know if you have any experience—but the trick is to *lead* the target. We're going up the middle again. All guns will fire as they bear."

Flares soared up into the sky, went off, and began to drift down. Then, as the hydrofoil caught up with her adversaries, Foley got his first look at the pirates. He couldn't see what was taking place to port, but the rigid inflatable boat on his side of the *Interceptor* was about thirty feet long and armed with heavy machine guns fore and aft. Both of which appeared to be aimed at *him*. As the muzzles flashed, he fired in return. The handles were sticky with the dead gunner's blood, but he ignored that to concentrate on the advice Prosser had given him. Because, like most officers in the space navy, he knew very little about littoral combat.

His shells kicked up geysers of white water out in front of the RIB boat as it skipped from wave to wave. But then the assault craft ran into the tracers, and Foley was pleased to see the forward gunner blown away. The windscreen, cockpit, and overarching light bar went next. With no one at the wheel, the pirate boat slewed away.

All of it took place within seconds. Someone uttered a whoop of joy over the intercom. Foley had no way to know if it was in response to his achievement or someone else's. The answer became clear as a burning boat appeared and was quickly left behind. "All hands prepare for the pickup," Prosser ordered. "The bugs are scrambling aircraft by now. I'd like to be somewhere else when they arrive."

The *Interceptor* slowed less than a minute later, came down off its foils, and began to wallow gracelessly as a boom swung out over the side, and two wet-suit-clad crew people dropped into the water. Connections were made, a winch whined, and it was only a matter of minutes before the thick, fifty-foot-long cylinder was hoisted up out of the oily-looking water. The divers rode it up and jumped to the deck as the glistening tube settled into its cradle.

Some of the crew strapped the drone down as others brought the boom back in. Once it was secured, Prosser advanced the throttles, and the *Interceptor*'s hull came up out of the water. Moments later, the hydrofoil was flying toward the southwest.

"The Ramanthians will expect us to head for the mainland," Prosser said over the intercom. "So we'll go to sea instead. We can shelter behind San Nicolas Island for a while. With any luck at all, the bugs will spend most of their time shooting at the pirate boats. Especially the one that's on fire. Then we'll sneak in, off-load our cargo, and return to sea. We lost some good people tonight. Don't forget them."

I won't, Foley thought to himself. *They will be avenged.*

DEATH VALLEY, CALIFORNIA

For hundreds of years, the entrances to the Lucky Fool mine had been sealed off to prevent hikers from falling down a vertical shaft, losing themselves in a maze of passageways, or being crushed by a sudden cave-in. But after months of war, the old digs were the top secret location from which Operation Cockroach would be launched. Margaret Vanderveen knew that much but nothing more. Partly because those in charge of the Earth Liberation Brigade were doing everything in their power to keep "the roach," as they referred to it, a secret—and partly because she was too busy working on her own project to pay much attention.

To call the gallery that Margaret and her team of doctors, microbiologists, and entomologists had taken over a "lab" was generous to say the least. Especially since the long, rectangular room had once been used to store timbers and other mining equipment. Harsh lights had been attached to the uncomfortably low ceiling, ancient pick marks were still visible on rock walls, and a pair of narrow-gauge tracks led from one end of the space to the other.

A workbench made out of raw lumber ran along one wall. It was divided into workstations, each having its own equipment according to the requirements of the person assigned to it. Power cables snaked this way and that, cots lined the other wall, and a crudely made conference table/lunch table/autopsy table occupied the center of the room. At the moment, it was occupied by a Ramanthian trooper. He lay belly-up on a blue tarp, eyes staring sightlessly at the lights above, while a couple of scientists argued over him.

One of them was a microbiologist named Dr. Howard Lothar. The other was a fiery entomologist named Dr. Catherine Woo. The subject of the heated discussion was whether the dead soldier was a victim of an Earth parasite called *Ophiocordyceps unilateris* or a microorganism that the invaders had brought along with them.

Though not a scientist herself, Margaret had been the first person to recognize the fact that some of the Ramanthians had the human equivalent of a skin disease. It was a malady she noticed while examining the body of a dead pilot. His chitin and, therefore, his exoskeleton had been very thin. And that was potentially important because, unlike humans, the insectoid Ramanthians had no internal skeletons. So if their outer shells were sufficiently weakened, they would literally fall apart. Which was exactly what the ex–society matron had in mind.

"Look," Margaret said, as the two antagonists took deep breaths and prepared to attack each other all over again.

"Fascinating though the question of causation is, let's focus on the task at hand. Regardless of whether the Ramanthians unintentionally brought a parasite with them or were infected by an indigenous bug, our job is to use whatever it is against them. So please return to work. We have a war to win."

Lothar had a head of thinning hair, a gaunt face, and a bad case of BO. He started to say something, evidently thought better of it, and turned away.

Woo was a tiny thing who had a tendency to wear too much makeup and cry when she thought the others were asleep. She looked at Margaret, and their eyes locked. There was not even a hint of compromise to be seen in Woo's unflinching expression. "I'm right," she said. And stalked away.

Margaret sighed and was about to return to the card table that served as her desk, when John appeared. He was a domestic android and had been part of the Vanderveen's household staff for more than twenty years. So when Margaret decided to torch the three-story Tudor rather than leave it for looters, the robot and a couple of employees had accompanied her on a cross-country trek to the family's ranch. There, after discovering the Ramanthian pilot, she had been able to hook up with the resistance. The android's chiseled countenance was forever expressionless. "Yes, John?"

"Commander Foley has returned, madam. People are lined up outside his office."

"Thank you, John. I'll head over right away."

So saying, Margaret stopped by her desk to grab her hand comp before following the rails back into the large cavern jokingly referred to as the grand ballroom. Banks of floodlights were angled to illuminate the chamber, welding torches flashed as slabs of steel were attached to ranks of waiting trucks, and, farther back, a scaffolding and curtain concealed still other preparations. "The roach?" Yes, probably.

Meanwhile, all manner of people came and went, the occasional robot sauntered past, and a steady stream of announcements were heard. The irony, in Margaret's opinion at least, was that thousands of bugs were living in an underground complex located fifteen miles away. Because unlike most humans, they *liked* to live under the surface.

Foley's office was located inside a steel shipping container that was supposed to protect the resistance leader in the case of a rock fall. No one knew if it would work, but the fact that they had gone to the trouble was indicative of how important the onetime thief and deserter had become. Everybody knew the story. Foley had been in Battle Station III's brig, awaiting a court-martial, when the bugs arrived.

The stories about how Foley and his followers escaped from the platform before it blew up varied. But even he agreed with the basic narrative. It had never been his intention to take part in the resistance, much less lead it. And Sergi Chien-Chu, who was a shrewd judge of character, had given Foley a choice. He could either participate in the resistance or pay the price for past crimes.

But as Margaret tagged on to the end of a long line of the people waiting to see Foley, she had to admit that he'd done a good job of pulling a number of disparate groups into a single organization focused on fighting the Ramanthians. Even if it had been difficult to capture his attention where the so-called Dead Bug project was concerned.

The line moved forward in a series of fits and starts as people were admitted to the resistance leader's office, stayed for a while, and left. There had been talk of having Foley delegate more authority to his subordinates. In spite of repeated promises, things were the same. So an hour and fifteen minutes had elapsed by the time Margaret stepped into the dusty shipping container and Foley rose to give her a hug. "Margaret! Here we are, living in what amounts to a cave, and you look wonderful. How do you do it?"

"I don't," Margaret replied. "But I like liars, especially charming ones, so keep it up."

Foley laughed and returned to his seat. The officer had changed a great deal over the last few months. His formerly full face was gaunt, his clothes hung loosely on his body, and he had the demeanor of a much older man. The changes were understandable but unfortunate. Margaret wondered what her husband Charles would think of her appearance when they met again. *If* they met again. "So, what can I do for you?" Foley wanted to know.

Was he being polite? Or had he forgotten? Margaret wasn't sure. "It's about the Dead Bug project," she replied. "I know you're busy, so I'll keep it short. My team has made progress. *Good* progress. In fact, I believe we're very close to being able to weaponize the disease. But we need more resources."

"That's good news," Foley responded brightly. "And I look forward to hearing the details. Unfortunately, I won't be able to give you more resources until Operation Roach is over. But that's only a day away, so you won't have to wait for very long."

Foley's eternal optimism was one of the things that made him a good leader. But there were times when it blinded him to other possibilities. Margaret frowned. "I don't know what Operation Roach involves. And I don't want to know. But what if something goes wrong? Could the Ramanthians track the effort back to the mine? Because if they could, my project is at risk."

Foley shrugged. "Anything is possible, Margaret. You know that. But no, I don't think that will happen. Come see me the moment the operation is over. I'll get what you need. I promise."

Margaret was lost in thought as she made her way back to

the lab. She had seen the certainty in Foley's eyes. He was so committed to Operation Roach, so certain of success, that he couldn't imagine failure. So what to do?

Margaret vacillated for a while. But her mind was made up by the time she arrived. The group was so small that only a couple of minutes were required to call a staff meeting. Once all of her people were gathered together, Margaret made her announcement. "Our work is very important. Because of that, Commander Foley wants us to move to an even safer location. I concur. Start packing."

Operation Cockroach was timed to kill as many Ramanthians as possible. That meant during the night, when most of the roughly twelve thousand troops that made up the Third Infantry Division were asleep. The problem was that they were deep underground within a complex that was safe from orbital as well as surface attacks. Or so they believed.

But as Foley stood on a platform deep inside the Lucky Fool mine and watched the specially manufactured weapons being loaded into their tubes, he knew there was one thing the bugs *weren't* prepared for. And that was an attack by computer-guided subsurface torpedoes. The ugly-looking weapons had been widely used back during the Hudathan wars but had fallen into disfavor since, largely because they were like a club. Effective but brutal, in a time when both military and political leaders wanted to minimize civilian casualties.

But such niceties no longer applied where the Ramanthians were concerned. So when Foley submitted his request through Admiral Chien-Chu, it was approved. And with no subsurface torpedoes in its inventory, the Confederacy had been forced to manufacture the weapons and ship them to Earth. Which was why the mission to pick up the drone in the San Pedro Channel had been so important. There weren't any backups.

Foley estimated that if four of the six torpedoes were able to reach their targets and only two of the tactical nukes went off, the explosions would kill six thousand Ramanthians. Because, thanks to escaped slaves who had been forced to build the underground complex, the resistance knew where to direct their weapons to inflict the maximum number of casualties.

But Foley wasn't satisfied with that. He wanted to kill *all* of the bugs in the 3rd Infantry Division. Once the torpedoes were detonated, thousands of Ramanthians would swarm up to the surface. And that was when a remotely piloted aircraft would drop a nuke right on top of them. Because the attack was slated to take place in Death Valley, the people on Algeron had been willing to green-light the plan. Even if the nuclear explosion resulted in a radioactive crater. Things were that desperate.

There would be survivors, though. Ramanthians lucky enough to survive both the subsurface *and* air attacks. And Foley had no intention of allowing them to escape. That was where the fleet of armed vehicles would come in. As the enemy soldiers attempted to flee, the resistance would be just outside the blast zone, waiting for them. And Foley planned to be there. The thought brought a smile to his lips as the last fusion-powered torpedo slipped into its horizontal launch tube. A whole lot of roaches were about to die.

A series of five underground explosions rocked Death Valley at 0302 in the morning. There were firsthand witnesses, but none of them lived for more than a few seconds as galleries caved in, tunnels collapsed, and life-support systems failed. Thousands of Ramanthians were buried alive, crushed, or killed by the nuclear explosions themselves. Survivors scurried toward the surface.

Foley, who was watching from miles away, felt the ground

shake and saw columns of fire shoot up out of ventilation shafts. A series of secondary explosions followed. A cheer went up from those standing around the trucks, and Foley felt a deep sense of satisfaction. After millions of human deaths and uncountable atrocities, the bugs were finally feeling some pain. Then Foley's sense of well-being was snatched away as a voice came over his headset. "Shoshone Six to Shoshone One. Over."

"This is One. Go. Over."

"We have a malfunction on the bird. Over."

Foley felt a sudden sense of foreboding. "What kind of malfunction? Over."

"It's in the air over the target—but the release mechanism is stuck. Three attempts were made to lay the egg. All of them failed. Over."

"You must be kidding."

"We weren't able to test-fly the bird," Six said defensively. "Over."

"All right," Foley replied tightly. "Crash the bird and trigger the egg on impact. Do it now. Over."

"Roger," came the reply. "Six to all Shoshone personnel. Protect your eyes. Over."

Foley turned his back and began to count. But 120 seconds later, the flash he'd been expecting to see had yet to appear. "Six? Report. Over."

There was a pause followed by the sound of Six's voice. "Sorry, sir. The bugs blew the bird out of the air. And two attempts to detonate the egg failed. Over."

Foley swore as he turned back again. More lights were visible. "This is Shoshone One. Initiate phase three. Repeat, initiate phase three. Kill as many of the survivors as you can. The bugs will send reinforcements. So we will withdraw at 0330. No exceptions. Over."

Unlike the Ramanthians themselves, most of their vehicles

were kept on the surface, where they could be accessed quickly. And rather than being wiped out as planned, the vast majority of them were combat-ready. Furthermore, unlike the partially armored civilian vehicles that the resistance was sending into the fray, the bugs were equipped with well-maintained Gantha hover tanks and Haba attack sleds. Both of which were well suited for the desert terrain.

The Ramanthians had what should have been another advantage as well. And that was a satellite-based command and control system that enabled their officers to track battles in real time and make adjustments as necessary.

But as hundreds of Ganthas and Habas left the protection of their revetments for the open desert, something strange occurred. Hundreds of duplicate symbols appeared on their screens. And that was when the Ramanthians realized the truth. The animals had installed emulators on their vehicles. Devices that made them electronically indistinguishable from their Ramanthian counterparts. A ruse that explained how they had been able to pre-position their forces without triggering any computerized alarms.

But effective though the emulators were on a temporary basis, they couldn't counter the fact that the bugs had numerical superiority and more offensive throw weight. So the humans were at a distinct disadvantage as the Ganthas and Habas sallied out to fight the old-fashioned way. Each file of three tanks was supported by six sleds. Their job was to protect the battlefield behemoths from rapacious T-2s. Except there weren't any cyborgs, so the Habas were free to protect their charges from other threats.

Emulators or no emulators, the Ganthas could fire on any target with a heat signature different from those that Ramanthian assets produced. So as they tracked enemy vehicles and fired on them with their 120mm guns, the hover sleds circled like anxious sheepdogs. Flares lit up the night, tracers arced back and forth, and the tankers scored a series of easy kills. Then the tactical situation began to change.

The Ganthas, which had been conceived as quad killers, were very effective at attacking large, relatively slow targets. So they took a heavy toll on the converted dump trucks, armored earthmovers, and other tank substitutes that the humans had pressed into service. But the Ganthas weren't nimble enough to dance with light trucks, dune buggies, and the motorcycles that sped at them out of the surrounding darkness.

The truck Foley was riding in ran up the side of a dune, caught some air, and came crashing down twenty feet beyond. A six-point harness held him in place as the driver swerved. An explosion lit the western horizon, and the *thump*, *thump*, *thump* of cannon fire came from somewhere off to the east. "Hang on to your panties," the driver said over the intercom. "And get ready to kick ass. We have a Gantha up ahead."

A rattling sound was heard as the woman in the front passenger seat began to fire the light machine gun bolted to the hood in front of her. But the six-barreled 1x20mm Gatling gun that comprised the truck's main armament wasn't high enough to fire forward over the cab. That meant Foley could engage targets on either side or to the rear but not straight ahead.

But this wasn't a problem for long as a swarm of sleds came out to meet the humans. The truck bucked wildly as the big bumper hit one of the Habas, and the right-hand set of tires rolled over it. Then more of the dimly seen machines appeared to either side. Each Haba had a fixed nose gun, minimissile launchers, and a rider armed with a grenade launcher or a Negar IV.

Foley saw a muzzle flash and used it as an aiming point. The minigun roared ominously, the hailstorm of bullets tore the

Haba to shreds, and its fuel tank blew as Foley's driver weaved in and out between the crisscrossing sleds. A minimissile exploded against the reinforced passenger door. That caused the front gunner to say some very unladylike things.

Then bullets began to ping the metal around Foley. He stomped on a foot pedal, which caused the gun mount to swivel right. Then it was time to fire at a Haba that was locked onto the truck's six. The sled's nose gun sparkled, Foley answered with a burst of his own, and the enemy vehicle exploded.

"To the right!" the driver shouted, as the truck skidded into a turn, and the black-on-black bulk of a Gantha tank appeared. "Hose it down!"

Foley did so. But the tank's skin was thick enough to protect it from 20mm shells. And the fans that kept the monster aloft were protected by an armored skirt. But that didn't matter because the truck's purpose was to serve as a distraction while off-road motorcycles closed in. One took a Haba-fired missile, erupted into flames, and flipped end over end. But the other came within inches of the Gantha's steel flank. So close that the rider seated in back could slap a magnetic disk onto the tank's hull.

Then it was time to accelerate hard as the seconds ticked away and the shaped charge exploded. Even the thickest armor wasn't proof against the jet of molten plasma that bored in through the Gantha's metal skin and found an ammo bin. There was a deafening roar as a dozen 120mm rounds cooked off, and a gout of flame propelled the turret ten feet into the air before allowing it to crash back down. "Good one!" the driver shouted, and Foley felt a sense of exultation as the truck sped away.

But things weren't going so well elsewhere. And that became apparent as a series of negative reports flowed in. At least two dozen attack trucks had been destroyed, the number of casualties was mounting, and the bugs were sending *more* vehicles into the fray. And that wasn't the worst of it. "Shoshone Two to Shoshone One," Foley's XO said, as gunfire rattled in the background. "The bugs located the mine. Hundreds of them are streaming inside. Over."

Foley felt sick to his stomach. Nearly every fighter he had was committed to phase three. So the only people in the mine were support staff, medical personnel, and their patients. All of whom were being slaughtered. And it was *his* fault. Because he'd been so sure of his plan, so certain that each phase would succeed, he had neglected to leave a sufficient security force at the mine.

With the sun about to rise in the east, and the increasing threat from Ramanthian aircraft, there was nothing he could do for the people being massacred in the mine. The most important thing was to save what he could and live to fight another day. Foley's voice cracked as he made his reply. "Shoshone One to all units. Break contact, retreat to your preassigned rally point, and await further orders. No one, I repeat no one, is to return to the mine. Over."

Having heard Foley's order, the truck driver turned and set off toward the west, with dune buggies and motorcycles throwing up rooster tails of dust all around. The group's rally point was the bombed-out ruin of what had once been the China Lake spaceport.

Meanwhile, in the back of the truck, Foley felt for the remote. He'd been carrying it for more than a month by then but never believed that he'd have to use it. He pushed the protective plate up out of the way. A red button was revealed. Then he closed his eyes. No one heard him say, "Please forgive me," over the roar of the engine and the rumble of the slipstream.

But there was no denying the roll of artificial thunder as a tactical nuke buried deep inside the Lucky Fool mine went off, and the ground above it gave way. The knowledge that hundreds of Ramanthians had been buried offered cold comfort. Operation Cockroach was over.

7

We should try to make war without leaving anything to chance. In this lies the talent of a general.

—Maurice de Saxe
Reveries on the Art of War
Standard year 1732

PLANET O-CHI 4, THE CONFEDERACY OF SENTIENT BEINGS

Two days had passed since the attack on Baynor's Bay. It was cloudy, a gentle rain was misting the air, and Santana welcomed it. Hopefully the bad weather would keep the Ramanthian fighters on the ground. Santana, Dietrich, and their T-2s watched from the top of a low rise as the O-Chi Raiders trooped through a coffee plantation and entered the verdant jungle beyond. Santana knew that the forest was going to be both a curse and a blessing during the days ahead. A curse because he would have to fight the planet before he could battle the bugs.

But the forest was a blessing as well. Because even though the enemy knew where the battalion was headed, it would be difficult to spot. Or, as Kimbo put it, "Finding us will be like looking for a blood tick in a dog's fur." Which was true although the Ramanthians weren't stupid and would be able to narrow the search.

Rona-Sa, Zarrella, and Alpha company had already passed the knoll by then. But as Bravo Company drew even with Santana, he had an opportunity to inspect Kimbo's command. A civilian earthmover led the way, blade up and ready to cut a path through the forest. It was loaded with a hodgepodge of gear, and two soldiers were perched behind the driver, ready to defend her from the local wildlife should any attack from above. Santana didn't think the tractors would make it all the way to the objective. But even a primitive trail would be welcome and make the initial part of the journey easier on his troops.

Sergeant Marlo Lopez came next. Servos whined with each step, her pods made a thumping sound as they made contact with the ground, and the acrid odor of ozone followed wherever she went. Like the other quads, Lopez was burdened with a full load of weapons, food, and ammo, most of which had been provided by the militia. A real blessing since most of the Legion's supplies was lost when the TACBASE had exploded.

There were two reasons to place the quads at the front of each company. The first was their ability to trample everything except the largest trees. And that would become very important if the battalion had to abandon the tractors. The second was that when it came to firepower, there was nothing on O-Chi 4 that was a match for the giant quadrupeds. In the case of an ambush, the lead cyborg would be able to fend the enemy off until infantry came forward to provide support. The idea was to rotate the companies every couple of hours so that each got its fair share of jungle busting.

Kimbo passed the rise next. He was mounted on a T-2 who was supposed to protect the company commander and provide him with mobility. The first, second, and third platoons followed. Santana was pleased to see the proper intervals between them. And judging from the marching ditty they were chanting, morale was good.

But as the third tractor appeared, followed by a quad named Jiro Yakumo, things took a turn for the worse. Captain Ryley was mounted on a T-2. But unlike his peers, who had distributed their T-2s at regular intervals along the length of the column, Ryley had surrounded himself with *seven* cyborgs. All carrying bio bods of various ranks.

Ryley nodded as he rode past and Santana nodded in return. When Santana spoke with Dietrich, it was over a private link. "Tell me something, Sergeant Major . . . Am I mistaken? Or are all of the people on those T-2s ex-members of the O-Chi Scouts?"

"You're correct, sir," Dietrich replied gravely. "It looks as though Captain Ryley thinks that his friends should ride rather than walk."

Santana felt a sense of disappointment. It was the sort of favoritism that was not only glaringly obvious but would soon stir resentment among the ranks. Something would have to be done. And that wasn't the worst of it. As the rest of Charlie Company trooped past, Santana saw that Ryley's first platoon was so bunched up it would take heavy casualties in a grenade attack. Meanwhile, the third platoon was so strung out that there were a hundred feet between some of them. And that was a significant problem since they were supposed to guard the fuel truck that brought up the rear and protect the column's six. Not Ryley's fault personally, but a sign of laxness since it was his responsibility to keep a watchful eye on his officers. "Go have a word with the PL," Santana said, knowing Dietrich had the same concerns he did. "Explain the importance of walking drag and tell her to close it up."

Dietrich nodded. "Yes, sir." His T-2 left tracks in the mud

as the rain fell harder. Santana looked up. The sun was little more than a yellow smear in the gray sky. The long march had begun.

The first day passed without major incident. Knowing that it would take extra time to set up the first encampment and having been advised that night fell quickly in the forest, Santana ordered a halt in midafternoon. With both the Ramanthians and wild animals to worry about, Santana knew it was important to construct a marching fortress each night. Given the variations in terrain, no two camps would be alike. But, wherever possible, the sites were to be located on high ground, both to provide good drainage in the case of a torrential downpour and to provide the battalion with a tactical advantage if it was attacked.

Once the boundaries of the encampment had been staked out and approved by Rona-Sa, the next step was to bulldoze a free-fire zone that would prevent attackers from getting too close without being seen. After a sufficient swath of jungle had been cleared, it was time to excavate a deep ditch around the encampment itself. The loose dirt was placed inside the newly created moat to create a berm. Quads were assigned to anchor three corners of the fort, and a force of three T-2s was sent to protect the fourth.

Two platoons of bio bods were to be on duty at all times and expected to stand two-hour watches. That meant most members of the battalion would get six hours of sleep one day followed by eight the next, a strategy that ensured there would always be enough people on duty to repel a sudden attack.

That was the plan. But just as Santana had anticipated, the battalion's first attempt to implement it took nearly three hours. Twice the length of time it should have taken given the fact that the unit had heavy equipment to dig the surrounding ditch.

Rona-Sa, who was responsible for the process, was anything but pleased. The two officers were standing outside the command tent at the center of the compound as fighting positions were excavated and pop-up tents were deployed. "I'm sorry, sir," the Hudathan said. "Tomorrow we will cut the time by at least an hour."

Santana nodded. "That would be wonderful. But even a half-hour improvement would be acceptable. Let's try to get the time down to an hour and a half during the next three days. Practice makes perfect."

"Yes, sir."

"And please pass the word. I would like all of the officers and senior noncoms who aren't on duty to gather in the command tent at 1900 hours. Pass the word."

"Sir."

Rather than eat by himself, or with his staff, Santana chose to roam the compound with empty mess kit in hand, mooching off the various units. Almost all of the squads had pooled their rations and added a variety of spices and other special ingredients to create communal meals. And, without exception, they were pleased to have Santana stop by.

The process gave Santana not only a feel for morale but an opportunity to put names with faces and occasionally pick up an interesting tidbit or two. Like the fact that some of the troops had seen enormous three-toed footprints in the mud next to a stream—and others were suffering from what they called "crotch rot." It was also apparent that Captain Ryley's troops were gathered together according to what outfit they had been pulled from rather than the squad they were assigned to.

Having completed the rounds, Santana made his way past the earthmovers and their fuel truck to the dimly lit command tent. Two of O-Chi 4's three moons were partially visible through the interwoven branches above. An occasional howl could be heard from deep within the forest, and some rather large insects were flitting about. Santana batted at one of them as he entered the hab's air lock and pushed through into the larger chamber beyond.

Thanks to Corporal Colby, the necessary preparations had already been made. So all Santana had to do was gather his thoughts as the battalion's officers and senior noncoms began to arrive. Once all of them had taken their seats on equipment cases, crates, and boxes, the meeting got under way. "We made some good progress today," Santana began. "But we'll need to increase the pace tomorrow—and cut the time required to set up camp. So let your people know. The faster they put everything together, the more downtime they'll have.

"But that isn't why we're meeting tonight," Santana said as he let his eyes roam the faces around him. "All of you know why we're here. And that's to take out the STS cannon on top of a mountain called Headstone. But what you may not be aware of is the fact that there are two ways to get the job done. With more on that, I'm going to hand the presentation off to Lieutenant Ponco. Lieutenant?"

There was a humming sound as Ponco rose and glided forward to hover a few feet to Santana's right. Besides serving as the battalion's S-2, Ponco was in charge of a small group of men and women designated as scouts. And, thanks to her ability to fly through the treetops, she could see things that no one else could. It was a capability for which all of the officers and senior noncoms were grateful.

"As you might imagine," Ponco began in her usual matter-of-fact manner, "an STS cannon requires a lot of power. That's why the bugs drove a thermal tap down to access the heat available in the planet's mantle. But rather than drill down through Headstone, which would have made the task that much more difficult, they chose a site located about fifteen miles west of the mountain. And according to information gathered by Colonel Antov and passed along to us through Captain Kimbo—the process of trenching, laying conduit, and backfilling the ditch was well under way three weeks ago. We don't have much imagery since the chits own such a large section of the sky, but here's a peek at the site."

Ponco deployed a tool arm, aimed a remote at the black box positioned on the floor in front of her, and pressed a button. A holo blossomed above the box and began to rotate. The picture had been snapped from the edge of space and enhanced. The audience could see the section of raw earth where the forest had been cleared away, the moatlike defensive ditch, and the carefully placed weapons emplacements. A com mast, a landing pad, and the top of what might have been a subsurface installation were visible as well. So was a trench that extended out from the compound and ran through the forest like an unhealed scar.

"So there you have it," Santana said, as the image imploded. "At first glance, the tap looks like it would be easier to attack than Headstone. Of course, all of the important stuff is buried Ramanthian style—so it's likely to be more difficult than it looks. The bugs are very good at building underground habitats as all of you know.

"At this point, we're far enough away that we could go for either target. So I'd be interested in your opinions. Or, put another way, which pile of shit would you like to step in first?"

That got a laugh, just as it was intended to, and the discussion began. It went on for twenty minutes or so. Most of the debate centered around a very important question: Was the geothermal tap the *only* source of power for the cannon? Or had the Ramanthian engineers installed a fusion plant or something similar on Headstone? If so, the bugs might be able to fire a shot or two even if the tap had been destroyed.

Although he had invited his subordinates to discuss the matter, Santana had been careful to reserve the final decision for himself. So once all of the viewpoints were aired, he stepped in. "Thank you for the lively discussion. It's my view that we have to go after Headstone because even a couple of shots fired at ships clustered around the O-Chi jump point could be disastrous. But now that you have considered the matter, you will be ready to answer questions from your troops. I think you'll agree that they deserve to know what we're doing and why. Questions? No? Then I'll see you at 0500. Let's see if we can break camp more efficiently than we made it. Captain Ryley . . . A moment of your time please."

Ryley, who was already on his feet, looked surprised. Some of his subordinates lingered, as if to stay with him, but left after Santana frowned at them. Ryley was a little over six feet tall. He had dark hair, beady eyes, and a sensual mouth.

According to what Santana had heard from others, Ryley was the well-connected son of a wealthy family who had been hired straight out of college and sent to O-Chi 4 to learn the pharmaceutical business from the ground up. Then, when the war began in earnest, Ryley had enrolled in the militia to avoid the draft back home. Once Earth fell to the Ramanthians, he was trapped on O-Chi 4 and couldn't get off-planet when the bugs landed. A not-altogether-complimentary biography.

However, on the flip side, Ryley was said to be intelligent and had distinguished himself during the failed assault on Headstone. As a result, he had won both a planetary defense medal and a field promotion prior to Temo's attempt to seize control of O-Chi 4's government. Plus, rather than stay with her, he had chosen to support the existing power structure.

"Have a seat," Santana said, as the hab emptied out. "How are things going?"

"Fine, sir. Thank you."

Judging from the look in his eyes, Ryley was wary and a bit suspicious. Why had he been singled out? Santana, who had been a captain only months before, understood how the other man felt. "Good. Captain Rona-Sa tells me that your people did a good job breaking trail today."

Ryley seemed to relax a bit. "Some of us have had quite a bit of experience, sir."

Was Ryley's comment a simple statement of fact? Or a slap at the off-world troops and the locals from south bay? There was no way to know. Santana nodded. "Yes, of course. Tell me something. I noticed that you chose to place all of your T-2s at the front of your column. I wondered why."

Ryley was immediately defensive. "I thought we were free to run our companies as we see fit."

"Within certain parameters, yes," Santana said mildly. "Now, perhaps you would be so kind as to answer my question."

Ryley shrugged. "The T-2s are fast and heavily armed. So they constitute the perfect fast-reaction force."

It was a reasonable answer. Even though it was Santana's belief that the cyborgs should be stationed at regular intervals throughout the column where they could provide immediate fire support. "I see. And the bio bods assigned to ride them? I noticed that all of them were ex-Scouts."

Resentment flashed in Ryley's eyes. "Is that what this is about? I chose those individuals I believed to be best qualified."

"And that makes sense," Santana replied. "Up to a point. However, what if your most qualified people are wounded or killed? Riding a T-2 takes some getting used to. Others must be ready to step in. Plus, there are appearances to consider.

Some might look at the situation and come to the conclusion that you have favorites. That would be bad for morale."

"Someone?" Ryley demanded resentfully. "Or *you*?"

The conversation was not going well. In fact, Ryley's combative manner could only be described as disrespectful verging on insubordinate, something Santana wouldn't tolerate. He frowned. "Unfortunately, your comments serve to confirm my worst fears. Beginning tomorrow you will integrate the T-2s into the column and rotate the bio bods assigned to ride them. And, when you address me, you will use the honorific 'sir.' Understood?"

Ryley stood. His face was flushed with anger. "Yes, *sir*. Am I free to go?"

"Dismissed."

Ryley did a neat about-face and marched to the lock. Moments later, he was gone. Santana heard a stir and turned to see Dietrich emerge from the walled-off cubicle that he shared with Colby. "That one looks like trouble, sir."

Santana frowned. "You were listening?"

Dietrich nodded. "Of course."

"Shouldn't you mind your own business?"

A smile appeared on Dietrich's cadaverous face. "I was."

The proximity alarms that had been placed around the perimeter were triggered by animals during the night—and one soldier managed to trip and take a tumble into the defensive ditch. A mishap that would dog him for days if not weeks.

Breaking camp was always easier than making it. So once the troops were fed and the pop-up tents came down, it was only thirty minutes before the march resumed. Unfortunately, the weather had improved, and as Joshi carried Santana up to the head of the column, he knew it was only a matter of time before the Ramanthian aerospace fighters found them. All the chits had to do was open a map and draw a straight line from Headstone to Baynor's Bay—knowing that the Confederate force would have to be within one or two degrees of it.

Fortunately, the enemy didn't have enough arms, legs, and beaks to launch a long-distance counterattack *and* work on the STS cannon at the same time. So the battalion was reasonably safe from a ground attack until it was a lot closer to Headstone.

Meanwhile, Bravo company's tractor roared loudly as its fifteen-foot-wide blade cut a swath through the thick undergrowth and threw waves of brown soil to either side. The crawler was about thirty feet long, fifteen feet wide, and thirteen feet high. That was large but not big enough to fell the forest giants that towered more than three hundred feet in the air. As a result, the temporary road snaked back and forth as it followed the path of least resistance in a consistently southeasterly direction.

The march was pleasant at first. The air was cool, birds sang from the trees, and the terrain was mostly flat. But as the sun rose higher in the sky and the humid air grew warmer, people began to tire. And what had been a pleasant walk was transformed into a mind-numbing trudge. A constant effort was required to keep the column moving, while noncoms worked to maintain the correct intervals and medics dealt with foot problems.

Adding to the difficulty was the need to conduct occasional drills. Because the question wasn't *if* they would be attacked but *when*. All of which kept Santana and his officers busy roaming the length of the column. And that was where Santana was, about halfway back, watching a tech repair a T-2's knee servo, when Ponco's voice flooded his helmet. "Zulu Seven to Zulu Nine. We have a casualty. One of my scouts is down. Over."

Santana frowned. "This is Nine. Was it due to an accident? Or enemy fire? Over."

"The latter . . . But the bugs weren't involved. Over."

"I'll come forward," Santana replied. "Keep your eyes peeled. Over."

Charlie Company had come to a halt, and Rona-Sa was already on the scene when Santana and Joshi arrived. Puffs of dust rose as Santana's boots hit the ground. Ponco glided in to receive him. "It was Atkins, sir. He was about a hundred yards in front of the tractor, and I was operating at treetop level. We were on the team push, and he was telling me about something he had found when the transmission was cut off in midsentence. That's when I came down to investigate. He was dead by the time I arrived."

Santana nodded. "Show me." Then, turning to Rona-Sa, he said, "Put the word out. The rest of the battalion will take a fifteen-minute break. Even-numbered platoons will remain on high alert."

"Sir, yes sir."

"Sergeant Joshi . . . Please keep your sensors on max and stay close."

With the T-2 bringing up the rear, Santana followed Ponco past the yellow tractor and into the bush. A trail of broken twigs and occasional boot prints led to a small, sun-dappled clearing. That was where Atkins lay, facedown in front of a tree, to which an oval wickerwork container was attached. As Santana approached the body, the cause of death was readily apparent. Bright blue feathers were attached to the six-inch-long dart that had penetrated the base of the soldier's skull. "Poison?"

"Probably," Ponco agreed. "I doubt the tip is more than three inches long. But look at where it went in. Below the edge of his helmet but just above his armor. Either the killer was lucky or an extremely good shot."

"I'd put my money on the second possibility," Santana said grimly. "I know there are indigs in the forest. Thousands of 'em. And you'd have to be a good shot to survive out here. What's the thing on the tree?"

"I can answer that," Ryley answered, as he arrived on foot. "If you look closely, you'll see a hand-carved spirit doll cradled inside. The sticks use them to mark territorial borders. Whenever we send teams out into the bush to gather raw materials, we have to pay the bastards off. This is what happens if you fail to do so. Our scientists turned the neurotoxin used for those darts into some very profitable products by the way."

"Thank God for that," Santana said sarcastically. "Put the body in a cool pack and load it on a quad. We'll hold a burial service tonight."

Santana kept the battalion moving, and the hours dragged by. The mood had changed. The forest felt oppressive. It was like a green hand that could close and squeeze the life out of them as the soldiers scanned the thick foliage above and kept their body armor zipped tight. They were scared, and that was a good thing so long as it didn't get out of hand. "Creative paranoia," was how Rona-Sa referred to it, and he should know, since Hudathans were hardwired for it. That was one of the primary reasons why his people had battled the Confederacy in the past.

Eventually, the battalion came to a river that, unlike the many streams and creeks encountered thus far, was too deep for the bio bods to wade through. Plus, the water was moving quickly enough to cause eddies and splash the boulders that poked up here and there.

Rather than take the time to fell trees and build a bridge, or construct a raft, Santana elected to ferry his troops across the barrier using quads, T-2s, and one-way trips on the tractors. Though time-consuming, the operation went fairly well.

The problem was the fuel truck. It lacked the clearance required to cross the river on its own and was too large for the quads. Even if one of them had been empty, which wasn't the case. They could leave the vehicle behind, but Santana wanted to keep the crawlers operational for as long as possible, and they required fuel. So what to do?

Santana and a group of his officers were standing next to the river gazing at the truck when Captain Ryley offered a possible answer. The officer had to raise his voice in order to be heard over the roar of the river. "What *we* do," he said in an obvious reference to Temo Pharmaceuticals, "is to strap bola logs to both sides of a vehicle and winch it over. Bola trees are strong but light. And they have thousands of air-filled cells inside their trunks."

"Okay, Captain. Make it happen. And the faster the better."

To his credit, Ryley was able to execute his plan in record time by ordering a T-2 to cut down a nearby bola tree with her energy cannon. The trunk was delimbed and sliced into sections the same way. Then, by using more cyborgs to drag the logs into place, Ryley was able to complete all of his preparations in half an hour.

Because of the strong current, Santana insisted on attaching cables to both ends of the truck so that it wouldn't be swept downstream, where it would slam up against the rocky riverbank. There was a scary moment when the fueler was about halfway across the river and a log appeared upstream. It was seemingly aimed at the truck. But a current jerked it sideways, and the troops cheered as the would-be battering ram slid past the back end of the tanker with only a foot to spare. That was when Santana exhaled and was surprised to learn that he'd been holding his breath.

Twenty minutes later, the battalion was snaking its way

between a series of widely spaced low-lying hills when Santana heard Ponco's now-familiar voice. Despite the fact that it was computer-generated, Santana could hear the tension in it. "Zulu Seven to Zulu Nine. I'm five miles southwest of your position, and I can see a Ramanthian drone quartering the area ahead of me. Over."

Santana swore softly and opened his mike. "Roger that, Seven. You have a decoy aboard, right? Over."

"Affirmative. Over."

"Drop it a couple of miles south and turn it on. Over."

"Understood. Over."

The decoy was designed to put out a steady stream of bogus radio transmissions similar to what a battalion of troops could be expected to produce. Then, assuming the bugs went after the decoy rather than the battalion itself, Santana would have one or two days of grace during which to move the unit forward.

But what if the strategy didn't work? And the chits were able to locate the *real* target? That was Santana's worst nightmare. Because an air attack on massed troops would produce dozens if not hundreds of casualties. Even with AA fire from the T-2 and quads. So Santana issued a new set of orders. "This is Zulu Nine. Alpha Nine will break north, Bravo Nine will break south, and Charlie Nine will hold position. Cyborgs will link up via the ITC and prepare to provide coordinated antiaircraft fire. The battalion will maintain radio silence until further notice. Over."

By breaking the battalion into three separate units and giving them time to prepare, Santana hoped to minimize casualties if the chits realized what was going on. Would his strategy work? Only time would tell.

The drills paid off as Zarrella and Kimbo led their respective companies into the bush and began to set up defensive positions. Santana followed Bravo Company, being closest to it as the evolution began, and watched approvingly as Kimbo built his defenses around Sergeant Marlo Lopez and her considerable weaponry.

There was a potential problem, however, and that was the screen of interlocking foliage directly overhead. It would help hide the quad from the air—but it would prevent her from firing her surface-to-air missiles as well since many of the branches were large enough to block the missiles, knock them off course, or cause them to detonate prematurely. The T-2s could use their energy cannons to create an opening, of course. Which to choose? Having given the matter some thought, Santana chose concealment over offensive capability and informed Zarrella and Ryley of his decision. That meant there was even more riding on the electronic decoy.

Kimbo and his people were busy digging defensive fighting positions by then. The pits would offer Bravo Company some protection in the case of either an air or ground attack. Rather than stand around and watch, Santana jumped to the ground and made his way over to where a squad was hard at work. "Can someone lend me a shovel? I could use some exercise." A corporal grinned, gave Santana an excavating tool, and went to work beside him.

Dietrich tried to remember if he'd seen another officer do something similar, couldn't, and dropped to the ground. *That's the problem with war,* the noncom thought to himself. *There's too much digging.*

As the battalion dug in, Ponco weaved her way through the sun-splashed treetops, heading south as quickly as she could. The drone was still visible on her sensors though still too far away to see with a vid cam. And based on the precise nature of the aircraft's movements—it appeared that a very methodical bug was piloting it. Ponco could imagine the Ramanthian, sitting in front of a console hundreds of miles away, guiding the airborne robot through a standard search grid.

Her job was to trick the bastard. And to do that, the recon ball would need to use some finesse. That meant letting the chit *discover* the bogus battalion rather than simply plopping the decoy down and turning it on. Because if what "looked" like a battalion of troops suddenly appeared out of nowhere, the operator would know he was being scammed. So Ponco had to pull up sooner than she would have liked, spiral down to the ground, and drop the decoy onto the forest floor below.

Then it was time to climb and wend her way back toward the battalion before activating the decoy. A steady tone indicated that the unit was operational. That was Ponco's cue to pause, take cover in the foliage near the top of a tall tree, and wait to see what would happen.

A good ten minutes passed before the silvery drone suddenly broke away from its back-and-forth search pattern to circle the decoy. The robot was visible, but just barely, on high magnification. Ponco would have smiled had she been able to do so. The Ramanthian pilot was excited by then and busy telling his superiors how smart he was. So would they bite? The next fifteen minutes would tell.

Rather than continue to hover, Ponco searched for a spot to perch and found one where a sturdy limb split into two smaller branches. The drone was still circling—and that was a good sign. Because there was no reason for the scout plane to linger unless the Ramanthians were hooked. And it wasn't long before two fighters appeared out of the south. They circled the area where the decoy was located and began their runs. They came in low, released canisters from under their wings, and accelerated away as the fuel bombs exploded.

A raging red-orange firestorm rolled over the jungle like a

wave hitting a beach. Those trees that weren't incinerated soon began to burn. The flames spread via interlocking branches, and it wasn't long before an enormous pall of smoke rose to throw a dark shadow over the land.

Ponco's first reaction was one of jubilation because the ruse had been successful. But that emotion was soon replaced by a growing sense of concern as thousands of birds rose from the foliage round the fire and flapped in every direction. Some were in flocks, others by themselves, all looking for safety.

And that raised a very important question. If thousands of birds had been displaced by the fire, what about animals? Ponco knew that the battalion was supposed to maintain radio silence. But this was important. *Very* important. So she opened a link and was careful to keep her message brief. "This is Zulu Seven to all units. The bugs went for it, but the fuel bombs they dropped set the forest on fire. Thousands of panicked animals could be headed your way. Over."

Santana was still in the process of absorbing Ponco's report when a swarm of small animals poured out of the undergrowth to the south of Bravo Company's position and surged into the clearing. They made all sorts of noises and scurried in every direction. Some of the soldiers opened fire but stopped when Kimbo shouted at them. "Hold your fire! Save your ammo for the *big* boys. They're on their way."

Kimbo was a local and knew what he was talking about. It was only a matter of seconds before the first velocipods burst out of the underbrush and rushed Bravo Company. The quad's minigun roared as it sprayed thousands of rounds into the surrounding forest. Many of the charging reptiles were torn apart, along with bushes, trees, and the ground itself, as the hail of bullets struck. But there were hundreds of targets, and some of the fleet-footed velocipods managed to make it through the curtain of lead.

The company's preparations began to pay off as Kimbo hollered, "Fire!" and the troops on the south side of the defensive circle let loose with crew-served machine guns, grenade launchers, and assault rifles. Santana stood shoulder to shoulder with Dietrich and a burly platoon sergeant as he fired short well-aimed bursts from his carbine.

Santana saw his bullets hit one of the yellow-eyed monsters and felt a stab of fear as it kept on coming. What was it Antov had said? Anything less than a .50-caliber bullet pisses them off? Something like that. Fortunately, *lots* of smaller-caliber bullets were effective. The velocipod stumbled and fell nose down. Forward momentum carried it all the way to the edge of Kimbo's fighting position where he put another bullet into the beast's head.

Then the earth began to shake as one of the locals yelled, "Here come the crushers!"

"Lopez will engage if necessary," Kimbo shouted over the company push. "Everyone else will cease fire. Get down and stay down."

The order didn't make sense. Not to Santana. And he was about to override Kimbo when lesser trees began to shatter and fall, fearsome screeches were heard, and the first triturator appeared. It was at least twenty feet tall and covered with overlapping sections of loose shell. The protective plates made a wild clattering sound as the behemoth lumbered north. Unlike the carnivorous velocipods, it was an herbivore and entirely focused on escaping to the north.

Now Santana understood why Kimbo had given the orders he had and realized that an off-worlder like Zarrella might make the mistake of opening fire on the crushers. A cloud of dust rose as a herd of the gigantic beasts thundered through the clearing, and Santana made contact with Alpha and Charlie Companies.

A second wave of animals, including a scattering of velocipods, followed. But Bravo Company was ready, and when the exodus finally came to an end, Santana was pleased to learn that with the exception of a fatality in Alpha Company and half a dozen minor injuries, the battalion had emerged unscathed. Not so the forest, however, which continued to burn. There had been casualties—and O-Chi 4 was one of them.

8

Life as a cyborg leaves a lot to be desired, but it sure beats the alternative.

—Sergi Chien-Chu
Former president of the Confederacy of Sentient Beings, Admiral, and Industrialist
My Life
Standard year 2840

THE CITY OF HEFERI, THE PLANET SENSA II, THE RIM

The first flush of dawn was barely visible in the east, so the air was still cool and relatively untainted by the stench of the city's open sewers as Chancellor Ubatha shuffled up a ramp onto the building's flat roof. A human lookout heard the sound and turned. The merc was wearing a sand-blasted helmet with a reflective visor and a one-of-a-kind uniform made out of secondhand body armor. There was no way to tell if the animal was male or female. All he could do was hope that he or she was competent.

"Good morning, sir," the guard said. Ubatha returned the greeting before making his way over to the spot where he liked to drink his morning Ta. The hot drink was one of the few pleasures he allowed himself.

His vantage point gave Ubatha a commanding view of the surrounding buildings, none of which was more than four stories tall. The city was very old, having been constructed hundreds of thousands of years earlier by the mysterious Forerunner race, then abandoned for reasons unknown. It was cradled in a valley between two gigantic sand dunes. According to the locals, the wind-driven mountains were traveling from west to east at a rate of about one mile per year. It was a phenomenon that forced residents of Heferi to constantly move east and led to never-ending violence.

Most of the residents made their livings as tomb raiders or by guarding tomb raiders or by stealing from tomb raiders. And the chaos meant that Heferi was a place where fugitives, even a *royal* fugitive, could hide. Not forever, but long enough to find someone who could either repair the Warrior Queen's broken body or provide her with a new one. And, after negative reports from more than a dozen highly qualified doctors, the second possibility was looking like the best one.

That was why Ubatha had to leave the fortresslike compound and make the dangerous trip to the spaceport, where he was scheduled to pick up a human geneticist. Unfortunately, that would make it necessary to take at least three bodyguards with him—thereby reducing the number of individuals available to defend the Queen. Of course, those who remained behind would have the benefit of four extremely expensive gun balls to help defend the complex, along with computer-controlled weapons positioned to fire on the most likely points of attack. As Ubatha sucked the last few drops of Ta through a straw, he heard the *pop, pop, pop* of distant gunfire and knew the day had truly begun.

It took the better part of an hour to ready what the animals referred to as "the gun truck." It was a thirdhand all-terrain vehicle that had been brought to Sensa II for some long-forgotten purpose years earlier. Since that time, a larger engine had been installed, along with a stiffer suspension and armor thick enough to stop anything short of an antitank round. The roof turret could traverse 360 degrees and the twin fifties could be depressed far enough to kill anyone more than ten feet away. All of which made for a very formidable vehicle indeed.

Even so, Chancellor Ubatha thought it wise to wear armor and carry a Negar III rifle himself. That was partly because the gun truck could attract trouble as well as deal with it, and there was always the chance that his mercs would turn on him. There hadn't been any signs of that. But there hadn't been any advance warning that a cabal including one of his mates was about to supplant the Queen either. The thought reminded him of the Egg Ubatha, and he felt a pang of regret. It had been a mistake to leave her on Hive. He prayed that she was safe but feared she wasn't.

"We're ready," Vasakov said, and gestured to the plank that led up into the gun truck. The animal had a prominent brow, a flat nose, and the rubbery lips typical of his race. Like most senior officials, Ubatha spoke excellent standard. "Thank you. And remember . . . Be careful."

Vasakov made a face. "Let's go."

Ubatha had spoken to Kai Cosmo, the animal in charge, regarding Vasakov's disrespectful manner the day before. The conversation had been far from satisfactory. After listening to Ubatha's complaints, Cosmo looked away, aimed a stream of black ju-ju juice at an iridescent beetle, and scored a direct hit. "Sorry about that, sir. But Vasakov was a Confederacy marine before he punched that lieutenant in the face. And he don't like bugs. Beggin' your pardon, sir."

So with no recourse except to fire the mercs and hire another band of equally dubious animals, all Ubatha could do was shuffle up the ramp and sit on the saddle chair that had been installed for his benefit. The lower half of Katika's body was visible below the turret. The mount made a whining noise as she stomped on a foot pedal, and the guns began to rotate.

Ubatha heard doors slam, felt the truck jerk into motion, and took the opportunity to peer out through the gun port immediately to his right. He caught a glimpse of the open gate, felt a jolt as the big tires rolled through a pothole, and heard Katika give a whoop of pure joy. According to Cosmo, she *liked* to shoot people. A desire Ubatha found hard to fathom. While he understood the need to kill for reasons of political expediency, he took no joy in it.

Given how restricted his view was, Ubatha couldn't see much other than sand-smoothed stone walls, the occasional glimpse of a barred doorway, and blips of color as the truck passed some laundry that had been hung out to dry. Then the shooting began. Nothing serious. Just target practice really, as guards stationed on rooftops took the opportunity to test their skills and break the monotony.

Thanks to the fact that most of them were pretty good shots, there was a series of loud clangs as bullets flattened themselves on armor plating. Large-caliber ammo was hard to come by, so Katika was supposed to hold back unless the truck came under a serious attack.

Holby shouted, "Roadblock!" from the front passenger seat as the vehicle screeched to a halt.

Vasakov was behind the wheel. He swore and put the truck into reverse.

The roadblock gave Katika the excuse she'd been looking for. As the fifties began to chug, empty casings cascaded down from above and clattered on the floor.

Roadblocks were common and shifted from day to day, making it impossible to choose a safe route in advance. The idea was to stop the vehicle and take possession of it and everything inside. That included passengers, who were typically held for the ransom. A very unpleasant prospect indeed.

"Hold on!" Vasakov shouted, and Ubatha barely had time to obey before the massive back bumper crashed into a barrier. An old wreck, probably, that had been pushed out into the street to bar their escape and might serve the same purpose the next day.

There was a *screech* of tortured metal as the obstacle was pushed out of the way—followed by a fusillade of bullets as the would-be bandits made a last-ditch attempt to trap their prey.

The gun truck jerked to a halt, surged forward again, and shell casings rolled to the right as they turned a corner. The first battle was over. There were others. But none that was quite so harrowing as Vasakov threaded his way through Heferi's deadly streets.

Fifteen minutes later, the gun truck left the sand-strewn streets of old town and sped up a ramp that channeled them into the heavily guarded parking area under the city's only spaceport. The component parts had been brought to Sensa II by a mining company more than half a century before. That operation had been forced to fold in the face of the planet's difficult environment. But because the self-propelled spaceport was large enough to crush whatever ruins lay in front of it, the facility was still in service.

The entrepreneur who owned the spaceport was said to be a Drac. No one knew much about the reclusive business being other than the fact that he made it a point to keep the spaceport open to anyone who had the ability to pay his exorbitant fees, and he could be quite violent when threatened.

That was evident as Vasakov parked the truck and half a dozen uniformed guards moved in to surround it. They were human. And as Holby deployed the ramp and Ubatha shuffled down onto the steel deck, one of them took the opportunity to brief the newcomers. "Leave all weapons other than sidearms in your vehicle," she said in a singsong voice. "And post a guard. If you attempt to interfere with our personnel, or another customer, we will smoke you. Any questions?"

The last was delivered in a cheerful manner, as if to follow up after a string of pleasantries rather than threats. "Yeah, yeah," Vasakov growled. "You eat steel and shit fire. Give me a fucking break. Katika, lock yourself in and stay on the fifties. Holby, you're with the bug and me. Okay, Mr. Ubatha . . . Let's go."

Ubatha surrendered the Negar III to Katika and sighed. Vasakov was hopeless. Then, with an animal on either side of him, Ubatha followed a clearly marked path to a lift. The elevator carried them upwards to a small but pleasantly furnished lounge. Huge plastasteel windows enabled them to look out on the blast-scarred landing pad, old town, and the sunlit back dune beyond. If one watched for a while, it was possible to see the occasional avalanche of sand slide down onto the west end of old town. Would the same buildings reemerge someday? There was no way to know.

The landing surface that occupied the foreground wasn't very large but didn't need to be given the limited number of ships that came and went. Two were visible at the moment. One was a beat-up shuttle from which cargo modules were being removed. The other was a courier ship with the sleek lines typical of Thraki vessels.

Ubatha watched as a hatch cycled open, stairs unfolded, and a Thraki named Bec Benjii appeared. He was dressed in a summer-weight mesh jacket, three-quarter-length trousers, and sturdy boots. Benjii paused for a second to look around before turning to speak with the person behind him. Then, as he made his way down the stairs, the human appeared. She was a tiny thing. A hood covered her hair, her eyes were invisible behind a pair of sun goggles, and her body was swathed in white fabric that billowed when the early-morning breeze hit it. Ubatha had never seen the animal before but knew he was looking at a renegade geneticist who styled herself as Carolyn Anne Hosokawa 1.3.

Was she really an illegal one-off of the female credited with creating the Clone Hegemony? Or an opportunistic pretender? Ubatha didn't care so long as she was competent. And Benjii swore that she was.

Doors slid open, admitting not only Benjii and Hosokawa but a wave of heat. Benjii was a diplomat, albeit a shadowy one, whose function had been to provide back-channel communications between the Ramanthian and Thraki governments prior to the Queen's injury.

So when Ubatha had been forced to evacuate the royal from Hive, he thought it best to contact Benjii rather than risk betrayal by cabal supporters like the War Ubatha. Since then, the Thrakies had been of considerable assistance. Not out of the goodness of their hearts but in order to curry favor with whatever Queen wound up on the throne. That meant they were probably working with the cabal as well. So Ubatha would have to come up with a counterbalance of some sort. "Please allow me to introduce Dr. Hosokawa 1.3," Benjii said, as his robotic form peeked out of a pocket. "Dr. Hosokawa, this is Chancellor Ubatha."

"It's a pleasure," Ubatha said, and delivered a formal bow.

Hosokawa threw the white hood back to reveal a head of bowl-cut black hair and the solid horizontal mark on her forehead. Ubatha knew it had been a bar code at one time, a standard practice inside the Hegemony prior to the revolution but currently out of favor. Especially for any scientist brave or foolish enough to work for the Confederacy's enemies. Her voice had a husky quality. "The pleasure is mine, Chancellor. I'm sorry it's necessary for us to meet under such trying circumstances."

It was artfully said, and Ubatha allowed himself to relax a little bit. At least Hosokawa came across as civilized as compared to Vasakov.

The trip back to the compound was less eventful than the journey out had been. Benjii had been through the process before. So he looked reasonably composed as bullets pinged against the truck's armor and a rocket-propelled grenade sailed past to explode against a building.

Not Hosokowa, however, who maintained a grim expression throughout the entire journey. But once the vehicle entered the compound, and the incoming fire stopped, she became more relaxed. "If you would be so kind as to follow me," Ubatha said, "we will visit the Queen. I know she has been looking forward to your arrival." The decision to reveal the Queen's true identity had been Benjii's. The Thraki felt that nothing less than the prospect of working with the royal would be sufficient to bring the geneticist all the way to Sensa II. And since he was willing to guarantee her silence regardless of how the meeting went, Ubatha had agreed.

The Queen's apartment was on the second floor, where the royal physician and a retinue of Ramanthian females took care of her daily requirements. The residence was roomy but sparsely furnished because it had been impossible to bring anything more than the bare necessities from Hive. A lady-in-waiting met the party at the door, bent a knee, and welcomed the visitors on the royal's behalf.

The aristocrat led them through a doorway into a large room. The metal sand shutters were open to the hot, dry air.

It was thick with the odors of sewage, rotting garbage, and exhaust fumes from a nearby factory. The Queen was in a horizontal position and supported by a framework designed to immobilize her exoskeleton. Her body was paralyzed, but her mind was clear. "There you are," she said, as the group approached, and Ubatha bowed. "Pardon me if I don't get up."

It was a joke, but none of them laughed. "As you can see, the Queen's sense of humor remains unimpaired," Ubatha said dryly.

"But everything else is numb," the monarch put in.

There was polite laughter this time. "Your Majesty, it is my pleasure to introduce Dr. Carolyn Hosokowa 1.3," Ubatha said. "As you know, the doctor is here to consult with you regarding the possibility that she and her associates might be able to grow a new body for you."

The ensuing conversation lasted for more than three standard hours. There were all sorts of issues to discuss, not the least of which was what would become of the clone's brain were the Queen to commission a copy of herself.

During that time, the sky darkened, the wind began to pick up, and it became necessary to close the sand shutters. A storm was brewing. But what kind? A class one, two, or three? The last being very serious indeed. The discussion continued as Ubatha went to find out.

Cosmo was up on the roof. The air was already brown with blown sand, and Ubatha had to lean into the wind as he shuffled over to where the animal was standing. The grit soon found its way into his clothes and the crevices between the plates of chitin that served to support him. Cosmo was wearing a helmet and full armor. He nodded. "The folks at the spaceport say we're in for a class-two blow, sir. And we have another problem as well."

"Why? What's wrong?"

"Based on video from the gun balls, it looks like people are closing in on the building," Cosmo replied. "I figure they plan to attack during the height of the storm. That's when visibility will be at its worst."

Ubatha felt a sinking sensation. There were sixteen mercs in all. Enough to protect the structure under normal circumstances—but far short of what would be required to repel a massed attack. "We've got to protect the Queen, her staff, and both of our visitors. Put two of your best people in her quarters and make sure they have plenty of everything. Then we'll close the blast doors and seal them inside."

Cosmo nodded. "Yes, sir. Where will you be if I need you?"

Ubatha could see a distorted image of himself reflected in the visor's mirrorlike surface. "I'll be right next to you," he answered. "If you're correct, we'll need every gun we can muster."

Cosmo said, "Hoo-rah," and Ubatha wondered what the words meant.

The storm grew steadily worse over the next twenty minutes. The wind made a persistent howling sound as it explored the streets of Heferi, searching for any signs of weakness. Sand slanted in sideways, and Ubatha was especially grateful for the goggles he wore since his eyes were the most vulnerable part of his chitin-covered body. And, true to Cosmo's prediction, hazy forms could be seen dashing from one hiding place to the next as they closed on the compound. Some of the shadowy figures were carrying ladders. And that made sense if they hoped to divide the defender's fire by coming up over two or three walls at once.

Fortunately, Cosmo had a plan that, if successful, could

disrupt the attack. From his command post on the roof, Cosmo was monitoring both the squad-level push and a bank of four monitors, each of which represented what one of his gun balls could "see." The truck was parked in the open courtyard below.

Seconds ticked by and eventually became minutes as Cosmo waited for what he believed to be exactly the right moment. Then, on his command, Vasakov pushed the main gate open. And left it open.

That was a completely unexpected development insofar as the bandits were concerned. So the better part of two minutes passed before they attacked. The opportunity to go through an open gate was too good to ignore. But the thieves weren't stupid. They knew that some sort of trap lay within. So rather than charge the gap on foot, they sent a sand crawler in first. Most of the machine was armored. The exception was the machine's belly. Or that was Cosmo's theory as he triggered the remote.

The IED (improvised explosive device) went off with a loud roar. The explosion lifted the tracked vehicle half a foot off the ground before allowing it to fall back. A secondary explosion rocked the machine from side to side. It was hard to say how many animals had been inside the crawler. But Ubatha figured three or four as more bandits rushed in to take cover behind the smoking wreckage. A gun ball opened up on them, and they blew the sphere out of the air.

But things were about to get even worse for the bandits as Katika opened fire with the twin fifties. As she traversed the courtyard, the .50-caliber shells left craters in the stone pavers and caused the wreck to tremble as the animals hiding behind it were torn to ribbons.

But even as Vasakov pushed the gate closed and another animal rushed in to place a bar across it, an urgent call came in over the radio. The rattle of automatic fire could be heard in the background. "Hey, boss . . . Holby here. We might have as many as three ladders against the east wall. Monson went to take a look, and they nailed him."

Cosmo swore. "Sounds like they're getting ready for a push. But remember . . . They can only come up three at a time. I'll send the bug over to replace Monson."

Ubatha didn't like being referred to as "the bug" but knew it wasn't the right moment in which to object and turned away. It was impossible to see more than a few feet ahead as he shuffled across the roof. And just in time, too, as a blurry Holby appeared on the right. A Hudathan named Fala-Ba was on the left and slightly more visible thanks to his size. Both mercs fired as dimly seen figures materialized in front of them.

But there was a middle ladder. And as Ubatha raised his rifle, a bandit came up over the waist-high wall, quickly followed by another. So Ubatha pinched the trigger, the rifle butt pummeled his shoulder, and a hail of bullets hit the surface of the roof. He was low! Too low.

But two factors conspired to save him. Some of the projectiles bounced up to hit their targets—and when fired on full automatic, the Negar III had a natural tendency to rise. So both animals jerked spastically and fell. "Nice work," Holby said admiringly. "Not bad for a chit."

Strangely, given its source, Holby's comment elicited a feeling of pride. Then Ubatha's thoughts were interrupted by the sound of a human voice. "Strider at eleven o'clock! Let's put some fire on that thing."

Ubatha looked up. The sun was little more than a yellow bruise in the sky. And there, like a shadow within a brown haze, a sixty-foot-tall machine could be seen. The walker looked like a human skeleton as it stepped over a neighboring building, and its rocket launchers belched fire.

Both missiles hit the roof. Ubatha was knocked off his feet, and Fala-Ba was blown to pieces. That left Holby, who ran to get the rocket launcher, which was resting next to the reserve ammo supply. But another bandit came up over the wall and shot the merc in the back. The impact threw Holby facedown as Ubatha brought the Negar to bear. A short burst sent the man on top of the ladder windmilling back to land somewhere below.

Another salvo of rockets struck. Explosions shook the building, and Cosmo was yelling over the radio. "Holby? Can you hear me? Kill that thing!"

Ubatha scuttled forward, put the assault rifle down, and was fumbling with the launcher when Holby returned from the dead. "Armor is important," he said as if lecturing a recruit. "Never buy the cheap stuff. Give me that thing and watch my six."

Ubatha didn't know how the number "six" played into the situation, but the need to protect the human was obvious. So he made a grab for the Negar III as Holby fired a rocket up into the sky. It struck one of the Strider's knobby knees and exploded with a bright flash.

"Good one!" Cosmo shouted, as the walker came to a stop. "Feed him another."

The second shoulder-launched missile was fired by someone down in the courtyard. It streaked upwards, hit the control cab dead on, and blew up. Ubatha watched in fascination as the Strider swayed, fell over backwards, and landed on two side-by-side buildings. A cheer went up from the mercs, and Ubatha clacked his approval as the machine broke into pieces. "Get back to your posts," Cosmo ordered sternly. "They may come after us again."

But as the minutes went by and the wind began to die down, it became apparent that the battle was over. It seemed the destruction of the Strider had been the deciding factor.

They would never know who had organized the attack or why. Except that the size of the complex and the presence of guards probably led them to believe that something very valuable lay within.

Ubatha turned to Holby. "I'm sorry about Fala-Ba," he said, and shuffled away. And, strangely enough, he meant it.

THE SPACE STATION *ORB I*, IN ORBIT OVER PLANET LONG JUMP, THE CONFEDERACY OF SENTIENT BEINGS

The planet Long Jump was located inside of the Confederacy's original borders. But just barely. Like Sensa II, where the Queen and her retinue had been hiding previously, Long Jump was a rim world. And one that was strategically located near a key nav point. But rather than force wayfarers to waste time and fuel landing on the surface, local entrepreneurs constructed an orbiting space station called *Orb I*, where customers could refuel before venturing out into the unknown. Or returning to the core worlds.

Over time, the space station had expanded to become more than a fuel stop. Now it was a mostly law-free zone in which just about anything that didn't threaten the habitat's well-being could be bought and sold. And thanks to some very robust defenses, *Orb I* had been able to defend itself against pirates, Sheen raiders, and—most recently—a Ramanthian destroyer.

In the wake of the attack, Ubatha knew it would be necessary to sneak aboard the space station, which loomed beyond the viewport next to him. Farther back, beyond *Orb I*, the planet Long Jump could be seen. It was mostly blue, with patches of brown. Not the sort of planet that Ramanthians preferred, but strategically important nevertheless.

The trip from Sensa II had been made aboard a Thraki

vessel called the *Dark Star*. The ship was fitted out to look like a freighter—but carried enough armament to be classified as a corvette. The perfect vessel for transporting a small but very important cargo. A *royal* cargo, which could be quite demanding at times. "You're sure that no one will be able to see me?" the Queen inquired. "I wouldn't like that." The metal cage that protected her now-frail body had been bolted to the deck in case the vessel's argrav generators failed.

Ubatha felt a tremendous desire to please the monarch and knew that the air within the cabin was thick with psychoactive chemicals. Something that could have an effect on his objectivity if he wasn't careful. "No, Majesty," he said patiently. "You and one of your ladies-in-waiting will be concealed inside a specially equipped cargo module. The rest of us will be put aboard the space station in the same fashion."

"And you're sure that this Tomko animal can help me?"

Ubatha had answered the question many times before. But the chemicals plus the sense of compassion he felt for the royal helped keep his annoyance under control. "Yes, Majesty, assuming you're willing to make the necessary sacrifice."

And that was the problem. Because prior to her injury, the Warrior Queen had been known to refer to human cyborgs as "freaks." It was a view shared by nearly all the Ramanthian population and frequently reinforced by the priesthood, who feared that the use of artificial bodies might disrupt family bonding and the race's reproductive cycle.

But with the entire empire at stake and no other options, the royal had been forced to consider what had previously been unthinkable. "My body is broken, but I don't know if I can give it up," the Queen said uncertainly, giving Ubatha a rare glimpse of the person behind the royal facade. She was a very real female, not that different from the Egg Ubatha. He felt the usual pang of regret and made an effort to redirect his thoughts.

"Well, that's why we're here. Once you've had a chance to consult with Dr. Tomko, you'll be in a position to make that decision. However, as you know, the cloning process that Hosokowa recommends would take a significant amount of time. And this approach would allow you to return to the throne more quickly."

There was a gentle bump as the ship made lock-to-lock contact with one of the many berths located around the disk-shaped space station. That was the cue for the unloading process to begin—and Ubatha could tell that the royal persona was back in place. "Don't let them drop me," she said crossly. "Or you'll be sorry."

Ubatha knew that the Queen would be helpless without him—and that *he* was the one in a position of power. But he bowed, and said, "Yes, Majesty, of course, Majesty." Not so much for the Queen as the empire. Because, for better or worse, Ubatha was a patriot.

After being unloaded onto *Orb I*'s "A," or cargo deck, the specially designed containers were placed on floating power pallets and towed onto a spacious lift. The elevator carried them up to "B" deck where the robo tug hauled them out onto the utility track that circled the space station's core.

Horizontal air slits had been cut into the cargo module that Ubatha was sharing with five other members of the Queen's retinue. So rather than focus on the uncomfortably close quarters and a growing sense of claustrophobia, Ubatha chose to peer through a nearby slot instead. He could hear announcements over the PA system, see the "zip" ads that slid across the electroactive walls, and smell the strange amalgam of body odors, perfumes, and lubricants that filled the air. Foot traffic had been relegated to a path farther out, and it was crowded with humans, Prithians, Hudathans, Dwellers, Thrakies, and androids. But no Ramanthians. Not a single one.

It was frightening to see how isolated the Queen and her retainers were. What if Benjii had betrayed them? What if they were about to be given over to the humans in exchange for a trade agreement? And what about Dr. Tomko? Could *he* be trusted?

There were so many dangers that Ubatha felt a great sense of foreboding as the robo tug took a right-hand turn—and towed the containers down a side passageway into a lift that was smaller than the first. It carried them up to "C" deck where, much to Ubatha's relief, Benjii was waiting to meet the royal party. Ubatha caught a glimpse of the Thraki and heard him say, "Follow me."

The tug started up again, passed a succession of numbered hatches, and took a hard right. That took the short train into what looked like a storage space with racks all around.

Moments later, some white-suited animals appeared, opened the containers, and went about the delicate task of moving the Queen into what one of the technicians referred to as "the clinic." Ubatha was in attendance throughout, doing the best he could to comfort the royal and satisfy her more reasonable requests.

Eventually, once the process was complete, the Ramanthians found themselves inside a high-tech lab. It looked like a combination operating theater and research laboratory, with adjustable lights overhead and workbenches against the bulkheads. All of which was intimidating and reassuring at the same time.

Moments after the Queen was positioned under the lights,

a human entered the room. Though no expert on such matters, Ubatha was sufficiently acquainted with animal culture to know that the individual who introduced himself as Dr. Tomko was both handsome and well dressed. Perhaps *too* well dressed, given how elaborate the clothing was. "Welcome!" Tomko said jovially as he went over to stand where the Queen could look up at him. "I understand you are interested in acquiring one or more electromechanical vehicles."

According to the cover story established by Benjii, the Queen was a wealthy Ramanthian who had been paralyzed as the result of a terrible hunting accident. And, if Tomko thought otherwise, there was no sign of it on his handsome face. "Yes," the royal replied, "I am. But before we proceed further, I have a question."

"Of course," Tomko replied. "Please ask it."

"Have you performed what I believe you refer to as a 'transfer' on a member of my race before?"

Tomko shook his head. "No, madam, I haven't. So that means there is some additional risk. But, should you decide to go forward with the operation, two highly qualified Ramanthian surgeons will be present to assist me. Plus, it may interest you to know that we will first practice the procedure using virtual-reality technology. Then, having perfected our techniques, we will perform simulated operations on a custom-built animatronic surrogate. So by the time we effect the actual transfer, the team will have had lots of relevant experience."

The Queen was silent for a moment, as if considering what had been said. Then she spoke. "Forgive me . . . My standard is less than perfect. But I believe there is a saying in your culture. Something regarding the possibility of human error."

Tomko grinned, reached up, and removed his head. Then, having been tucked under an arm, the object continued to speak. "There is always an element of risk, madam. But we will do everything in our power to reduce it. And, as you can see, I am living proof of how good the technology is."

The Queen scented the air with chemicals that made her retainers feel good. "You are most persuasive, Doctor. But, if it's all the same to you, I would like to keep my head firmly in place."

9

> The skillful tactician may be likened to the Shuai-jan. Now the Shuai-jan is a snake that is found in the Ch'ang mountains. Strike at its head, and you will be attacked by its tail; strike at its tail, and you will be attacked by its head; strike at its middle, and you will be attacked by head and tail both.
>
> —*Sun Tzu*
> The Art of War
> *Standard year circa 500 B.C.*

PLANET O-CHI 4, THE CONFEDERACY OF SENTIENT BEINGS

The sky was so dark, it could have been evening. Occasional bolts of lightning strobed the sky, thunder rolled across the land, and the rain fell in relentless sheets. Most of the water was intercepted by the uppermost layer of foliage. Then it trickled from leaf to leaf before eventually reaching the already-soaked ground. That was why the O-Chi Raiders were temporarily trapped on a rise that had been transformed into an island. The defensive ditch had become a moat that was subsequently subsumed by steadily rising water. "We won't be going anywhere today," Rona-Sa predicted sourly. "Not even the tractors could plow through this mess. Never mind the cyborgs and the bio bods."

Rona-Sa was correct, and Santana knew it, as the officers stood next to Alpha Company's quad and looked out over what some wag had dubbed "Lake No-go." Santana was wearing a bush hat plus a poncho, but his uniform was wet nevertheless. Two days had passed since the Ramanthian attack and resulting stampede. And, insofar as Santana could tell, the bugs believed that the battalion had been destroyed.

That perception wouldn't last forever, of course, which was why it was imperative to close the distance between the Raiders and their objective as quickly as possible. *Before* the Ramanthians discovered the truth. Something sinuous snaked through the turgid brown water about twenty feet offshore. Santana looked at the Hudathan. He wasn't wearing any raingear and seemed unfazed by the weather. "The least you could do is look miserable like the rest of us."

"You should visit Hudatha," Rona-Sa replied humorously. "First it rains, then it begins to snow."

Santana knew that his XO's home world was in orbit around a star called Ember, which was 29 percent larger than Terra's sun and well on the way to becoming a red giant. That, plus the fact that the planet Hudatha was locked into a Trojan relationship with a Jovian binary, produced a wildly fluctuating climate. Something that Rona-Sa's people had evolved to cope with. "I'll put a visit on my list of things to do right after we win the war," Santana replied dryly. "In the meantime, let's use the day to perform maintenance and rest the troops."

"It'll be *two* days minimum," the Hudathan said gloomily. "Because once the rain stops, we'll be up to our asses in mud."

Santana sighed as Rona-Sa turned away. The battalion still had a long way to go, and he was beginning to wonder if he had bitten off more than he could chew. Rainwater trickled down his neck, and mud sucked at his boots as he turned to leave. If there was an answer, it continued to elude him.

The downpour stopped shortly after the noon rats were issued. The clouds parted, the sun appeared, and the ground began to steam. It was still too muddy to go anywhere, however, so all the battalion could do was eat lunch and watch the waters of Lake No-go start to recede.

It was a very frustrating time for Santana, who was aching to get under way but knew it would be foolhardy to do so. The solution was to stay busy, which he did by visiting each company, supervising things that didn't need to be supervised, and generally making a pest of himself. So Santana was kneeling next to a tractor, inspecting a huge bogie wheel, when he heard a squelching sound and turned to find Corporal Colby at his side. "Sorry to interrupt, sir . . . But an urgent call came in."

"A call? From whom?" Santana responded, as he came to his feet.

"A Colonel Farber, sir."

"He was on the hypercom?"

"No, sir. The radio, sir. The colonel is in orbit and asked for our coordinates."

Santana frowned as they crossed the compound together. "He's about to drop?"

"Yes, sir."

Santana's thoughts churned as he stepped under a widespread tarp and made his way over to the folding table where the battalion's com gear had been set up. Farber was a much-decorated officer, best known for leading a raid on Worber's World in a futile attempt to rescue a group of Confederacy diplomats being held there. Unfortunately, all of the prisoners had been killed by the Ramanthians along with more than four hundred of Farber's five-hundred-person landing team.

Some of the press referred to the mission as "Farber's Folly" and claimed that the officer was incompetent. Others portrayed Farber as a misunderstood hero. And because Earth had fallen and the Confederacy was badly in need of heroes, the second perspective won out. Major Farber received a Medal of Valor from President Nankool and was promoted to colonel. Now he was in orbit around O-Chi 4 and about to land. The question was, why?

The com tech gave Santana a headset with a boom mike attached. He put it on. "This is Zulu Nine. Over."

The voice that filled his ears was bright and confident. "Farber here . . . Glad to meet you, Major. Sorry about the short notice, but there's a war on, eh what? There will be two of us. The navy types assure me that we'll put down within two miles of your position. Once on the ground, we'll stay put until your pickup team arrives. Over."

Given the circumstances, there wasn't anything Santana could say except, "Yes, sir. Over."

The next thirty minutes were spent assembling a pickup team and getting it ready to go. In addition to Lieutenant Ponco, Santana chose to take Dietrich and four cyborgs, including Joshi. After that, it was simply a matter of waiting for the computer-guided drop pod to enter the atmosphere. Then, assuming that it held together, parachutes would be deployed, and a homing beacon would come on. Ponco was ready and waiting when the time came. "It looks like the pod is going to land about a mile out, sir. The swabbies did a nice job."

Santana nodded. "Let's hope the bugs are taking a nap. Because if they aren't, the pod will show them where to look for us. Let's get going."

Ponco did what she could to lead the group along a path that kept them up out of the water and the worst of the mud. The result was a snaking route that made the trip longer but prevented the heavy cyborgs from becoming trapped in the muck. But it wasn't raining, and Santana might have enjoyed the shafts of sunlight that slanted down through the trees if it hadn't been for the sense of foreboding that hung over him.

Joshi's foot pods made sucking sounds as Ponco led the team along a rise, through a screen of vegetation, and into the clearing beyond. That was where Santana spotted the two-man pod. Or what remained of it. The egg-shaped capsule had been blackened while falling through the atmosphere and dented by a succession of thick branches as it crashed through the jungle canopy. Then, after hitting the ground with what had probably been a resounding *thump*, the petal-like side panels had opened, revealing the passengers within.

One of them was still seated, one leg over the other, smoking an old-fashioned pipe. The officer was wearing a green beret complete with the winged-hand-and-dagger emblem of the *2nd Regiment Etranger De Parachutistes*, which legionnaires referred to as the 2nd REP. It was an organization that didn't include cyborgs and no longer used parachutes except to slow their combat pods just prior to landing.

Farber was dressed in the shimmery "ghost" camos that Santana's troops were supposed to have but didn't. The fabric sought to match the background as Joshi came to a halt and Santana jumped to the ground. He saluted. "Welcome to O-Chi 4, sir. I'm Major Santana."

Farber knocked the tobacco out of his pipe and raised it by way of a reply. "Nice of you to drop in, Major. I was beginning to wonder. Well, better late than never as they say. Perhaps you would be so kind as to have one of your people cut that parachute down. We wouldn't want to attract any bugs, would we?"

There was a strong possibility that the Ramanthians had tracked the pod electronically and knew exactly where it was. But there was no point in saying so, and Santana didn't. He looked up to where the fabric was caught in the foliage above. "I believe Lieutenant Ponco is working on that, sir," Santana said. A branch snapped as the last cord was cut, and the chute came slithering down to puddle on the ground.

"Good," Farber said, as he removed a pack from the pod. "Which machine will I be riding?"

Santana didn't want to get crosswise with Farber but knew his legionnaires hated being referred to as "machines" and felt compelled to say something. "They are cyborgs, sir . . . And you will ride Corporal Batta. He fought on Gamma-014. So you'll be in good hands."

"Yes, of course," Farber replied. Although it was clear that he couldn't see the hulking T-2 as anything other than a piece of equipment.

"I was told to expect two people," Santana said tactfully.

"Here I am," a sandy-haired man in civilian clothes said, as he emerged from the bushes. "I was taking a leak. The name is Smith. Harry Smith."

Something about the hard planes of Smith's face, his well-worn body armor, and the businesslike submachine gun that he held across his chest screamed special ops. The kind of man who had worn a uniform at some point in the past and was way too savvy to reveal himself until he got a good look at whatever appeared out of the jungle. Santana nodded. "It's a pleasure to meet you, Mr. Smith. You'll be riding Private McKay over there."

Smith turned toward the T-2. "Thanks for coming out to

fetch us, McKay. You volunteered for this mission if I remember correctly. What's wrong? Are you crazy?"

The last was said with a grin, and Tena McKay laughed. It had a strangely feminine sound given the size and shape of her electromechanical body. "Sir, yes sir."

Santana was impressed. It seemed that Smith had done his homework and then some. That meant the civilian was familiar with *his* background as well. Something to keep in mind during the days ahead.

"What about the pod?" Dietrich inquired as he gathered the parachute into an untidy bundle. "Should we leave it as is?"

The question was directed to Santana, but Farber chose to answer for him. "There's no way to destroy the pod, so shove the chute inside and let's go."

Dietrich didn't even glance at Farber. "Sir?"

Santana could see the writing on the wall. Farber had been sent to take command of the battalion in the wake of Antov's death. But even though Santana knew that was to be expected, he felt a sense of loss because he'd come to see the O-Chi Raiders as belonging to *him*. Plus, there had been the secret hope that a replacement wouldn't be available. He was careful to keep his voice professionally neutral. "You heard the colonel, Sergeant Major. Hide the chute and mount up."

Dietrich did as he was told, and Santana saw what might have been a look of satisfaction flicker across Farber's face. His authority had been questioned and affirmed. Everything was as it should be.

Once Farber and Smith were aboard their respective T-2s and properly strapped in, Ponco led the party back along the path taken before. They arrived at the encampment thirty minutes later. Farber jumped to the ground and turned away from the cyborg without so much as a thank-you. "So," Farber said, as he looked around, "I know we're in the jungle, but that's no reason to tolerate laxness. Surely we can tidy up a bit, eh what? Maintaining a military appearance is critical to morale."

Santana, who was standing a few feet away, felt a rising sense of anger. He thought the camp was very well organized thanks to Rona-Sa's ceaseless efforts. But he knew that to say so would sound defensive. "Yes, sir."

"We'll tackle that later," Farber said breezily. "Please pull your officers together. I have some announcements to make."

By that time, Santana was positive that Farber had been sent to take command. A development that would make him Farber's XO. But rather than share his orders with Santana first, as most commanding officers would, it appeared that Farber was going to tell everyone all at once. Was that an intentional slight? Or a matter of personal style? There was no way to know. "Yes, sir," Santana replied. "I'll have Corporal Colby track them down."

"Ten minutes," Farber said sternly, as he produced his pipe. "Time is critical."

Santana already knew that. Or thought he did. And wondered what sort of news Farber was about to deliver. Twelve minutes later, all the officers were gathered in the muddy headquarters area. Some stood and some sat on gear boxes as Farber eyed their faces. "Good afternoon. My name is Colonel Max Farber. I was sent to O-Chi 4 to take command of this battalion in the wake of Colonel Antov's unfortunate death. As a result, Major Santana will assume the role of Executive Officer—and Captain Rona-Sa will take on the responsibilities of the S-3 or operations officer. Both appointments are effective immediately."

"Now," Farber said, "let's talk about the task before us. It's my duty to inform you that the time frame for this mission has changed. I believe the orders issued to Colonel Antov called for him to capture or destroy the Ramanthian STS cannon 'as soon as practically feasible.' Or some mumbo jumbo to that effect. Now, based on strategic necessity, a hard deadline has been imposed. Mr. Smith . . . Perhaps you would be kind enough to explain."

Smith had been seated on a box of ammo. As he stood, his blue eyes swept the group. "I assume most of you are aware that the bugs are in the midst of a population explosion so significant that they were forced to acquire more real estate. In the simplest terms possible, that's why we're fighting the bastards."

Santana was watching from the back row. What was Smith's role anyway? Subject-matter expert? Or a minder sent to keep an eye on Farber? Time would tell.

"And making the situation even more difficult for them," Smith continued, "is the fact that newly hatched Ramanthians can be *very* destructive. So much so that the bugs don't want them on Hive and plan to raise them on nursery planets. Jericho is a good example of that. Having gained control of the world, the chits planted hundreds of thousands of eggs there. And when the nymphs hatched, they ran wild. You can ask Major Santana about that. He led a successful mission to rescue President Nankool from a POW camp there."

All eyes swiveled to Santana. Including those that belonged to Colonel Farber. Some of the officers were aware of the mission, and some weren't. But judging from Farber's frown, he was cognizant of Santana's combat record and how it compared to his own.

Santana felt a sense of relief as Smith continued, and all of the heads turned back. "So one way to cause the enemy grief, and force them to divert critical resources away from our core worlds, is to launch attacks against Ramanthian nursery planets. And that's what we're going to do.

"In twelve days, a group of Confederacy vessels will assemble at the O-Chi jump point and depart for bug-controlled space. That means that if the STS cannon on Headstone is still operational, the ships will be sitting ducks. But that won't happen because this battalion is going to destroy it."

Farber nodded. "Thank you, Mr. Smith. I'd say that sums things up rather nicely. The 'so what,' as they say, is that you and your troops will no longer be able to dillydally. From this point forward, we will march day *and* night toward our objective, taking only those breaks that are absolutely necessary. So it will no longer be possible to establish elaborate camps like this one. But do not fear . . . The battalion will still be able to defend itself."

Farber waved his pipe like a wand. "Company commanders and staff will remain. Platoon leaders will rejoin their troops and prepare to depart at 1800 hours local."

Once the platoon leaders had departed, Farber took up the next item on his agenda. His eyes sought Santana and found him. "The plans submitted by Colonel Antov called for a direct assault on Headstone. That, in spite of the disastrous attempt to dislodge the Ramanthians shortly after they put down. Is that correct?"

Santana nodded. "Yes, sir. Although we . . ."

Farber dismissed what Santana was about to say with a wave of his pipe. "Save that thought, Major. We'll come back to it. First, I want to share the *new* plan. Rather than attack Headstone, we're going to destroy the geothermal tap that provides the facility with power. That will be faster and prevent unnecessary casualties."

Santana raised a hand and spoke without being called on. "Excuse me, sir . . . We considered that approach and ultimately decided against it."

Farber sighed. His expression was that of a parent coping

with a recalcitrant child. "You are no longer in command, Major Santana. I really must remind you of that."

"Yes, sir. I know sir," Santana replied doggedly. "But our reasoning still holds. Even if we cut power to the cannon by destroying the tap, the bugs might be able to get off a couple of shots using an alternative power source. A fusion generator, for example. And even one energy bolt could play hell with the ships gathered around the jump point. Should we take that chance?"

"He has a point," Smith put in mildly.

But Farber was far from convinced. "That's true," he said contemptuously. "And the Ramanthians may have a plan to crash an asteroid into one of our ships. Or place a curse on us. But neither possibility is very likely. So I suggest that we apply some common sense." The meeting came to an end ten minutes later.

Dietrich spoke to Santana as the company commanders departed. "I told Colby to record the meeting, sir."

Santana knew what the noncom was thinking. Later, if Farber's plan blew up, a record of what had been said could be valuable. Especially if Farber attempted to shift the blame. Though uncommon, such things weren't unheard of. Santana nodded. "Thank you, Sergeant Major. Let's hope everything goes as planned."

Night-vision technology enabled the battalion to travel during the hours of darkness although doing so entailed more risk. Especially where the possibility of accidents was concerned. Farber had reduced the amount of rest the troops got, so they began to tire. That had a negative impact on situational awareness. And without any defenses to protect the battalion while it was at rest, Santana feared what would happen if they were attacked.

Yet as the hours passed, and the battalion continued to make steady progress toward its goal, none of Santana's fears was realized. The troops performed well in spite of a lack of sleep, there weren't any serious accidents, and nobody attacked them. So that by early morning of the third day, Santana was beginning to think that he'd been too cautious. The battalion had covered thirty-six miles since Farber had taken command, which was no small accomplishment given the difficult terrain.

In the meantime, as the potential pathways to Headstone and the geothermal tap began to diverge, Lieutenant Ponco reported that the bugs were searching along the first route. And had Santana been in command, that was where the battalion would have been. All of which took a toll on his self-confidence and raised the same question. He could lead a platoon, and he could lead a company, but what about a battalion? The jury was out.

Temo was tired and had every right to be. For the past five days, she and a tribe of O-Chi natives had been following a straight line from the Ramanthian geo tap back to Baynor's Bay. And that was a complete waste of time because Antov had been planning to attack Headstone and there was no reason why his off-world successor would do otherwise. But Commander Dammo wanted to make sure. Especially after falling for an electronic decoy and toasting fifty square miles of forest. So while the bugs searched the line of march that led from their base to Baynor's Bay, she had been sent out to beat the bushes south of that route.

Still, Temo thought to herself, it felt good to sit between the roots of a towering Ba-Na tree and relax for a moment. Birds sang their songs, shafts of sunlight splashed the forest floor, and insects hummed as they darted from place to place. All of which was better than hanging around Headstone waiting for the Ramanthians to win the war.

The daydream was shattered as foliage rustled overhead and an O-Chi named Fither dropped out of the tree to land on the ground in front of her. The warrior's face was decorated with diagonal slashes of white bird dung, an antiquated Negar I assault rifle was slung across his back, and a knife was strapped to his right thigh. Fither was a member of the Otha tribe. And the Temo clan had been doing business with them for more than twenty years. "I see you," Temo said respectfully.

"And I see you," Fither responded. "The forest knows."

"Yes," Temo said gravely. "The forest knows."

That was nonsense, of course, because if the forest *knew*, it would have destroyed all of the sentient creatures on O-Chi before they could cut down trees or sink geothermal taps down through the planet's crust. But that was the sort of crap one had to tolerate in order to interact with the sticks.

"So, Fither," she said patiently. "What have you got for me?"

"There are walking machines," Fither answered. And then he pointed. "That way."

"Walking machines, huh?" Temo inquired skeptically. "A few days ago you told me that an army of ghost warriors was about to attack."

Fither shrugged. "Dream. So sorry. Have picture this time."

"Excellent," Temo said approvingly. "Let's see it."

Fither removed the small device from a belt pouch and gave it over. By providing each of her scouts with Ramanthian-manufactured cameras, Temo had been able to increase the accuracy of the information they provided to her. Temo pressed the bug-style dimple switch, and video blossomed. The image was fractal, in keeping with the way that the chits normally saw things, but came together when a second button was pushed.

The viewpoint was from up in a tree looking straight down. Temo felt her heart start to beat faster as she saw a column of soldiers pass beneath the lens, followed by a T-2, and a hulking quad. Had the cyborgs "seen" the blob of heat high above? Probably. But the assholes couldn't shoot everything in the forest. Temo remembered the attacks on Signal Hill and the family's hunting lodge. She smiled grimly. "Thank you, Fither. Good job."

It had been a long, hard day, and Farber was riding near the head of the column. The troops were tired. He knew that. But if he could wring one more mile out of them before the evening rest break, then so much the better. Farber was used to riding a T-2 by that time. The main problem was low-hanging branches and the need to duck frequently. So it was a relief when the column entered a long corridor in which there was no undergrowth to speak of, and Ba-Na trees grew on both sides of the path. Farber noticed that the forest giants were spaced too evenly to have occurred naturally and turned toward the man on the T-2 next to him. "Look at those trees, Mr. Smith. I think they were planted."

Smith opened his mouth to reply. But that was when a blue-feathered dart penetrated his left eye, and whatever he had been about to say was transformed into a scream. Farber watched in horror as Smith plucked the dart out of his eye and a dollop of viscous goo dribbled down his cheek. Then, having examined the tip with his good eye, Smith said, "Poison." He might have said more but was prevented from doing so as his body jerked spasmodically and the neurotoxin spread through his circulatory system.

Farber wanted to shout a warning, but there wasn't any

point in doing so as hundreds of missiles sleeted down out of the foliage above. Bio bods screamed, some having been hit a dozen times, as they fell kicking to the ground.

That was bad enough. But the moment the dart storm stopped, the O-Chies opened fire with their Ramanthian-supplied Negar assault rifles. Many of the natives were piss-poor shots—and some of the rifles failed to work properly. But they had the element of surprise on their side, not to mention the high ground, and the range was relatively short. Farber hit his harness release, jumped to the ground, and ran for cover as his T-2 fired at targets above. The slaughter had started.

Santana was at the very end of the column when the ambush began. The idea was to make sure that both segments would have leadership if the battalion was cut in two. That was a good thing. But bit by bit, as the day progressed, the column had been allowed to stretch. So as the enemy fire lashed down from above, Santana was a good half mile from Farber, who, according to the information displayed on his HUD, was alive but strangely silent.

All Santana could do was jump in and try to save the battalion. There wasn't enough time in which to pull everyone together into a single formation. So he chinned the switch in his helmet. "This is Zulu Nine. Rally around the quads! Use them for cover. Over."

Then, having switched to the intercom, he spoke to Joshi. "Take me forward, Sergeant. And kill as many of those bastards as you can."

"Roger that, sir," Joshi replied stoically, as he began to jog and fire both of his arm-mounted weapons at the same time. A half-slagged body fell as blips of blue light stabbed the foliage—and a second attacker was transformed into a bloody mist as a burst of machine-gun fire tore his body apart. Joshi's fire combined with all the rest tore holes in the jungle's green canopy. Bits of leaves, twigs, and chunks of wood rained down on the troops, along with O-Chi bodies and parts of bodies.

But it wasn't enough. Because as the O-Chies fired down on them, dozens of bio bods staggered and fell until Joshi was forced to jump over their bodies. Then what looked like black dots fell out of the trees, hit the ground, and bounced back into the air. "Grenades!" someone shouted, as a bright explosion cut a T-2's legs out from under her. The cyborg's rider was dead, but the T-2 continued to fire up into the foliage as a pair of bio bods towed her body toward cover.

Santana took note. First automatic weapons, then grenades. The bugs were supplying the O-Chies with arms. Were the Ramanthians providing leadership as well? That seemed likely. The ambush had been well planned and executed.

Then the time for analysis was over as Joshi rounded a curve and Alpha Company's quad came into sight. Most of what remained of Zarrella's company and the tail end of Bravo Company were gathered around the cyborg. His name was Coto, and his minigun roared defiantly as it sent a steady stream of projectiles up into the ragged canopy.

By then it was clear that the battalion was up against hundreds of native warriors, there wasn't anyplace to hide, and, even though they were impervious to the poison darts, the T-2s were taking damage from Ramanthian grenades. It was tempting to send the troops into the surrounding jungle, where they might be able to take shelter, but Santana knew that danger lurked there as well. The O-Chies knew the forest in a way that his troops never could—and would presumably like nothing better than to pick them off one at a time.

So as Joshi came to an abrupt halt and Santana bailed out, the situation was bleak. Bullets pinged as they hit Coto's armor, geysers of dirt leapt into the air as an O-Chi warrior fired blindly from above, and someone screamed over an open mike. "Medic! I need a medic!"

Santana looked up, saw what might have been a shadow jump from one branch to the next, and fired his carbine. A warbling cry was heard, and branches broke as an O-Chi hit the ground a few feet away. There was some satisfaction in that but not much since it did nothing to alter the underlying situation.

That was when Captain Ryley arrived on the scene. Charlie Company had been in the lead, with Farber tucked between the squad on point and the second platoon, when the shit hit the fan. Now, as Ryley's T-2 carried him back in the direction they had come from, it looked as though the ex–militia officer had decided to run. Santana swore, raised his carbine, and was about to take a shot at Ryley when the other officer's cyborg swerved. Seconds later, Ryley was on the ground and sprinting toward the quad. "Major! Order the quads to fire missiles at the Ba-Na trees. They're the tallest ones. Do it *now*."

Santana didn't like Ryley. And couldn't see how firing missiles at trees was going to help. But if the battalion went down, Ryley would too. So, desperate to do *something*, Santana gave the necessary order. "Zulu Nine to all quads. Target the tallest trees and fire missiles at them *now*. Over."

There was a pause as the cyborgs processed the unexpected order and launched their missiles. Then came a series of loud booms as the weapons struck, the trees were severed, and the tops began to fall. "More!" Ryley demanded. "Fire again."

The quads obeyed. The first trees were falling in slow motion by then. There was a loud, crackling noise as hundreds if not thousands of branches broke, a multitude of vines snapped, and the forest was torn asunder. The ground shook as the gigantic trunks struck, a T-2 and its rider disappeared as a massive Ba-Na tree fell on them, and a vast cloud of dust rose. And then, as it began to settle, the incoming fire ceased.

That was when Santana understood. Being the tallest structures in the forest, the Ba-Na trees had been supporting the parasitic plants and the snakelike vines that provided the O-Chi warriors with what amounted to elevated highways. Scores of indigs had been killed as an entire layer of the environment was destroyed. A few survived, only to be cut down by vengeful troopers.

Finally, as the gunfire died away, it was time for the surviving platoon leaders and noncoms to begin the bloody business of salvaging what they could. Santana had been kneeling next to the quad. He stood, raised his visor, and looked at Ryley. "Thank you, Captain. You saved a lot of lives today. I won't forget."

Ryley produced a crooked smile. "You're welcome, sir."

"You were up front when they hit us," Santana said. "What happened to Colonel Farber?"

"He ran into the jungle," Ryley replied coldly. "The bastard."

Santana nodded. "We'll send someone to look for him as soon as we can. In the meantime, there's a lot of work to do. We'll spend the night here. I want a ditch, a berm, and all the rest of it."

"You'll have it, sir," Ryley said. And both men went to work.

The battle was over, and an eerie silence had fallen over the forest. In fact, it seemed as if all the jungle creatures had fled or gone into hiding. But Dietrich knew that danger lurked all around him as he followed a trail of broken twigs, crushed plants, and occasional boot prints deeper into the green maze. In spite of the damage inflicted on the area to the west, this part of the forest was still intact. So, alert to the possibility that O-Chies could be watching from above, the noncom kept his rifle up and ready to fire.

While Sergeant Major Dice Dietrich wasn't a native, he had fought on LaNor, Savas, Jericho, and Gamma-014. Often under hellish conditions. So he knew a thing or two about how to stay alive in a variety of environments.

But there weren't any snipers, trip wires, or man traps waiting for him. Just the zigzag trail of destruction Colonel Farber had left as he ran pell-mell into the jungle, looking for a place to hide. Not that the noncom needed such evidence. He could "see" Farber's location projected on the inside of his visor. He paused next to a small stream and took a long look around before stepping over the flow of water onto some soft mud. His right boot obliterated one of the tracks Farber had left.

Then it was time to make his way up a gentle slope, climb over a rotting log, and push his way through a grove of spindly tree trunks to a point where he could look down into a small clearing. And that was where Farber was. His helmet lay on the ground, most of his shirt was missing, and he had been tied to a tree. "Thank God!" Farber said feelingly, as Dietrich appeared. "I chased one of the bastards into the forest. That was when they captured me."

It was a simple story. And Dietrich might have been willing to believe it if he hadn't seen Farber run with his own eyes. Now that Dietrich was closer, he could see the writing on the officer's bare chest. "Go back or die. Maj. D. Temo."

"So Major Temo led the ambush . . . Now that's interesting."

"Cut me down," Farber growled. "That's an order."

"I'd like to," Dietrich responded, as he sat on a moss-covered log. "I really would. If only to testify at your court-martial. But that would be way off in the future, wouldn't it? After this mission fails—which it surely will if I leave you in command."

Farber's face was bright red. "How dare you? I'm a colonel! And you are a noncom. You will do as you're told or pay the price."

Then, as if thinking better of his words, the tone became more conciliatory. "But, if you free me now, we'll pretend that this conversation never took place."

"Thanks, but no thanks," Dietrich replied. "That STS cannon needs to be destroyed—and Major Santana is the man who can get the job done. We wouldn't be in this fix if the brass had left him in command."

"Santana is *nothing*," Farber said contemptuously. "He has some medals, but so what? So do dozens of others. I'm slated to be a general. Do you hear that? A *general*. I could take care of a man such as yourself. Think about it. Would you like a commission? I can make you a lieutenant today. Right now."

"I was a corporal when I met Santana," Dietrich said reflectively. "He was a second lieutenant back then—having been busted from first. That was because a superior officer ordered him to fire on a group of civilians, and he refused. So I stuck with him, saved his ass a couple of times, and he saved mine. Hell, he saved me from *myself*. From becoming the kind of person you are. So I owe him. And that's going to be real hard on you."

"They'll hang you," Farber said, as the full import of

Dietrich's words sank in. "You'll die with your feet kicking in the air."

"Maybe," Dietrich conceded as he stood. "And maybe not. But one thing's for sure. *You* won't be around to see it."

"No!" Farber screamed, and wet his pants. *"Help me!"* A single gunshot rang out. The battle was over.

10

Though not very pretty to look at, diplomacy is superior to war, which is the only alternative.

—Lin Po Lee
Philosopher Emeritus, The League of Planets
Standard year 2164

PLANET TREVIA, THE POONARA PROTECTORATE

Some parts of the *Regulus* were more than a hundred years old. But, thanks to the fact that her drives were relatively new, the tramp freighter continued to eke out a profit by hauling cargoes to places where the regular lines weren't willing to go. And that included planets like Trevia, which was located in a remote sector of the Confederacy known as the Poonara Protectorate.

As Vanderveen stood at the center of the crew lounge and stared up through a viewport, she could see the pale, slightly orange orb floating above her. The sight of the planet, and the knowledge that she would likely be stuck there for a couple of years, filled her with a sense of gloom. If the president and the secretary of state intended to punish her, then Trevia was the perfect choice. Because it was not only remote but inhospitable. Though roughly the same size as Earth, the planet's atmosphere was much colder, and there was half as much oxygen in the air. Plus, there was just one population center of any size on Trevia, and that was the aptly named Dome City. A sealed habitat that was home to roughly six thousand residents, many of whom were political exiles, eccentrics, and outcasts. And that made sense because who else would want to live there?

Vanderveen's thoughts were interrupted by a low whistle as Captain Eric Canther entered the lounge. He was about ten years older than she, handsome in a largely unkempt sort of way, and had been coming onto her since the beginning of the trip. "You make that suit look good," Canther said. The leer was intentional.

Vanderveen was attired in a so-called skinsuit. Meaning a mechanical counterpressure suit rather than traditional space armor. It was tight and left very little to the imagination. Something Canther clearly enjoyed. "It's not too late, you know," he added suggestively. "I could put a thirty-minute hold on the shuttle."

"Thanks, but no thanks," Vanderveen responded. "It took longer than that to put my pressure suit on. Plus, I'm looking for something more than recreational sex. Or do you plan to propose, give up your job, and live on Trevia?"

Canther laughed and held up his hands. "No, anything but that! Get the rest of your stuff and board the shuttle. We'll be back in a month or two. And I'll look better to you by then."

Vanderveen stuck her tongue out at him and went aft to collect her helmet, carry-on bag, and the hypercom set she had been issued. The trip to the surface was largely unremarkable. There weren't any other passengers. Just cargo modules filled with food, spares, and all manner of personal items that had been ordered by the city's diverse population.

After descending through the relatively thin atmosphere and braking for what seemed like a prolonged period of time, the shuttle leveled out over a rocky plain. As an ugly complex of buildings and smokestacks flashed by below, Vanderveen knew she was getting a look at one of the solar-powered greenhouse-gas-producing factories scattered across Trevia's surface. The plan was to raise the planet's temperature by pumping chlorofluorocarbons, carbon dioxide, and methane into the atmosphere. Then, having melted some of the ice at the poles, it would be possible to separate oxygen and hydrogen from the resulting water and begin the lengthy process of creating a breathable atmosphere.

In the meantime, the locals were forced to live under a huge duraplast dome. Light glinted off the surface of the half bubble as the shuttle banked, circled, and came in for a vertical landing. The Class III spaceport was necessarily outside of the dome and located a mile away for safety reasons.

As Vanderveen placed the helmet over her head, she felt it self-seal to her skinsuit's neck ring and eyed the HUD that appeared in front of her. All of the indicator lights were green. She felt a solid thump as the shuttle put down next to the blister building that served as combination passenger terminal and maintenance facility. A wreck and a couple of beat-up air cars were visible off to one side.

Having received a go-ahead from the pilot, it was time for Vanderveen to pass through the ship's tiny personnel lock and make her way down a set of roll-up stairs. She could feel the additional pressure as the skinsuit began to hug every square inch of her body.

A small crowd was waiting as the shuttle's cargo hatch cycled open. But as a pair of space-suited humans and half a dozen worn robo loaders came forward to unload the ship, a solitary figure remained. Vanderveen recognized the machine as a standard Class II Admin droid. At least one or two such robots were standard equipment at every consulate. It was about five and a half feet tall, vaguely humanoid in appearance, and clad only in its dull alloy skin. "Consul Vanderveen? My name is Ralph. Welcome to Trevia."

Vanderveen heard the voice via the speakers in her helmet and knew that the robot could communicate on various frequencies using a dozen different languages if required to do so. Androids didn't have feelings. Not really. But it was hard not to treat them like people because their accumulated experiences produced what came across as individual personalities. She responded accordingly. "Thank you, Ralph. Just out of curiosity, where is FSO-3 Price? He's the acting consul I believe."

Like all of his kind, Ralph had a very limited inventory of facial expressions, none of which was on display. So there was no body language to analyze as the android made its reply. "The consul pro tem is indisposed. May I take your bag?"

"No, thank you," Vanderveen replied. "But I would appreciate it if you could collect my luggage."

"It has already been loaded onto our ground car," Ralph said matter-of-factly. "Please follow me."

"What about customs?" she wanted to know.

"There are no customs inspections," Ralph replied. "But you will be required to register as you enter the dome."

So Vanderveen followed the android around the shimmery blister to a large lot with only three vehicles parked in it. All were skeletal affairs, clearly intended for use by people wearing pressure suits. True to Ralph's claim, Vanderveen's trunks had already been loaded into the cargo bed and strapped down. "Would you like to drive?" he inquired politely. "Or should I?"

"I'll leave it to you," Vanderveen replied as she climbed into the passenger seat. There weren't any other cars on the road, and it was arrow-straight. So the trip from the spaceport to the dome took less than ten minutes. In order to enter, it was necessary to pass through a spacious lock. That was followed by a mandatory stop at the city's access-control station. Like most of the structures inside the habitat, the facility didn't have a roof nor was there a need for one.

Interestingly enough, a Ramanthian was in charge of the registration process. That was reminiscent of the days prior to the war, when bugs could be found throughout the Confederacy performing a variety of tasks. And the alien's presence was consistent with what Vanderveen had been told on Algeron. There were quite a few Ramanthian expats on Trevia. The original colony had been founded when a religious cult was forced to leave Hive. Now, more than seventy years later, the settlement included people from many races and backgrounds.

Having been entered into the city's database and welcomed in what could only be described as a perfunctory manner by the registrar, Vanderveen followed Ralph out to the vehicle. Like all of the vehicles permitted inside the dome, it was powered by an electric motor.

The streets were laid out like spokes on a wheel and tied together by circular boulevards, each identified by a letter. Space was at a premium, so most of the structures shared walls with each other and were backed up to other buildings.

Because most of the dwellings were modular, they would have been boring to look at had it not been for the way they were painted. Pastel colors were most popular. And a plentitude of well-maintained plants and trees brought a much-needed touch of green to the community while throwing off additional oxygen as well.

The Confederacy's consulate was located at the very center of the dome's circular footprint along with the city hall, a medical facility, and some major stores, most of which were set up to serve the needs of the contract workers who were paid to service the greenhouse-gas factories. Dangerous jobs given the harsh working conditions—but ones they could depend on for a long time.

As Ralph guided the car into one of four parking spots in front of the two-story consulate building, Vanderveen saw that the windows were equipped with adjustable shutters. For privacy probably—since there wasn't any weather to worry about.

"So tell me what I'm looking at," Vanderveen said. "What's on the first floor?"

"Offices," Ralph replied. "Living quarters are located above."

"That will make for a short commute," Vanderveen observed, as she followed the android through a pair of security doors. The lobby didn't have a ceiling, and the furnishings were a bit shabby, but the floor was spotlessly clean. And there, positioned directly below the Confederacy seal, was a massive desk. The woman seated behind it appeared to be in her sixties. She had fluffy pink hair and was dressed in the sort of two-piece outfit that had been popular on Earth three years earlier. She smiled and stood. "Good morning, ma'am . . . And welcome to Trevia. I'm Nina Crosby."

Vanderveen smiled and went forward to shake the receptionist's hand. That was when the pistol caught her eye. It was sitting in Crosby's in-box. "Are we expecting trouble?" she inquired mildly.

Crosby followed Vanderveen's gaze. "Oh, *that*," she said dismissively. "There used to be a sergeant and a squad of marines stationed here. But they were taken off Trevia three months ago to help with the war. So we're on our own now. Dome City is a peaceful place for the most part. But we do get the occasional nutcase. I shot one three weeks ago. Just in the leg, mind you . . . There was no reason to kill the poor bastard."

Having read Crosby's P-1 file, Vanderveen knew the

receptionist was a retired master chief. "We're lucky to have you," Vanderveen observed. "I will feel quite secure knowing you're on the job."

Crosby nodded. "Don't worry, ma'am. There ain't nobody that's going to see you without an appointment."

Vanderveen wondered if Crosby might do too good a job of keeping people at bay and resolved to keep an eye on that possibility. "Ralph tells me that the vice consul is indisposed?"

Crosby gave a snort of derision. "I guess you could call it that. But I'd say that flat-assed drunk is more like it."

"Is that a common occurrence?"

"Yup," Crosby answered cheerfully. "Fortunately, the place pretty much takes care of itself. No offense, ma'am."

"And none taken," Vanderveen assured her. Then she turned to give her helmet to Ralph. "Would you show me to Mr. Price's office? And take my belongings up to my quarters?"

"Yes, ma'am," Ralph replied obediently. He led her past the desk and into a hallway. The vice consul's office was the second one back and on the left. "This is it," Ralph announced. "Your office is next door."

Vanderveen looked inside. She saw the predictable wall seal, a desk, and two guest chairs, one of which was clearly intended for use by Ramanthians. As for the man himself, he was laid out on the couch with a half-empty bottle of booze on the coffee table beside him.

Vanderveen placed her carry-on on the cluttered desk before making her way over to the couch. Then, having pinched Price's nostrils together, she waited for the natural reaction. He awoke with a splutter. "What the hell? Who are *you*?"

"I'm your new boss," Vanderveen answered sweetly. "Now get up off that couch. This may be the ass end of nowhere—but you're getting paid. And that means you're going to work. Understand me?"

Price swung his feet over onto the floor, winced, and stood. He looked embarrassed. "Sorry about that . . . It isn't the way it looks."

"Oh, but I think it is," Vanderveen countered, as she sat in a guest chair. "I read your P-1 file. And the previous consul rated you as ineffective—and ordered you to seek help for what he called 'a serious drinking problem.'"

Price was seated behind his desk by then. He was in need of a haircut, had a bulbous nose, and there was at least two days' worth of stubble on his cheeks. Resentment could be seen in his bloodshot eyes. "Consul Zachariah had it in for me. And, if you're such a hotshot, how come *you're* here?"

Vanderveen smiled grimly. "I'm in the official shithouse just like you are. The difference is that I'm sober. *And* planning to work for a living. Go to your quarters, get cleaned up, and come back. Or, if you prefer, submit your resignation. It's all the same to me."

There was a long moment of silence. Then Price stood and stalked out of the room. Vanderveen got up, went over to the desk, and pressed a button. "Nina?"

"Yes, ma'am."

"Please contact all of our people and inform them that there will be a staff meeting at 1500 hours. Do we have a conference room?"

"Yes, ma'am."

"We'll meet in the conference room then. And Nina . . ."

"Ma'am?"

"Please keep your pistol in a drawer."

Vanderveen's airtight trunks were in her residence when she arrived. The two-bedroom, two-bath suite was larger than she had expected or needed. And while a latticework of crisscrossing laths had been installed over the bedrooms and both baths in place of a ceiling, Vanderveen felt somewhat exposed as she struggled to peel the skinsuit off and took a shower. After toweling herself dry and donning a fresh set of clothes, it was time to go down and confront her staff.

The conference room was large enough to accommodate three times as many people. Ralph had been stationed at the front desk, so Crosby could attend. Price was present as well. He looked better. But Vanderveen could see the brooding hostility in his eyes.

There were only two other staff members. They included a technician named Hiram Wexel, who was responsible for keeping the consulate's electromechanical systems running, and a very junior FSO-5 who had clearly been doing most of the vice consul's work. Her name was Missy Sayers. She had dark shoulder-length hair, a pinched face, and all the hallmarks of a workaholic. A trait Vanderveen planned to take full advantage of.

The staff members were given an opportunity to introduce themselves, with Vanderveen going last. She made no mention of being in the State Department's penalty box and knew she didn't have to. That was obvious. The trick was to convince the men and women on her staff that they could accomplish something in spite of the circumstances they found themselves in.

So once the introductions were complete, Vanderveen asked each staff member to comment on their needs and activities. Price said Vanderveen should request more staff. Crosby said things were fine. Wexel was in dire need of spare parts. And Sayers wanted to know how her reports had been received at the State Department. Vanderveen replied by saying, "What reports?" and looked at Price.

The vice consul frowned. "The people on Algeron have enough to do without reading the drivel submitted by an FSO-5 on Trevia."

Sayers, who had clearly been told that her reports were going in, looked crestfallen. Vanderveen made eye contact with her. "Do you have copies?"

Sayers nodded miserably.

"Please resubmit them to me by 0900 in the morning. I will read every one of them from beginning to end. And, if I think they have value, you can rest assured they will be sent to Algeron. Okay?"

Sayers avoided looking at Price. She forced a smile. "Yes, ma'am. Thank you."

"Okay," Vanderveen said. "I can't say that I have much hope for additional personnel. Not given the exigencies of the war. But if Mr. Price will provide me with some supporting documentation, I'll see what I can do. Mr. Wexel . . . I hear you regarding the spares. If you would be so kind as to prepare a high-priority request, I will shoot it to the supply people via hypercom. Ms. Sayers . . . We'll have a talk after I read those reports. I think that's enough for today. Thank you."

Vanderveen returned to her apartment after that and spent the next couple of hours putting things away. Then, having made herself a meal from items that Consul Zachariah and his wife had left behind, she took it out onto a small balcony. It was evening by then, stars glittered beyond the gentle curve of the dome, and she was very much alone. Could she see O-Chi 4? No, Vanderveen decided. She couldn't.

Vanderveen spent her first two days on Trevia dealing with a variety of administrative issues and reading the Sayers reports. They were *very* dense. Too dense to pass up the chain of command without some serious editing. But they were also quite valuable. Because Sayers had not only been out meeting with people in the various subcommunities, she had gone to the effort of documenting everything they had to say and collected copies of news stories sent to them from their home planets. More than that, she had organized the material, cross-indexed it, and written hundreds of annotations. All of which might have seemed boring to Price but was like gold to Vanderveen.

But Sayers didn't know that. And being used to the way Price did things, she looked scared as she entered the consul's office and took a seat at the conference table. "Good morning," Vanderveen said cheerfully, as they settled in. "I want you to know that I read your reports, and you're doing an outstanding job. Such a good job that I'm going to put you up for an early jump to FSO-4."

Sayers, who hadn't heard any positive feedback in a long time, looked surprised, then pleased. "*Really?* That would be wonderful! So the reports are okay?"

"The quality of the data and the analysis in the reports is outstanding. However, they need to be summarized and submitted with the detail as backup. Once you do that, the reports will be better than okay. I'll use them as justification for a promotion."

Sayers nodded eagerly. "Yes, ma'am. I'll get right to work."

"Good . . . In the meantime, I'm going to need your help setting up a round of courtesy calls."

"Yes, ma'am. I would be happy to set them up. Do you have any priorities I should be aware of?"

"Yes. For obvious reasons, the Ramanthian community is of particular interest to our superiors. And, as I read your reports, the name Hamantha Croth crops up more than once. What do you recommend? Should I begin with him?"

Sayers was thrilled to be asked for her opinion, and it showed as the light in her eyes grew brighter. "Yes, I think you should. There are a number of interesting things about Croth, starting with the fact that, even though he's a relative newcomer, the expat community treats him like a well-established leader."

Vanderveen's eyebrows rose slightly. "As measured by what?"

"He's a much-sought-after speaker," Sayers replied. "But as you know, Ramanthians have a tendency to defer to people of superior rank. And when he's around, the rest of them clam up. So I wondered why."

"And?"

"And I did some research," Sayers replied. "Some of the locals get news summaries from Hive, which they keep at their community center for others to read."

Vanderveen smiled broadly. "Don't tell me. Let me guess. You went there and read a bunch of back issues. Or did you? There aren't many people who can read Ramanthian script."

"That's true," Sayers replied, "but Ralph can. The news summaries were full of government propaganda. But Ralph found a fractal image of Croth, and we asked Wexel to convert it. And guess what?"

There was something infectious about Sayers and her girlish enthusiasm. Vanderveen smiled. "What?"

"His *real* name is Bebo Hoknar. And prior to the Warrior Queen's death, he served as her majordomo. It's my belief that the locals are well aware of that, which is why they defer to him. He's the most senior ex-official on Trevia."

"Brilliant," Vanderveen said. "Excellent work. But why use a false name?"

Sayers shook her head. "I don't know, ma'am. Unless he wants to keep non-Ramanthians in the dark about his identity for some reason."

"Well, maybe we'll find out," Vanderveen replied. "Please set up a meeting."

"Yes, ma'am."

"And Missy . . ."

"Ma'am?"

"Thank you."

* * *

The Thraki ship *Light Runner* landed on Trevia without any fanfare and began to discharge its passengers an hour later. There were six of them, all but one of whom were Ramanthians, the sixth being a Thraki, who remained with the ship.

The rest, led by a richly robed merchant named Ortu Bacula, were transported into the dome. According to the information provided to the city's registrar, Bacula and his party planned to meet with local officials regarding the construction of a pollution-spewing factory that would not only create jobs, but complement their efforts to produce greenhouse gases.

So it wasn't surprising to the few people who were paying attention when Bacula and his retinue checked into a hotel at the heart of what the local humans referred to as "bug town." It was a section of the city where Ramanthian cuisine, sand baths, and entertainments were widely available.

But, contrary to appearances, Bacula was the lowest-ranking member of the party, and one of his servants was in charge. The servant role was one that the War Ubatha had chosen for himself so that while all eyes were on Bacula, he would be free to look for the Warrior Queen. Because, thanks to the information extracted from the Egg Ubatha, the soldier knew his quarry was hidden nearby.

That didn't mean the process would be easy, however. Most of the roughly twenty-five hundred Ramanthians who lived in Dome City were exiles, nonconformists of various stripes, or outright criminals. None of them was likely to cooperate with government agents. Especially a group of resident denialists who continued to send antigovernment tracts to Hive and other Ramanthian planets. Though careful not to claim that the Warrior Queen was still alive and living on Trevia, they liked to natter on about how "the memories of our rightful monarch will never die." The key word being "rightful."

Since he couldn't go door to door searching for the Queen, the War Ubatha would have to use a less-direct approach. And that was to keep an eye on the individuals that a resident intelligence agent thought were most likely to know where the royal was hiding. Then, having identified such a person, the War Ubatha would follow him or her to the Queen's hiding place.

To accomplish that, Ubatha had brought a surveillance expert plus a trunkful of very sophisticated equipment to Trevia. Devices which would not only allow his team to remain in the shadows—but greatly increase the number of suspects they could track.

The first step was to set up a command center in Bacula's hotel suite. Once that was accomplished, hundreds of tiny self-propelled spy balls were launched into the air with orders to seek out the addresses of the individuals on Ubatha's list and take up positions inside their homes. The process was delightfully simple thanks to the absence of roofs.

So, within one rotation of landing, the War Ubatha and his team were not only established but on the receiving end of a steady flow of information. Most of which was mind-numbingly dull. As a result, Ubatha had to take frequent breaks lest the banality of the incoming conversations drive him mad. That was why he was in his room, practicing crosscuts with his sword, when Ras Qwen appeared in the doorway. The surveillance technician was clearly excited. "Sorry to interrupt, sir. But subject Six has a human visitor."

Each suspect had been assigned a number by the intelligence agent who had compiled the list of names. The lower the number, the more important that individual was thought to be. And since the agent was also the city's registrar—he was in a position to know who was who. So a meeting between a human and Six was clearly of interest.

The warrior followed the technician into the central living area, where a bank of monitors had been set up. "This is the one," Qwen said, indicating screen three. The picture showed a room decorated to resemble a home on Hive, a Ramanthian functionary who looked vaguely familiar, and a pair of human females. All three were seated.

Ubatha lowered himself onto a saddle chair and settled in to watch. "Names," he demanded.

"The functionary calls himself Hamantha Croth. But his actual name is Bebo Hoknar. He served as the Warrior Queen's majordomo and fled Hive two days *before* her death was announced to the public. According to the data supplied by the registrar, both of the animals work for the Confederacy's consulate. The creature on the far right is Consul Christine Vanderveen. She arrived a week ago and appears to be making a round of courtesy calls."

"And Hoknar is at or near the top of her list."

"It appears that way—yes."

"Back it up. I want to see it from the beginning."

Qwen complied. Ubatha watched and listened as the pleasantries came to an end and the *real* conversation began. And it was painfully mundane as the Vanderveen animal probed Hoknar for information, and he fended her off. "She knows something," Ubatha observed. "Or believes she does."

"Perhaps," Qwen allowed. "But if so, she isn't getting anywhere."

And that was true. Because fifteen minutes later, as the humans got up to leave, nothing of any real consequence had been said. "Sorry, sir," Qwen said, as the visitors left and the door closed behind them. "I thought we were onto something."

"Quiet," Ubatha ordered, as a female Ramanthian shuffled into the picture. The Egg Hoknar? Yes, the warrior thought so.

"What did they want?" the Egg Hoknar inquired.

"It was a courtesy call," Hoknar answered. "But the new animal seemed to be after some sort of information. We must be very careful. What if the animals were to learn the truth? There's no telling what might happen."

"Come," the Egg Hoknar said. "Your lunch is ready."

Ubatha felt the slow, pleasurable flush of victory as the couple shuffled out of the room. He still didn't know where the fugitive Queen was. But he knew whom to ask.

Thanks to the spy ball in Hoknar's home, the War Ubatha was very familiar with the expat's habits. So the home invasion took place at two in the morning. A time when both of the Hoknars would be sound asleep.

It took less than a minute for Qwen to neutralize the alarm system and pick the lock. A few moments later, Ubatha and his team were inside. It was a simple matter to enter the bedroom and turn the lights on. The couple was sleeping on floor bolsters facing the door. Hoknar awoke with a start and was trying to get up when Ubatha placed a foot on his back.

Meanwhile, the Egg Hoknar did something completely unexpected. She reared up, produced a pistol, and fired. The bullet nicked one of the troopers. So he shot her in the head. She collapsed in a heap.

"You fool!" Ubatha said, and brought a closed pincer around. There was a loud clack as chitin made contact with chitin and the soldier staggered backwards. Suddenly, some of Ubatha's leverage, not to mention a possible source of information, was gone. There was one benefit, however—and that was Hoknar's reaction to his mate's death. Judging from his body language, he was both shocked and terrified.

"Check to see if the noise woke anyone up," Ubatha ordered. "Take Hoknar into the eating area and secure him to the table. But leave his tool arms free so he can talk."

Troopers were busy tying Hoknar to the table when Qwen returned. "There isn't any activity in the area, sir. If other residents heard the Egg Hoknar's shot—they didn't recognize the noise for what it was."

"Good," Ubatha replied. "Stay out front. Let me know if you see anything."

With his subject secured to the table, Ubatha was ready for the interrogation. By pulling a chair around, he could sit only inches away and stare into Hoknar's face. "This could be quite painless," Ubatha said. "And that would be my preference. Your name is Bebo Hoknar. Not Hamantha Croth. You served as the Warrior Queen's majordomo. And shortly after she left Hive, *you* left Hive. And followed her here. That much is obvious. And admirable in a way . . . because loyalty is a virtue. But there is something else to consider. And that is loyalty not to a single person but to our entire race. So tell me where the Queen is, and we will leave you in peace."

The last was a lie, of course. Because Ubatha had no intention of allowing Hoknar to live. But it was necessary to lie in order to achieve a higher purpose. Hoknar blinked rapidly. A sure sign of stress. "I don't know what you're talking about. Truly I don't."

Ubatha tilted his head in a way that signaled pity. "Your egg mate is dead. Who will arrange for her funeral once you're gone?"

"I would tell you if I knew," Hoknar insisted pitifully. "But I don't."

"Okay," Ubatha responded. "Perhaps what you say is true. But my duty is clear. I have to make sure."

Then, looking up at one of his troopers, Ubatha gave the necessary orders. "Tape his beak and remove his wings."

Hoknar screamed. Or tried to. But he couldn't open his mouth, so no sound came out. "Now," Ubatha said, as he held one of the severed appendages up for Hoknar to examine. "Are you ready to tell me what I need to know?"

Hoknar had no choice but to communicate via click speech. *"Please,"* he said. "How can I tell you what I don't know?"

"You are starting to annoy me," Ubatha said heartlessly. "Remove his left foot."

Hoknar struggled. Or tried to as a trooper took hold of his left foot and pulled. Having grabbed a meat cleaver from a rack, a second soldier raised it high above his head. There was a solid *thunk* as the blade cut through Hoknar's ankle and sank into the wood tabletop. Blood spurted and began to pool on the floor.

Hoknar fainted at that point. He came around when a trooper dumped a panful of water onto his head. "I'm waiting," Ubatha said grimly. "Tell me what I want to know."

And Hoknar did. The ensuing conversation lasted for more than ten minutes. And by the time it was over, Ubatha knew the truth. The Warrior Queen had been smuggled into the city in a cargo module. But it was apparent to Hoknar and others that she wouldn't be able to hide on the planet for long. The Ramanthian community was simply too small. Somebody would notice. Plus, there was the hope that a cure could be found. And that was why she had been taken to Sensa. "By whom?" Ubatha demanded. "*Who* took the Queen to Sensa?"

"Chancellor Ubatha," came the reply. "And a Thraki named Benjii."

The War Ubatha wasn't surprised to hear his mate's name. But a Thraki? That was news. Especially since the fur balls were providing him with assistance as well. *They're supporting both sides,* Ubatha thought to himself. *So they win either way. The eggless scum.*

The warrior stood and made eye contact with one of the troopers. "Shoot him. Use your silencer."

There was a soft *phut* as the soldier fired, Hoknar jerked, and his body went limp. The entire party would be aboard the Thraki ship and in hyperspace before the bodies were discovered. Then the long, tiresome business of killing the Queen would continue. But, as Nira had written, "In order to achieve strength we must conqueror resistance." And that made him feel better.

11

An army is a team, lives, sleeps, fights, and eats as a team. This individual hero stuff is a lot of horseshit.

—*General George S. Patton Jr.*
Standard year 1944

PLANET O-CHI 4, THE CONFEDERACY OF SENTIENT BEINGS

Trees had been cut down. Ground had been cleared. And graves had been dug. Seventy-six in all. Santana still had difficulty believing it. Nearly a third of the battalion had been wounded or killed in a single engagement. Yet as the sun sent hesitant rays of pale yellow light slanting down through what remained of the forest canopy, the evidence was clear to see.

Each hole was seven feet long, six feet deep, and four feet wide. They were spaced exactly two feet apart and laid out on a grid. Bodies and parts of bodies had already been placed in the graves. And with the exception of those assigned to guard the perimeter, the rest of the battalion stood at attention as soil was shoveled into the neatly excavated holes.

Captain Zarrella occupied one of the graves as did the mysterious Mr. Smith. But missing, and still unaccounted for, was Colonel Max Farber, who had last been seen running into the jungle as the fighting began. Dietrich had gone into the forest looking for the officer and returned with Farber's still-functional helmet. But there had been no trace of the man himself. Dead probably. Killed by the O-Chies. Santana's thoughts were interrupted by the sound of Dietrich's voice. "The battalion is ready, sir."

The holes had been filled in, laser-inscribed metal markers had been placed at the head of each grave, and the troops were waiting for him to say something. Santana knew that some of them believed in God and some didn't. But all of them believed in each other and those who had gone before. So Santana read the words that Legionnaire Alan Seeger had written before his death in World War I on Earth. It began:

I have a rendezvous with Death
At some disputed barricade,
When Spring comes back with rustling shade
And apple-blossoms fill the air
I have a rendezvous with Death
When Spring brings back blue days and fair.

And ended:

But I've a rendezvous with Death
At midnight in some flaming town,
When Spring trips north again this year
And I to my pledged word am true,
I shall not fail that rendezvous.

"It is," Santana finished solemnly, "our way. The way of the Legion. And it has been for more than a thousand years."

Ponco, who like others present had already died in battle, felt a special kinship with Seeger. And a sad longing as she looked at Santana. Because even though both of them were alive, it was in very different ways, and what her heart wanted could never be.

Santana allowed a moment of silence. Then, conscious of what had to be done, he spoke again. "As is so often the case in war, there is no time to grieve. And won't be until our mission has been accomplished. After discussing the matter with Captains Rona-Sa, Kimbo, and Ryley, I have come to the conclusion that the only way we can realistically hope to accomplish our objective is to divide the battalion into two groups.

"The first section under the command of Captain Rona-Sa will include the tractors, quads, and those bio bods who were severely wounded during the ambush. They will be accompanied by two platoons of troops who will provide security. Once group one arrives in Baynor's Bay, they will seek additional medical attention for the wounded and establish a firebase.

"The second section, under my command, will consist of Captain Ryley, Lieutenant Ponco, and a force of thirty-four people. Half of them will be T-2s. This team, which will operate as two platoons, will be able to move quickly and take the bugs by surprise. And, even if we fail to accomplish that, the presence of seventeen T-2s will provide the company with overwhelming firepower. Thank you for your bravery and constancy. That will be all."

The troops were dismissed a few seconds later. And as they took their places in their newly re-formed squads and platoons, Santana made his way over to the place where Rona-Sa was talking to Kimbo. Both officers had been wounded. They came to attention as Santana arrived. "As you were, gentlemen. I'm sorry to say that both of you look like hell warmed over."

Rona-Sa was leaning on a homemade crutch. He had been hit by three darts during the ambush. But thanks to both his size and Hudathan physiology, he had survived. Kimbo had a bloodstained bandage wrapped around his head. "There's no need to add insult to injury, sir," he said with a grin. "Haven't we suffered enough?"

"Sorry," Santana replied contritely. "Now remember . . . I want you to maintain a high profile as you withdraw. We know the bugs supplied the O-Chies with weapons, so it's logical to suppose that the indigs will be watching. And while the Ramanthians track you back to Baynor's Bay, we'll run straight down their throats."

Rona-Sa was anything but happy with the assignment. "If you say so, sir. But I can still ride and respectfully request permission to accompany group two."

"Permission denied, Captain. Your job is to get well—and get the rest of the battalion back safely. There is a very good chance that your column will be attacked by the O-Chies or Ramanthian aircraft, or both. So it's very important that the group has an experienced officer to provide leadership."

Rona-Sa's face was expressionless, but Santana could tell that he was somewhat mollified. "Sir, yes sir."

Confident that group one was in good hands, it was time for Santana to turn his attention to group two. Preparations were already under way. The first step was to repair all of the T-2s that could be repaired, a process that often involved using parts salvaged from cyborgs killed in action. So that in some cases the neatly mounded graves held little more than a badly mangled brain box.

Then, once the T-2s were fully operational, it was necessary to perform preventive maintenance on them. That included replenishing their ammo bins and mounting missile launchers on every other unit. There wouldn't be any reloads. But the SAMs would give the company a limited ability to engage enemy aircraft. Meanwhile, those T-2s not encumbered by missiles were equipped with backpacks. That didn't leave much room for the flesh-and-blood riders, but it couldn't be helped.

The company's bio bods were equipped with helmets, body armor, and a variety of weapons. More than half of them were legionnaires who were not only combat veterans—but had the technical skills required to keep the cyborgs up and running. Ryley came forward to meet Santana as he approached the column. The former militia officer still had a supercilious air, but the legionnaire had come to trust him. "We're ready, sir."

"Excellent. Let's mount up. I'll take the point, and you ride drag. We'll switch places in two hours. Remember . . . If I fall, carry on. The Confederacy will be counting on you."

Ryley nodded. "Yes, sir."

"Good. Keep it closed up back there."

Five minutes later, both officers were mounted, strapped in, and all of the radio checks were complete. A new reporting structure had been put into place. That meant new call signs and the need to memorize them. "This is Alpha One," Santana announced. "Alpha One-Three will provide our eye in the sky—and Alpha One-Four has the lead on the ground. Maintain visual contact with the team in front of you at all times. Let's move out. Over."

And with that, Dietrich and his T-2 went into motion. They could see Ponco's alphanumeric symbol on their HUDs as well as those of the people behind them. So their job was to follow the recon ball while keeping a sharp eye out for obstacles on the ground and any threats the Intel officer might have missed.

Ponco was flying about fifty feet off the ground as she wound her way in and out of the trees. The task was to stay ahead of the column but not too far ahead, and monitor the level of the forest that the O-Chies liked to use as their arboreal highway.

Because it was important to not only prevent another ambush but kill any scouts before they could get back to the Ramanthians and report the truth: Part of the battalion was in retreat, but the rest was coming on fast. And Santana was counting on her.

The first couple of hours were exhilarating. Having been freed from the constraints imposed on them by the slow-moving column, the cyborgs were free to run. Once the correct intervals were locked in and a suitable rhythm had been established, the T-2s were able to make a steady twenty-five to thirty miles per hour. That pace couldn't be sustained, of course, since there were rivers to cross and other obstacles to deal with, but the average speed was still much higher than anything the battalion had been able to manage during the previous week. So Santana felt good.

His surroundings were little more than a green blur, there were moments of what felt like weightlessness as Joshi jumped over fallen trees, and the occasional *pop* as an insect came into violent contact with Santana's visor. But after a couple of hours had passed, Santana began to tire. And he knew that the rest of the troops felt the same way. However, it was important to push the company, and he did. So that by the time the light had begun to fade and Santana called a halt, the team had covered nearly two hundred miles. It was an accomplishment that put them only two days out from the G-tap.

But to maintain that pace, Santana knew it was important to perform maintenance on the cyborgs. So rather than eat, pee, and push on, he granted the company an eight-hour respite. Although once the bio bods consumed their rations, carried out repairs, and stood an hour of guard duty, they would be lucky to get five or six hours of sleep. Instead of taking the time and energy required to build a marching fort, Santana had the troops put out sensors and sleep within a circle of watchful T-2s.

The hours of darkness passed uneventfully, but Santana hadn't been able to sleep as well as he would have liked and was unexpectedly sore as he made the rounds. Months had passed since he had spent a full day on a T-2 that was running cross-country. But everyone else had sore muscles as well, and it gave the bio bods something to bitch about as they ate their rats, drained their bladders, and strapped in. Moments later, they were under way.

Ponco had her sensors on max. That was a good thing to the extent that it enabled her to "see" the occasional group of grazing triturators and lead the company around the massive beasts. But there was a downside as well. Cranking her sensors up to high gain resulted in a lot of visual clutter. That included the presence of arboreal animals that were of little or no threat to the company, hot spots where the sun had been baking a tree trunk for an hour, and, in one case, the wreckage of an air car that had been hanging in the canopy for years.

So when Ponco "saw" the scattering of heat blobs at a distance, she didn't take them very seriously. Not until she got close enough to make a positive ID. That was when she took cover behind a Ba-Na tree and put out the call. "This is Alpha One-Three. I have approximately twelve—that is one-two—indigs in sight, and suggest that the column pull up while I deal with them. Over."

Santana's voice was concerned. "This is Alpha One. I read you. Can you handle them alone? Over."

"Affirmative," Ponco replied, although she wasn't as confident as she sounded. "I'll give you a holler if I need help. Over."

"Roger that. The column will take a break. Over."

Ponco's first task was to circle around the O-Chies and place herself between them and the G-tap. Because if this particular group of indigs was hostile, she wanted to prevent them from making contact with the Ramanthians. But were they? Unfortunately, there was only one way to find out.

So Ponco darted from tree to tree until she was as close as she dared to go. Then she showed herself. The result was almost instantaneous, as the natives opened fire on her.

Ponco took evasive action, secured a good vantage point, and prepared to fire. Rather than pull the trigger manually, she chose to bring her .50-caliber weapon online and marked three targets for the onboard computer to shoot at. Then it was a simple matter to give the order, feel the recoil, and watch the symbols disappear.

Then the survivors came straight at her. Now that they knew off-world troops were in the area, they were determined to report the invasion. But they fell one after the other as Ponco marked them for death, and the computer did her bidding. Then the target blobs began to coalesce as the O-Chies banded together and charged her. They were moving up, down, and sideways as they swung from vines and jumped branch to branch.

But Ponco could deal with that, or believed she could, until a shrill tone sounded inside her "head." The computer's voice was emotionless. "Incoming missile. Incoming missile. Take evasive action."

Ponco obeyed in hopes that she could shake the weapon. "Type?"

"Type R89 fire-and-forget with hunt/pause capabilities."

Ponco wasn't scared anymore. She was terrified. Apparently, one of the O-Chies had been armed with a Ramanthian Type 89 missile. The weapons were easy to fire and could not only track their targets but wait for a clean shot if necessary. "This is Alpha One-Three. A Type 89 missile has a lock on me. Estimated six hostiles on the loose. You're on your own. Over."

Then it was kill or be killed as Ponco was forced to switch her attention away from the O-Chies to the computer-controlled killing machine that was stalking her. She triggered all of the electronic countermeasure gear she had on board but knew it wouldn't be enough in a situation where the enemy had visual contact with her.

As Ponco flitted from tree to tree and from shadow to shadow, she caught brief glimpses of the deadly thing as it darted through the foliage. It was shaped like an elongated bullet. But unlike a projectile fired from a gun, the 89 could hover before speeding in for the kill. Such were Ponco's thoughts when Santana's voice came over the push. For the first time in memory, he made use of her first name. "We're ready for the little bastard, Sally. Home on my signal and come straight in."

Ponco felt a sudden surge of hope as she swerved, flew under a thick branch, and weaved her way between sun-splashed tree trunks. "The missile is closing," the computer announced dispassionately. "Ten to impact. Nine, eight, seven . . ."

Then Ponco was down at ground level, following a game trail through the woods, as gunfire erupted from the right flank. The missile, which had been suckered into flying past a rank of four T-2s, exploded. Pieces of the machine flew for another thirty feet before plowing into the ground.

A cheer went up as Ponco soared into the treetops. She was giddy with relief and surprised to be alive. "This is Alpha One-Three. Thank you. Over."

"You're welcome," came the reply. "Close with those O-Chies and kill them. Over."

Ponco was alive, but the job was far from over.

The next couple of days were not only physically demanding but emotionally exhausting. As the company continued to race toward the Ramanthian geo tap, a series of scrambled radio messages had come in from Rona-Sa. The larger group had been attacked by Ramanthian aircraft twice. But thanks to the heavily armed quads, two fighters had been shot down, and casualties were relatively light.

Did that mean the bugs believed *all* of the Confederacy troops were retreating toward Baynor's Bay? He couldn't be sure. But as Santana lay belly down at the edge of the forest and looked toward the geothermal power plant, there was reason to hope. Because there had been no further contact with the enemy or its auxiliaries subsequent to Ponco's nearly fatal encounter with the Ramanthian missile. Having carried out a reconnaissance during the hours of darkness, the recon ball was hovering inches off the ground to the officer's left.

As Santana peered through a pair of binoculars, he saw a stretch of open ground, X-shaped monster barriers similar to those he'd seen in Baynor's Bay, and weapons blisters between them. Farther back a windowless, one-story building hugged the ground. There was a landing pad on the roof. That was flanked by three vertical stacks, all leaking what might have been steam into the cool morning air. The only other feature worth noting was a com mast that poked straight up from the south side of the installation.

That was what Santana could see from the edge of the forest. But he knew that in keeping with both the power plant's function and the Ramanthian preference for living underground, most of the facility would be below the surface. And that, he figured, was where most of the troops were housed.

The general impression was that of a well-fortified installation but one the battalion would have been able to take had the entire force been present. Unfortunately, that wasn't the case. "So," Santana said, as he panned the glasses from left to right. "There's no way to take this thing head-on. Not given the force at our disposal."

"No, sir," Ponco agreed. "I circled the entire facility last night and concluded that we would need the quads to beat their defenses down."

Santana knew he had allowed himself to engage in wishful thinking where the installation was concerned. He had hoped that the geo tap's defenses were only partially completed. Or maybe they were poorly built. But no such luck. The Ramanthians had done their work well. So what to do? Quitting wasn't an option. Not with so much at stake.

Think, Santana told himself. *Every fortress has a weakness. All you have to do is find it.* But there weren't any weaknesses. None Santana could see anyway. So he and Ponco were forced to withdraw without formulating a plan.

After being undermined by a rain-swollen stream many years earlier, a giant Ba-Na tree had fallen over and left a deep hole where its root ball had been. By stretching a camo net over the depression, the company had been able to create a serviceable hiding place. The key was to keep both their electronic and physical activity to a minimum.

Even so, Santana knew the Ramanthians could be depended on to send patrols out into the surrounding area on a regular basis. And that meant the company couldn't stay where it was for more than a day. The second platoon was on duty, and the first was trying to get some sleep as Santana held the net for Ponco. "I'd like to see the video you shot last night," Santana said. "Maybe I'll see something we can use." Ponco might have harbored doubts about that, but if so, she kept them to herself.

So as Santana sat on a rock with a cup of hot caf in his hand, Ponco projected a three-dimensional image into the air in front of him. It had been shot at night, so everything had a greenish hue. He was intrigued at first, but after the first couple of minutes the footage became very boring. Santana forced himself to pay attention as the recon ball skirted the perimeter of the Ramanthian base. And what he saw served to make him even more depressed. Because in addition to the defenses he'd seen firsthand, it soon became clear that the free-fire zone in front of the weapons blisters was mined, razor wire had been put in place to protect the approaches to the gun positions, and slit trenches zigzagged from one bunker to the next.

But then, just as Santana was about to give up in disgust, something caught his eye. "Roll that last twenty seconds again." Ponco responded, and Santana watched the recon-ball view of the jungle floor slide past as the cyborg skimmed across bare dirt. Then the view changed as the forest closed in around the camera again.

"The bugs cleared a fifty-foot-wide swath of forest that leads east," Ponco explained, as the video stopped. "It's my guess that they dug a trench and buried the power conduit in order to protect it from both animals and air attacks."

"Of course they did," Santana said, as his mind began to race. "They would have to. And that could be the opportunity we've been looking for. What's to stop us from digging down into the ground and cutting that conduit?"

Ryley had been listening in. "My guess is that they positioned sensors all along the length of the conduit, sir. We start digging, and they come a-running."

"Right," Santana said, as he continued to think about the problem. "But what if we pretend to attack the base at the same time? That might bottle them up. And, or, reduce the number of troops they can send to stop us. Plus, we'd be waiting for them when they arrived."

"It's an intriguing idea," Ponco replied carefully. "But it has a lot of moving parts."

"So does an automatic weapon," Santana said grimly. "And, in the right hands, it will kill you."

* * *

It had been a long day. The waiting was the worst part. Because the company's hiding place was so close to the G-tap that it wasn't a question of *if* they would be discovered but *when*. And if that occurred prior to nightfall, Santana's plan would go up in smoke. Worse yet, he and his troops would have to run, the STS cannon would remain functional, and an entire battle group would be at risk.

But, thanks to strict radio discipline and some good luck, they made it through the day undetected. So as darkness fell and the platoons parted company, they still had the element of surprise on their side. Santana and the first platoon followed Ponco into the jungle. Ryley led the rest of the company west. It took half an hour for Santana and his troops to make their way to the point where the fifty-foot-wide scar cut through the forest.

The location was about a mile east of the power plant. The Ramanthians were methodical creatures, so Santana figured the power conduit was buried at the center of the pathway. Once a security screen was established, a pair of T-2s began to dig. They were equipped with the only sets of shovel hands that the company had brought with it. But they were making excellent progress. Santana glanced at his watch. The time had come to send a scrambled message to Ryley. And the result was spectacular as two missiles struck the power station's com mast, and it collapsed. Predictably enough, the bugs fired back.

Meanwhile, Santana was standing a few feet away from the steadily deepening hole, battling the urge to issue unnecessary orders. Speed, that was the most important thing, and the cyborgs were already digging as fast as they could. "This is Alpha One-Three," Ponco said over the radio. "There are three airborne targets inbound. They're too small to be aircraft."

"Track 'em and kill 'em," Santana said, as a scraping sound

was heard and Private Sam Voby's shovel hand came into contact with concrete. "Over."

The T-2 was up to his shoulders in the hole by then—which meant that the containment was about six feet down. The other cyborg said, "Bingo," as she ran into concrete as well. They were close. *Very* close. But could they crack the tunnel open quickly enough?

Based on the data provided by her sensors, Ponco figured that the incoming targets were flying robots. Which made sense because while the Ramanthian command structure opposed the use of cyborgs, they had some very effective attack drones in their inventory. So Ponco, a T-2, and a couple of bio bods were waiting for the enemy machines as headlights appeared and three cylindrical robots came sailing down the path. They were equipped with argrav units, nose cannons, and a variety of sensors. The lead unit managed to get off two blobs of coherent energy before it ran into a hail of bullets and exploded.

Having been warned, the second and third machines took evasive action. Ponco went after one of them, saw an opening, and took it. A flash of light strobed both sides of the forest as the robot exploded.

Meanwhile, the surviving drone was driving in toward the hole in the ground and the T-2s working there. It was clearly determined to sacrifice itself if necessary. But the T-2 assigned to assist Ponco fired its fifty and blew the machine out of the air. Santana was so focused on the effort to access the cable vault that he was only dimly aware of the red-hot bits of metal and plastic that fell on him.

Light flared as Private Hopson made use of his energy cannon to slice into the concrete containment. The weapon wasn't designed for that purpose and quickly began to overheat. But not before it cut through into a hollow interior. That was when another cyborg took over.

Santana felt a rising sense of excitement. Rather than simply dropping the conduit into a trench and pouring concrete over it, the Ramanthians had constructed a relatively spacious tunnel. That meant his troops could not only cut the conduit whenever they chose, but follow it back to the geo tap, and attack the plant itself! And that was important. Because while the bugs might repair the cable before the Confed ships arrived, they wouldn't be able to replace the G-tap itself. "Hurry!" Santana said, conscious of the fact that the order was unnecessary. "Cut a hole large enough for a T-2 to drop through. We're going in."

Temo was in the cell-like room that had been assigned to her, lying on the pallet she had created for herself and staring at the ceiling when Sub Commander Hutlar Remwyr threw the curtain aside and entered without warning. He didn't like having a human living in his power plant but had been forced to tolerate Temo's presence because Commander Dammo had ordered him to do so. The result had been a sort of chilly civility between the two of them.

But now Remwyr put all pretences aside as Temo turned in his direction. "Get up," he ordered. "Animals are attacking. Why?"

All of the Ramanthians had looked alike to Temo until she'd been forced to live with them. And as the renegade came to her feet, she found herself looking at what she knew to be an especially short officer whose left leg had been replaced by a prosthesis. Because of Remwyr's reference to "animals," she thought a group of velocipods were attacking the base at first. Then she realized that the officer meant humans. "Because they want to get in?" she inquired innocently.

Though short and stocky, Remwyr was tough. His right pincer stabbed forward, hit Temo in the stomach, and caused her to double over. Then his good knee came up to strike her chin. She dropped like a rock. "I know they want to enter the base, filth . . . You told me that they had been defeated. And were retreating toward the west. Now they're attacking. How is that possible?"

Temo had lurched to her feet by that time. Something warm was dribbling down her chin. When she wiped it, her wrist came away red. "My report was correct," she insisted. "And you know that. Your planes attacked the retreating column *twice.* So it looks like they tricked you. Part of the battalion continued this way. And they got past my scouts. Or killed them. But so what? The force they sent is bound to be small and lightly armed. So they won't be able to force their way in."

"Wrong, animal," Remwyr responded. "They already have."

Temo was genuinely surprised. "*Really?* How?"

"One group pretended to attack us while a second dug their way down to the tunnel east of here. Now they're inside and headed this way."

"Well, I'll be damned," Temo said admiringly. "Somebody has a brain."

"Get your soldiers," Remwyr said. "Follow Section Leader Sotim. You will stop them."

"Or?" Temo said defiantly.

"Or I will kill you."

Temo sighed. "That's what I like about you Sub Commander Remwyr. You have a way with words."

It was dark inside the tunnel. But the combination of the work lights thrown forward by the lead T-2s, and the less powerful spots projected by the helmets the bio bods wore, was sufficient to illuminate the next thirty feet or so. The passageway was so narrow that only two cyborgs could advance, with no more than a few inches between their massive shoulders. Santana and the rest of the troops followed.

The power conduit ran down the center of the tunnel. It was about the same diameter as a man's thigh and had an oily appearance. The cable was shielded but caused Santana's radio to crackle and pop. Shiny tracks ran to either side of the conduit. That suggested that the bugs could send some sort of vehicle up the line to carry out repairs on the conduit.

Rather than cut the cable, which would alert the forces on Headstone to the fact that something was wrong, Santana had elected to follow it back. The bugs weren't going to like that. So he knew it was only a matter of time before the enemy attempted to block him and wasn't surprised when a bright light appeared up ahead. "This is Alpha Four-Four," Corporal Pryde said. "A vehicle is coming our way. It's picking up speed. Over."

That was bad news. What if they destroyed the vehicle but couldn't squeeze past the wreckage? But Santana knew that was a chance they'd have to take. "Stop it," he ordered tersely. "And do it now."

Both of the lead T-2s fired, but it didn't make any difference. The light kept coming, slammed into them, and blew up. The powerful blast ripped the cyborgs apart. But their bodies served to shelter Santana and the rest of the platoon to some extent. The blast wave threw him onto his back as Dietrich and the T-2s immediately to his rear opened fire. A dozen Ramanthians had been following along behind the sled. They jerked spastically as the bullets tore into them. Then it was over as more cyborgs crowded past and Dietrich paused to give Santana a hand. "Are you all right, sir?"

"Bruised, that's all," Santana replied. "We need to clear the tunnel and do so quickly."

"I have a better idea," a female voice said over the platoon push. "This is Major Temo. You might be able to save a few of your people if you pull back *now*. Otherwise, we're going to kill every single one of you."

Santana felt a sudden surge of anger. "Wait right there, you traitorous bitch . . . We'll see who kills who."

The answer was a burst of defiant laughter followed by a *click* as the contact was broken. Now Santana knew who had been responsible for sending the sledload of explosives up the tracks. Major Temo had a lot to account for, and the bill was overdue.

The replacement T-2s pushed what remained of their dead comrades aside, tore into the wreckage beyond, and ripped it apart. The resulting hole was large enough for a single cyborg to pass through. But that was sufficient, and the surviving members of the platoon began to stream through. "Ponco," Santana said, as the recon ball appeared at his side. "Scout the tunnel ahead. Look for booby traps."

Ponco didn't want to do it. She'd been blown up before. But she couldn't refuse Santana.

Ponco was about to move forward when somebody opened fire from the other end of the tunnel. Thanks to the lights mounted on the T-2s, Santana could see that a hastily constructed barrier had been thrown across the passageway. And judging from the number of ricochets that were zinging around him, the defenders were trying to bounce bullets off the walls as a way to score hits on the people sheltering behind the T-2s.

Ponco was forced to retreat, and the T-2s paused as projectiles pinged off their armor. They fired in return, but it appeared that the barricade was serving its purpose. "This is ridiculous," Dietrich said disgustedly, as he stepped in between the cyborgs.

His grenade launcher produced a *ka-chunk* sound followed by a couple of seconds of silence. Then came an explosion loud enough to deafen unprotected ears. The firing from the far end of the passageway stopped. "That's better," Dietrich said. "Stomp 'em!"

The T-2s went forward, with Ponco right behind them. They tore the barricade apart and kept going. Santana had to step over three human bodies all dressed in militia uniforms before he could proceed. None of them appeared to be female, so he knew Temo had survived and was on the run.

A steel door marked the end of the tunnel. It had been open but began to swing closed as somebody pulled on it. A T-2 made a grab for the handle as Dietrich fired a grenade through the gap. There was a flash, followed by a bang and the clatter of shrapnel hitting the door. Then the T-2s led the way into the staging area beyond the door. As Santana entered, he saw chunks of meat lying around, blood-splattered walls, and a wounded Ramanthian. The trooper raised a pistol, and Santana shot him.

Then it was time to call a momentary halt so that the rest of the platoon could catch up. And that's where Santana was when Lieutenant Grisso prodded a militiaman into the room with her assault rifle. "This one was playing dead, sir. Jordin was going to kill the bastard, but I said you'd want to talk to him."

Santana realized how stupid he'd been. It was a basic rule. Dead bodies aren't dead until they're proven to be dead. He'd been so eager to move forward that he had forgotten to check. He was lucky to be alive. "Thank you, Lieutenant. Good work."

Having turned to the militiaman, Santana frowned. "You have one chance to survive—and that's to cooperate. Where is the control room? And where did Major Temo go?"

The soldier had lost his helmet. There was blood on one

side of his face. Someone else's probably—and he had a furtive look. "The control room is two levels below us. I can take you there. As for the major, I don't know. There's a landing pad on the roof. She might be headed for that."

Santana turned to Grisso. "Take everyone but Lieutenant Ponco and Sergeant Major Dietrich. Go to the control room, place the charges, and meet us on the roof. If this man is lying shoot him."

"Yes, sir," Grisso said eagerly. "Come on people . . . You heard the major. Let's rig this place to blow."

"Okay," Santana said as he looked from Ponco to Dietrich. "Let's hustle. We need Temo alive if possible. If anyone can give us a status report on the STS cannon, she can. Plus, I want to see her hang."

A Klaxon was bleating, bursts of click speech could be heard over the PA system, and the floor trembled as something exploded outside. Ryley? And the second platoon? Yes, Santana thought so. It seemed they were making good progress.

Ponco led the way, with Santana and Dietrich close behind. They followed a ramp up along the side of a wall. It led to a dead body. A *Ramanthian* body. Santana was determined not to make the same mistake twice so he stopped to check it. "Either Temo and her people killed this bug, or he committed suicide. My money is on the first possibility."

"Mine, too," Dietrich said. "It looks like the love affair with the bugs is over."

That theory was borne out as the threesome followed a trail of bodies out into the main corridor, where they came under immediate fire from a group of Ramanthian troopers who were hiding behind an improvised barricade. Weapons clattered madly as bullets flew, and Ponco was forced to back up.

Dietrich threw a grenade at the opposite wall. The angle was such that it bounced out of sight and blew up. Santana followed the noncom's example, heard a second explosion, and entered the corridor ready to fire. But there was no need. The Ramanthians were not only dead, but doubly so, as Dietrich put an extra bullet into each one of them. Meanwhile, having jerked some furniture loose, Santana made a hole in the barricade.

Then it was onwards and upwards toward the roof and the sound of fighting outside. "This is Alpha One to Alpha Two-One," Santana said. "We're inside the plant and about to exit onto the roof. Alpha Three is setting charges in the control room. Use fire from the T-2s to plow a path through the minefield and enter the building. Over."

"This is Alpha Two-One," Ryley replied. "Roger that. We'll join you as soon as we can. Over."

Santana heard a roaring sound punctuated by the sound of gunfire as Ponco led them onto a flat roof. A Ramanthian transport was parked at the far end of the space. Its engines were running, and a side door was open. And there, with their backs to Santana, three humans could be seen. They were crouched behind a pile of cargo modules, firing at a group of Ramanthians who had taken cover behind a waist-high blast wall. "The bug pilots are waiting for someone," Santana shouted. "A VIP of some sort, and Temo is trying to hijack his ride. Dietrich, watch our six. Ponco, circle around. See if you can enter the transport from the other side. Take control of it if you can."

Dietrich turned back toward the ramp, and Ponco flew away as Santana raised his weapon. The CA-10 wasn't a sniper rifle. Far from it. But the range wasn't too bad, and he was a good shot. The key was to leave Temo alive.

He looked through the scope, selected the man on the left, and fired. The target toppled forward and collapsed. Temo was in the process of turning in that direction when the man to her right fell. Having realized where the fire was coming from, the renegade turned. Santana was waiting. The bullet flew straight and true. Temo's left knee exploded in a spray of blood. She made a grab for it and fell over backwards.

Santana heard a couple of explosions as he ran forward, knew that Dietrich was taking care of business, and figured that the VIP was dead. Bullets whipped past his head as the Ramanthians fired at him. The projectiles sounded like angry bees.

Temo had managed to sit up by that time. She was trying to bring her weapon to bear on him when Santana arrived to knock it away. "Oh, no, you don't!" he said, as the rifle clattered onto concrete. "Stay where you are."

Then he was down behind the cargo modules as Ramanthian bullets hammered them. Temo pulled her belt loose and began to wrap it around her leg just above the knee. "I suppose you're Alpha One," she said through gritted teeth. "Congratulations. I don't think Antov could have accomplished what you have."

"I'm glad you approve," Santana said, as he raised his visor. "Now tell me about the STS installation."

"What do you want to know?" Temo said as she pulled the tourniquet tight.

"I want to know what kind of backup power supply they have."

"Smart," she said. "Very smart. What's it worth to you?"

"Nothing," Santana said coldly, as Dietrich arrived and ducked down beside him. "But you could save the other knee."

Pain was etched into Temo's face. Her eyes were locked with Santana's. "You wouldn't."

"He would," Dietrich put in, as a series of loud reports were heard from the direction of the transport. "If not, I'd be happy to do it for him."

Temo closed her eyes and opened them again. "The head bug is a fanatical bastard named Commander Dammo. He has a fusion reactor on Headstone. Chances are that he could fire two or three shots without using power from the geo tap."

Santana felt his spirits fall. He'd been hoping that if the power plant went off-line, the STS cannon would be rendered useless. "This is Alpha One-Three," Ponco said over the radio. "The transport is ours. Over."

"Roger that," Santana replied. "Keep the engines running."

"It won't work," Temo said tightly. "Headstone is crawling with bugs."

"Well, you'd better hope that it does," Santana replied grimly. "Because you're going with us."

Dietrich grinned wolfishly. "Welcome to the Legion, Major Temo. The pay sucks, but there's plenty to do."

12

Death follows life just as life follows birth.

—*The Thraki* Book of Yesterdays
Date unknown

PLANET EARTH, THE RAMANTHIAN EMPIRE

The military spaceport at China Lake, California, had been attacked shortly after the Ramanthians destroyed Earth's orbital-defense platforms. Now the base was little more than a sprawling junkyard. The once-proud control tower lay like a fallen tree across the remains of an in-system freighter and the moonscape beyond. And the multitiered terminal building hadn't fared any better. It had taken a direct hit from a missile that plunged down through five stories and exploded in the parking garage. So while the periphery of the structure was intact, the center was a burned-out hole.

Ironically enough, it was the destruction that made for a perfect hiding place. Despite the fact that just about all of China Lake's surface installations had been destroyed, part of the spaceport's underground storage-and-maintenance facility remained intact. The subsurface maze had been occupied more than once. But never for very long because shortly after a group of humans moved in, the bugs would attack. Roughly 10 percent of the much-disputed complex was still inhabitable so long as one didn't mind the constant threat of a raid.

Navy Commander and Earth Liberation Brigade Leader Leo Foley knew that. So guards were in place all around the hideout, and a fast-response team was ready to respond within a matter of minutes. All of that was nice but brought him very little comfort given the extent of the threat. Still, there were only so many places where the ELB could hide.

Such were Foley's thoughts as he left the utility room that served as his quarters, paused to collect a mug of caf from the makeshift cafeteria a hundred feet down the corridor, and followed a series of duracrete hallways back to the onetime storeroom that served as his office. Much to his surprise, the door was open, and a man was seated behind his desk. He had blond hair, a rigidly handsome face, and appeared to be in his midtwenties. However, Foley knew that Sergi Chien-Chu's brain was well over a hundred years old—even if his cybernetic vehicle was much younger. It was one of many such "forms" he could call on. "Good morning," Chien-Chu said cheerfully. "Sorry about the lack of advance notice, but coming and going from Earth is a rather complicated process these days, and my security people won't let me publish a schedule."

Foley understood but wished he'd been given time to prepare a report or at least get his thoughts in order. Of course, there was a distinct possibility that Chien-Chu wanted to catch him off balance. He was a very savvy businessman and ex-politician after all. "Yes, sir," Foley replied. "Welcome to China Lake. Can I get you a cup of caf?"

Chien-Chu smiled. "Coffee is hard to come by these days. Why waste it on someone who can't enjoy it?"

Foley said, "Yes, sir," and took what normally served as his guest chair.

"Congratulations on Operation Cockroach," Chien-Chu said. "The Ramanthian propaganda machine claims that you and your people killed five thousand of their supposed 'peacekeepers.' And we know that when it comes to casualties, they always subtract about twenty percent from the *real* number. So it's safe to say that you nailed at least six thousand of the bastards."

"It was supposed to be nine or ten thousand," Foley said bleakly. "And I lost 423 people."

"That's a lot," Chien-Chu admitted. "But, cold as it may sound, that's something like fourteen of them for every one of us. Had we always done so well, the war would have been over a month ago."

"Maybe," Foley allowed, as his eyes drifted away. "But more than a hundred of the casualties were the direct result of my stupidity. I should have evacuated the mine *before* the attack. Or, failing that, left a significant force behind to protect it. I did neither. And lots of people died as a result."

"That's true," Chien-Chu conceded. "You made a mistake. One born of hubris and overconfidence."

"So you're here to relieve me of my command," Foley said dully, as his eyes swung back. "And you're correct to do so."

"Nice try," Chien-Chu replied dryly. "But you aren't getting off that easily. If we were to cashier every officer who made a mistake, sergeants would be in charge. Nope, your punishment is to stay right where you are and hatch more plans like Operation Cockroach. You really put the hurts on them with that one, son. Keep it up."

It was strange to have what looked like a younger man call him "son." "Yes, sir," Foley replied, even though he didn't have the foggiest idea of what to do next.

"Good," Chien-Chu replied. "Nothing attracts resources like success. If you need something, let me know. You have a hypercom. Use it sparingly—but use it."

"Yes, sir."

"And Commander . . ."

"Sir?"

"Go get something to eat. You look like a skeleton."

The so called Dead Bug Lab was a step up from the grubby room that Margaret and her scientists had been forced to share deep in the bowels of the Lucky Fool mine. According to signs neatly stenciled onto duracrete walls, the large, rectangular space had once been the home of the 321st Aerospace Fighter squadron's in-service training facility. And, thanks to the fact that the team was already present when Foley and the rest of the survivors of Operation Cockroach arrived, they had been able to hang on to the precious square footage. Power was flowing from a portable reactor, running water had been restored, and there was little to no chance of a cave-in. The bugs could attack, of course—but that was true anywhere.

So Margaret was sitting in her tiny office when Dr. Howard Lothar stomped in and dropped a head onto the surface of her metal desk. "There it is," he said triumphantly. "Just like I said."

"There *what* is?" Margaret wanted to know, as the dead Ramanthian glared at her. "And how many times have I told you? Put something *under* body parts. They leak."

Lothar continued as if Margaret hadn't spoken. "See the growth on the back of this specimen's head? That's called a stroma—or a fruiting body."

One of the problems associated with supervising scientists, but not being one herself, was that there were frequent occasions when Margaret didn't have a clue as to what they were talking about. "I'm sorry, Howard," she said. "Please go back and lay the necessary groundwork, so I'll know what you're talking about."

Lothar sighed. Then, in the manner of an adult instructing a child, he gave a minilecture. "We know that some Ramanthians are dying from the equivalent of a human skin disease. For a host of reasons I won't bore you with, it's my hypothesis that after arriving on Earth in large numbers and spreading out across the globe, they came into contact with a fungus called *Ophiocordyceps unilateris*. Probably in the equatorial jungles where our friend *Ophio* finds its way into carpenter ants and forces them to leave the forest canopy for the vegetation lower down. Then, having taken control, it compels its victim to bite onto a leaf.

"The ant dies," Lothar added, "but continues to hang there, as the fungus grows inside of it. Eventually, a stroma like this one breaks through the anterior surface of the ant's head. A couple of weeks later, spores begin to fall—each one of which can infect a new host. And that's what happened to Marvin," Lothar added, as he patted the head. "Although it's my guess that the Ramanthians unknowingly made *Ophio*'s task easier by flying their troops hither and yon all over the world. Who knows? Marvin could have been infected right here rather than down south somewhere."

"I don't know," Margaret said doubtfully. "I'm not a scientist—but don't parasites and their hosts coevolve? Plus, the Ramanthians just arrived."

"You've been listening to Woo," Lothar said accusingly. "She thinks the bugs brought the parasite with them. But that, like most of the stuff she says, is pure bullshit. I admit that the odds are stacked against an Earth parasite having the capacity to exploit an off-planet host, but it appears that *Ophio* is very resourceful. And I can prove it."

"Really? How?"

"I took spores from a stroma produced by a specimen named Larry and used them to infect Marvin. He did everything a carpenter ant would do except clamp onto a leaf. He is, or was, a sentient with a very complex nervous system. So the course of the disease was different. Marvin experienced some pretty bad seizures before he died. I enjoyed that."

Margaret was horrified. She knew her team had requested and been given control of Ramanthian POWs for study—along with the bodies of dead bugs found here and there. But the methods Lothar had been using were way over the moral/ethical line. And she was responsible for allowing it to happen. "I hope you're joking."

"Hell no, I'm not joking," the scientist replied defiantly. "*What?* You're feeling all gooey about the scum who took our planet, killed my wife and millions of your fellow citizens? Have you forgotten what they did to your daughter on Jericho?"

Margaret hadn't forgotten. And she wondered where her daughter was. "I understand, Howard. I really do. But if we aren't careful, we'll wind up just as bad as they are."

"So, shoot me," Lothar said tightly, as tears began to stream down his cheeks. "I would do it myself if I had the guts."

Margaret got up, circled the desk, and put an arm around Lothar's shoulders. "What you need is some rest. Come on . . . I'm giving you the day off."

"What about the fungus?" Lothar demanded stubbornly as he wiped the tears away. "We can weaponize it. I know we can. All we need is a large supply of *Ophio*."

"I'll work on it," Margaret promised.

"And Woo? Will you tell her to shut the hell up?"

Margaret remembered the way Woo occasionally sobbed in the middle of the night. "No, Howard. I won't tell Woo to shut the hell up. Actually, I think you two have a lot in common. But I will instruct the entire staff to follow up on your research."

That seemed to do the trick as the tension went out of the scientist's shoulders, and he allowed himself to be led away. The head, which was leaking goo onto the surface of Margaret's otherwise-clean desk, was understandably mute.

As usual, there was a line out of Foley's door, down a hall, and around a corner as Margaret barged into his office. The officer in command of the brigade's nonexistent air force was seated in the guest chair. Margaret nodded to him and smiled pleasantly before dropping Ralph's head onto the desk with a muted *thump*. The increasingly smelly object was sealed inside a bag and stared out through foggy plastic. "Sorry to interrupt," Margaret said, "but I need to speak with you before Ralph here begins to rot."

The pilot looked appalled—and Foley was annoyed. Because even though it wasn't perfect, the line outside his office was part of an effort to make himself accessible. Something that was very important in an organization that was quasi-military at best. So line jumpers were a problem. Yet the head, combined with the fact that it was Margaret who had been toting it around, was an irresistible draw. Foley made eye contact with the pilot. "Would you excuse us, Major? If you would be so kind as to wait outside, we'll resume our conversation in a few minutes."

The pilot left, Margaret took his seat, and Foley frowned at her. "This had better be good, Margaret . . . Especially after the way you lied to the guards as you and your team left the mine. I didn't order you to set up shop at this location, and you know it."

"No, you didn't," Margaret agreed unapologetically. "But what if we had remained there? Where would we be now?"

The challenge was obvious. As was her meaning. Margaret

and her scientists would have been dead had they remained in the mine. Foley winced. "That hurts."

"Sorry," Margaret replied. "It wasn't my intention to be judgmental. But I felt compelled to defend my actions."

"And you did," Foley observed ruefully. "So what's with the head?"

"The head is part of an experiment," Margaret replied. "A morally questionable experiment. But important nevertheless."

Having said that much, Margaret went on to repeat what Lothar had told her. She finished by saying, "So, here's where the matter stands now. We have a weapon. One the planet gave us. All we have to do is use it. And if we do so quickly enough, it's possible that the Ramanthians will be forced to withdraw. But odds are that they're working on a defense. So we've got to hurry."

Foley looked at the head and the space black eyes that seemed to bore into him. His thoughts were churning—and he felt a growing sense of excitement. What if Margaret was correct? What if they *could* force the bugs to withdraw from Earth? That would be a victory so important it could change the course of the war. "But *how*?" Foley wanted to know.

"We need a large supply of *Ophiocordyceps unilateris*," Margaret answered matter-of-factly. "And since we don't have the time or means to grow the fungus in a lab, we'll have to get spores from donors like Marvin here."

Foley frowned. "Okay . . . But how the heck would we do that?"

Margaret smiled sweetly. "That, Commander Foley, is *your* problem."

Two days had passed since Margaret had entered Foley's office and placed the Ramanthian head on his desk. Since that time,

Foley had requested all of the information that his Intel people could provide on Ramanthian health problems, the status of their medical-support system, and an estimate of how many troopers were dying of natural causes versus combat-related trauma.

Hard data was difficult to come by. But some operatives believed that the Ramanthian mortality rate had increased even though they had a firm grip on the planet and combat-related casualties should have been down. So if the anecdotal evidence was true, there was a very real possibility that the bugs were losing a significant number of personnel to the fungus that Margaret and her team referred to as "Ophi." But what if such reports had been exaggerated by amateur operatives who were eager to believe the worst?

That was a significant danger. Foley was determined to go out and get a firsthand look at what was taking place. So he was following a local named Pete Sawyer along a drainage channel in almost complete darkness. It was dry and would remain that way until spring, when the rains might or might not fall. In the meantime the floodway functioned as a nocturnal highway for rodents, coyotes, and the occasional human. Although, except for a few hardy souls like Sawyer, there weren't many people who were brave or foolish enough to venture near the enemy-occupied town of California City. Prior to the war, it had been a bedroom community for nearby military bases. Now the bugs lived there.

With no moonlight to go by, Sawyer was forced to use occasional blips from a handheld torch to confirm their position. And when one such check revealed the wreckage of a human shuttle lying crosswise over the channel, he held up his hand. "This is where we go up and over," Sawyer whispered. "The best vantage point is the old water tower. The bugs left it intact. Probably on purpose. So we put a hole in it about three weeks after the city was overrun. Now they store their water underground. The point is that they don't care about it. So there aren't any guards. Bit of a climb, though . . . Have you got a head for heights?"

Now you ask me, Foley thought to himself. "I'll be fine," he lied. "Lead the way."

So Sawyer led the way up the concrete slope to the point where a ragged hole had been cut in the security fence. After crawling through on hands and knees, Foley followed Sawyer on a zigzag path that took them between abandoned houses, through a much-looted minimall, and up to the base of a duracrete tower. Foley assumed there was a globular tank higher up. But he couldn't see it. Sawyer said, "Wait here," and vanished into the night.

Foley's hand rested on the silenced pistol that rode under his left arm until Sawyer returned carrying an aluminum ladder over his shoulder. "I keep it hidden," he explained. "No point in letting the bugs know what I've been up to."

Then, with the ease of someone who had plenty of practice, Sawyer put the ladder up against the support tower and checked to make sure that it was solid. "Okay," he said hoarsely. "Follow me up. The rungs start about ten feet off the ground. After that, it's a climb of 130 feet or so. Oh, and one more thing. If you fall, try not to scream. That could attract the wrong sort of attention." And with that, Sawyer disappeared into the gloom.

Foley looked up, swore softly, and followed. It was easy at first, and because Foley couldn't see much, the height didn't bother him. But his legs weren't used to that kind of exercise, and it wasn't long before he began to feel the burn. Then he saw the scattering of lights that represented the Ramanthian base and realized that he was at least fifty feet off the ground. That triggered fear—and it took all of his willpower to keep climbing.

Don't look down, Foley told himself. *Look up.* And it worked. To some extent at least, as the resistance leader forced himself to reach, pull, and push. Finally, after what seemed like an eternity, a strong hand took hold of his wrist and pulled him up onto a circular walkway. "There you are," Sawyer said. "What took so long?"

"I had to pause every now and then to shit my pants."

Sawyer laughed softly. "So you *don't* have a head for heights. Well, you have balls, that's for sure. Come on . . . Let's walk around to the other side of the tower. The sun's about to rise, and it should be quite a sight."

As the men watched, a horizontal ribbon of pink light appeared in the east, followed by the first rays of sunshine as a new day began. But before the sun could part company with the horizon, Sawyer led Foley around to the south side of the bulbous tank. It was painted green, and as Foley craned his head to look upwards, he could see the jagged hole where a human missile had struck. "The show's about to start," Sawyer said. "We'd better sit down, or the bugs might spot us. Did you bring a pair of binoculars?"

Foley was wearing a knapsack. He shrugged it off and lowered himself onto the grating. The glasses were inside, and he took them out. It was hard to ignore the fact that he was more than a hundred feet off the ground, but Foley did the best he could as he brought the device up to his eyes.

Seated as they were, Foley could see under the metal railing. That gave him a nearly unobstructed view of a large crater and the road that spiraled up around a cone-shaped hill to the fire-blackened grating on top. It was loaded with hundreds of plastic-wrapped bodies all stacked like spokes on a wagon wheel. Heads in and feet out. And as he watched, more dead Ramanthians were being unloaded from a truck. There were so many that it was necessary to layer the corpses.

"It's like this every Thursday morning," Sawyer put in. He was seated with his back against the tank, peering through a pair of beat-up binoculars. "Except that the bugs are processing more bodies every week. And there's one more thing. Look at how they're dressed."

Foley looked and saw what Sawyer meant. The Ramanthians were wearing the bug equivalent of hazmat suits! A sure sign that they were concerned about a contagious disease of some sort. "So they didn't wear protective clothing before?"

"Nope. And the bodies were wrapped in something that looked like linen rather than plastic."

The reports were true. And he was looking at a very generous supply of *Ophiocordyceps unilateris*. Foley felt a rising sense of excitement as the last body was unloaded from the truck before it pulled away. The vehicle circled the hill, crossed the crater, and passed through a gap in the rim. What might have been an honor guard of roughly a hundred Ramanthian troopers was evenly spaced around the top of the depression.

The truck vanished for a moment, then reappeared as it made for the base beyond. As Foley scanned the fortress, he saw a defensive ditch, weapons blisters, and high walls. The hint of a duracrete dome was visible beyond that.

That was impressive enough. But the knowledge that the base was like an iceberg, with most if its mass located below the surface, was quite sobering. Because any attempt to rush the crematorium and hijack the bodies there would be met with a counterattack from within the walls. Foley's thoughts were interrupted by Sawyer. "Now watch this," the civilian said. "They always do it the same way."

Foley heard the faint squeal of something akin to bagpipes, followed by a sequential round of rifle shots from the troops stationed around the crater, and a loud *whump* as a tongue of fire shot up from deep inside the cone-shaped hill. Smoke poured up into the sky as the bodies began to burn. And the flames were so hot that all of the corpses were fully cremated in less than five minutes. "The ash falls down through the grate into some sort of bin below," Sawyer explained. "They empty it every couple of weeks."

Once the ceremony was over, the honor guard shuffled down off the rim of the crater, where they boarded a waiting truck and soon left for the base. The military funeral was over. "Well," Foley said, "that was very interesting. Thank you for bringing me. Let's get the hell out of here."

Sawyer's face was brown and wrinkled from years spent working outdoors. His eyes were blue, and, judging from the look in them, he thought Foley was crazy. "No can do. They'd spot us for sure. As the sun comes up, we'll move west to place ourselves in the shadow thrown by the tank. It'll be cooler that way. Later, once it gets dark, we'll climb down. That's why I told you to bring water and something to eat."

Foley sighed. It was going to be a long, hot day.

LOS ANGELES, CALIFORNIA

It was Wednesday morning. Six days had passed since Foley had climbed to the top of the water tower and been witness to the mass cremation in California City. Now he was eighty miles south of there, belly down on a hill, looking west as the sun rose behind him. The HOLLYWOOD sign had been rebuilt many times over hundreds of years. The first five letters still stood off to his right. The others had been destroyed during the invasion. But that was the least of the damage.

Los Angeles, Hollywood, Beverly Hills, Pasadena, Alhambra, Monterey Park, and Montebello were history. And there, at the very center of a blackened crater, was an enormous starship. So large it would never be able to lift off. Foley assumed that the vessel had been intentionally sacrificed to provide the Ramanthians with an instant fortress.

The ship had a black, slightly iridescent skin that shimmered in the early-morning light. Artificial lighting crackled around it from time to time, killing any bird unfortunate enough to venture close and suggesting that the ship's defensive screens were still operational.

Dirt ramps had been constructed so that hover vehicles could drive up into what had originally been the vessel's launch bay, and all manner of prefab structures had been set up around the brooding globe. As Foley swept his glasses across them, he saw what looked like supply dumps, temporary mess halls, and rows of perfectly spaced troop habs.

The whole thing was more than impressive. It was terrifying. Because there, right in front of him, was the very core of the Ramanthian presence on Earth. And to touch it was to die. But that was exactly what he and thousands of others were about to do. Not because they had any real hope of conquering the beast, but in order to throw a scare into the invaders and get them to rush reinforcements into the area. Reinforcements from places like California City.

During the process, Foley hoped to kill a lot of Ramanthians—while suffering as few casualties as possible. And this time he had been careful to seek advice from key subordinates and plan for every imaginable scenario. Or so he hoped.

Foley and his security detail were all clad in precious ghost camos, which, along with some other specialized gear, had been shipped in for the occasion. They were covered with special netting that was designed to conceal both their heat signatures and a certain amount of electromagnetic activity.

Would the special-ops gear work? Foley hoped so as the radio reports began to come in. Each voice represented a group of resistance fighters, some of whom were at war with each other for one reason or another but had agreed to a temporary truce in order to participate in what promised to be the first really important attack on the Ramanthians.

They weren't aware of the *real* purpose behind the attack, however, and Foley felt guilty about that, even though security demanded that only a few people be in on the secret. *Still,* Foley told himself as the calls came in, *we're going to kick some Ramanthian ass, and that's for sure.*

Most of the groups were made up of civilians, which meant that they weren't that big on military radio procedure. "This is Commander Marcos," a booming voice said. "The Conquistadores are ready."

"This is the Hammer," another chimed in. "We're ready to fall. Over."

"The Rats are in position," a female voice said. "Just say the word."

And so it went until more than a dozen groups had reported in. Then it was Foley's turn. "This is Shoshone One. I promised you a surprise, and it's on the way. Keep your heads down. Over."

What followed was a long, agonizing three minutes, during which nothing happened and all sorts of negative scenarios ran through Foley's mind. What if the whole thing had been called off for some reason? Or some sort of technical glitch had occurred?

The possibilities ate at him, and he was just about to place a hypercom call when a clap of thunder was heard. Seconds later, the incoming missile struck the Ramanthian ship dead on and exploded. Shields flared, and some of the energy was dispersed, but the explosion was powerful enough to scorch the ship's skin.

The capability had been there all along of course. Because if the Confederacy could send supply drones through hyperspace, it could send missiles, too; but it had been reluctant to do so, knowing that the slightest miscalculation could result in collateral damage. And even if each weapon landed on target, everyone knew that the bugs would react by placing hostages in and around any installation that might be worthy of an intersystem missile.

But now, with a one-of-a-kind strategic opportunity in the offing, Foley had requested and been granted an intersystem strike. There was another clap of thunder followed by a second hit. The missile struck the huge side hatch just as the bugs were starting to close it. The explosion slagged the door, scoured the vehicle park inside the warship, and triggered a series of loud booms. "This is Shoshone One," Foley said over the radio. "So far so good. Stand by for one more. Once it hits, you will be free to attack. Over."

Foley had requested nine missiles and been granted three, which, as Chien-Chu pointed out, cost five hundred million credits each and would require the Confederacy to sacrifice hyperdrives that otherwise could have been used in destroyer escorts or other ships of a similar size.

But all things considered, Foley was satisfied. Because even though he liked killing Ramanthians, the real prize lay elsewhere, and the completely unexpected attack would almost certainly have the desired effect.

The last missile missed the ship but fell in the middle of

the encampment just east of it. The weapon went off with a brilliant flash and a resonant boom. Secondary explosions rattled like firecrackers, what looked like a firestorm swept hundreds of evenly spaced habs away, and at least a thousand bugs were killed. All things considered, that was better than a direct hit on the grounded vessel. Because, in spite of its size, the battleship's weapons were designed for space battles. And there was no way to know where the incoming missiles were coming from and, therefore, no way to respond.

Smoke was pouring up into the air, and the destruction was still under way when the second phase of the attack began. Predictably enough, Ramanthian troops began to pour out of the ship like ants escaping a ravaged nest. Bloodthirsty resistance groups came after them. Some swept into the crater on light trucks with weapons blazing. Others, the Rats in particular, surfaced from Metro tunnels, which ran *under* the crater and were supposedly blocked off. All were supported by a wild assortment of aircraft that had been rolled out of their hiding places and launched for the occasion. Foley saw air cars with the word POLICE painted on the side, crop dusters, and even ultralights, all climbing, turning, and diving as they dropped hand grenades and homemade bombs on the aliens below.

But the battle was far from one-sided. The same aircraft were very vulnerable. And it wasn't long before some of them were blown out of the air or simply shot to pieces.

The situation on the ground wasn't much better. Brave though the resistance fighters might be, they were no match for heavily armored Ramanthian veterans, who were not only enraged by the sneak attack, but led by fanatical members of the *Nira* cult urging them to fight to the death. They met the humans and drove them back.

Foley put out a final message. "Shoshone One to all allied forces. Withdraw . . . I repeat, break contact and withdraw. A major battle was won here today. The Confederacy thanks you. Over."

Then, having done all that a leader could, Foley threw the protective net off and stood. "Come on," he said to the men and women around him. "There are wounded down there. Let's collect as many of them as we can."

CALIFORNIA CITY, CALIFORNIA

It was cold and dark—an early Thursday morning. Margaret was scared as Pete Sawyer led the resistance fighters up the dry channel toward the Ramanthian base. According to the reports from Foley, the attack on the ship had been a success. Heavy casualties had been inflicted on the bugs, and the aliens had been forced to bring in reinforcements from as far away as California City. In fact, a convoy estimated to include at least three hundred troops had departed late the day before. So assuming that the adjoining base had been sufficiently weakened, then a force of about fifty security people should be able to raid the crematorium without too much trouble. The problem, Margaret thought to herself, was the words "should be."

The column stopped suddenly, and Margaret ran into the man in front of her. He swore, and she whispered, "Sorry." Then the line was moving again with nothing but the glittering stars to light the way. Her husband, Charles, was out there somewhere, on Algeron probably, fighting a war of words. And Christine? Well, she had followed in her father's footsteps, even if her methods had a tendency to raise eyebrows. Wouldn't they be surprised, Margaret thought, to know that she was packing a pistol and part of an effort to raid a crematorium!

Margaret's thoughts were interrupted as the column turned left and scrambled up a steep slope. The line slowed as people were forced down on their hands and knees to crawl through the hole that had been cut in the fence. The empty pack on her back caught on the wire and had to be freed by the person behind her.

Once Margaret was through and back on her feet, there was a short wait while the rest of them arrived. Then the column surged ahead, and it became difficult to keep up as Sawyer led his charges between houses, down deserted streets, and past a fire-scorched high school.

The sun had started to rise by then, and Margaret could see the water tower and the volcano-shaped hill off to the right of it. The miniature mountain grew larger, and an embankment appeared as they arrived at the crater wall. The facility was unguarded. And why not? The bugs had no reason to think anyone would want to attack it.

So Sawyer took them along the edge of the embankment to the point where a well-packed section of dirt road cut through the obstruction. That led them into the circular arena where the ambush would take place. The whole thing had been rehearsed back at China Lake, so everyone knew what to do. "Remember," Sawyer cautioned them, "it's important to kill the honor guard silently. The last thing we need is to have more bugs arrive on the scene."

Margaret and her team weren't expected to fight. So they were directed to take cover behind the pieces of earthmoving equipment that were parked next to the crater's wall. Lothar was there, as was Woo, each of whom seemed determined to ignore the other.

Margaret's thoughts were focused on the plan. Would the Thursday-morning cremation ceremony actually take place? Especially in the wake of the battle in LA? Sawyer thought so. "What are they going to do?" he had demanded earlier. "The base is clearly being used as a mortuary. So unless they burn the incoming bodies, they'll start to pile up. Plus, they know some of them are diseased. Don't worry, ma'am. They'll come." But despite Sawyer's unwavering certainty, Margaret continued to worry.

The resistance fighters had intentionally arrived fifteen minutes early to allow for the possibility of delays along the way. So time seemed to crawl by as the sun inched higher in the sky and finally rose over the east rim of the crater. And it was then, right on time, that the distant sound of engines was heard. Margaret felt her heart start to beat faster as the noise grew steadily louder and eventually turned into a roar as the first hover truck floated into the arena. It paused for a moment before following the spiral road to the top of the miniature mountain. The second and third trucks followed.

Then the fourth truck arrived, pulled over to one side, and settled onto its skirts. Just as it had many times before. Except Sawyer said there had been a *fifth* vehicle in the past. A transport loaded with troops. Did that mean the base was running low on personnel? Margaret hoped that was the case, as Ramanthian troopers shuffled down out of the fourth transport and formed two ranks.

The noncom who began to inspect them was about halfway along the first rank when the resistance fighters emerged from their various hiding places. All were armed with silenced weapons. Some of the noise suppressors were military issue, and the rest were homemade. But all of them were reasonably effective. The Ramanthians began to jerk and twitch as a hail of bullets hit them.

Margaret closed her eyes. She understood the necessity of what was taking place and knew that the enemy had done worse, but she was still sickened by the cold-blooded slaughter. It took less than a minute to put the entire honor guard down.

But the bugs up on top of the hill were still alive and could theoretically alert the base. Sawyer was about ten feet away from Margaret holding a radio up to his ear. She knew that two snipers, both positioned up on the water tower, were supposed to neutralize the troopers on the hill. Sawyer nodded. "Good, good, *what*? Well, shoot the bastard!"

That was when one of the men to Margaret's left pointed up into the sky. "Look! One of them is flying!"

And it was true. Even though Ramanthians, especially older ones, couldn't fly very well, they could get aloft for short periods of time. And this individual was not only young, judging from the energy with which he was flapping his wings, but had the advantage of a hill from which to launch himself into the air. So he was already gliding over the crater wall by the time the humans opened up on him from the ground. But the fusillade of bullets had no visible effect on the trooper, who quickly disappeared from sight. "Goddamn it to hell!" Sawyer raged. "The idiots on the tower missed. I'll go after him."

"No, you won't," Margaret said sternly. "Phase one is over so *I'm* in command. He's halfway to the base by now, so it's very unlikely that you'll catch up with him. Prepare another ambush—and whack the bastards when they arrive. In the meantime, my team will go up and collect what we came here for. Let's get to work."

Sawyer opened his mouth as if he was about to say something, clearly thought better of it, and closed it again. "Yes, ma'am. Maybe we can get that hover truck running. If so, it might come in handy."

Margaret nodded, turned to her team, and waved them

forward. "Come on . . . We have a hill to climb." The scientists weren't in very good shape. So there were lots of complaints as Margaret sent them huffing and puffing up the spiral road to the top of the conical mountain where the trucks were parked. Bodies lay sprawled where they had fallen. One of the vehicles had been partially unloaded. Margaret, who was out of breath herself, pointed at the first transport. "Get the rest of the bodies off that truck. Lothar and Woo will identify donors."

The team went to work. The bodies were sealed in plastic. They made thumping sounds and sent up little clouds of dust, as Margaret went over to supervise the sorting process. Woo made a face as she cut a body bag open and the stench of decomposing bug filled her nostrils.

Then, with help from Lothar, Woo took a close look at the back of the bug's head. It had a normal appearance. So Lothar spray painted a red X onto the soldier's bag. The second body had a bullet hole in its forehead and had clearly been killed in combat. But the third had the very thing they were looking for. An attempt had been made to cover it with a bandage, but a stroma was visible on the back of the soldier's head. "Sistek!" Lothar shouted. "Over here."

Sistek was a burly lab tech who had been selected for the job of harvester because of his upper-body strength. He motioned the scientists out of the way and raised a razor-sharp machete over his head. The blade generated a solid *ka-thunk* sound as it came down.

Lothar made a grab for the head as it rolled free, got hold of a stubby antenna, and held his prize aloft. "Pay dirt!" he proclaimed proudly. "Just one of these melons contains enough spores to infect a hundred bugs—each of whom can infect a hundred more. Margaret—turn around. You're the boss, so the first head goes into *your* pack."

The grisly business of harvesting heads continued after that, as the scientists examined bodies, and the machetes fell. But as Margaret made the rounds and urged her team to work faster, she knew it was only a matter of time before Ramanthian reinforcements arrived. So it came as no surprise when the radio in her pocket burped static, and Sawyer spoke to her. "Look toward the base, ma'am. It's time to pull out. The hover truck is running, and we'll use it to make our getaway."

Margaret looked south, saw the airborne transport, and realized that she'd been wrong about a ground attack. The Ramanthians had a faster way to respond. Worse yet, it was a sure bet that the boxy aircraft had at least thirty troopers on board. And it was coming straight at her. Shells kicked up dirt on top of the hill as the pilot fired his nose cannons. "Run for the truck!" Margaret shouted to the team as she pointed downhill. "Run like hell."

That was easier said than done since every one of them was carrying a pack loaded with Ramanthian heads. Some made the trip in well-calculated leaps. Others tripped, fell, and skidded downhill. Margaret caught a glimpse of Lothar pausing to help Woo as she ducked behind one of the hover trucks.

But the improvised escape plan wasn't going to work because the ship would land, the troops would get out and fire down on the humans before they could board Sawyer's truck. Unless . . .

As the ship flared in for a landing, Margaret hurried over to a small platform she had noticed earlier. Then she pulled her pistol and fired. It was impossible to miss. But the small-caliber bullets had no effect as the transport settled onto the grate, and a ramp hit the ground. That was when Margaret pulled the lever on the side of the control station. It released a roaring blast of fire that shot upwards and wrapped the ship in flames.

There wasn't much time. No more than a second or two in which to think about Charles and Christine. Would her daughter marry Antonio Santana? Was he still alive? Then there were no more thoughts as the ship's fuel supply went up, and the resulting explosion swept the top of the hill clean.

13

We must take the current when it serves, or lose our ventures.

—William Shakespeare
Julius Caesar
Standard year 1599

PLANET TREVIA, THE POONARA PROTECTORATE

Vanderveen was asleep when the com set began to beep. She fumbled for the handset and swore as it clattered to the floor beside her bed. Having retrieved it, she rolled over onto her back. It was daytime but just barely. Sunlight streamed down through the slats of wood over her head and threw long, narrow shadows across her blanket. "Hello? This is Christine Vanderveen."

"It's Missy," Sayers said. "Sorry to call so early, ma'am, but we need to get to the hospital *now.*"

Vanderveen sat up and swung her feet over onto the tile floor. Her first thought was for her staff. "Why? What happened?"

"It isn't one of our people, ma'am. Somebody tortured Hamantha Croth. Then they shot him and left him for dead. Except he *isn't* dead. Not yet anyway. A neighbor saw some Ramanthians leave his place in the middle of the night and called the police. They brought Croth to the hospital. And he's asking for *you*. I think this is important, ma'am. We need to hurry."

"I'll meet you in the lobby in ten minutes," Vanderveen replied. "And bring some sort of recorder."

The diplomats entered the hospital twenty minutes later. There was a slight delay at the front desk. Shortly thereafter, a Ramanthian doctor arrived to escort them up to the second floor. He spoke standard with a heavy accent but could still be understood. "We must hurry. Citizen Croth is dying. We did everything we could, but it won't be enough."

Croth/Hoknar had a room to himself. He was belly down on a Ramanthian-style bolster bed. He was hooked to an IV, and there was machinery all around. His eyes were closed, and a rasping sound could be heard each time he took a breath. A patch of sealant marked the spot where he'd been shot, one of his wings was missing, as was a foot. To say that Croth/Hoknar had been tortured was an understatement. It made Vanderveen feel sick as she knelt next to him. "Citizen Croth? Or should I say Majordomo Hoknar? This is Consul Vanderveen. You wanted to speak with me?"

There was no response at first, and Vanderveen wondered if the Ramanthian was conscious. Then his eyes opened and seemed to roll into focus. Hoknar's voice was so faint that Vanderveen had to lean forward in order to hear it. "Listen carefully . . . The Warrior Queen is still alive. And in hiding. But a cabal led by ex-Governor Parth managed to place their own Queen on the throne. Now, because of my weakness, they know where she is. Go to Sensa II, find the rightful Queen, and return her to power. Both sides will have to make concessions. But, if you do as I say, peace is possible."

Vanderveen felt a rising sense of excitement. If what Croth,

AKA Hoknar, said was true, the mere fact that the Warrior Queen was alive represented an important opportunity. Because by publicizing that fact, it might be possible to sow the seeds of dissent within the Ramanthian population. And, if the Warrior Queen would be willing to negotiate a truce in order to regain her throne, that could end the war. She glanced at Sayers and was relieved to see that she was aiming a camcorder at Croth/Hoknar. "Around my neck," he rasped. "The royal seal. Take it. Tell the Queen what I said. She may not like your proposal, but she will listen."

"I will try," Vanderveen promised.

Croth/Hoknar closed his eyes, shuddered as if in pain, and opened them again. "Thank you. And one more thing . . ."

"Yes?"

"Tell the Queen I'm sorry. So very, very sorry. The pain was too much."

Vanderveen started to reply but saw the light in the Ramanthian's eyes start to fade and knew he was gone. A tone sounded and stopped as the doctor pinched a switch. He had been responsible for the Queen's medical care during her short stay on Trevia and liked her. His eyes made contact with Vanderveen's. "So you'll help?"

"If I can."

He nodded. "Please hurry."

Two hours after Croth/Hoknar's death, Vanderveen was seated at her desk staring at the hypercom in front of her. Assuming the device worked, it would allow her to have a real-time conversation with people on Algeron. Interestingly enough, the basic technology had been stolen from the Ramanthians by none other than Major Antonio Santana. And now, a year and a half later, it was revolutionizing interstellar communications. Because prior to the advent of the hypercom, it would have been necessary to send a message torp to Algeron and wait for a reply. A two-week process if everything went well.

Now she could make an FTL call. But would Assistant Secretary Holson take the opportunity seriously? And react to it quickly enough? She feared that he wouldn't.

There was another way of course. And that was to try for Secretary of State Yatsu. Or the president himself. But if she went over her supervisor's head, the move could be seen as further evidence of what her superiors perceived as a rebellious nature. Vanderveen sighed. There was no way in hell that she was going to call Holson and run the risk that the bastard would try to block her.

First, she had to enter a five-digit access code into an alphanumeric keypad. Then it was necessary to slip a finger into the ID port. The finger prick hurt. What seemed like a very long ten seconds passed as the device verified her DNA and opened an FTL link. Eventually it would become possible to call discrete locations from the field. But for the moment, *all* Foreign Service calls were routed through a computer on Algeron. Its female persona had black hair and brown skin. The image shivered, broke up into a thousand motes of light, and came back together again. "Good evening, Consul Vanderveen. Who are you calling?"

"The president."

A human might have registered surprise, but the simulacrum's expression remained unchanged. "Priority?"

"One."

"Please hold."

The operator, if that was the correct word, disappeared. A Confederacy seal appeared in her place. Vanderveen held and held some more. Fifteen long minutes passed. Finally, with no advance warning, Nankool appeared on the screen. He looked disheveled and had clearly been asleep. "I'm taking this call because of what we went through on Jericho," he said grumpily. "But it had better be important. Because if you're calling to whine about conditions on Trevia, this will be a very short conversation. Come to think of it, why call *me*? You report to Assistant Secretary Holson."

Vanderveen felt sick to her stomach. Was the Croth/Hoknar thing *real*? What if he had been lying? But why would he do that? "I'm sorry to wake you, sir," Vanderveen said, as she battled to keep her voice steady. "But I have evidence that a Ramanthian cabal forced the Warrior Queen into hiding on Sensa II—and replaced her with a monarch of their own choosing. Given how important such a development would be, and the urgent need to protect the Warrior Queen from a team of assassins, I thought it best to call you directly."

Nankool looked stunned. His mouth opened and closed, but nothing came out. Finally, having regained his composure, he was able to speak. "You mentioned evidence. *What* evidence?"

"The Ramanthian you are about to see is named Bebo Hoknar. He called himself Hamantha Croth while in hiding. He was the Warrior Queen's majordomo prior to her supposed death. After being tortured, shot, and left for dead, he sent for me. Here's what he had to say."

Vanderveen's right index finger stabbed a button. Video from Sayer's camcorder followed the carrier wave through hyperspace to Algeron. She watched as Croth/Hoknar told his story all over again. Once it was over, Nankool reappeared. There was a frown on his face. "How long have you been there? A few weeks?"

It was actually considerably less than that—but Vanderveen could see where things were headed. "Something like that, sir."

"And you're already causing trouble."

Vanderveen didn't see it that way, but said, "Yes, sir."

"We don't have a consulate on Sensa II, do we?"

"No, sir."

"And you want to go there. Am I correct?"

"It seems like an important opportunity, sir."

Nankool grinned broadly. "Holson will be pissed."

"Yes, sir."

"Okay, I'll talk to the navy. Hopefully, they have a suitable vessel in the area. They will contact you."

"Yes, sir. Thank you."

At that point, Vanderveen expected Nankool to break off the conversation, but he didn't. A serious expression appeared on his face. "Christine . . . There is a dispatch on the way to you via normal channels. And I'm sorry to say that it contains some very bad news."

Vanderveen felt the bottom drop out of her stomach. Santana. It had to be Santana. Nankool knew him, as did her father. She bit her lower lip in an effort to fight back the tears. "Yes?"

"It's your mother, Christine . . . She was killed in action during a raid. The nature of the mission is classified, so I can't give any details. But suffice it to say that a number of people owe their lives to her bravery. Margaret was an extraordinary woman."

Vanderveen managed to say, "Thank you for letting me know," though she was crying as the little screen went black. Her mother dead? It didn't seem possible. Her father would be devastated.

Vanderveen wanted to retreat to her quarters but couldn't do so without being seen. So she locked the door to her office and curled up on the couch. Sobs racked her body, shadows crept across the room, and the war continued.

ABOARD THE CONFEDERACY MINESWEEPER *IO* IN ORBIT AROUND SENSA II

According to all of the information that Vanderveen had been able to get, the city of Heferi was a very dangerous place. For that reason, the *Io*'s commanding officer, LTJG Craig Sullivan, insisted on going with her. Which should have been fine except that the diplomat couldn't tell if Sullivan was going to be an asset or a liability. He looked as if he wasn't a day over eighteen. But as his XO, a chief warrant officer named Lopez, had told Vanderveen during the trip out, "Don't let the schoolboy looks fool you. It takes balls to disarm a mine. And brains, too. He's a little uptight, but that will wear off."

Except now, due to Vanderveen's need to reach Sensa II quickly, the boyish officer was about to accompany her down to the surface of a very dangerous planet, a task that was very different from neutralizing mines. Was he up to it? There wasn't any choice. He had to be.

The officer eyed her skeptically as First Class Petty Officer Mubu entered the *Io*'s tiny mess and dumped an armload of weapons onto the metal table. "No offense, ma'am, but are you familiar with small arms?" Sullivan wanted to know.

"Never seen one before," Vanderveen deadpanned as she chose a semiauto handgun and released the magazine. Then, with the expertise born of considerable practice, she began to slip cartridges into the clip. "This will do as a primary—assuming you have more magazines for it. But I'd like something smaller for a backup. Plus a decent flick-blade."

Sullivan smiled wryly. "Who knew that diplomats were so familiar with weapons?"

Vanderveen smiled. "It helps to speak softly and carry a big gun. Speaking of which, what have we got for heavy artillery? From what I hear, the people on Sensa II are well armed."

"That's where this bad boy comes in," Mubu said, as he cradled a pulse cannon in his arms. He had dark skin, broad cheekbones, and extremely white teeth. "I could stop a tank with this puppy."

Vanderveen nodded. "I hope you won't have to. Let's get ready, gentlemen. The sooner we get dirtside, the better."

It took all of three hours to complete their preparations, get the necessary landing clearances, and enter the planet's frequently turbulent atmosphere. Rather than bring the navy minesweeper down and get the locals all stirred up, Sullivan had elected to use one of the ship's two shuttles. He had the cockpit to himself, and the others were seated behind him in the multipurpose cargo compartment.

Heferi was on the dark side of the planet at the moment. And since it was the only city on Sensa II, Vanderveen found herself staring out a viewport into stygian blackness as the tiny vessel leveled out over what she assumed was desert. And that was how things remained until Sullivan's voice came over the intercom ten minutes later. "I have visual contact with Heferi—and we've been cleared to land. Check your harnesses, say your prayers, and don't soil my seats. You'll clean 'em if you do."

With that cheerful admonition, the shuttle began to slow, dropped down into the valley that lay between two mountainous dunes, and circled the cluster of lights below. As Vanderveen looked out through the viewport, she saw three red tracers blink into existence and curve toward the ship. Target practice perhaps? Or someone hoping to bring the shuttle down so they could loot the wreckage?

She could only guess as the cannon shells sailed past and vanished from sight. The shuttle seemed to pause in midair as Sullivan fired the repellers, and the ship settled onto a brightly lit "X." Then, acting on instructions from air traffic control, Sullivan took off again and scooted the boat into a slot between a Thraki freighter and a disreputable-looking yacht. "Welcome to Heferi," Sullivan said, as the skids touched down for the second time. "I hope we find the Queen quickly. The locals charge two hundred credits an hour to park here."

Vanderveen wasn't too worried about money, having signed for fifty thousand back on Trevia, but she was in agreement nevertheless. The Ramanthian assassins could have been on the ground for a full rotation already. She felt a rising sense of impatience as she came up out of her seat. "Let's gear up and hit the dirt. We have work to do."

After leaving a large cash deposit with the spaceport's heavily guarded cashier, the threesome was free to leave the facility and enter the dimly lit streets beyond. They were dressed in civilian clothing to blend in with the local population.

A dozen would-be bodyguards were waiting to greet them as they emerged, along with a bevy of drug dealers, prostitutes, and guides. They rushed to surround the newcomers but fell back when the heavily armed Mubu stepped forward.

Vanderveen eyed the people arrayed in front of her, spotted a one-legged man on crutches, and pointed at him. "*You.* Yes, you. We need a guide. I'll pay fifty credits for the next five hours of your time."

The man grinned broadly. His cheeks were unshaven, half his nose was missing, and his teeth were brown. "You chose well," he cackled. "I know Heferi like the back of my hand."

"Are you sure about this?" Sullivan wanted to know. "Why *him?*"

"Because he can't outrun us," Vanderveen replied.

Sullivan gave her an admiring glance as the newly hired guide hopped toward them. His clothes were ragged, and a sour smell surrounded him. Vanderveen wrinkled her nose. "What's your name?"

"It's William. But everybody calls me Billy."

"Well, Billy . . . We're looking for some bugs. Some of them arrived in the last day or so. Ring any bells?"

Billy shook his head. "No, ma'am. Sorry, ma'am. But that don't mean they ain't here. I work nights. It's cooler then. Maybe they landed during the day."

Vanderveen nodded. "How 'bout bugs who have been here for a while? They would be secretive and well protected."

"Nope," Billy said. "I'm not aware of anything like that. But I know where we can find out."

"Good. What have you got in mind?"

"It's a bar called Homer's. All kinds of people hang out there. If your bugs are in Heferi, someone knows."

"Okay," Vanderveen agreed. "Take us there."

It was only a three-block walk—but a scary one nevertheless. There were no streetlights. Just the occasional internally lit sign, the momentary spill of light from an open door, or the glow of luminescent graffiti. Billy's crutches made a rhythmic thumping sound as he led the visitors around a corner, past a group of dimly seen men, and toward the sign beyond. The H had gone dark so it read as OMER'S.

A scattering of locals were standing around outside. Some of them traded greetings with Billy. The rest eyed the trio in the speculative manner that predators reserve for their prey.

Two heavily armed Hudathan bouncers were on duty at the front door. One of them raised a large paw. "Hold it right there, Billy. Homer wants his twenty credits. You got it?"

Billy turned to look at Vanderveen, who removed a small roll of money from a pocket and subtracted a twenty. She gave it to Billy, who passed it along. "There," he said triumphantly. "Billy always pays his debts."

"Yeah," the bouncer replied. "And it's going to rain beer in the morning. Don't skip out on your bar tab again. Not unless you want to lose the other leg, too."

Billy made a face, waved his clients forward, and entered the bar. Vanderveen felt warm, fetid air wash around her as she and her companions were enveloped by a miasma of stale beer, mixed body odors, and the fumes from greasy food. There were twenty or thirty tables, and about half of them were in use. A brightly lit bar could be seen against the far wall—and a tired-looking stripper was orbiting a pole off to the right. The music had a prominent backbeat and was too loud for comfort.

Vanderveen scanned the crowd for Ramanthians, didn't see any, and felt an insect land on her cheek. She slapped and it buzzed way. "Sand flies," Billy said disgustedly, as if that explained everything. "Where would you like to sit?"

"In a corner," Sullivan answered, and Vanderveen nodded. It would be good to put their backs against a wall if that was possible.

Having located an empty table and ordered a round of drinks, the threesome settled in to watch the crowd as Billy went out to speak with the people he knew. None of whom was likely to share information with strangers. And, because there was a constant flow of individuals in and out of the bar, that kept him busy for quite a while. But eventually he was forced to return to the table with nothing meaningful to report. A few Ramanthians had been seen here and there over the last month, but nobody was sure where they were or why they were in Heferi. And nobody cared.

So being tired, and with no leads to follow up on, Vanderveen had Billy take them to a nearby boxtel, where she paid him. In keeping with its name, the hostelry consisted of about fifty lockable cargo modules all stacked in tiers. They were located inside what might have been a Forerunner temple, judging from the vaulted roof, an altarlike structure at one end of the room, and rows of stone benches. Each box had an air vent with a mattress and clean bedding. The last was a welcome surprise.

Like the other two, the diplomat had little more than a toothbrush with her. So it didn't take long to get ready for bed and crawl into her "room." Then, after removing her body armor, it was time to curl up with a gun in her hand. That was when Vanderveen thought about her mother, father, and Santana. A sand fly was trapped inside the box, and it buzzed from time to time. Eventually, she fell asleep.

When Vanderveen awoke, the air was warm, she needed to pee, and she could hear the *pop, pop, pop* of gunfire in the distance. After pulling her gear together and crawling out of the box, the diplomat discovered that Billy was waiting on the floor below. He nodded respectfully. "Morning, ma'am. I found someone who can tell you about the bugs."

Vanderveen jumped down onto the sand-scattered floor. "How much?"

"Two hundred."

"One hundred."

"One-fifty."

"One-twenty-five. And that's final."

Billy nodded happily. "Done. But my source will want something, too."

"Wait here."

Having roused her companions, Vanderveen spent fifteen minutes in a rented shower stall, toweled off, and put the same clothes back on. When she returned to the main room, the others were ready. "Okay," Vanderveen said. "Where are we going?"

"To a bar," Billy announced.

"I *like* this job," Mubu said approvingly.

The heat fell on them like a hammer as they left the boxtel and entered the streets beyond. Vanderveen could see the lead dune by looking left—and the back dune by looking right. Both had steep slopes and were hundreds of feet tall. The ground shook, and a dull *thump* was heard. "Tomb raiders," Billy explained. "Fighting it out somewhere below us. That's how I lost my leg. Follow me."

Sand flies buzzed all around as the foursome picked their way through the debris-littered streets. Empty shell casings lay everywhere. Billy led them around a body at one point, and a horrible stench filled Vanderveen's nostrils. The city was, she decided, the worst hellhole she'd ever been in. And that was saying something.

It took ten minutes to reach the ladder that led down into the bar called the Mummy's Breath. "I'll wait here," Billy announced. "Just ask for Kai Cosmo. He'll tell you what he knows."

Vanderveen descended the ladder first and was surprised by the flow of cool air that rose to greet her. The mummy's breath perhaps? Yes, she thought so. The air had a dry, musty quality—as if emanating from ancient chambers far below.

A human bouncer was positioned at the foot of the ladder. He nodded and pointed Vanderveen toward a rough-hewn passageway. It had been excavated by tomb raiders as part of their efforts to find Forerunner artifacts.

Vanderveen followed a series of dangling glow strips to a set of stairs that led down into what might have been a rectangular swimming pool thousands of years before. That's where two dozen tables had been set up. It was early in the day, so most of them were empty. A badly dented one-eyed utility droid clanked over to greet them. "Good morning," the machine said gravely. "A table for three?"

"We're looking for Kai Cosmo," Vanderveen responded.

"Of course," the robot replied. "Please follow me."

Vanderveen and her companions followed the machine to a table where a man was in the process of assembling a submachine gun (SMG) from the newly oiled parts laid out in front of him. He had a hard face, a dark tan, and was dressed in military-style body armor. There was an audible *click* as one assembly mated with another. "Mr. Cosmo?" the diplomat inquired. "My name is Vanderveen. Billy sent us."

Cosmo directed a stream of ju-ju juice at a spittoon and nodded. "Have a seat. Sorry about the parts. It's a good idea to clean your weapons once a day around here. The goddamned sand gets into everything."

"You sound like a marine," Sullivan said stiffly. "A deserter perhaps?"

"And *you* sound like a tight-assed navy officer," came the reply. "And a junior one at that."

Sullivan was seated by then. He looked offended. Or tried to. "A navy officer? What makes you say that?"

"The academy ring on your left hand," Cosmo answered dryly.

Sullivan looked embarrassed and began to rotate the face of the ring inwards.

Cosmo jerked a thumb toward Mubu. "And, judging from the CSN tattoo on Mr. Plasma Cannon's forearm," Cosmo continued, "he's one of your men. Not the play pretty though . . . She's a civilian."

Vanderveen smiled as the merc continued to put the SMG back together. "How so?"

"You're wearing your sidearm in a cross-draw holster, your hair is too long, and you smell nice."

Sullivan scowled and Vanderveen laughed. "You're good. I'm impressed. Billy says you have some information for us."

"Maybe," Cosmo allowed warily. "I led a group of mercs who were hired to guard a complex occupied by some very snooty bugs. One of them was sick and confined to a cagelike apparatus. Sound interesting?"

"Yes," Vanderveen replied, as her heart began to beat a little bit faster. "*Very* interesting. Where are they?"

"Ah," Cosmo said, as he slipped a magazine into the SMG. "That's the question, isn't it? Let's talk price."

"What do you want?"

"A ride," Cosmo said simply.

"Why?" Sullivan wanted to know.

"Why not?" Cosmo answered. "Would *you* want to stay here? I made some money, and I'd like to live long enough to spend it."

"You have a deal," Vanderveen responded.

"What about sailor boy?" Cosmo wanted to know, as the wad of ju-ju migrated from one cheek to the other. "What's to keep him and his swabbies from throwing me into the brig?"

"He takes his orders from *me*," Vanderveen replied. "And you have my word."

Cosmo looked from face to face. Sullivan scowled but didn't deny it.

"Okay," the merc replied. "The bugs took off for *Orb I*. That's a space station in orbit around Long Jump in case you aren't familiar with it."

"You're sure?"

Cosmo nodded. "One hundred percent. My team and I took the bugs to the spaceport. They had a Thraki in tow. *He* mentioned the name. And they left on his ship."

Vanderveen was about to reply when a buzzing sound was heard and Cosmo made a grabbing motion. "Well, look at this," the merc said, as he held the object up for the others to inspect.

And there, rather than the sand fly that Vanderveen expected to see, was a tiny spy ball. It hummed and began to vibrate in a futile attempt to escape Cosmo's grasp.

The diplomat felt a sudden emptiness in the pit of her stomach. Someone had been listening to the conversation. But *who*? Locals? Hoping to make money off what they heard? Or the assassins who had been sent to murder the Queen? "Come on," she said grimly. "Let's get out of here."

Cosmo stood, placed the spy ball under his boot, and placed his weight on it. Electricity crackled, and there was a crunching sound.

As they left the bar, Cosmo paused to give the bouncer a couple of credits in exchange for a dusty backpack, which he hoisted up onto his shoulders. "I never sleep in the same place twice," he explained. "It's safer that way."

The ladder shook as Vanderveen climbed up into the hot sun. Then, having stepped off to one side, she put on a pair of sunglasses. Billy had been waiting in a scrap of shade on the other side of the street. He waved and began to hop his way across the open area. A hundred and twenty-five credits was a lot of money, and he was eager to collect it.

Then a black shadow slid over him, Vanderveen heard a thrumming sound, and a rocket struck the street. There was a flash of light followed by a loud *boom*. And when the smoke cleared, there was nothing more than some bloodstains and a blackened crutch to mark the place where Billy had been.

There wasn't time to think, much less duck. So it wasn't until after the explosion that Vanderveen realized she'd been hit by tiny pieces of shrapnel. They stung as she looked up and saw the air car. Cosmo yelled, "Follow me!" and with no one else to rely on, Vanderveen obeyed.

The merc ran down the block with the others right behind

him. Vanderveen realized they were heading in a northwesterly direction, toward the spaceport. The air car's shadow caught up with her from behind, bullets kicked up puffs of dust all around, and Cosmo turned to fire the SMG at the attackers.

Then the air car was gone, and Cosmo was leading them through the ruins of a partially collapsed building. People were camped there, making it necessary to zigzag through a maze of tents, clotheslines, and fire pits. Some of the residents yelled obscenities but stopped as the tubby aircraft reappeared, and a stream of machine-gun bullets sent everyone diving for cover.

"This way!" Cosmo said, as he trampled someone's meal and ducked into a doorway. The others followed, and Vanderveen found herself on the ground floor of a tower. They were safe for the moment. But she knew that if they ventured out, the car would pounce on them again.

"Who the hell is shooting at us?" Sullivan wanted to know.

"The people who sent the spy ball," Cosmo answered pragmatically. "Hey, you . . . Cannon guy. Are you any good with that thing? Or do you carry it to look tough?"

Mubu frowned. "You're starting to piss me off, jarhead. Yes, I'm good with it. What's on your mind? Assuming you have one."

Cosmo grinned. "Climb the stairs and get set. When the car comes, blow it out of the sky."

Mubu looked quizzical. "But what if it doesn't come?"

"Oh, it'll come all right," Cosmo assured him. "Now get up there."

Mubu turned and began to climb the stairs. "Okay," Cosmo said, as he replaced the SMG's partially used magazine with a fresh one. "I'm going to invite the car to return. Feel free to shoot at it." And with that, he was gone.

"Stay here," Vanderveen said to Sullivan. "And guard the stairs. I'll provide covering fire for Mubu."

Sullivan opened his mouth to protest, but Vanderveen had already turned her back on him. She took the stairs two at a time. They turned, and turned again, before delivering her to the top of the tower. Judging from a corner heaped with trash and the strong odor of urine that hung in the air, someone had been camped there until very recently. But they were nowhere to be seen as Vanderveen drew her pistol and thumbed the safety off.

Mubu glanced her way before raising the cannon on his shoulder. "There's Cosmo," Vanderveen said, as she peered over the waist-high wall. "He's standing in plain sight."

"Crazy bastard," Mubu mumbled, as he turned a slow 360.

"There it is!" Vanderveen said, as the car emerged from between two buildings and sunlight glinted off the driver's windscreen. "To your left at two o'clock."

Mubu swiveled as the aircraft appeared and opened fire on the ground below. Geysers of dust erupted all around Cosmo, who ducked behind a block of stone. That was when Mubu fired. Everything seemed to go into slow motion as the blob of coherent energy sailed toward the air car and missed by less than a foot. "Damn it!" the sailor said, as the shot blew a huge divot out of the building beyond.

"Uh-oh," Vanderveen said, as the air car began to turn. "You pissed them off."

Mubu made a slight change to his stance and took careful aim as the airborne vehicle turned and the bow-mounted machine gun began to chatter. Vanderveen swore and emptied an entire magazine into the car. That was when she saw the Ramanthians and knew Cosmo was correct. The bugs knew where the Warrior Queen was and were determined to reach the monarch first.

Bullets sang all around. But having missed once, Mubu was determined to score a hit this time. So he stood fast even as Vanderveen shouted, "Fire!" Then, at what seemed like the very last moment, he pressed the firing stud. The bolt flew straight and true. There was a flash as it hit. The car flipped onto its starboard side, and a Ramanthian fell free. He attempted to deploy his wings, but there wasn't enough time. Dust exploded upwards as the body struck the ground.

Meanwhile, the engine screamed in protest as the air car slip-slid down into the plaza below, where it crashed and burst into flame. Black smoke poured up into the sky.

"Nice work, sailor," Vanderveen said, as she patted Mubu on the back. "I owe you a beer."

Cosmo and Sullivan were waiting when the twosome reached the ground. "You said you were good with that thing," the merc said with a grin. "I was beginning to wonder."

"The first round was a ranging shot," Mubu replied with a straight face. "I'll bet the driver shit himself."

"I know I did," Cosmo said, as he offered Vanderveen a scrap of fabric. "Here . . . I took it off the bug who landed on his head. He was wearing civvies—but look at what was stamped into his body armor."

Vanderveen accepted the offering and removed her sunglasses in order to see it more clearly. A dark delta shape had been imprinted onto the bullet-resistant fabric. Cosmo's eyes were waiting when she looked up. "A file leader?"

"An *assistant* file leader," he responded. "But good for you. And it amounts to the same thing."

"They were Ramanthian regulars. Not tomb raiders."

"Exactly."

Vanderveen put the glasses back on. "I wonder if we got all of them."

“I don’t know,” Sullivan responded. “But I wouldn’t count on it. Once they’re in your house, bugs can be real hard to get rid of.”

Cosmo laughed, but Vanderveen didn’t. A sand fly landed on her arm. She slapped at it and was rewarded with a bloody smear. “We got what we came for. Let’s get off this crud ball.”

14

> They died hard—these savage men—not gently like a stricken dove folding its wings in peaceful passing, but like a wounded wolf at bay, with lips curled back in sneering menace, and always a nerveless hand reaching for that long sharp machete . . .
>
> —*General Douglas C. MacArthur*
> Reminiscences
> *Standard year 1964*

PLANET O-CHI 4, THE CONFEDERACY OF SENTIENT BEINGS

The Ramanthian transport was badly overloaded. Engines strained as they struggled to lift twenty-eight bio bods and cyborgs off the power plant's roof. Lieutenant Ponco was at the controls, and Santana was standing in the doorway behind and to the left of her. "You're sure you can fly this thing?" he inquired doubtfully.

"I can't, but my computer can," Ponco replied confidently. And, as if to prove it, the transport staggered into the air.

"I'm glad to hear it," Santana said dryly, as the aircraft banked to starboard and began to spiral upwards. "Keep up the good work."

Santana turned and made his way into the crowded cargo compartment. Captain Ryley was on his feet. Their eyes met. "Go ahead," Santana said. "Blow it."

Ryley grinned. "Yes, sir!" The remote was already in his hand. He flipped a cover out of the way and thumbed a button. The charges in the geo tap's control room went off one after the other. While the ship continued to climb, Santana caught a glimpse of three secondary explosions followed by a tongue of fire that shot straight up. Then a thick cloud of black smoke closed in around the site as if to conceal it.

"Nice work, Captain. My compliments to the second platoon," Santana said. He intentionally put the comment out over the company push, so that Ryley's people would be able to hear it. The bio bods grinned proudly.

Satisfied that the power plant was off-line for good, Santana turned his attention to Major Temo. The renegade had received some first aid by that time and sat with her injured leg resting on a Ramanthian ammo box. Santana went over to stand in front of her. "It's time for you to earn your keep. I want you to go forward and get on the radio. Who was the bug in charge of the power station?"

"Sub Commander Remwyr," she answered sullenly.

"Okay. Tell Commander Dammo that Remwyr was badly wounded during a surprise attack on the power station—and that you're bringing him to Headstone for medical treatment. If you say anything else, Sergeant Major Dietrich will show you to the door. And the first step is a lulu."

"It won't work," Temo replied stubbornly.

"You said the attack on the G-tap wouldn't work," Santana observed. "Yet here we are. Now get your ass up to the cockpit—or start flapping your wings. Which is it going to be?"

Temo stared up at him. Her hatred was plain to see. Then, with some difficulty, she stood. Santana helped her forward and into the cockpit. "Sit there," he said, and pointed to a Ramanthian-style saddle chair. "Do you know how to use the radio?"

"Yes," Temo said, as she pushed her leg out in front of her.

"All right. Make the call. I'll be listening."

So Temo took hold of the cylindrical mike, squeezed the handle to activate it, and identified herself. It took less than a minute for a com tech to summon Dammo. It quickly became clear that the officer knew that power had been cut. So he was pissed, and what Temo had to say did nothing to improve the officer's mood. He was still ranting and raving when Headstone appeared in the distance, and Santana drew a line across his throat. Temo mumbled something about giving Dammo a full report and broke the connection.

"Okay," Santana said. "I think he bought it. Return to your seat."

Once Temo was back in the cargo compartment and had been secured to a seat, it was time for the rest of them to get ready. "Listen up," Santana said over the company push. "The landing pad is about a hundred feet below our objective. But if we work things correctly, we'll be able to ride an elevator up to the cannon. Of course, the bugs won't like that, so you'll have to kick their pointy asses. Any questions?"

"Yes, sir," Lieutenant Grisso said. "Once the cannon has been destroyed, how do we get off the mountain?"

"I'd like to say that we'll be able to board the transport and fly off," Santana replied. "But the odds are against that. So the simplest thing to do is kill *all* of the chits and move in."

That got some chuckles but not very many. Santana saw their expressions and smiled grimly. "Those of you who served in the Legion will remember that Captain Danjou and a company of sixty-two men were attacked by two thousand Mexican soldiers in the village of Camerone and fought 'em to a standstill."

It was true, and the legionnaires gave the traditional shout of "CAMERONE," thereby lifting the spirits of the ex-militiamen and -women as well. Santana smiled approvingly but felt guilty. Because he knew that only a handful of legionnaires had survived the fateful battle on April 30, 1863.

The transport had to climb in order to reach the landing pad located a hundred feet below the summit. Santana had seen a model of Headstone in Colonel Antov's study. And that had been impressive enough. But as the slipstream buffeted his face and he looked out at the mountain's sheer cliffs, he realized that any attempt to scale Headstone under fire would be a waste of lives. Even with a thousand troops and air support. Which was why the first attempt to do so had failed.

Now, as the ship gained altitude, all of the missile batteries continued to track it. Was that because they were programmed to follow movement? Or because Dammo was aware of the ruse and about to blow the transport out of the sky? What felt like a steel fist took hold of Santana's stomach and refused to let go as the landing pad appeared. "Get ready!" Santana shouted, as a crosswind hit the transport and caused it to wobble. "T-2s first. There aren't any friendlies on this mountain. Kill anything that moves."

The tension in the cargo compartment was palpable as bio bods checked their weapons, and the transport touched down. "Now!" Dietrich shouted from his place next to the door. "Go! Go! Go!"

The cyborgs hit the ground first. A stretcher party had been sent to fetch Remwyr. Half a dozen troopers were lounging next to a double-barreled antiaircraft weapon. And the ground crew was waiting to refuel the aircraft as the engines spooled down. All of them were swept away as the T-2s leveled their weapons and opened fire.

The result was a bloody mist as the Ramanthians ceased to exist, and what looked like pink confetti fell onto the landing pad. The surprise was complete. And by the time the bio bods jumped out of the transport, all the enemy troopers were dead.

But the advantage wouldn't last for long, and Santana knew that as he waved the troops forward. "This way! Follow Lieutenant Ponco. The cannon is above us."

Temo had been forced to sketch the complex. So Santana, his officers, and their NCOs knew that a tunnel led from the landing pad back into the heart of the mountain. That was where they hoped to seize control of a lift that would take them straight up and into the STS battery. By doing so, they could avoid the need to climb a very steep slope while being fired on from above. But as with everything else, the plan required speed, overwhelming firepower, and a measure of good luck.

So time was critical as the troops surged off the pad, entered the mouth of a dimly lit tunnel, and followed a row of ceiling-mounted lights toward the back. When they were fifty feet in, double doors parted at the other end of the passageway to reveal a group of Ramanthian troopers. But rather than standard infantry, these bugs were members of an armored unit. Their helmets had side-mounted bubbles through which they could see, hook-shaped protrusions to accommodate their beaks, and chin flares designed to protect their neck seals. Their bodies were protected by what looked like high-tech chain mail. It shimmered and flared as energy bolts struck it.

Santana knew that, while the Ramanthian warriors might lose a toe-to-toe contest with a T-2, their power-assisted armor could rip a bio bod apart. Never mind the offensive capability resident in the Negar IV assault rifles they were carrying. Both sides fired as they began to close with each other.

What ensued was a horrible melee in which both T-2s and Ramanthian troopers fired at point-blank range, powerful bodies grappled with each other, and any bio bod unfortunate enough to get caught in the middle was torn apart.

Having led his troops forward, Santana found himself at the very center of the fracas with no way out. So he fired his carbine at an advancing Ramanthian, saw dimples appear on the trooper's armor, and waited to die.

The Ramanthian raised a bulky arm and was about to deal the human a crushing blow when Ponco entered the gap between them. The pincerlike fist struck, penetrated her globe-shaped body, and produced a shower of sparks. Ponco was killed instantly.

But as the Ramanthian attempted to free his pincer from the recon ball's housing, Santana took advantage of the opportunity to step in close and press the muzzle of his weapon up against a bulbous eye guard. He pulled the trigger repeatedly. The second and third bullets blew holes through the clearplas bubble and went straight through the Ramanthian's brain.

Santana was going to turn his attention to another trooper when a T-2 plucked him out of the mix and harm's way. "Sorry, sir," a voice rumbled over the speakers in Santana's helmet. "But it isn't nice to hog all of the fun. Leave some bugs for us."

The tide began to turn as a phalanx of cyborgs shouted "CAMERONE" and pushed forward. It was hard to get traction on the bloody floor, but they were so tightly packed together that there was no room in which to fall. The cyborgs were angry, a bit stronger than the Ramanthians, and their armor was thicker. Taken together, these advantages made a critical difference as they shoved, kicked, and stomped their opponents into submission.

Even as the Ramanthians were forced to give ground, Santana saw the double doors start to close—and knew that if the lift rose without his troops on board, they would be trapped in the tunnel as the enemy flooded in behind them. "The elevator!" he shouted. "Stop the elevator."

But the T-2s were still locked in combat, and the doors

were only two feet apart when they came to a stop. Santana heard a girlish voice over the radio. "This is Alpha Six-One. I have control of the lift. Over."

Santana knew the voice belonged to Leesha Stupin. By crawling on her hands and knees, the bio bod had been able to scuttle between the battling giants above and enter the elevator unopposed. And that was wonderful. But once the chits backed onto the platform, Stupin would be easy meat. "I need two T-2s on the lift *now*," Santana said over the company push. "Execute."

As it turned out, three cyborgs were able to break through the crush and attack the Ramanthians from behind. That was the turning point, as all of the remaining enemy soldiers went down. They lay in broken heaps, but a price had been paid. In addition to Ponco, the company had lost three bio bods and a T-2. Gradually, bit by bit, the already-small unit was being whittled down to nothing. "Board the elevator," Santana ordered grimly. "There's more work to do upstairs."

"Reload if you need to," Santana ordered, as the doors slid closed. The lift had been used during the construction process and was large enough to accommodate twice their number, had that been necessary. "They'll be waiting for us," he warned. "And they'll pin us down inside the elevator if they can. So charge out and get in among them. Remember the ambush, remember the people we buried, and remember what we came here to do."

Someone shouted, "Camerone!" And this time legionnaires and militia responded as one. "CAMERONE!"

"T-2s first," Santana said, as the lift jerked to a halt. "And remember . . . If you're a bio bod, get in there and protect your cyborg's six."

Then the doors opened, a vertical slice of sky appeared, and all hell broke loose. Some enterprising officer or noncom had ordered his troops to reposition an auto cannon so it could fire on the elevator. It roared as the T-2s charged into the open. Three of them fell in quick succession. But by that time the *fourth* cyborg, a private named Willy Haber, was on top of the gun crew hosing them with gunfire. He screamed epithets the Ramanthians couldn't understand, stomped their dead bodies, and turned one of them into paste.

Then Dietrich and a bio bod named McTee arrived to slew the weapon around so that it was pointed at the Ramanthians. A corporal stepped in to fire it. Half a dozen enemy troopers were blown away as the rest took cover behind the STS cannon's dome-shaped housing. "Chase the bastards down!" Santana roared. "Captain Ryley . . . Take some people, get inside that housing, and plant the demo charges. Let's finish the job before the bugs can counterattack."

Ryley tossed a casual salute. "Sir! Stupin, Rajuta, Praxo . . . Follow me."

Certain that the lift had been put out of commission by the Ramanthians themselves, Santana knew that the bugs would have to climb upwards to try to retake their mountain aerie. But by which route?

Sporadic gunfire was heard as the last of the defenders were tracked down. Santana took a quick tour of the mountaintop. The need to do so reminded him of Ponco and how she had given her life to protect him. The thought of it made his throat tight and threatened to choke him. *Later,* he told himself. *Focus.*

There were two ways to approach the cannon. The first was to climb uphill from the landing pad, which was back under Ramanthian control. Enemy bullets pinged the ramparts around Santana whenever the officer showed himself.

The second way to reach the cannon was over a narrow path that zigzagged up the northeast side of the mountain to the antiaircraft batteries located there. Santana figured that if he was in command of Ramanthian forces, he would send a small force up the path, try to draw the defenders to that location, and send the majority of his troops up from the landing pad. Because even though the slope was steep, it was wide enough to accommodate fifteen or twenty soldiers marching abreast. And they would be harder to stop than a column of twos at the top of the mountain path. But would Dammo, or whatever bug was in charge, see things the way he did?

There was no way to be sure. But Santana had to do something. So he sent a single T-2 plus a couple of bio bods to seal off the trail while the rest of his soldiers took up positions west of the gun turret. Ryley's voice flooded his helmet. "This is Alpha Two-One. We're ready. Over."

"Pull out and execute," Santana replied. "Over."

Ryley and his troops emerged a minute later. The officer thumbed a remote, and a series of muted *thumps* was heard. Smoke poured out of the dome and was snatched away by the wind. "That should do it, sir," Ryley said, as he made his way over to join Santana. "We destroyed the controls, part of the track that the turntable rests on, and the cannon's accumulators."

"Good work," Santana said gratefully. "It seems that you have a natural talent for blowing things up. Now, no matter what happens next, we can . . ."

Santana never got to finish his sentence. There was only one Ramanthian fighter. Perhaps that was all the enemy had left. Whatever the case, it came out of the sun, fired a missile, and immediately pulled up. The T-2s detected the threat but too late. The cyborgs were just starting to respond when the weapon struck the west side of the dome and exploded. The blast killed a T-2 and two bio bods.

Santana understood the nature of his error. By destroying the cannon, he had inadvertently freed the enemy to employ airpower. Now that the cannon was off-line, it was all about honor. Even if that meant doing damage to their own fortress.

There was no need to give an order as the T-2s equipped with missiles fired them. The sleek-looking weapons leapt into the sky, snaked away, and converged on the fleeing plane. There was a flash of light followed by a puff of smoke as bits of wreckage twirled toward the ground.

Meanwhile, in concert with the air attack, the Ramanthian counterassault began. And, as Santana had anticipated, they came from two directions at once. He was standing above the landing pad, shoulder to shoulder with his troops, when the Ramanthians marched upslope. Weapons rattled as the legionnaires fired down into the undulating mass of bodies. Many fell, but the bugs kept coming. They were led by a very brave officer. He was waving a sword and seemingly invulnerable to the bullets that kicked up puffs of dust around him. Dammo? Yes, quite possibly.

The officer was flanked by two noncoms. One of them held a Ramanthian battle flag aloft just as one of his ancestors might have a thousand years earlier. The other was carrying a pole with Temo's head on it. Her eyes were staring sightlessly uphill, the wooden shaft was drenched in gore, and the message was clear: The chits wanted revenge. And they were willing to face a hail of bullets, climb over the bodies of their dead, and even take to the air if required. Those who chose to unfurl their seldom-used wings made excellent targets and were soon shot down.

The order to charge didn't originate from Santana. It came from a private named David Pynn. His T-2 had been killed during the assault on the auto cannon. And like the enemy in front of him, he was motivated by a desire for revenge. So when he shouted, "Come on! Let's kill the bastards!" it wasn't the result of careful thought. But as he jumped the waist-high wall and started downslope, it began a chain reaction. Santana was powerless to do anything other than join them as the rest of his troops followed Pynn, their weapons chattering madly.

The Ramanthian officer was directly in front of Santana. And as bullets whipped past and grenades exploded downslope, Santana made for the Ramanthian. Then, as the two lines clashed and penetrated each other, the bug raised his sword. Santana pulled the trigger on his carbine but nothing happened. He was out of ammo.

There was barely enough time to raise the otherwise-useless weapon and use it to block the descending blade. The strength of the blow sent a jolt down both of Santana's arms. He grimaced and brought a knee up. It struck the chit in the thorax and threw him off balance. Santana took advantage of that by clubbing the other officer with his rifle butt.

The Ramanthian was stunned. He just stood there for a second as Santana drew his sidearm and fired. The bullets entered through the bug's thorax and blew bloody divots out of his back. He fell over backwards and slid downhill to join a drift of bodies.

The Ramanthian standard-bearer went down shortly thereafter, as did the noncom supporting Temo's head. That was when the tide of battle turned. All opposition melted as the T-2s descended the slope like avenging gods. Their weapons continued to fire as their foot pods turned the fallen into a bloody slush.

According to the information available on Santana's HUD, only sixteen members of the company were still alive. A victory had been won. But the price was so steep there was no joy in it. And he wondered how many more people would have to die before the war finally came to an end. Blood from both sides of the conflict ran downhill, seeped out onto the landing pad, and painted it red.

THE SPACE STATION *ORB I*, IN ORBIT OVER PLANET LONG JUMP, THE CONFEDERACY OF SENTIENT BEINGS

Vanderveen was on "B" deck, letting the crowd of spacers, merchants, and crew people carry her in a clockwise direction around the center of the *Orb I* space station, when a holographic image appeared directly in front of her. The man was about her age and very handsome. "Hey, babe . . . If you're looking for a good time, my name is Mark. How 'bout we get together? I'm on . . ."

Vanderveen never found out where Mark was located because the image exploded into a thousand motes of light as she walked through it. And there were other distractions, too. Including the "zip" ads that circled the bulkheads, the exotic scents that misted the air, and the arrows that appeared on the floor in front of her. Each of them represented a business and was trying to lead her somewhere. All of which made it difficult to concentrate on the task at hand. And that was to find the Warrior Queen.

After receiving permission from Secretary Yatsu to travel from Sensa II to *Orb I* aboard the minesweeper *Io*, Vanderveen had been forced to part company with Sullivan and his crew half an hour earlier. Kai Cosmo was at her side as she left the ship. But once aboard the space station, it was only a matter of a few seconds before he said, "Thanks for the ride, ma'am," and promptly disappeared. Which made sense because he was almost certainly a deserter, and there were military personnel in the constantly swirling crowd.

That meant Vanderveen was alone. For the moment at least. Although Secretary Yatsu had promised to send a security team—people who could help her and protect the Queen. Assuming Vanderveen was able to find the monarch. *And how hard can that be?* she thought to herself. *There are only so many places to hide on a space station.*

It was a comforting thought, and one that helped boost her spirits as she paused in front of an information kiosk. There were more than a dozen entries under HOTELS. She chose a midpriced hostelry that promised to provide "a comfortable bed, a full suite of electronic conveniences, and a private bath."

The Sweet Sleep was located on "D" deck right next to a zero-gee gym. After checking in, Vanderveen made her way down a short hall to room four, slid the keycard through the reader, and entered what turned out to be a very small cabin.

The unit included a bunk barely large enough for one person, a fold-down desk, and a tiny bath. But that was enough. So Vanderveen shrugged the backpack off her shoulders and locked the hypercom in a drawer. Then, having unpacked to the extent she needed to, she went looking for something to eat.

The stand-up eatery was located about fifty feet from the entrance to her hotel and was clearly popular with the space station's crew beings. And that was a reliable indicator of good food at reasonable prices.

So she bellied up to a counter, made her selections from the list on the menu that appeared in front of her, and touched SUBMIT. A utility droid arrived with the food ten minutes later. The meat-and-veggie wrap was excellent.

As Vanderveen ate and washed her food down with occasional sips of tea, she was in a perfect position to watch the passing crowd. She saw humans, Thrakies, Prithians, Dwellers, Hudathans, and LaNorians. But no Ramanthians. And that made sense inside the boundaries of the Confederacy. It also served to illustrate a very important point. If the Warrior Queen and her retinue were aboard *Orb I*, they were hiding.

But why would the Ramanthian monarch enter enemy territory? To get help perhaps. But what *kind* of help? According to the Ramanthian doctor on Trevia, at least a dozen experts had examined the Warrior Queen and arrived at the same conclusion. Her condition was hopeless. Which brought Vanderveen full circle. Why hide on *Orb I*?

Vanderveen had eaten her fill and was about to return to her room when a cyborg wandered past. Not a military form but what looked like a one-of-a-kind civilian who was equipped with four arms. A technical specialist of some sort, she supposed. Somebody with a need for extra limbs.

Suddenly, like a bolt from the blue, Vanderveen had it. Of course! Having given up on finding a cure, the Queen wanted to purchase a custom-designed vehicle. And all of the very best cyberneticists were human, which would explain the royal's presence on *Orb I*. Or maybe not. But it was a theory. And the only one Vanderveen had.

Vanderveen felt a rising sense of excitement as she paid her tab with a swipe of the hotel's guest card and went looking for an information kiosk. A quick search produced three hits.

After jotting the names down, Vanderveen paid quick visits to each, her theory being that one of the cyber labs would be visibly larger and theoretically more successful than the others. And that was the case. TOMKO CYBERNETICS was located on "C" deck. If external appearances meant anything, it was at least twice the size of the other two businesses combined.

Since TOMKO CYBERNETICS seemed best suited to satisfy the needs of a presumably demanding monarch, Vanderveen resolved to start with them. But how? Vanderveen knew that the lab's employees would stonewall her if she walked in and asked for information regarding the Queen. And they would strengthen their security measures as a result. She could force them to answer her questions by calling for some legal assistance, of course. But that would take weeks if not longer.

So Vanderveen purchased a cup of tea from a vendor and watched people come and go from the lab as she sipped it. Then, having concocted a plan, she went back to her room and made the necessary preparations. She would need the right look and some basic supplies to be successful. An hour later, she was dressed and carrying her briefcase as she entered TOMKO CYBERNETICS and presented herself to the receptionist. Bio bod? Or cyborg? It was impossible to tell. The woman looked pleasant either way. "Yes? How can I help you?"

"I work for ANCO Electronics," Vanderveen lied. "We're about to release a new line of synthiskins. I'd like to speak with one of your lead engineers regarding the possibility of a beta test."

"Everyone is busy at the moment," the receptionist replied. "Would you care to make an appointment?"

"Can I wait?" Vanderveen inquired. "I'm on a very short layover, and I think your engineers would be interested in what we have to offer."

The receptionist had clearly dealt with pushy salespeople before. She shrugged noncommittally. "As you wish. But it could be hours."

"That's okay," Vanderveen responded cheerfully. "I understand."

So Vanderveen took a seat in the small lobby and pretended to do some work on her hand comp as people came and went. Then, after a long, boring twenty minutes had passed, the moment Vanderveen had been waiting for arrived. The receptionist left her desk to visit the restroom or run an errand.

Vanderveen took a quick look around to ensure that she had the lobby to herself, slipped the comp back into her briefcase, and stood. Then, with the quick, confident steps of a person who knows exactly where she's going, Vanderveen rounded the reception desk and took a hard right. Partly because the receptionist had gone left and partly because people wearing white coats had a tendency to turn right. And the closer she could get to the lab, the better.

A door hissed as it slid out of the way, and she entered a short hall. Another door was visible some twenty feet farther on. But she could see the biometric security scanner located next to the portal labeled CYBER LAB and knew she wouldn't be able to get past it. Fortunately, the plan didn't require her to do so. All she had to do was confirm a Ramanthian's presence.

Vanderveen continued down the hall and checked the signs on the doors that opened left and right before choosing the one labeled STORAGE. As the barrier slid open and the lights came on, Vanderveen felt her heart try to leap out of her chest. Because there, standing with their backs to the walls, were at least a dozen people!

Then she realized that rather than office supplies, the storage room was filled with cybernetic bodies or "forms." Prototypes perhaps? Experimental units? There was no way to know. Nor did Vanderveen care as she went to the very back of the room and made a place to sit down. The lights went off when she ordered them to, and with the exception of the glow from some LEDs, the compartment went dark. The waiting began.

Vanderveen awoke with a start. She was curled up on the floor. How long had she been asleep? A quick glance at the luminous dial on her watch provided the answer. A good three hours had elapsed since she'd given herself permission to take a fifteen-minute nap. That meant the lab was closed for the day. So why could she hear the characteristic clatter of click speech?

At that point, Vanderveen realized that at least two Ramanthians were right outside the door and might enter at any moment. She got to her feet and was busy trying to come up with a way to hide when the barrier slid open, leaving only one option. The diplomat froze as the lights came on.

Vanderveen could see the Ramanthian from the corner of her eye as he shuffled into the storage compartment. He was holding a pistol in his left pincer. Not one of the Queen's people, then. Because they wouldn't have any reason to burglarize TOMKO CYBERNETICS. So *who*? The assassins. Having listened in on her conversation with Cosmo and heard what the merc had to say, Croth's killers were on *Orb I* looking for the monarch. But how did they move around without being spotted? They clearly had help of some sort. She could smell wing wax. Would the Ramanthian realize she was a bio bod rather than a form? Blood began to pound in her ears.

The Ramanthian took a long look around, lowered the pistol, and turned to go. As the door closed, Vanderveen allowed herself to take a deep breath. Then, conscious of the fact that the bug could return at any moment, she opened her briefcase and removed a weapon of her own. The weight of it was comforting as she went to stand just inside the door.

It was tempting to sneak out and shoot the Ramanthians. But how many of them were there? And what would happen if *she* was killed? The effort to find the Queen would come to a sudden halt. And the lost opportunity could be the difference between war and peace.

So Vanderveen stood with an ear pressed against the door and listened. There was a series of *thump*s, followed by a muted crash and a storm of click speech. Was someone getting chewed out? Maybe.

Finally, after five minutes or so, the noises stopped, and Vanderveen opened the door. The briefcase was hanging from her shoulder, the pistol was raised, and she was ready to fire. But there were no targets in sight.

What she *could* see was all sorts of stuff that had been pulled out of various rooms and dumped onto the floor so that Ramanthians could sift through it. Had they found what they were looking for? Or left disappointed? There was no way to know. And what about alarms? Had they tripped any? If so, security people were on the way and would assume that the messy search was Vanderveen's doing. The State Department would eventually bail her out, but that would take time.

So, determined not to leave empty-handed but aware of the fact that she lacked the expertise to hack TOMKO'S computer system, Vanderveen went to a secondary information source. And that was the room marked GARBAGE. The door was unlocked, and the refuse bins were untouched. Was that because garbage and sewage were traditionally handled by members of the Ramanthian Skrum class? Or because the bugs assumed that garbage was garbage?

Vanderveen stuck the handgun into her waistband, went over to the container marked SHREDDER, and dumped the paper onto the floor. Then, having dropped to hands and knees, she began to paw through the pile. Most of the printouts were routine items of the sort any business would produce. And Vanderveen was beginning to wonder if TOMKO's employees had been extra diligent regarding materials having to do with the Queen, when she came across a page titled, "Field Trial Four."

And there, right in the foreground, was what looked like a Ramanthian without any chitin. But rather than the internal organs one would expect to see, all sorts of electromechanical components were visible. Of equal interest were the buildings in the background and the green hills beyond. Were the structures on the planet below? Vanderveen was determined to find out.

There wasn't enough time to do more than glance at the sheet before stuffing it into her briefcase and coming to her feet. Then, conscious of the fact that security could arrive at any second, Vanderveen followed a trail of debris to a side door. It was closed. But a Ramanthian-sized hole had been cut through the center of it. And that allowed the bugs to enter without tripping the alarm.

Vanderveen was able to duck and step through as well. Then it was a simple matter to stand up straight and follow the corridor out to the main thoroughfare. Had she been photographed by the lab's security cameras? Without a doubt. So it was time to do some research and get off the space station quickly. She hurried away.

ABOARD THE FREIGHTER *INTHEON*, OVER PLANET LONG JUMP, THE CONFEDERACY OF SENTIENT BEINGS

After performing the necessary research, Vanderveen had been able to confirm that Dr. Tomko not only had a home on the planet below but a well-equipped research facility as well. And assuming that the assassins knew what she knew, it was extremely important to reach Tomko's estate before the Ramanthians did. And that was why she was aboard the *Intheon*. The freighter was so large that she barely qualified for a landing on a planet with something close to Earth-normal gravity. But the *Intheon* was the only ship Vanderveen had been able to hire on short notice. The elderly vessel shook like a thing possessed as she dropped into the atmosphere. Not having wings, the ship couldn't glide. So it was all about brute force as the freighter's engines roared and battled to keep the *Intheon* from cratering on the surface below.

The captain's name was Nora Perthy. And judging from the explosion of gray hair around her head, she was almost as old as the ship. Perthy owned the *Intheon*, but just barely, and couldn't afford luxuries like a pilot. So the crew consisted of Perthy, a robotic load master, and a rarely seen engineer.

As Vanderveen sat with her hands clenching the chair's

armrests, Perthy was conning the ship. A necessity since the ship's NAVCOMP was on the blink. The process involved manipulating a small joystick, stabbing various buttons, and coaxing the *Intheon* to do what Perthy wanted. "That's right, honey," she said softly. "Slowly, slowly, keep it level. You can do it. Remember the landing on Alto? You did it there, didn't you? Hmmm. What have we here? There's a battle going on."

The last was directed to Vanderveen, who was seated in the nav officer's chair to the left of and slightly to the rear of Perthy. Six curved screens were arrayed above the banks of controls. The camera mounted on the ship's rotund belly was up on the main screen at the moment, and as a wisp of low-lying cloud blew through the shot, Vanderveen could see that a Thraki-style ship was already on the ground.

Tiny figures were scurrying toward the main complex as smoke poured out of two outbuildings. And from what Vanderveen could see, it looked as though the attackers were about to overrun the largest structure. "See those people?" she inquired. "Take them out."

Perthy turned to stare at Vanderveen. She looked incredulous. "You must be joking. My ship isn't armed. But even if it were, I wouldn't do that."

"Oh, yes you would," Vanderveen said, as she pulled the pistol from under her jacket. "Look closely. They're Ramanthians. On one of the Confederacy's planets. Attacking some innocent citizens. So you will stop them, or I will blow your brains all over the control panel."

"But then both of us will die!"

Vanderveen smiled thinly. "That's correct."

"You're crazy."

"Yes, I am. Now kill them."

"But *how*?" Perth demanded desperately.

"Use your repellers. Walk the ship back and forth. Burn anything that moves."

Perthy swore some very unladylike oaths as she turned back toward the controls. Vanderveen's chair seemed to rise to meet her as the *Intheon*'s descent slowed, and the globe-shaped vessel began to hover some twenty-five feet off the ground.

The attackers had broken off their assault by then and begun to shuffle away from the main building as the *Intheon*'s repellers plowed black furrows in the ground. One of the Ramanthian soldiers disappeared in a flash of fire, quickly followed by another, as the freighter chased them down. "The ship!" Vanderveen shouted. "It's lifting. Stop it."

But it was too late. The Thraki vessel was not only a lot smaller, but much more agile, and it had little difficulty making its escape. "Damn it," Vanderveen said. "You were supposed to kill all of them."

"I will do no such thing," Perthy said primly. "That's what the navy is for. I'm going to land, and you're going to pay me. Then I'm going to lift."

Vanderveen lowered the gun and put it away. Some of the would-be assassins had escaped. But the Queen was still alive. Or so she hoped.

Vanderveen was on the ground ten minutes later. She followed a still-smoking furrow up a slight incline toward the building beyond. Judging from appearances, the much-abused facade had been struck by hundreds of bullets and at least one rocket.

When she was a hundred feet away, Vanderveen stopped, and a Ramanthian shuffled out to greet her. He was nicely dressed and bowed formally. "Greetings. And thank you. Dr. Tomko's security people weren't prepared for such a concerted attack. And you are?"

"My name is Vanderveen. Christine Vanderveen. I am the Confederacy's consul on Trevia. The planet where you and the Warrior Queen were in hiding before you left for Sensa II. How is her majesty? Well, I hope."

There was a long silence as they looked into each other's eyes. The Ramanthian was the first to speak. "So your government knows?"

"At a very high level—yes."

"And you were dispatched to make contact?"

Vanderveen nodded. "I was. The Ramanthian cabal wants her majesty dead. And the Queen plans to retake the throne. We can help."

"But for a price."

"Of course."

The Ramanthian nodded. "My name is Ubatha. Chancellor Ubatha. I think it's time that you met the Queen."

15

The enemy of my enemy is my friend.

—Human folk saying
Date unknown

PLANET ALGERON, THE CONFEDERACY OF SENTIENT BEINGS

It was dark at the moment and so cold that President Nankool could see his breath fog the air as the Thraki shuttle lowered itself onto the VIP pad. He was standing on one of Fort Camerone's ramparts looking downwards as the ship was enveloped by a cloud of steam. The entire area had been cordoned off, and security was extremely tight; all hell would break loose if word of the meeting were to leak out—both in the Confederacy and in the Ramanthian Empire. Because fanatics on both sides weren't willing to settle for anything less than total victory. And in their minds, peace talks would equate to treason. Plus, there were those who were benefiting from the war and wanted the conflict to continue. They included arms manufacturers, senior members of the military, and the rapacious news combines, which continually fed off the conflict.

As for regular folks, if they heard that peace talks were under way, expectations would soar. Then, if the negotiations fell apart, Nankool feared that morale would sink even further. So rather than conduct preliminary conversations in the harsh glare of the public spotlight, he was about to meet with Chancellor Parth in private. And it pained him to do so because there was general agreement that the bugs were winning the war. And that meant he and his staff would be forced to negotiate from a position of weakness.

As the handpicked ground crew surged forth to service the shuttle, Nankool glanced to his right. Judging from all appearances, Charles Vanderveen was just fine. But Nankool knew that the death of the diplomat's wife had hit him hard. So much so that there were reports he'd been drinking a lot lately. And the fact that his daughter had put herself back in harm's way didn't help either. All of which had a bearing on Nankool's decision to include Vanderveen on the negotiating team. Maybe some hard work plus the passage of time would help him to heal. A rectangle of light appeared as a hatch opened, and half a dozen backlit figures shuffled down a ramp to the place where Secretary Yatsu and some of her staff were waiting to receive the Ramanthians. Vanderveen said, "Bastards," under his breath, and Nankool pretended not to hear.

"Come on, Charles . . . We're serving live grubs in hot sauce—and you wouldn't want to miss out."

Very few Ramanthians had been allowed on the surface of Algeron, and with the exception of a few POWs, all of their visits had taken place prior to the war. As Parth shuffled down the ramp onto the landing pad, he was struck by how cold the air was, the glare of the surrounding lights, and the alien feel of the place. There were members of the cabal, Admiral Tu Stik, for example, who felt that the trip to Algeron was a mistake. As a member of the *Nira* cult, he opposed any form of negotiation. But if overruled, he preferred that the meeting take place on a Ramanthian battleship, so the animals could feel the full weight of the empire's military might.

But Parth was a politician. And a pragmatist. As such, he knew that while his willingness to visit Algeron could be viewed as a sign of weakness, there were potential benefits as well. The primary one was to place the animals in a receptive frame of mind. And that was important because even though the Ramanthian military had won battle after battle since the beginning of the war, there was a very real possibility that dark days lay ahead.

The burgeoning alliance between the Hudathans and the Confederacy was bad enough. But now that the Clone Hegemony had placed its genetically bred warriors under General Booly's command, and some sort of horrible disease was spreading among the troops on Earth, Parth feared the military momentum was starting to swing the other way. So it made sense to negotiate a deal while in a position of undeniable strength. *Besides,* Parth thought to himself, *we can always break the truce and attack the animals later on.* Members of the *Nira* cult would object at first but ultimately go along.

Parth's thoughts were interrupted as a small human with lots of black hair came forward to greet him. "Welcome to Algeron," Yatsu said solemnly. "I'm Secretary of State Yatsu. It's an honor to meet you. We often greet guests with a formal ceremony. But given the temperature and the need for security, I suggest that we go indoors."

Parth bowed. "Chancellor Parth. The honor is mine. By all means, let's put comfort before ceremony. We can continue the introductions inside."

Both diplomats made small talk as a phalanx of cybernetic monstrosities led them through an open door into the brightly lit warmth within. The higher temperature felt good, but Parth's sense of smell was quite acute and the mixed odors of human perspiration and food caused him to gag, a reaction he sought to conceal as he and his staff were escorted through a maze of hallways and into a large conference room.

A formally set table occupied the center of the space, round so as to put everyone on an equal footing. Even if that was a bit delusional where Parth's hosts were concerned. Six saddle chairs were available as well, and he wondered where they had come from. A Ramanthian world perhaps? Where they had been looted along with everything else that wasn't nailed down? Yes, he thought so.

Nor did the preparations end there. In place of the offensive odors encountered earlier, the reassuringly familiar scent of Ramanthian cooking hung in the still air. And Parth could see a row of gleaming warmers sitting on the tables that lined one wall. It seemed that the humans had gone all out in an effort to please their superiors. A propitious sign indeed.

But before refreshments could be served, introductions had to be made on both sides. A tiresome business that had just concluded when President Nankool entered the room with another human at his side.

Parth felt a sudden flush of pride. Because rather than meet with the Queen, who was technically his peer, Nankool had been forced to negotiate with a lesser power instead. That was a sure measure of Ramanthian dominance. Although, had the human been aware of it, the two of them were actually equals since the Warrior Queen was in hiding and her successor was at Parth's beck and call. Secretary Yatsu made the necessary introduction. "President Nankool, please allow me to introduce His Excellency, Chancellor Parth."

Having been briefed by Charles Vanderveen, Nankool knew that a bow was in order, and delivered one as Parth bent a knee. Then it was time to meet the Chancellor's staff and prattle about the weather, even as the Ramanthians continued to slaughter the Confederacy's citizens. And that was the crux of it. Which was better? To negotiate a peace deal of some sort? And trade sovereignty for safety? Or to refuse and fight to the last man, woman, and child?

It would have been a difficult decision regardless. But now, based on the information that Christine Vanderveen had submitted, there was a very real possibility that the Warrior Queen was still alive. That would make the sitting Queen a pretender who, according to Christine Vanderveen, was being controlled by Parth and a group of his cronies.

So what to do? Make some sort of deal on the theory that even if she was alive, the Warrior Queen wouldn't be able to regain the throne? Or refuse whatever terms were offered in hopes that the current government would fall? Millions of lives hung in the balance as Yatsu spoke.

"It's lunchtime for us, and on the chance that you might be hungry after your long journey, we took the liberty of preparing some Ramanthian delicacies. Fortunately, from our perspective at least, a prisoner of war named Inbo Haknu is being held on Algeron. He, if I'm not mistaken, is a master chef. We asked chef Haknu if he would be willing to cook for you, and he agreed. He was quite demanding where the ingredients were concerned, and though unable to fulfill all of his requests, we did the best we could."

Parth felt a combination of anger and grudging respect. Here, clad in the form of a diplomatic nicety, was both a compliment and a boast. Because even as the animals went to considerable lengths to please their guests, they were sending a not-so-subtle message: "We may be losing the war, but we have hundreds of thousands of Ramanthian POWs, and their fates hang in the balance."

"You are very kind," Parth lied. "The food smells wonderful. And you are correct. Chef Haknu is very well-known and highly respected. I look forward to eating whatever he prepared."

As Nankool's guest of honor, Parth was the first person to sample what the buffet had to offer. The human food came first. And revolting though it was, Parth forced himself to take a few small samples. Then came the warmer filled with sautéed grubs, all of which were still wiggling, and there were more favorites, too.

After filling his plate, it was off to the round table, where waiters stood ready to serve a variety of liquids. Having been seated next to Nankool, Parth tied the Ramanthian-style napkin around his neck and speared one of the grubs with a single-tined fork. It was still struggling as he held it up for Nankool to inspect. "Have you ever had one? They're quite active—but a single bite is sufficient to subdue them."

Having opened his beak, Parth placed the morsel in his mouth. Then, having flipped the extra-large napkin up over the top of his stubby antennae, the Ramanthian bit the morsel with his beak. Parth heard the characteristic popping sound as a mixture of blood and intestinal matter spurted against the inside surface of the napkin. The rich, fatty taste combined with the hot sauce was on a par with the best cuisine available on Hive. The food was, all things considered, an unexpected pleasure.

Prior to the war, when the Ramanthians had been part of the Confederacy, Nankool had been present when grubs were served at ceremonial dinners attended by a dozen sentient races. So he was ready for the napkin ritual. But what about the statement that preceded it? Was Parth's comment what it seemed? A simple observation? Or was there something more to it? A warning perhaps . . . A veiled way of saying that, struggle as the Confederacy might, the empire could consume it with ease.

Nankool wasn't sure. But when Parth's napkin came down, the human was waiting. Secretary Yatsu, Charles Vanderveen, and the rest of the Confederacy's staff members watched in horrified fascination as Nankool placed a grub between his front teeth and held the wiggling creature there for a full three seconds. Then, rather than flip a napkin over his head, he held it in front of his face. There was no mistaking the loud *pop* or the blood on the formerly pristine cloth. He swallowed, and a big grin appeared on his face. "That was yummy."

The rest of the meal was polite if not pleasant as both sides sought to avoid any sort of faux pas, knowing that the *real* discussion was to follow. And Nankool was pleased to see that regardless of whatever emotions were churning inside of him, Vanderveen had been able to maintain his composure.

Finally, once the dishes were cleared away, it was time for the talks to begin. And, since the Ramanthians were the ones who had suggested the meeting, it was agreed that they would go first. Nankool took note of the fact that Parth spoke without notes. Was that because he'd gone to the trouble of memorizing them? Or was that an indication of how powerful the Chancellor was? So powerful that he could say whatever he pleased. That would line up with the information provided by Christine Vanderveen.

"Thank you for agreeing to meet with representatives of the Ramanthian Empire," Parth began. "Sadly, for those on both sides of the conflict, millions of sentients have lost their lives or been injured. In fact, my mate, the War Parth, fell during the opening days of the war. So my surviving mate and I are in an excellent position to understand the terrible price that families on both sides have paid.

"That makes our task all the more urgent," Parth said earnestly, as his space black eyes roamed the faces around him. "So, acting in the best interest of our people as well as yours, we would like to propose the outline of a treaty. Of course the devil, as humans like to say, is in the details. But I think you'll agree that there can't be any details without the creation of an overarching accord.

"Now," Parth continued, "I know that this is a delicate and very difficult subject. But the facts are clear. Given the strategic realities, we are winning the war."

Secretary Yatsu started to object, but Parth raised a pincer. "Please . . . Allow me to finish. Let's begin with the human home planet. We conquered Earth and presently occupy it. I'm sure that's very painful for you. Just as it would be for me if the situation was reversed. So as a gesture of goodwill and to signify the beginning of a new relationship, we are willing to withdraw our troops from the surface of the planet. That would limit casualties and allow your citizens to resume their normal lives under the protection of the Ramanthian fleet."

Nankool frowned. "'The protection of the Ramanthian fleet'? What does that mean?"

"It means," Parth replied evenly, "that the citizens of Earth will be confined to their planet for the time being. But that could change later on depending on how they behave and the structure of the final treaty."

Nankool felt a sense of barely contained rage. Parth's proposal would reduce Earth to a virtual prison planet. So his first instinct was to slam his fist down on the table and say, "No!" But, unfortunately, he couldn't allow himself to show any emotion whatsoever. And, like it or not, Nankool had to consider the Ramanthian proposal. Especially since the bugs *were* winning the war—and getting them off Earth would represent a victory of sorts. One likely to appease a large part of the electorate. He battled to keep his voice level. "And the rest of the Confederacy's planets? What about *them*?"

Parth delivered the Ramanthian equivalent of a shrug. "A great deal of staff work would be required to establish some appropriate criteria. But I think it's safe to say that if we are able to reach an agreement regarding Earth, the same sort of arrangement could be extended to other worlds as well, the exception being those designated as nursery planets. They would remain under Ramanthian control."

At that point, Charles Vanderveen produced an inarticulate cry of rage, stood, and threw himself across the table. A water carafe tipped over, hand comps flew sideways, and Parth uttered a squawk of fear as Vanderveen's hands closed around his throat.

Pandemonium broke out as Parth's staff came to his defense, security people rushed to intervene, and Vanderveen took three stunner bolts in quick succession. His eyes rolled back in his head, and his muscles seized up, but the diplomat's fingers were still locked around Parth's scrawny neck. So as the Ramanthian battled to get enough air, it was necessary for a military policeman to pry the offending digits loose one at a time.

Finally, as Vanderveen was carried away, order was restored. In a perverse sort of way, Nankool was grateful for the attack on Parth since it provided him with an excellent opportunity to declare a break. Parth was still in the process of recovery as Nankool spoke. "Please accept my deepest apologies for Undersecretary Vanderveen's unforgivable actions. But, having lost a mate yourself, perhaps you will be able to empathize with his situation. It was only a few days ago that Secretary Vanderveen received news that his mate had been killed during a battle on Earth. I suggest that we adjourn, and if you're willing, resume our discussions in ten hours. Lieutenant Hiro will escort you to your quarters."

In spite of the fact that the last part came across as a command rather than a request, neither Parth nor any member of his party offered an objection. Once they had been led out of the room, Nankool turned to Yatsu. "Round up General Booly, Admiral Chien-Chu, and Madame X. We have a very important decision to make."

The meeting took place in Nankool's well-appointed office. Legion General and Military Chief of Staff Bill Booly was seated to the president's left. He was a legendary figure by then, a man who had fought countless battles on behalf of the Confederacy and had the scars to prove it. He had his mother's gray eyes and his father's lean body, but his hair was almost entirely white. Deep lines were etched into his face, his skin was pale, and he looked tired.

The woman seated to Booly's left was generally referred to as "Madame X," by government insiders. But her real name was Margaret Xanith. She had a head of well-coiffed gray hair, and despite the perpetual frown that she was known for, her face was surprisingly youthful. As head of the Confederacy's Intelligence organization, she knew most of the things worth knowing and had long been one of Nankool's most trusted advisors.

Admiral and industrialist Chien-Chu sat elbow to elbow with Xanith. Rather than the youthful vehicle chosen for trips to Earth, he was wearing a slightly portly body similar to the way his bio body had appeared at age fifty-five. He never wore a uniform unless forced to do so although his dark business suit was so similar to the rest of his attire that it was equally predictable.

Secretary of State Yatsu was present as well. And Nankool could see the strain around her eyes. "How's Charles?" he inquired.

"He's better now," Yatsu answered. "The worst effects of the stunner bolts have worn off. He wanted me to apologize on his behalf. He's very sorry."

"Tell him to squeeze a bit harder next time," Nankool said with a grin. "And tell him I can see why Christine is such a troublemaker."

"A rather *useful* troublemaker," Xanith observed. "She filed a report while you were meeting with Chancellor Parth. Not only was she able to find the Warrior Queen, the two of them met, and we have the makings of a deal. The Queen's throne in exchange for peace."

Nankool gave a low whistle. "That is very interesting. Of course, Parth is offering peace as well. But at a high price."

"According to Christine, the Warrior Queen is willing to accept something close to a complete reset," Xanith explained. "Meaning a return to prewar conditions, boundaries, and relationships. The exception is the nursery planets. They would continue to be part of the Ramanthian Empire."

"Most of them were largely unsettled prior to the war," Yatsu observed. "And now that they're infested with Ramanthian nymphs, I'm not sure we want them."

"True," Booly agreed soberly. "Although one-third of those nymphs will grow up to be Ramanthian warriors. And that means trouble in the future."

"The general makes a good point," Chien-Chu said flatly. "But the Warrior Queen's proposal would give us time to prepare. And, with support from both the Hudathans and the Hegemony, our military should be strong enough to counter the potential threat."

"That's true," Nankool allowed cautiously. "But let's flip this over. All of you know that I have a soft spot for Christine Vanderveen. But it sounds like she's out there cutting deals all by herself again. So will her verbal agreement with the

Warrior Queen hold up? Or will her 'supreme buggyness' suddenly decide to disavow it? We're talking about an outcast here. Someone who's on the run from her own people.

"Then there's the question of feasibility. Let's say Christine is correct—and the Warrior Queen keeps her word. What's to say that an attempt to put her back on the throne would be successful?"

"I can answer that," Xanith replied. "To some extent anyway. Thanks to our resistance people, the effort to infect Ramanthian troops with *Ophiocordyceps unilateris* has been a tremendous success. Thousands of troops have been killed, thousands are sick, and thousands are tied up caring for those who are ill. In fact, it's my guess that has a lot to do with Chancellor Parth's willingness to pull their troops off the planet. The truth is that the Ramanthian command structure has very little choice. And don't forget . . . so long as the bugs have ships in orbit, they can not only watch everything that takes place on the surface but glass the planet anytime they feel like it. So, in a weird sort of way, we're better off with soldiers on the ground. Or, put another way, this offer is no offer at all.

"Furthermore," Xanith continued, "there's reason to believe that hundreds of thousands of so-called denialists refuse to believe that the Warrior Queen is dead. So if we could give them hope, they might rise up against the pretender. Or, failing that, offer passive support. All of which leads me to believe that even if our efforts fail, we can still sow seeds of dissension throughout Ramanthian society. And that would be fun."

It was as close to a joke as any of them were likely to hear from the Intel chief, so Nankool smiled. "An excellent summary. Thank you. However, I feel it's my duty to point out that, attractive though such a strategy might be, the cabal controls all the levers of power. That includes not only the government but the military. So we might be better off with the bird in hand, so to speak. General Booly? You've been relatively quiet up to this point. What's your opinion?"

Booly looked up from the tabletop. His expression was bleak. "We're losing the war. We got our asses kicked on Earth, Gamma-014, and a dozen other planets as well. The resistance is making remarkable progress on Earth, but it would take a fleet to force the bugs out of the solar system. Thousands of ships are under construction deep inside the Hegemony. But it will be months before they're ready. And we will continue to be very vulnerable in the meantime. And if the Ramanthians think we're about to make a comeback, there's an excellent chance they will glass some of our worlds as part of a last-ditch attempt to avoid defeat."

"Of course, that's why we're going after their nursery planets," Chien-Chu put in. "Once we control one or two of them, the Ramanthians will think twice before using nuclear weapons against us."

"Okay," Nankool said. "So, given all that has been said, what should we do? Continue on? Accept Parth's proposal? Or back the Warrior Queen?"

There was a moment of silence followed by a voice vote. Secretary Yatsu had the last word. "So there you have it. God help us if we're wrong."

In spite of all the efforts that had been made to provide the Ramanthians with comfortable quarters, Parth was very unhappy as he looked out through a floor-to-ceiling window. The sun was obscured by a thick layer of gunmetal gray clouds. He had been attacked, his personal dignity had been violated, and his request to have the offender beheaded had been refused. That was bad enough.

But all the members of his party had been restricted to their quarters. That made it next to impossible to gather intelligence regarding Fort Camerone. And the final outcome of the mission was still in doubt. *Well, it's up to them,* Parth thought grimly. *If they want to die, all they have to do is say, "No."*

Parth's thoughts were interrupted as an aide shuffled into the room. "It's time, Excellency."

Hail rattled against armored glass, causing Parth to wonder why the humans would bother to colonize such an unpleasant planet. They were welcome to it. "Thank you. Has everything been packed? I will want to depart the moment the meeting is over."

"Yes, sire. All is ready."

"Excellent. Please lead the way."

But it was a squad of legionnaires who actually led the way, and Parth felt very vulnerable as he and the members of his party were led back to the same room where negotiations had broken off ten hours earlier. Thankfully, there was no sign of the animal who had attacked him—and Secretary Yatsu apologized all over again. Parth interpreted that as a positive sign.

A round of greetings followed, and food had been served by the time Nankool arrived. He made a point of greeting each Ramanthian by name before taking his seat. A droid poured some caf into his cup, and he eyed Parth over the rim. "I believe you had the floor when our meeting was interrupted. Is there anything you'd like to add?"

"No," Parth replied. "In spite of the barbaric attack on my person, we remain open to a bilateral cessation of hostilities followed by what might be called local sovereignty for some of the Confederacy's more populous planets. The exact list would be subject to negotiations carried out under the supervision of Thraki intermediaries—but would exclude nursery planets. Space travel, if any, would be conducted with prior approval from our government and would be subject to supervision by the Imperial navy. These are nothing more than rough outlines, of course. But if they are generally agreeable, the effort to formalize them can begin."

"Thank you," Nankool replied. "We appreciate the empire's willingness to enter into discussions—even if we can't agree to the initial terms that you laid out. So, in the spirit of good-faith negotiations, we would like to propose an alternative plan."

Parth didn't want to listen to Nankool's plan but forced himself to do so. Perhaps the animals were hoping to save face in some minor way. If so, he would be willing to consider their offering so long as they agreed to the essence of his proposal. He nodded. "Go ahead."

"Under the treaty we have in mind," Nankool responded, "the empire would agree to an unconditional surrender. All of your military personnel and civilians would be protected by Confederate law and treated with respect."

Parth could hardly believe what he was hearing. "Is this some kind of human joke?"

"No," Nankool replied firmly. "It's a serious offer. And the best one you're going to get."

Parth was stunned. The response made no sense. Not unless the animals were crazy. Or knew something he didn't. His eyes flicked from face to ugly face. Then it came to him. He spoke impulsively. "You have the Warrior Queen."

Nankool looked surprised. "The Warrior Queen? That's impossible. She's dead. You had a state funeral. Remember?"

"It won't help you," Parth said as he stood, and his staff did likewise. "The real Queen sits on the throne—and you're losing the war. Nothing will change that. In weeks, months at most, you will be forced to surrender. And when that day comes, I will take your head myself."

"Perhaps," Nankool allowed. "But in the meantime I suggest that you get your pointy ass off this planet. Lieutenant, show the bugs out."

Parth was furious. And remained so as he and his companions were escorted out of the fort and onto the VIP landing pad, where their shuttle was waiting. A few minutes later, they were on board, cleared for takeoff, and strapped into their seats. Shortly after that, repellers roared, and they were pushed down into their seats.

Parth wanted to make the hypercom call immediately but felt he should wait, lest the animals manage to intercept it. So all he could do was sit and fume until the shuttle entered orbit, where it was taken aboard the Thraki ship *Rift Runner*. The larger vessel got under way twenty minutes later. Once free of Algeron's gravity well and secure within his private cabin, Parth made the call. It took a couple of tries, and what seemed like an agonizing ten minutes passed before the War Ubatha appeared on the tiny screen. He raised a pincer to speak, but Parth cut him off. "Where are you?"

There was a slight lag followed by a burst of static. "On the planet Long Jump, sire."

"And the Warrior Queen? Is she there?"

"Yes, sire."

"Then why haven't you killed her?"

"We tried, sire. But the animals attacked just as we were about to break into the building where she had taken refuge."

"So, they have her?"

"Yes, sire. Or so it appears."

"Then kill all of them. And one more thing . . ."

"Sire?"

"Should you fail, be sure to kill yourself. There will be no place for you in the empire."

The image of Ubatha shivered. "Yes, sire. It shall be as you say."

16

Once the sword has been drawn, a cut must be made. For to show steel, and withhold it, is to signal weakness.

—*Haru Nira*
The Warrior
Standard year 289

PLANET LONG JUMP, THE CONFEDERACY OF SENTIENT BEINGS

The air inside the low, one-story building was warm and thick with the throat-clogging stench of death as Christine Vanderveen crawled across the floor on hands and knees. The heavy canteens thumped and bumped on both sides of her as empty shell casings skittered away from her knees. She paused, and her right hand came down on a patch of half-dried blood.

The facility, which was cradled within a U-shaped valley, was intended to function as a retreat for Dr. Tomko and a proving ground for his latest cyber forms. Now the formerly idyllic setting had been transformed into a war zone. Fortunately, Vanderveen had been able to prevent the Ramanthian hunter-killer team from entering the TOMKO complex during their first attack. But that hadn't prevented the bugs from launching a *second* assault eight hours later. Now there were only half a dozen of Dr. Tomko's people who could be classified as effectives plus an equal number of walking wounded to defend the complex when the time came. They were seated with their backs to the front wall, talking to each other in low tones, as Vanderveen eyed the section of sun-dappled floor that was marked by dozens of divots and splashes of blood. Because of the windows located just below the roofline at either end of the building, a six-foot-wide swath of duracrete was visible to the snipers positioned on the surrounding hillsides. They fired at anything that moved and had two kills to show for their efforts.

There was no science to it. Just luck, as Vanderveen summoned all of her courage and threw herself forward. The canteens flew all about her as she plunged through the hazy sunlight, and a distant *crack* was heard. The bullet missed by inches, bounced off the floor, and smacked into the ceiling.

Vanderveen landed hard, and all the air was knocked out of her lungs. Her legs were still in danger, but a pair of strong hands was there to pull her into the shade. "The trick is to slide," Cathy Kor said, once the diplomat was safe. "That was a belly flop."

Kor had been second-in-command of Dr. Tomko's security force before the bugs killed her boss. Now the square-faced merc was in charge. She had a buzz cut, green eyes, and a spray of freckles across her nose. A series of dashes were tattooed around her neck along with the words "cut here."

"I'll remember that," Vanderveen said, as she began to untangle the canteens and pass them out. "Anything new?"

"Nothing good," Kor said phlegmatically. "The bugs popped most of our spy cams. But they missed a couple, and Sparks tells me they're massing for another attack. Humans this time."

Vanderveen knew that Sparks was a skinny tech who had been in charge of the facility's electronic surveillance system back when there was one. He and two other men were holed up down in the basement, where they represented the last line of defense for the Queen and her staff. In case the bugs got inside. "Humans?" she inquired. "That's weird."

"Port scum, probably," Kor said disapprovingly. "There isn't much law on Long Jump. That's why Dr. Tomko hired us."

"Can we hold 'em off?"

Kor shrugged. "Maybe. But I doubt it."

Shattered glass lay everywhere and made a crunching sound as Vanderveen stood and turned to peek out a window. She jerked away as a bullet slapped the back wall. Where were the reinforcements she had requested? There was a war on, and the government was short of everything, but surely the Confederacy had some sort of resources in the area. Even a contingent of customs agents would be welcome if they could fight. "Uh-oh," Kor said ominously, as she looked over a windowsill. "Here they come."

Having checked to ensure that the Queen was safe, or as safe as she could be under the circumstances, Chancellor Itnor Ubatha shuffled past the animals assigned to protect her into the chamber beyond. Sparks was sitting in a chair, staring up at a bank of video monitors. One showed the scene on the floor above, where the mercs were beginning to fire at the oncoming attackers. And two provided shots of the grounds. The rest were black.

Having heard Ubatha's approach, Sparks spoke without turning to look at him. "Here comes another attack, sir. It looks like your friends hired a group of mercs."

"They aren't 'friends,'" Ubatha grated. "They're enemies. Mine as well as yours."

"Roger that," Sparks replied. "Look! One of them has a sword!"

Ubatha felt something cold grab onto his guts. "Zoom in on the soldier with the sword."

* * *

Sparks did so. The Ramanthian in question was standing near one of the holes that had been blown in the fence, waving the mercs through. "What's so special about him?" the tech inquired. There wasn't any answer. And when Sparks turned, Ubatha was gone.

As Vanderveen took a peek through the blown-out window, she saw dozens of tiny figures passing through the gaps where the security fence had been holed. "Kill them," she ordered grimly. "And remember . . . They won't take prisoners."

The comment was intended more for Kor's men than the officer herself. Because they were mercs. And like hired guns everywhere, they were bound to put themselves first. Fortunately, none of the men and women showed any signs of running as the snipers opened fire from the hills and the attackers swept forward. "*Aimed* fire," Kor said grimly. "We're starting to run low on ammo. Hey! Where's the bug going? He'll get his ass shot off."

As Vanderveen turned to her left, she saw that Chancellor Ubatha had exited through the hole where the front door had been. He was holding a pistol. And, judging from appearances, he was about to join the battle. She shouted, "No! Stop!" But it was too late.

Vanderveen grabbed one of the assault weapons that were leaning against the front wall and made for the front entrance. Not because Ubatha was a friend, but because he was an important link to the monarch and the only member of her retinue who had the capacity to stand up to her.

A bullet pinged off the door frame as she darted outside. The formerly pristine lawn was a mess. Kor's mercs were firing out through the windows. And Vanderveen knew there was a very real danger of being shot from behind. But it was too late to worry about that as one of the attackers opened up on Ubatha with a submachine gun. Geysers of dirt rose all around the Chancellor as he continued to plow his way forward, and Vanderveen dropped to one knee.

There wasn't enough time to use the scope. All Vanderveen could do was bring the rifle up and fire instinctively. One of her bullets struck the man with the SMG in the shoulder and turned him around. Another threw him down. Ubatha, seemingly unaware of the manner in which his life had been spared, continued to shuffle forward.

As bullets kicked up puffs of dust around him, the War Ubatha felt a terrible sense of shame. For to lead animals into battle was to *be* an animal. But such was the fate that the gods of war had allotted him. And the alternative was even worse. If he failed, the entire empire would be at risk. The War Ubatha's thoughts were interrupted by a series of overlapping sonic booms. All of the beings around him paused to look up at the sky. "Drop pods!" a noncom shouted. "Destroy them."

And the mercs tried. But there wasn't much point in doing so. The chutes used to slow the containers had already been released, and the containers hit the ground one after another. Plumes of gas jetted away from them as the pods began to open. "Now!" the War Ubatha shouted. "Attack them *now*. Before they can defend themselves."

What ensued was a horrible free-for-all. Each drop pod contained two legionnaires—a cyborg and a bio bod. Once on the ground, they were supposed to exit, come together, and prepare for combat. A process that should take less than sixty seconds. But while some of the containers landed in front of the Ramanthian-led force and some landed behind it, the rest came down practically on top of it. T-2s were struck by multiple rockets as they lurched out of their pods. And many bio bods fared even worse. They were shot while still strapped into their seats. But try as they might, the mercs couldn't kill *all* of the legionnaires, and it wasn't long before they were taking casualties as well.

The War Ubatha saw one of the containers hit fifty feet away, raised his sword, and charged. There was a flash followed by a loud *boom* as the pod took a direct hit. A panel blew off as the blackened vehicle toppled over onto its side. It appeared as if the cyborg was trapped in the wreckage. But a human rolled free and struggled to rise.

The War Ubatha had arrived on the scene by then. He raised the blade high, knowing that when it fell, the animal's head would roll free.

Chancellor Ubatha wasn't a very good shot. Nor did he need to be from only a dozen feet away. He looked down the barrel, squeezed the bulb-shaped handle, and felt the resulting recoil. The bullet struck the War Ubatha's right thigh, shattered his chitin, and dumped the warrior on the ground. Meanwhile, as the revengeful T-2s and their riders made use of their superior firepower to cut the mercs down, the tide of battle began to turn. In fact, the battle was nearly over as the legionnaire whom the War Ubatha had been so determined to behead raised his carbine. "No," Vanderveen ordered as she stepped in. "Hold your fire. That's an order." The soldier complied.

The War Ubatha still had his sword and was trying to lift it when a second bullet shattered his arm. *"Now,"* Chancellor Ubatha said, as he stood over his fallen mate. "Now you will pay. There is only one way you could have followed us here. And that is with information obtained from the Egg Ubatha. Information you would have had to force out of her. Is she still alive?

"Answer me," Chancellor Ubatha demanded as he placed a foot on his mate's chest. "Did you kill our mate?"

The War Ubatha had been wounded before. But never so badly. And the pain was intense. He could hear the other Ubatha. But the words sounded as if they were coming from a place a million miles away. "We are at war," he answered. "Each must do his or her part. I asked, and she refused. Sacrifices must be made. That is the way of the warrior."

Chancellor Ubatha made a strange, choking sound. He fired again and again until the pistol was empty—and the War Ubatha was nothing more than a bullet-riddled corpse. Then, having thrown the pistol down, he turned away. Vanderveen looked at the legionnaire as a T-2 fought its way clear of the wreckage. "Follow him. Keep him safe."

The legionnaire's face had been hidden behind his visor until that point. But as he removed his helmet, she saw something remarkable. "Tony? Is that *you*?"

Santana smiled. "Sorry we took so long. But we were on a transport en route to Adobe when orders came in to divert. They said a diplomat was in trouble. I should have known."

Vanderveen's eyes were full of emotion. "Yes," she replied joyfully. "You should have known."

PLANET ALGERON, THE CONFEDERACY OF SENTIENT BEINGS

Days were short, so timing was critical; as the sun rose in the east, the shuttle temporarily designated as *RAM 1* settled onto the VIP pad at Fort Camerone, and a contingent of Naa blew the spiral-shaped horns that had traditionally been used to announce the arrival of an important chief. A large group of dignitaries, including President Nankool, Secretary of State

Yatsu, and Military Chief of Staff Bill Booly, were on hand to greet those aboard the incoming ship.

Intersol vid anchor Danny Occuro was stationed on the ramparts above the landing pad. One of the news network's flying cameras was focused on him. The rest were providing the director with shots of the scene below. Occuro felt nervous and for good reason. He had been chosen over many others to provide pooled coverage of the most important news story since the destruction of the *Friendship* and the beginning of the war with the Ramanthians. It was a weighty responsibility and one that would put his name in the history books. Because, assuming that what he'd been told was true, the Warrior Queen had survived her injuries by becoming a cyborg. And pictures of her new body were about to be sent throughout the Confederacy for the first time.

As the shuttle's skids made contact with the repeller-scorched tarmac and the engines spooled down, it was time to begin his narration. "This is Danny Occuro, reporting live from the planet Algeron, with breaking news. I am referring to the arrival of the Ramanthian monarch, often referred to as the Warrior Queen, who, having been injured on Earth, had reportedly died of her wounds. In fact, it was only a little more than a month ago that the Ramanthians held a state funeral for her and chose a new Queen to replace her.

"But according to highly placed government sources, the Warrior Queen was actually on the run, hiding from a team of Ramanthian assassins. That suggests that the present Queen is little more than a pretender, a tool placed on the throne by a cabal of senior officials, all of whom want to run the government themselves. I'll have more on that as additional information becomes available."

The picture dissolved to a shot of the landing pad. "The hatch is opening now, and President Nankool is going out to meet the monarch, even as a formal twenty-one-gun salute can be heard in the background. That's an honor reserved for the president and visiting heads of state. A sure sign that the Confederacy plans to recognize the Warrior Queen as the legitimate leader of the Ramanthian people. Doing so would open up the possibility of a truce although there aren't any assurances that the present Queen would agree to step down."

As the director took a wide shot and the camera zoomed in, Occuro described what he saw. "This is it, gentle beings . . . Our first look at the Queen's new human-designed body. It's our understanding that this is one of three vehicles the monarch can wear, each of which offers certain advantages."

At that point, a split-screen comparison appeared showing file footage of the Queen right next to the live feed. What the audience saw was a richly dressed Ramanthian who had already exchanged formal bows with the president and was making her way along the reception line. A small coterie of staff members followed behind. Two were human although Occuro had no idea who they were. "However," he said, as the split screen disappeared, "even though the Queen's body *looks* normal, I have it on good authority that the design incorporates bullet-resistant materials as well as communications gear that is consistent with both Confederacy and Ramanthian protocols. That, too, seems to suggest some sort of diplomatic accommodation is in the works or has already been agreed to.

"I suggest that you remember this moment. There are all sorts of uncertainties, not the least of which is how the Ramanthian people will respond to the sudden resurrection of their once-popular leader. But it's possible that we are witnessing a pivotal moment in history."

Never, in all of her twenty-seven years, had the Warrior Queen been in the presence of so many animals. Their ugly faces surrounded her. Harsh voices assailed her ears. And the putrid stench of their filthy flesh made her want to vomit. Except that she couldn't vomit. Not anymore. Because her electromechanical body had no need to consume food or get rid of it.

It was an amazing vehicle, with which she had developed an almost immediate love-hate relationship. Love because of the way in which it had freed her from the metal rack, and hate because she was an incomprehensible monster now. All of which was made more painful by the knowledge that without the aid of the disgusting creatures around her, she would already be dead. Murdered by members of her own race. That fact and more swirled through her mind as the last introduction was completed, and President Nankool escorted her into the fort.

Airborne cameras were everywhere. They zipped, darted, and even rolled along the floor as the animals sought to capture every moment of her shame. But the publicity was necessary. The Warrior Queen knew that. Parth and his cabal would try to block the incoming broadcasts. But the soon-to-be-reinvigorated denialists would find a way to make the truth known. Bootleg copies of the broadcast would be made and secretly distributed to all of the empire's planets.

Parth and his cronies would declare them to be propaganda and insist that the creature seen meeting with the animals was a robot rather than a cyborg. And what else *could* the traitors say? Since they had declared her dead?

So, in the end, it would come down to what she said, how she said it, and testimonials from the expat experts that Chancellor Ubatha was going to bring in. In the meantime, the royal would do what she had been taught to do since birth. And that was to play her part to perfection.

Vanderveen and Santana had been relegated to the very end of the processional, and the diplomat was happy to be there. Having successfully defended the monarch from assassins and negotiated an interim agreement with the royal, it was a relief to hand her charge off to more-senior officials. That plus the fact that Santana was walking along next to her combined to put Vanderveen in a very good mood. So when the president, the Queen, and the rest of the party entered a conference room and left her outside, she was thrilled. "We're going to have dinner with my father," Vanderveen said, as she turned to Santana. "If you don't mind, that is."

"I would love to have dinner with your father," Santana said. "I haven't seen him since the day I left Algeron for Jericho. He came out to see me off. He was very worried about you."

"He's still struggling with my mother's death," Vanderveen replied. "Let's see if we can cheer him up."

Santana nodded. "And then?"

Vanderveen put her hands in his. "Then we'll have some time to ourselves."

Santana smiled. "*That* sounds good. Very, very good."

For the first time in many months, President Marcott Nankool had reason to hope. His decision to back the Warrior Queen rather than accept Parth's offer looked as if it might pay off. Assuming that he and his staff could convince the frequently cantankerous monarch to do all the right things. And that would be no small feat because, in spite of the words that came out of her beak, it didn't take an empath to detect the underlying contempt she felt for all humans, including him.

They were seated around a circular table. It was the same one that had been used during the meeting with Parth. Even Christine Vanderveen's detractors had to agree that the high-level verbal agreements she had negotiated with the Ramanthian royal were quite solid. The most important of them was that the Confederacy would help restore the Warrior Queen to her throne in return for "a reset to prewar conditions."

If implemented, the agreement would force the bugs to surrender all the worlds they had captured, with the possible exception of certain nursery planets. And the Confederacy would do likewise. The exact wording of the agreement would have to be hammered out. But there wasn't much doubt as to the outcome since the Confederacy was in the driver's seat.

No, the problem was a difference of opinion regarding *how* to begin the upcoming PR offensive and *where* to do so. This was why Chien-Chu was making the Confederacy's case for the second time. "With all due respect, Your Highness," he said patiently, "Earth is the perfect place to launch your campaign because it's the human home world. And in order to succeed, we need buy-in from our citizens. That will require some effort since nearly all of them blame you for starting the war.

"Yes," Chien-Chu said, as Chancellor Ubatha opened his beak to speak, "I know . . . The *previous* Queen, sometimes referred to as the great mother, set events in motion prior to her death. But perceptions are important. And Earth is the place where you were wounded, thereby cementing your unofficial title of Warrior Queen and earning you a permanent place in the hearts of all Ramanthians. By going there to make your first speech, you will evoke strong emotions on both sides. Although they may have reservations, most humans will rejoice over the prospect that their home world will be freed. Meanwhile, those Ramanthians who have grown tired of the war and understand the strategic realities, will realize that a reset represents a good outcome given what could occur otherwise."

Nankool couldn't read the Queen's nonverbals but suspected that she wasn't used to much, if any, push back. So when she spoke, he was interested to see what she would say. "I continue to have reservations," the royal replied. "The planet Trevia would be a better choice in my mind. A great many Ramanthian expats live there, a significant number of whom would welcome my return. But I place a great deal of trust in Chancellor Ubatha and his opinion."

All eyes went to the Ramanthian official, and although Nankool fully expected him to echo the Queen's opinion, he was in for a pleasant surprise. "Thank you, Highness," Ubatha said. "I believe Earth would be a good location for all of the reasons Admiral Chien-Chu put forward plus one more. Assuming that the Confederacy can put you on the surface and provide sufficient security, the visit will not only highlight the physical courage that you're known for, but the cabal's dishonesty as well. Because Parth and his cronies have lied to our citizens about conditions on Earth. And your presence there will make that clear."

Perhaps it *was* Ubatha's vision. Or maybe his comments gave the Queen a chance to save face. But whatever the reason, she agreed. "We will assign a senior diplomat to travel with you," Yatsu declared. "And General Booly will arrange for security."

"Thank you," the Queen replied. "But I would like to retain Consul Vanderveen's services—and those of Major Santana as well. I wouldn't be here today if it weren't for them."

"Of course," Nankool replied, before anyone could object. "Consider it done."

The top of the windswept pinnacle was lost in darkness until the private air car swooped in to hover above it, and a pair of powerful floodlights came on. They served to illuminate part of the ancient ruins that covered the top of the plateau and threw hard shadows toward the east. As the aircraft lowered itself onto the ground, the pool of light shrank. "You're sure about this?" Santana inquired, as the skids touched down. "We could stay somewhere warm."

"Oh, it'll be *warm*," Vanderveen promised. "And private.

As you know, Fort Camerone is like a small town. Everybody knows everything about everyone else."

"Maylo Chien-Chu knows," Santana pointed out, as the single crewman tossed a large duffel bag out onto the rocky ground. "This is her air car."

"That's true," Vanderveen agreed. "But she can keep a secret."

"Then so be it," Santana said, as he jumped to the ground. "I'm looking forward to our first camping trip."

Vanderveen dropped into his waiting arms, *another* duffel bag hit the ground, and the crewman waved good-bye. The engine screamed, and the pool of light began to expand as the air car took off. It snapped out of existence a few seconds later. "Two days," Vanderveen said. "I'm going to have you to myself for two whole days. Then it's off to visit Earth."

"If we don't freeze to death first," Santana cautioned. "Come on . . . Let's find a place to hole up." And find it they did. There were a number of underground dwellings to choose from, all excavated by the Naa hundreds of years earlier.

Having inspected half a dozen possibilities, Santana and Vanderveen settled on a snug chamber accessed via a spiral stairway carved out of solid rock. They didn't have any dried dooth dung to use as fuel, but thanks to a friendly supply sergeant, Santana had something better—a quantity of military F-1. A single block would provide a hot fire for six hours. So it wasn't long before firelight began to dance on the walls, a pleasant warmth suffused the room, and the odor of cooking filled the air. "Our relationship could end right here," Vanderveen said, as she dropped the final ingredients into a pot. "In spite of having servants most of her life, my mother was an excellent cook and tried to pass her skills along to me. But I never paid much attention."

"If memory serves me correctly, you have other talents,

however," Santana said, as she stood and entered the circle of his arms. Her lips seemed to melt beneath his, the clean smell of her filled his nostrils, and the kiss lasted for a long time. Eventually, she pushed him away.

"No dessert until you finish your dinner," she said sternly. "No matter how horrible it may taste."

The stew was surprisingly good. And as Santana ate, sitting with Vanderveen only two feet away, he couldn't remember a time when he'd been so happy. But that was bad in a way because the war was far from over, and Vanderveen would go wherever her duties took her, including war zones like Earth. He couldn't imagine anything worse than to find something so precious only to have it snatched away. He was thinking about Charles and Margaret Vanderveen when their daughter turned to look at him. "You're awfully quiet."

"I was thinking."

"About what?"

Santana looked at the fire, then back again. "I love you."

Vanderveen smiled gently. "Yes, I know. And I love you."

The fire hissed, shadows were joined, and time seemed to stop.

PLANET EARTH, THE RAMANTHIAN EMPIRE

The battle began moments after the Confederacy cruiser *Cygnus* and her escorts popped out of hyperspace. That was to be expected since elements of the Ramanthian fleet had been in orbit around Earth since the invasion months earlier. But, thanks to a diversionary attack on bug-occupied Mars, half the Ramanthian ships normally assigned to the human home world were a hundred million miles away when the *Cygy* arrived. And that plus the element of surprise gave Admiral Kurtz the advantage she needed.

The ensuing action was brief but violent and resulted in the destruction of twelve Ramanthian vessels, which was probably very painful for the Warrior Queen. Although Santana couldn't detect any expression on her carefully molded face as the assault boat designated *RAM 1* departed the cruiser's brightly lit hangar bay for the blackness of space.

The Queen's assault boat had an escort comprised of twenty-one Dagger 190s, all of which were under strict orders to defend *RAM 1* regardless of the cost. Once on the ground, it would become Santana's job to protect the Warrior Queen from both humans *and* Ramanthians, a task he was determined to carry out because it was his duty to do so and because Christine was part of the royal's retinue. She was seated a few feet away from the Queen. Christine's eyes met his, and she smiled.

The assault boat shuddered as it entered the atmosphere, and the pilot's voice came over the intercom. "Our formation is under attack, but our escorts are keeping the enemy at a distance. We should be on the ground in about ten minutes." A *click* served to punctuate the paragraph.

Santana knew that Commander Foley's resistance fighters were supposed to provide most of the security while his team served as the ultimate backup. And while that was fine in theory, the officer knew that Foley's patriots were the very people most likely to try to assassinate the Queen. Which meant it would be foolish to let anyone other than members of his own team get close.

They were a piratical-looking platoon, led by second-in-command Lieutenant Bushnell, Dietrich, and two reliable sergeants. There were eighteen legionnaires in all, not counting himself, all of whom were combat veterans and had been carefully screened. It wasn't a large force compared to what Santana could have requested, but he feared that a full company would be *too* large and might get in its own way.

And, making the situation even more interesting, there was the fact that General Booly had given him orders to kill the Queen if she tried to make unauthorized contact with Ramanthian forces or if it appeared that she might fall into the wrong hands. Or pincers, as the case might be.

Santana's thoughts were interrupted as the ship banked, circled, and came in for a landing. "We'll be on the ground in a minute or so," the pilot announced. "Please remain in your seats until the green light comes on."

There was a solid *thump* as the assault boat put down. The green light came on, and the stern hatch cycled open. That was the cue for Santana and his platoon to exit the transport and take up defensive positions all around. It quickly became clear that Lieutenant Bushnell knew what he was doing. That gave Santana time to examine his surroundings.

The first thing he noticed was that the assault boat was sitting on a rise near the center of the vast wreckage-strewn crater that had been Los Angeles. The ship was surrounded by a company of ragged resistance fighters. They were dressed in whatever bits and pieces of military gear they had been able to pull together, and all of them were facing outward. Just as they should be in order to defend the Queen.

To the west, beyond the resistance fighters, the blackened remains of what had once been a sizable starship could be seen. "You're looking at the *Hive Defender*," a male voice said. "It was at the center of a large base. We went after it, and the bugs drove us off, but only after we inflicted a lot of damage. In spite of repeated attempts, they haven't been able to reconstitute what they had. My name's Foley. Commander Foley. And I'm guessing that you're Major Santana."

The naval officer was so lean that he looked more like an animated skeleton than a man. And although his voice was friendly, his eyes were like dark pools. It was a look Santana had seen before, both on the battlefield and in hospitals later on. Foley had seen too much, made too many life-and-death decisions, and would never be the same again. "Yes," Santana replied. "It's a pleasure to meet you. And congratulations on your victory. Taking that ship down is an amazing accomplishment."

"It cost a lot of lives," Foley said bleakly. "But the *Hive Defender* will provide the perfect backdrop for the Queen's speech. The wreckage will send a message to humans and Ramanthians alike."

The Queen and her party were filing out of the ship by then and being herded into position by an overly officious Public Relations (PR) officer. Danny Occuro was present as well. Three airborne vid cams bobbed around him. "Speaking of the Ramanthians," Santana said, "where are they?"

"About five miles away," Foley answered casually. "We spent the last two days clearing the landing zone, and I lost five people doing it."

"So when will they counterattack?"

Foley shrugged. "Who knows? Our efforts to employ biological warfare against them have been very successful. So there are a lot less of them than there used to be. If we're lucky, they won't respond until the Queen is back in orbit. And the fact that we have a significant amount of air cover should slow them down."

As if to illustrate Foley's point, there was a loud roar as three Daggers passed overhead. They fired rockets at an unseen target, and smoke billowed up into the sky. That was when Vanderveen arrived on the scene. "Commander Foley? I'd like to introduce myself. My name is Christine Vanderveen."

Foley looked surprised as he shook her hand. "It's a pleasure to meet you, ma'am. Your mother was a very extraordinary woman. And a brave one. I was telling the major how successful our biological warfare campaign has been. That's thanks to Margaret and the team she assembled. The Confederacy owes her a deep debt of gratitude."

Vanderveen was about to reply when the PR officer began to bellow instructions over his megaphone, and the diplomat was forced to rejoin the Queen's party. The message had been agreed to in advance, but it was her job to make sure that the royal stuck to it.

As Foley issued orders to his troops via a handheld radio, Santana made the rounds and was pleased to see that all of the T-2s and their riders were properly placed. And thanks to the open area all around, the enemy would have very little cover if they tried to attack over the ground. Having assured himself that everything was as it should be, he paused to listen as the broadcast began.

"I am standing on the planet Earth," the Queen said, "at the center of what was the city of Los Angeles. A battle was fought here in the recent past. It was a symbolic battle in the sense that while our brave troops won, the human resistance fighters did a great deal of damage to our base, and we've been unable to rebuild it.

"Why *is* that?" the Queen demanded, as her dark eyes stared into the camera. "It's because the pretender who sits on the throne and the cabal who placed her there are incompetent and don't know how to lead.

"Worse yet is the fact that thousands of the troops serving on Earth are suffering from a life-threatening and highly communicable disease. That means they are essentially trapped here since the cabal is afraid to bring them home, where they could infect the general population. You didn't know that, did you? Well, there are a great many things the cabal wants to hide from you, including the fact that I am still alive."

That was when a transmission came in over Santana's headset. "This is Blue Leader . . . There is a Ramanthian combat assault platform (CAP) coming your way. It was submerged off Malibu and surfaced about a minute ago. It's *huge.* Over."

Santana swore. The warships orbiting high above were supposed to protect the ground party from that sort of surprise—but they had no way to see down through the water. Nor had he been aware that the enemy CAPs were capable of submerging themselves. It made sense, though, since they were probably designed to function on water worlds when necessary. "Roger that . . . Slow it down if you can. We'll wrap up and pull out as quickly as we can. Over."

Santana heard two *click*s by way of a reply and turned to Foley, who was standing a few feet away. "Tell your people to stand by. A CAP is headed our way. And we won't be able to stop it. Not without firing on it from space. And that could result in a lot of collateral damage."

Foley's eyebrows rose slightly, but that was all. "Where was it?"

"Underwater. Off Malibu."

Foley shook his head in amazement. "So that's where they hid it. Every night they brought the blasted thing out and attacked anything that had a heat signature. Then, come dawn, it disappeared. Now we know."

"Yeah," Santana said, "I guess we do. The Daggers will attempt to delay it. I'll notify the PR officer. We're pulling out."

"Sounds good," Foley replied casually. "You do that."

The Queen was still talking as Santana approached Vanderveen. She was standing next to the PR officer and Bushnell. "Tell the Queen that it's time to leave. What amounts to a flying fortress will arrive here in a few minutes."

Vanderveen looked worried. "I'll pass the message through Chancellor Ubatha."

"But the Queen hasn't finished yet!" the PR officer objected.

He had a red face, a carefully trimmed mustache, and a very nonmilitary paunch.

"She'll get killed if we don't pull her out of here," Santana countered. "Tell her. I want everyone on the assault boat two minutes from now. Lieutenant Bushnell, please prepare to withdraw."

"Look at that!" Bushnell said, and pointed toward the northwest. The combat assault platform was the size of a skyscraper turned on its side. It was heavily armed and could launch aerospace fighters, which were already climbing up to do battle with the Daggers. Something about the fact that the monster was only two hundred feet off the ground and traveling at a mere twenty miles per hour made the ship all the more frightening. There was a flash of light and a loud report as one of its main batteries fired. What sounded like a freight train roared overhead. Half a second later, the ground shook as a column of soil shot up into the air a thousand yards east of the boat. Fortunately, Vanderveen, Ubatha, and the Queen were halfway up the ramp by then. And the assault boat's engines were beginning to spool up.

It was then, as the air surrounding the Ramanthian vessel shimmered and electrical discharges crackled all around the ship, that something completely unexpected occurred. Carefully camouflaged missiles produced what sounded like a combined roar as they shot almost straight up, struck the assault platform in quick succession, and exploded.

The combined impacts proved to be too much for the ship's defensive screens, and at least one of them was able to punch a hole in the CAP's belly. The resulting explosion was not only deafening but produced a shock wave that could be felt miles away. The ship's stern hit the ground first, soon followed by the bow, which crushed what was left of a hotel. A cloud of dust billowed up to conceal the vessel's final death throes.

It took Santana a moment to absorb what had taken place and figure out why. That was when he turned to Foley. The resistance leader had a big grin on his face. "Nice, huh? The bugs never knew what hit them."

"Why you rotten bastard," Santana replied. "You knew where the CAP was hiding all along! And you used both the Queen and the rest of us as bait."

The grin vanished from Foley's face. "Welcome to *my* world, Major . . . Or what's left of it. And give this message to the Queen. If she ever puts a foot on this planet again, I will personally blow her fucking head off."

And with that, Foley walked away. The dust cloud had cleared a bit, and bright flashes could be seen as what sounded like thunder rolled, and a series of secondary explosions destroyed what remained of the CAP. The royal visit was over.

17

The gods favor the bold.

—*Ovid*
Metamorphoses
Standard year A.D. *5*

ABOARD THE CONFEDERACY BATTLESHIP *EARTH AVENGER*
NEAR PLANET HIVE, THE RAMANTHIAN EMPIRE

The battle began as a hole opened in space and two dozen computer-controlled asteroids came shooting out of the void. They were equipped with hyperdrives as well as in-system propulsion systems. And if one of them managed to hit Hive, a tremendous amount of damage would be done.

That wouldn't happen, of course, because the bugs had been attacked before and were prepared for such an eventuality. But ready or not, they would still have to use a significant portion of their defensive capability to destroy the incoming rocks, and that was part of General Booly's plan.

Then, once the asteroids arrived in-system, another hole opened, and thirty-six Vulcan missiles accelerated out of the inky blackness. Like the asteroids, they were computer-controlled, but the similarity ended there. Each Vulcan was equipped to detect and zero in on Class A targets.

It was assumed that most, if not all, of the Vulcans would be intercepted. But the Ramanthians would be forced to choose between the asteroids and missiles, which might or might not be armed with nuclear warheads. Did the bugs have enough warships and orbital battle stations to block the incoming swarm? Maybe. But as Booly sat above and behind the *Earth Avenger*'s bridge, and imagined how the battle would unfold, he felt reasonably sure that *something* would get through.

Of course, the real point of the exercise was to suck up as much of the enemy's defensive capabilities as possible—thereby clearing the way for the fleet of 275 Confederacy warships that would arrive minutes later. Their task, in turn, was to bore in and clear a path for the ground troops that were to land on Hive. The final objective was to return the Warrior Queen to the throne and effectively end the war.

Booly turned to look at the Queen. No matter what the outcome, hundreds of thousands of Ramanthians were going to die. How did she feel about that prospect? he wondered. Sad? Perhaps. But not sad enough to call the invasion off.

More than two standard months had passed since the broadcast from Earth. And a great deal had occurred during that time. A series of speeches had been made, and according to reports from inside the empire, the anticabal messages were beginning to gain traction. There had been demonstrations in large cities, followed by scattered acts of sabotage, and three cases of well-publicized self-immolation. And the cabal reacted to the protests just as Booly thought they would—which was with poorly-thought-out mass reprisals that brought even more Ramanthians over to the denialist cause. Thereby feeding the unrest.

Meanwhile, hundreds of ships were being completed deep inside Hegemony-controlled space even as more than five million clone soldiers came under the Confederacy's control, along with a quarter million Hudathans. All eager for revenge.

But the Confederacy was *still* outnumbered. And for that reason there were many in the Senate who favored waiting for a few months before attacking Hive. Fortunately, Booly, Chien-Chu, and others had been able to convince a majority to support an immediate attack because political support would be critical. Especially if the attempt failed.

The battleship's primary Command & Control (C&C) computer was generally referred to as "the Preacher" because of its deep, melodious voice and a perpetual desire to tell everyone what to do. "The ship will drop hyper in three minutes," the Preacher intoned as the final seconds ticked away. "Secure all gear, check space armor, and strap in. Primary weapons systems, secondary weapons systems, and tertiary weapons systems have been armed. All fighter aircraft are prepared for immediate launch. I repeat . . ."

The Preacher's spiel became a meaningless drone as Booly fought a battle within himself. The attack was the right thing to do. He felt certain of it. Then why did he feel a sense of impending doom? Maybe it was the Naa blood that coursed through his veins or the fact that he was older now. His thoughts turned to Maylo, the fear in her eyes when they had said good-bye, and the sweet taste of her lips. *This is the last one,* he promised himself, *then I'll retire.*

Booly's thoughts were interrupted as the Preacher spoke again. "Stand by for normal space." The bridge crew, including Captain Jonathan Alan Seebo 514,234, were seated in what was generally referred to as "the tub." Meaning a U-shaped enclosure located half a level below the observation deck on which Booly, the Queen, and various staff members were seated. Or, in the royal's case, strapped to the deck since the body she had chosen for the occasion was far too large for a Ramanthian-style saddle chair.

Then the waiting was over as Booly's stomach lurched, the

NAVCOMP shut the hyperdrive down, and a starscape appeared on the curvilinear screen above and in front of the tub. It was meaningless, really, since the ships that were vectoring in on them were too small to see and wouldn't become visible to the naked eye unless they attempted to ram the *Avenger.*

No, the real action could be seen in the holo tank directly in front of the captain, where red and blue symbols had already begun to clash. But it was difficult to make out the details of what was taking place, so Booly took advantage of his rank to release his harness and make his way over to the so-called admiral's pulpit, located above and behind the command chair. From there he could look down into the tank and hear the orders that were given. He could also access the ship's command channel if necessary, but he didn't plan to do so, knowing that it would make the crew self-conscious.

Most of the conversation between Captain 234 and the crew was professionally matter-of-fact. But they were people and people have emotions. So a mutual groan was heard as the blue box that represented the carrier *Iridian* winked out of existence. The battle had only been under way for a minute and a half, yet 3,467 allied personnel were dead. Booly felt an almost overwhelming sense of sorrow, but he knew that even though he bore responsibility for the deaths, generals weren't allowed to cry.

PLANET HIVE, THE RAMANTHIAN EMPIRE

Chancellor Parth was deep within the warm embrace of a sand bath when his majordomo entered the room to inform him that multiple flights of computer controlled asteroids and enemy missiles had entered the solar system via hyperspace. And worse yet, an entire fleet of warships was headed toward

Hive, preceded by thousands of robotic drones, all of which were transmitting a message from someone or something that claimed to be the Warrior Queen. In spite of the warm sand that was vibrating against his chitin, Parth felt something cold enter his bloodstream. "Show me," he ordered.

The majordomo aimed a remote at the wall screen, and video blossomed. What Parth saw was both unexpected and frightening. Because there was a picture of the legendary Kathong standing on what appeared to be the Plain of Pain but probably wasn't. The monster was at least three times the size of a normal Ramanthian and equipped with four arms rather than two.

"Hear me," the monster demanded, "or suffer my wrath. For I am the *real* Queen, the Warrior Queen, and this is but one of my bodies. Can you hear the thunder? Look to the skies. I am on the way. Those who hunger for my return have nothing to fear. Those who are corrupt, or feed off corruption, should prepare to die."

There was a sudden eruption of sand as Parth came up out of the bath and accepted a robe. "Get Admiral Stik on the com. And do so quickly."

The servant was expressionless as always. "Yes, Excellency."

"And one more thing," Parth added. "It may be necessary to evacuate the Queen to Hive Home. Notify the commander of the Imperial Guard and tell him to make all the necessary preparations."

"Yes, sire," the majordomo replied. "It shall be as you say."

ABOARD THE RAMANTHIAN BATTLE CRUISER
***NEW EMPIRE* OFF PLANET HIVE**

Rather than concentrate most of a ship's critical personnel in one place the way the humans did, Ramanthian naval architects preferred to distribute them throughout their vessels. For that reason, the battle cruiser *New Empire*'s control room was relatively small. *Too* small in Grand Admiral Stik's opinion as he shuffled back and forth between two bulkheads as a way to relieve the tension he felt. It had always been his dream to command the Ramanthian navy. But as hundreds of enemy ships poured out of hyperspace and he waited for Chancellor Parth's visage to appear on the com screen, Stik wished his predecessor was still in charge.

But like so many other members of the Warrior Queen's administration, Grand Admiral Imba had been forced into retirement and was said to be raising grubs on his country estate. *The eggless bastard.* Stik's thoughts were interrupted as a com tech spoke. "Chancellor Parth is on-screen, sir."

Stik turned and made his way over to the com station even as a steady flow of reports came in from the ship's command center. "Most of Battle Group 12 has been neutralized. Repeat, Battle Group 12 is presumed lost. Battle Group 3 is under pressure but continues to hold, and reports that one enemy carrier has been destroyed."

As Stik eyed Parth's face, he could tell that the civilian was angry. And, judging from the set of his antenna, scared as well. "Yes, Excellency . . . What can I do for you?"

"That's a stupid question," Parth replied caustically. "You can kill all of the animals before they land on Hive. That's what you can do."

Stik sighed. Civilians, especially *senior* civilians, could be rather thick at times. And the fact that both of them were members of the cabal did nothing to change that. "I'm sorry to say that won't be possible, Excellency."

Parth was visibly shocked. "You're serious? You believe the animals will seize control of Hive?"

"No," Stik replied patiently. "I didn't say that. I said that we won't be able to prevent them from landing. As you know, it has been necessary to weaken the home fleet in order to prosecute the war. That, plus the number of incoming ships, means that the animals will probably succeed in putting some troops on the ground. But General Amm and his forces will be waiting for them. So there's little if anything to fear."

"Good," Parth replied stolidly. "But, just in case, I think it would be prudent to evacuate the Queen to Hive Home. I will accompany her to make sure that the government remains up and running smoothly."

Of course, you sniveling coward, Stik thought to himself. *Hide behind the Queen.* But there was no point in stating the obvious or placing his career in jeopardy. "Understood, Excellency."

"Kill them," Parth said unnecessarily. "Kill all of them." Then the screen snapped to black.

The *New Empire* shook like a thing possessed, and Stik very nearly lost his footing as a symphony of Klaxons began to sound. "Torpedoes!" a voice declared. "Dozens of them. The screens are falling. Quick! We need to . . ."

But the officer never got to finish his sentence. Because that was the moment when a missile hit the ship; a jet of plasma burrowed through hull metal and found one of the ship's magazines. The *New Empire* ceased to exist.

ABOARD THE CONFEDERACY BATTLESHIP *EARTH AVENGER*
OFF PLANET HIVE

Ever since the moment that *Earth Avenger* left hyperspace, the destroyer escort (DE) *Fury* and a squadron of twelve Dag 190s had been sitting in the battleship's launch bay waiting for orders to depart. And now that the capital ship and her escorts had successfully fought their way through wave after wave of nearly suicidal defenders, the time was at hand. The evolution had to be carried out with considerable care, however, because it was necessary for the *Avenger* to drop her shields momentarily to retrieve or launch smaller vessels. And that would open the battleship to attack.

So even though Booly, the Queen, and her retinue had boarded the DE and were strapped in ready to go, they had to wait for the right moment before the *Fury* could take off. Finally, after what seemed like an eternity, the warship rose on her repellers and followed three Daggers out into the cold blackness of space. The rest of the escorts took up positions all around to protect the ship from enemy fighters.

The little vessel was a good choice for the mission at hand, or so it seemed to Santana. Though small, it packed a lot of firepower for its size and was very maneuverable. That virtue paid immediate dividends as four Chak fighters bored in, the Daggers took them on, and the *Fury*'s captain sent her ship corkscrewing through the fray.

The baby-faced lieutenant was no more than twenty-one or twenty-two years old, but, thanks to all the casualties the Confederacy had suffered, she was already in command of her own ship. And had clearly performed well in the past given how important her cargo was. "Hang on," the officer said via the ship's PA system as something hit the screens and the *Fury* shuddered. "I have Landing Force Alpha on visual."

Santana knew the officer was referring to one of three globe-shaped formations. Each landing force was comprised of heavily armored gunboats, transports, and hundreds of assault craft. All were important, but none more so than Force Alpha, which was to include the ship carrying both Booly and the Warrior Queen. Her scorpion-like Kathong body was strapped to the center of the cargo deck. Vanderveen was seated on the other side of the compartment from Santana and appeared to be in deep conversation with Chancellor Ubatha.

Dietrich was slouched a few feet away and, based on appearances, was taking a nap. In addition to his other duties, the noncom had agreed to watch over Vanderveen on the battlefield. Santana knew she would be furious if she found out about the arrangement but didn't care so long as she survived.

Farther back, with his helmet on the seat next to him, General Booly sat staring into space. What was he thinking? There was no way to know. Some senior officers were as transparent as glass. But not this one. He was competent though. Very much so. And having suffered under General-453's incompetent leadership on Gamma-014, Santana was thankful for Booly's presence.

"We're in," the captain announced, as the *Fury* took her place at the center of Landing Force Alpha's globe-shaped formation. "And I just received word that the Hudathan Pathfinders were able to board and take control of Battle Platform 5."

A reedy cheer went up. Everyone knew that at least one of the enemy's orbital battle stations would have to be captured or destroyed before Landing Force Alpha could enter Hive's atmosphere. Now, thanks to the Hudathans, there was a large hole in the Ramanthians' multilayered defense system. That would allow the globe-shaped formation to morph into a beelike swarm that would pour through the gap and battle its way down to the planet's surface. "Here we go," the captain announced, and the *Fury* began to buck as she entered the atmosphere.

ON THE SURFACE OF PLANET HIVE, THE RAMANTHIAN EMPIRE

As Chancellor Parth's ground car plowed its way through the mob of citizens hurrying to leave the city for the countryside beyond, the sound of overlapping sonic booms rolled across the land, and white contrails clawed the otherwise-pristine sky. "Damn them!" the Chancellor said feelingly, as the car's wheels bumped over what might have been a body. "Damn them to all of the hells."

It wasn't clear who the official was referring to. The refugees? The denialists who were urging them to flee? Or the animals who, in spite of their well-known inferiority, were about to land? The driver didn't know. Fortunately, the Egg Haka was already out in the country near the small town where they had been hatched. As for the War Haka, he was off-planet somewhere, serving in the *Death Hammer* Regiment. A source of pride for the entire family.

Thanks to occasional blips of sound from a hidden siren, plus the flashing lights behind the car's grille, the driver was able to force a path to a downward-sloping ramp, where two soldiers were stationed. A sure sign that the panic hadn't infected the military.

The troopers came to attention as the government car rolled past them. Then, as the driver steered the heavy vehicle down into the maze of subsurface passageways where most of the city dwellers lived, it was like a return to sanity.

Because of a strong military and police presence, those citizens who wanted to leave had to do so via spiraling pedestrian ramps rather than the streets. That allowed the driver to make better time, and it was only a matter of a few minutes before he passed through a checkpoint and entered the spacious garage that was located beneath the Queen's official residence.

Three armored cars and a contingent of brightly armored Imperial Guards were gathered around the entrance. That was a sure sign that the royal was waiting within. The driver brought the car to a smooth stop—and was surprised when Parth opened the door himself. *Perhaps,* Haka thought to himself, *we're in more trouble than I thought.*

* * *

Parth shuffled into the lobby, saw that the Queen was dressed in the same armor that was standard for her guards, and instinctively understood what she hoped to accomplish. Even if she couldn't be the Warrior Queen, she could *look* warlike, and that would be good for morale. Parth's respect for her went up a notch as she spoke. "You're late."

"Sorry, Majesty," Parth replied as he bent a knee. "The roads are full of refugees. But never fear. Our motorcade will take us to a secured landing pad where a military transport is on standby. From there it is only a ten-minute flight to Hive Home. And once underground, you will be safe from everything up to and including a direct hit from a nuclear weapon."

"Don't be ridiculous," the Queen replied contemptuously. "There won't be any nuclear weapons. The Warrior Queen is ruthless, but she wants to rule over something more than a radioactive wasteland. No, if you've seen the propaganda broadcasts, then you know what she intends to do."

Parth *had* seen the broadcast but had no idea what the Warrior Queen planned to do other than reclaim her throne and kill him. There was a horrible emptiness in the pit of his stomach. "I've seen the footage, Majesty . . . But I'm not sure what you're referring to."

"I should never have allowed myself to listen to you or to go along with your traitorous plans," the royal said bitterly. "But, like you, I'm ambitious. And I believed I could use the cabal and ultimately take control of it. That was naïve. We still have a chance, however. Not much of one, but a chance nevertheless. And that is to go to the Plain of Pain and confront the Warrior Queen."

"The Plain of Pain? Why there?"

"Because she is playing the part of the Kathong," the Queen

answered impatiently. "She *has* to go there. Then, once we kill the Kathong," the royal continued, "the Ramanthian people will know who the *true* Queen is. And even if the animals succeed in taking control of Hive, they will still have to deal with the person in charge. *Me.*"

It was an audacious plan. Parth felt humbled. Here, rather than an empty vessel, was a monarch reminiscent of the great mother. And, thanks to the cloud of psychoactive chemicals that enveloped him, Parth discovered that he *wanted* to serve her. He bowed deeply. "I am your servant, Majesty. Your car awaits."

According to current military doctrine, three conditions had to be met in order to carry out an opposed landing on a Class III planet: (1) Secure orbital control, (2) Achieve air superiority, and (3) Place enough troops on the ground to hold the landing zone (LZ) while more troops and supplies are brought down through the atmosphere.

Unfortunately, allied forces didn't have complete control of the battle platforms in orbit around Hive—nor did they have unchallenged air superiority. But what they *did* have was a hole through which Landing Force Alpha could pass in order to establish an LZ on the Plain of Pain, a desolate place that had a special significance for the Ramanthian people.

But there were other reasons for establishing a beachhead on the Plain of Pain as well. First, there was no civilian population to worry about. And that was of considerable importance to the Queen because a great deal of collateral damage would make it difficult, if not impossible, for her to rule. Second, there were no localized defenses to deal with. And why would there be? It was, as one senior officer put it, "a goddamned desert." And third, there was plenty of elbow room, which Confederacy forces were going to need if they hoped to put enough people and equipment on the ground to hold the LZ.

To accomplish that, Booly had ordered his generals to drop eight fully equipped TACBASEs onto the plain first. The so-called drop boxes formed a defensive ring five miles across and were ready to do battle within minutes of landing. And that was a good thing because no sooner had the last TACBASE thumped down and leveled itself up than the fortresses came under attack by Ramanthian armor. The bugs weren't stupid. They knew what the off-worlders hoped to accomplish—and were determined to prevent it.

But because the high command hadn't anticipated the possibility of *any* landing, much less a landing on the Plain of Pain, all they could do on such short notice was to rush lightly armored vehicles and troops into the area. Their job was to hold the animals in place until a battalion of Gantha tanks could arrive on the scene.

The problem was that each TACBASE included four quads as well as sixteen T-2s and their riders. Within ten minutes after landing, the highly mobile legionnaires were dispatched to plug the gaps between the drop boxes. And thanks to their superior firepower, they were able to lay waste to the attacking vehicles even as dozens of Confederacy ships put down inside the circle of steel. The *Fury* was one of them. The ship landed on a low rise around which troops were starting to mass.

Vanderveen was no stranger to violence, or to warfare for that matter, but had never been part of a planetary invasion. And she was nearly overwhelmed by the assault on her senses as Booly, the Warrior Queen, and the rest of them clattered down a ramp and onto the reddish soil. Half a dozen senior officers were waiting to update Booly on the tactical situation as Santana and his soldiers formed a protective cordon around the VIPs. Vanderveen took the opportunity to look around.

A complicated tracery of white lines carved the blue sky into dozens of abstract shapes as the life-and-death struggle for air superiority continued, and the ground shook as artillery rounds fired from twenty miles away marched across the LZ. The first couple of explosions did little more than throw fountains of reddish soil high into the air. But the third scored a direct hit on a troop transport and blew it apart. Chunks of flying metal cut an entire squad down, struck an assault boat that was in the process of landing a hundred yards away, and destroyed that as well.

It all happened so quickly that Vanderveen was still trying to absorb it as a pall of smoke rose to obscure the scene, the artillery shells continued to march across the LZ, and a newly arrived quad lurched past. It was surrounded by a pack of rakish T-2s, all armed with shoulder-mounted missile launchers, ready to defend the larger cyborg from speedy attack vehicles. The stench of smoke, fuel, and ozone was thick in Vanderveen's nostrils as servos whined, a Dag screamed past, and a series of explosions were heard.

Vanderveen's thoughts were interrupted as Santana approached on a T-2 with another cyborg at his side. "It's time to saddle up. This is Corporal Haskins. She'll take good care of you."

Vanderveen had ridden T-2s before though not recently. But old habits returned quickly as the diplomat circled around behind the cyborg and made use of the recesses built into the back of the trooper's legs to climb upwards. A helmet was waiting for her. Once she put it on and the safety harness was fastened, it was time to say hello. "Thanks for the ride, Corporal. I've done this before, but it's been a while. Don't hesitate to boss me around."

The voice on the intercom was female. "Roger that, ma'am . . . Just keep your head down. The major told me that I'll be stationed on a one-woman asteroid if anything happens to you."

"I'll do my best," Vanderveen promised and made a mental note to complain about the special treatment later. Although the truth was that she was equally guilty, because she had known Dietrich for as long as she'd known Santana and given the non-com similar instructions. With the exception of the Queen, who was larger than a T-2 and fully capable of keeping up with one, the rest of the party was strapped onto cyborgs and ready to depart. Chancellor Ubatha had been ordered to remain behind and assume control of the Ramanthian government if necessary. Booly gave the group a last-minute briefing via the company-level push. "The enemy is trying to pin us down long enough to bring their heavy armor to bear. They plan to win the battle in orbit, establish air superiority, and trap us in the LZ.

"So we're going to break out, use our speed to flank their tanks, and kill them. Meanwhile, a flight of vid cams will follow her majesty into battle and live footage of her return will be fed to the Ramanthian population. Questions?"

"Yes, sir," Santana replied. "What happens if her majesty gets killed?"

Booly was about to respond when the Queen interrupted. "In that case, her majesty will have a very bad day."

The human-style joke produced nervous laughter. Booly spoke once it died down. "I think that covers it, Major . . . But since it's *your* job to keep her alive, we don't have anything to worry about, do we?"

There was an edge to Booly's words. And Vanderveen understood why. Like it or not, the general had to obey Nankool's orders. And the need to protect the Queen in the midst of a planetary invasion was a heavy burden. So Santana's skepticism was like salt in an open wound. For some reason, she was reminded of the lunch with Maylo Chien-Chu and the Wula Sticks. What was it the seer had said? "Your fates are bound together?" That was certainly the case.

"No, sir," Santana replied levelly. "Nothing at all."

"Good," Booly said. "Pass the word . . . The regiment will advance."

Parth was going to die. That was clear to him as the open command car that he and the Queen were riding in led a powerful wedge of Gantha tanks forward. The only question was *how*. Would he be blown up? Burned to death? Or simply shot? There was no way to be sure of anything but the final outcome. Because the animals had not only been able to land in force but had established a foothold on Hive's sacred soil and destroyed the quick-response force sent to stop them. All in a matter of hours rather than the days or weeks the generals had first predicted.

That was why the Queen was determined to do battle with the invaders before night fell. Because if she didn't, the invaders might have so much momentum it would be virtually impossible to stop them. So Parth was there, sitting directly behind the royal as the wind whipped past him and a salvo of long-range surface-to-surface missiles came sleeting in from the east. They were receiving guidance from Confederacy vessels high above, so most of the weapons hit their marks. Explosions flashed all around as Gantha tanks began to die, and the rest of the formation was forced to circumvent.

But the huge multitiered steel monsters were far from helpless. Their 120mm guns made a sound similar to rolling thunder as they sent "smart" artillery shells racing downrange. Parth knew, because General Amm had explained it, that the precision-guided munitions were equipped with fins, steering rockets, *and* an integrated GPS tracking system. All of which enabled them to strike targets well over the horizon. Plus, imperial forces had vehicle-mounted missile launchers that could track the incoming weapons and use the resulting data to fire at enemy launchers. So even though Parth couldn't *see* the damage, he knew that the enemy was suffering casualties as well.

But that knowledge was scant comfort as the side-to-side line of bipedal monster-things appeared in the distance. Each of the horrors was carrying a rider and running an unpredictable zigzag pattern. Sparks appeared as they fired shoulder-launched missiles, which made sinuous snakelike turns as they locked in on Ramanthian vehicles and left trails of light gray smoke behind them. Parth closed his eyes and waited for the inevitable explosion of light, but nothing happened. So he opened his eyes just in time to see a scout car fly apart as an entirely new threat lumbered out of the smoke ahead.

Parth knew that the four-legged walkers were called quads. They carried missiles, guns, and troops. Human troops, Clone troops, and Hudathan troops. The latter were the most terrifying because of their reputation for ruthless savagery. The cyborgs fired, explosions rippled across the battlefield, and the command car was still unscathed. *We'll be in among them soon,* Parth thought to himself as he fumbled with the rifle he had been issued. Could the weapon stop a Hudathan? Such were Parth's thoughts as General Amm's voice sounded inside his helmet. "You can watch live video of the imposter on channel three. The animals are broadcasting it far and wide. They *want* us to see her."

Parth switched the heads-up display on the inside surface of his visor to video and selected channel three. There he saw raw footage of what looked like a Kathong. The creature was running with the tireless efficiency of what it was: a machine. And even though Parth knew he was looking at a cybernetic vehicle, and even though he knew the animals were using Ramanthian mythology for their own perverted purposes, the image still had power.

The Queen had been looking at channel three as well. And her voice was contemptuous. "It's a costume and nothing more. We'll bury her in it."

Once again, Parth was impressed by the Queen's clarity, courage, and purpose. A flight of missiles came flashing in, a Gantha vanished in a slow-motion ball of flame, and the command car rocked as a wall of displaced air rushed past it. Parth gripped his rifle and experienced a moment of hope. Maybe, just maybe, he would survive the day.

Everything was clear. Booly could see the clouds of smoke that were boiling up into the air, the columns of dust generated by thousands of vehicles that were coming straight at him, and what the ancient Zulus called "the horns of the bull" to his left and right, as the Legion's *2nd Regiment Etranger De Cavalerie*, and elements of the Hegemony's 1st Armored Division, sought to flank the Ramanthians. And the T-2's power was *his* power as the machine carried him forward. He gloried in the way the air flowed around him, the way every sense had been fully awakened, and the rush of adrenaline that coursed through his veins.

Then the time for reflection was over as the two armies collided and penetrated each other. A wild free-for-all ensued. It was the kind of battle that the Legion's cavalry hungered for. And in that moment the wild conglomeration of fugitives, criminals, and idealists who made up the Legion wanted to kill. And Booly, who had spent his entire adult life among them, was no different. Finally, after years spent behind a desk, he was a soldier once again.

As the quads and Ganthas continued to trade earthshaking blows, the T-2s and Haba attack sleds dashed in and out, using their larger cousins for cover. Meanwhile, in the midst of the surrounding madness, a battle within a battle was under way.

Having claimed a slight rise as her own, the Warrior Queen was putting on a fearsome display of what her Kathong body was capable of. Not only could it take repeated hits from a variety of weaponry, it had considerable offensive capability as well. That could be seen as she fired green energy bolts from the trident clenched in her scorpion-like tail. The blasts were powerful enough to destroy anything less than a Gantha tank. But it took thirty seconds to recharge her accumulators, so it was necessary that she defend herself with the machine guns built into her tool arms between salvos.

The Warrior Queen would have been overrun, though, along with the rest of her party, had it not been for Santana and his platoon of legionnaires. They formed a cordon around the rise and were kept very busy. And as the radio message came in, Santana was starting to worry. There had been casualties. Lots of them. And the bugs kept coming. "Orbital Control to RAM Six," a voice said in his ear. "An enemy ship is closing on your position from the west. The Dags are trying to shoot it down but no luck so far. We think they plan to crash it on top of you. Over."

Santana looked west, but the incoming ship hadn't broken the horizon yet. "This is RAM Six. Roger, that. But how would they pick us out of the crowd? Over."

"We believe they are homing in on the signals being broadcast from the vid cams," came the answer. "We recommend that you destroy them immediately. Over."

Santana looked at the Warrior Queen, saw that three of what had been six vid cams were still buzzing around her, and swore. "Atkins . . . Destroy those vid cams. And do it *now*."

"No!" came Booly's voice, as he and his T-2 materialized out of the drifting smoke. A group of aides and bodyguards could be seen immediately behind the officer. "Kill two of the cameras and delegate the third to me," Booly said.

"But sir," Santana objected, "that would . . ."

"That's an order," Booly growled. "Do it."

Santana glanced toward the west. The Ramanthian freighter was visible and getting larger with each passing second. Tiny, insectlike Daggers were attacking the behemoth, and smoke trailed behind it, but it continued to bore in. "You heard the general, Atkins. Kill two of the cameras."

The T-2 fired two shots in quick succession and the cameras exploded. Then, having delegated the last machine to Booly, Santana turned to tell him as much. But the general and his aides were already on the run, with the globe-shaped vid cam in hot pursuit.

The essence of Booly's plan was clear. If he could lead the camera away from the Warrior Queen, the Ramanthian ship would follow. But could he execute the move in time? The freighter had come much closer. Santana could see the flare of the vessel's repellers, the dust they churned up, and flash after flash as missiles hit the already devastated hull.

Should he take the Queen and make a run for it? Or would that make the royal even more vulnerable? Santana was still thinking about the pros and cons as the wedge-shaped ship began to turn its nose away from the rise and toward Booly. Then, with increasing speed, the freighter entered a shallow dive and followed the signal in.

Booly looked up, saw the huge mass coming straight for him, and ordered his party to scatter. Then his thoughts turned to Maylo. *Good-bye, dearest, good-bye . . . I'll be waiting.*

Then the ship was upon him, crushing all that he was under its unimaginable weight, as the freighter's blunt nose began to plow its way across the Plain of Pain. Waves of dirt curled away from the bow as the hull slid for the better part of two miles before the ship finally came to rest. And, in addition to killing the Confederacy's highest-ranking general, the spaceship obliterated two quads and more than a dozen T-2s. That opened a path that ran deep into the Confederacy's ranks. A road to victory.

"Now!" the Queen shouted, as the freighter struck. "Follow it in." The original plan had been compromised. She knew that. But the way was open, and that meant it was possible to salvage victory from the jaws of defeat. So with a company of Imperial Guards for support, and careless of the bullets that buzzed all around her, the Queen stood as the command car pursued a zigzagging course between smoking wrecks, groups of combatants, and occasional rock formations.

And then the command car was there, within sight of the bodies that lay in bloody drifts, and the defiant creature that stood on top of the rise. It produced a bloodcurdling chittering sound, sent a ball of coherent energy flying at the royal vehicle, and scored a hit. The impact sent the Queen and several members of her party tumbling out onto the ground.

Then the Queen was up and moving forward as the Kathong creature came out to meet her. And neither one of the royals were alone. A dozen animals were present to support the Warrior Queen and an equal number of Imperial Guards were gathered around the other royal as she and her standard-bearers advanced.

Vanderveen and her T-2 were right behind the Warrior Queen and moving forward when a Ramanthian rocket struck the center of Haskins's chest and exploded. Owing to her position on the cyborg's back, Vanderveen was sheltered from the blast. But as the cyborg fell over backwards, there was a very real possibility that she would be crushed under the T-2's considerable weight.

So Vanderveen hit the quick-release button located at the

center of her harness and threw herself sideways. The ground came up fast and knocked the wind out of her as the two groups of combatants came together. Projectiles kicked up geysers of dirt all around her as Vanderveen struggled to rise.

Then Dietrich was there, standing over her, firing a grenade launcher. More than half a dozen Ramanthian soldiers had circled around the center of the battle, hoping to attack the Warrior Queen from behind. Four of the charging Ramanthians were killed as Dietrich's grenades exploded around them. But the noncom's luck ran out as the two survivors emerged from the smoke. They were so close that he couldn't employ the launcher. So Dietrich was in the process of reaching for his pistol when a bug, who was carrying a lance, thrust the needle-sharp weapon at him. The legionnaire produced a grunt as the spearpoint penetrated his armor, passed through his abdomen, and emerged on the other side with the bloodied pennant still attached. Then, having taken hold of the shaft with both hands, Dietrich fell.

Vanderveen was back on her feet by then, firing her carbine. Bugs came at her, and she fired. A hail of bullets took them down. One of them tried to rise, and she put another bullet through his visor.

As Vanderveen knelt next to Dietrich and pulled his helmet free, she saw that his eyes were open. They blinked rapidly as blood trickled from the corner of his mouth. "So you're alive," he croaked. "That's good. *Real* good. The major told me to make sure."

"You were supposed to watch over *him*," Vanderveen said gently. "But thank you."

Dietrich forced a smile. "Sorry, ma'am . . . But I report to the major. Or I did. And I was honored to do so. You tell him . . ."

"Yes?"

There was no answer. Dietrich was gone.

Vanderveen stood, began to turn, and felt something strike her head. There was an explosion of pain, followed by a long fall into endless darkness.

18

For there among the fallen lie the best and the brightest, their blood forever comingled with our sacred sand and the sky above.

—*Poet Tras Aba*
The Plain of Pain
Standard year 313

PLANET HIVE, THE RAMANTHIAN EMPIRE

As the bloodred sun began to set in the west, the Warrior Queen uttered a primal chittering sound and threw herself forward. It appeared to be an uneven match because the Kathong body was so large. But, because the usurper was wearing a suit of power-assisted armor, she was nearly as strong as a T-2. So as the two of them clashed, the outcome was anything but certain.

Santana's platoon had suffered more than 50 percent casualties by that time, which meant there were only six T-2s and an equal number of bio bods left to guard the Warrior Queen as two dozen Imperial Guards sought to flank her. Having run out of ammo for his rifle, Santana fired his pistol into an enemy visor from less than four feet away. It shattered. But as the Guard fell away, the legionnaire felt an unexpected weight land on his back. A Ramanthian! The bugs could fly for short distances, and this individual had taken advantage of that.

Santana swore as the soldier managed to pull his helmet back and began to saw at his neck seal with a serrated knife blade. All he could do was bring the pistol up and fire blindly. Suddenly, the additional weight fell away. And not a moment too soon as more "fliers" landed on the Kathong-like body and began to attack it with high-speed power drills. It was a very savvy choice of weapons and one that suggested advanced planning.

Meanwhile, the Warrior Queen was using one set of electromechanical pincers to hold her rival in place while the other pair sought to throttle her. But the usurper brought both of her tool arms up, broke the chokehold, and delivered a very serviceable punch to the Warrior Queen's face. Sparks flew as an eye was destroyed, and the cybernetic body lurched in response.

Having jumped from his T-2 onto the Warrior Queen's back, Santana shot one of the fliers in the back. The Ramanthian jerked spastically and fell away as the other flier struggled to withdraw his drill bit. Santana aimed the pistol and fired. The bullet went wide as the Warrior Queen jerked away from a blow calculated to blind her remaining eye.

Once he'd freed the drill, the Ramanthian soldier shoved it forward. Santana felt a stab of pain as the spinning bit went through his armor and entered his flesh. Having shed his armor in order to save weight, the Ramanthian's head was bare. So Santana snapped his head forward. There was a satisfying *thud* as the helmet made contact with chitin. As the trooper fell backwards, he took the drill with him. Santana fired again. That bullet flew true, passed through the trooper, and hit the Queen. She bucked both of them off. Santana hit the ground, felt a jolt of pain, and rolled away.

* * *

The Warrior Queen was dying. That was how it felt, and the readout on her HUD confirmed it. The drills had gone deep into her body and damaged the elaborate life-support system that kept her brain alive. So unless she could end the fight quickly and receive some cybernetic first aid, her effort to reclaim the throne would be over. So she brought her tail all the way forward.

The trident-shaped energy weapon struck the pretender's helmet and drove pieces of it down into her brain. Thanks to the armor she was wearing, the royal remained vertical for a moment. Then she fell. And, having lost consciousness, the Warrior Queen collapsed a few seconds later.

Chancellor Parth was watching from only feet away as the Queen's body hit the Plain of Pain. An armored shoulder had been struck a glancing blow by a bullet, and he had chosen to go down rather than invite certain death by remaining vertical. Now, shocked by what he had witnessed, Parth rose and began to shuffle west. He fully expected to receive a bullet in the back and was grateful when he didn't. Especially since General Amm's armor had clearly been flanked, and the animals were sweeping in from both sides.

Had Parth taken a moment to lift his head and look around, he would have seen the battle-scarred quad that was approaching him from the right. But he didn't. So when the enormous foot pod came down on him, the brief moment of pain came as a complete surprise. Hive had fallen.

It was dark. Or very nearly so. Occasional flashes of light lit up the western horizon, and the subdued mutter of artillery could be heard as Confederacy forces under the leadership of General Mortimer Kobbi continued to battle what remained of General Amm's home-defense force. But all of the orbital battle platforms had fallen, more and more allied troops were landing with each passing hour, and the Warrior Queen was not only alive but safely resident in a less warlike form. So within days, weeks at most, she would be able to reclaim her throne. And hostilities would end.

None of which was of any interest to Santana. He had been plucked off the battlefield by a medical unit, treated for his shoulder wound, and sent off to join a group of walking wounded that was scheduled to be evacuated in the next couple of hours.

But the moment the medic in charge of the group turned his back, Santana slipped away. Now, along with the robots that had been assigned to "tag and bag" more than a thousand dead bodies, he was prowling the battlefield, looking for Vanderveen and Dietrich. According to what he'd been told, both were missing and presumed dead. And the likelihood was like a lead weight in the pit of his stomach.

Hundreds of helmet lights bobbed and seemed to flicker as the robotic graves-registration teams went about their grisly business, and a few, like Santana, went in search of fallen comrades. Humans, Hudathans, and members of less numerous species lay everywhere. Some of their faces were empty. Others were no longer recognizable or still contorted in pain.

Bodies lay in heaps where terrible minibattles had been fought or, in some cases, lay all alone. And there were Ramanthians, too . . . Hundreds of them. Some had gaping wounds, but others looked so peaceful it seemed as though they might rise to fight again.

Finally, after a nightmare journey, Santana stepped over a dead Seebo, circled a burned-out quad, and entered the area where the battle royal had taken place. Both of the would-be monarchs had been removed from the battlefield, but the robots were just beginning to filter into the area, so the rest of the bodies lay where they had fallen.

As the blob of light projected from his helmet played across one of the Ramanthian "fliers" he had battled earlier, Santana knew he was very close to the place where the final confrontation had taken place. Using that as a center point, he began an ever-expanding-circle search.

Two minutes later, he saw the lance, recognized the body as being Dietrich's, and felt a huge lump rise to block his throat as he looked down into Dietrich's face. They had served together for years by that time, shared uncountable dangers, and been friends, even if that friendship had never been formally acknowledged and couldn't be, given the nature of their professional relationship.

Servos whined as a pair of androids arrived. Santana stood. "Please treat this man with great care. He was my friend."

The robots were programmed to treat *all* bodies with respect and to ignore redundant orders. So they made no reply as Santana turned away. That was when the light from his helmet speared a smaller body. Santana's heart leapt as he knelt next to it, wrestled the badly damaged helmet free, and saw Vanderveen's bloodied face. Then, hardly daring to hope, his fingers sought her jugular. There was nothing at first. Just her yielding flesh. But just as Santana was about to give up, he felt what he'd been hoping for. A single surge of blood. "Medic!" he shouted. "Over here! Hurry."

PLANET EARTH, THE CONFEDERACY OF SENTIENT BEINGS

Six months had passed since the cessation of hostilities, a massive recovery effort was under way, and even though things would never be the same, a sense of normalcy had returned. The wedding was held on an island in the Pacific Ocean. The bride wore a beautiful white gown, the groom was in uniform, and more than five hundred formally attired guests were in attendance. The celebrants included President Nankool; Admiral Chien-Chu; his niece, Maylo; Triad Doma-Sa; and many, many others. All of whom had come to wish Undersecretary Christine Vanderveen and Lt. Colonel Antonio Santana a long and happy marriage.

Once his part of the ceremony was over and the happy newlyweds were being mobbed by well-wishers, Charles Vanderveen was able to slip away for a barefoot walk on the beach. His wife, Margaret, wasn't there. *Couldn't* be there. But he could sense her presence. And the warmth of it went deep into his bones. Waves broke offshore and he was at peace.

AUTHOR'S NOTE

This is the ninth and final volume of the original Legion of the Damned series, which began in 1993. But if it's an end, it's also a new beginning, because I am under contract to write a prequel trilogy set before the book *Legion of the Damned.* The first book is titled *Andromeda's Fall* and centers around a young socialite named Catherine Carletto, who is forced to join the Legion under the nom de guerre Andromeda McKee after the emperor is murdered and her parents are killed in a purge. This is a time when Trooper Is are still being integrated into the Legion, the Hudathans are still on a paranoid rampage, and the Ramanthians are allied with humans in opposition to them. *Andromeda's Fall* is available now. So the Legion lives on!

In the meantime, I would like to once again thank physicist Dr. Sheridan Simon for his advice and assistance in creating the primary planets in this universe as well as the races native to them. Unfortunately, Sheridan didn't live long enough to appreciate how durable our creations would be, but I haven't forgotten him.

Last, but not least, I would like to thank all of my faithful readers for sticking with me over all the years. And a special word of appreciation to the men and women of the United States armed forces, who put themselves in harm's way—and fight the *real* battles that keep us free. Wherever you are, thank you.

For more information about William C. Dietz and his books, visit: williamcdietz.com.

From national bestselling author

WILLIAM C. DIETZ

AT EMPIRE'S EDGE

In a far-distant future, the Uman Empire reigns, conquering worlds across the stars and beyond, ruling with a benevolent hand . . . and an iron fist.

On one planet, the remnants of a violent, shape-shifting race called the Sagathies are kept captive by Xeno cops, who have been bioengineered to see through the aliens' guises. Still, sometimes one manages to escape.

Jak Cato is a Xeno cop. He's returning a fugitive Sagathi when things go horribly awry. Saved from being slaughtered with the rest of his men because he is drunk, Cato must now become the hero he was created to be, recapture the Sagathi, and exact revenge. . . .

Praise for the novels of William C. Dietz

"A tough, moving novel of future warfare."
—David Drake, author of the Hammer's Slammers series

"When it comes to military science fiction, William Dietz can run with the best."
—Steve Perry, author of the Matador series

penguin.com

M890T0511

LEGION OF THE DAMNED™
www.legionofthedamned.com
Available on the iPhone
App Store
Now available as
a strategy game.

FROM NATIONAL BESTSELLING AUTHOR

WILLIAM C. DIETZ

The Andromeda Trilogy

ANDROMEDA'S FALL

The Legion of the Damned™ Series

LEGION OF THE DAMNED
THE FINAL BATTLE
BY BLOOD ALONE
BY FORCE OF ARMS
FOR MORE THAN GLORY
FOR THOSE WHO FELL
WHEN ALL SEEMS LOST
WHEN DUTY CALLS
A FIGHTING CHANCE

PRAISE FOR THE AUTHOR AND THE SERIES:

"William C. Dietz raises the bar of excellence for military science fiction with every book he writes . . . a superb, action-packed thriller." —*Midwest Book Review*

"Dietz has created an intricate tapestry of local and starfaring culture with top-notch action sequences." —*Publishers Weekly*

williamcdietz.com
penguin.com

M491AS0712